AMBUSHED

It was definitely time to leave. I'd been here too long as it was. According to my watch, the ten minutes I'd planned to stay had turned into twenty.

I returned to the kitchen and mopped up the water stains on the floor, stuffed the paper towels in my pocket and headed for the side door. I was too tired and stiff to try to get back out the way I'd come in. I was standing in the little vestibule next to the door, putting on my wet sneakers and thinking about what an unpleasant sensation slipping into wet canvas is, and vowing that from now on in I would buy leather sneakers, when I noticed what I thought was a red spot on the floor.

I hunkered down to get a better look.

Thinking back, I don't know whether I heard something or smelled it or felt the air around me move, but suddenly I knew with absolute certainty that someone was behind me.

But before I could even move my hand in the direction of my pocket, a pain exploded in my head.

I heard an odd gasp, which I realized was mine. Lights flashed. Then there was nothing . . .

ENDANGERED SPECIES

BARBARA BLOCK

KENSINGTON BOOKS
KENSINGTON PUBLISHING CORP.
http://www.kensingtonbooks.com

Although the city of Syracuse is real, as are some of the place names I've mentioned, this is a work of fiction. Its geography is imaginary. Indeed, all the characters portrayed in this book are fictional and any resemblance to real people or incidents is purely coincidental.

For Dora Bruckner, my grandmother.
If she hadn't made the trip, none of us would be here.

I would like to gratefully acknowledge the substantial contributions of Lawrence Block, without whom this book would not have been concluded.

Chapter
1

I was sitting behind the counter of Noah's Ark, watching two crows peck at the black plastic bags of garbage I'd just put out on the street, while I half listened to the boy standing in front of me.

"Me and my friends," the kid was saying. "We could close down your store, you know. Just like that." He brought his right hand up and snapped his fingers.

"Really?" I smiled sweetly. "Be my guest."

In the mood I was in, I'd consider being rid of this place an act of mercy. At the moment, the thought of not having to clean cages, restock shelves, answer questions about the feeding habits of hermit crabs, or fill out the three thousand government forms New York State inflicts on the small business owner had a lot of appeal.

The boy frowned. "I'm serious. We shut down the fur store on Salina."

According to the newspaper account I'd read they hadn't, but I wasn't going to call the kid a liar.

"So am I." I threw the key to the front door of my store on the counter. "Here you go, kid . . ."

"Jeff . . ."

"Whatever."

"Jeff," he repeated, his voice cracking in a preadolescent squeak.

"Fine. Jeff, then." I massaged a cramp in my shoulder while I moved my arm around. The damn thing had been bothering me all day. I must have slept on it wrong. "I'll make it easy for you." I pointed to the key. "Take it. The place is yours. Oh, and by the way, good luck returning the fish to their natural environment. The guy that bred most of them lives out in B'ville."

Jeff swallowed. His eyes searched the room for an answer that wasn't there. What should he do? Take the key? Not take it? He didn't know. The PETA manual had obviously never covered a situation like this. I felt a pang of guilt. The kid was what? Fifteen at the most? And that was being generous.

I was telling myself I shouldn't be giving him such a hard time when he swallowed, straightened his shoulders, and did what any politician would have done in similar circumstances: ignored what I'd said and kept on going with his spiel. My guilt disappeared. Admiration took over. Damn, the kid was good. Who knew? I could be talking with the next mayor of New York City.

The boy was tall and extremely slender. His thinness was emphasized by the clothes he'd chosen to wear: green-and-yellow plaid polyester bellbottoms, a tight-fitting orange shirt, and an enormous black ski parka that came down to his knees, all of which, judging from their condition, I was certain he'd gotten at the Goodwill store. He'd completed his ensemble with a string of yellow plastic beads around his neck, black nail polish on the fingernails of his left hand, a nose ring, plus five earrings on his left earlobe, which served, perversely, to underline the essential sweetness of his face.

Some of my academic friends would have called this kid's style of dress tribal, others would have called it postmodern, I called it bad early seventies. Most of the people I know would have thrown him out by now, but I couldn't. He reminded me of myself at that age. Dressed in thrift store odds and ends to my mother's everlasting mortification, I'd harassed people on street corners and in stores, begging them to sign my petitions for everything from nuclear disarmament to animal rights. I was thinking about what an insufferable little prig I must have been when I became aware that the kid was talking again.

"You think what you do is right?" he said. "You think it's okay to own living creatures, to buy and sell them as if they were chattel?"

"Yes." I reached for my lighter and lit a cigarette. I couldn't seem to help myself. The kid was bringing out the worst in me. "I do."

He leaned across the counter. I exhaled in his direction. He coughed and moved back. I lied and told him I was sorry.

I expected him to start lecturing me about the dangers of secondhand smoke. Instead he pointed to the caged tarantula sitting in the corner. "Would it be all right for me to buy one of those and burn it?"

"No. Of course not." I gently tapped the cage. The spider waved its two front legs at me. "They still experience pain."

"Even if it is just a spider."

"Yes," I agreed reluctantly. I could see where this conversation was going. "Even if it is just a spider."

"Well, what happens when people mistreat something you sell them?"

"I try to make sure that doesn't happen."

"But when it does," the kid insisted.

"Then of course I feel bad." I rubbed my forehead. I was getting a headache and I'd left my Motrin back at the house. Good resolutions aside, the kid was going to have to leave.

"Why do you do it then?"

"Sell livestock?"

Jeff nodded.

"Because it's part of my business." About forty percent of it, to be exact. The rest consists of pet supplies of one kind or another.

"That's totally bogus."

"Is it now?" I raised an eyebrow. "I'll tell the bank that's holding the mortgage on my house that."

"You could earn a living doing something else if you wanted to."

"I'll go down and get a job flipping burgers at the mall right now." I wasn't going to tell this kid that in my former life I'd worked for the newspaper, or that this store hadn't been my idea, it had been my husband's, or that I'd been against the whole thing from the start, or that I'd gotten stuck with the place when he died, mostly because it was none of his business.

Jeff flushed. He gestured at the cage full of canaries. "They should be out flying around."

"They would be dead if they were," I retorted. "They're captive born and bred. They've never even seen a worm, much less built a nest."

"Some would make it," the kid insisted.

"Yes, some would, but most won't."

I had to raise my voice to be heard over the blare of the police car speeding up the street. I wondered if it was going to another shooting. We'd had two fatal drive-bys not too far away from here in the past week, a record for Syracuse this time of year. Some people put it down to the weather. Usually by the end of January everyone's inside shivering, but for the last two weeks we've been averaging a very unseasonable forty degrees.

Other people say the New York City cops have a new policy. It's called share the wealth. They buy upstate bus tickets for gang members and tell them to get out of town. As for me, I ascribe the rise in crime to the economy. Thirty years ago, Syracuse was a manufacturing town, but most of those plants have moved to Mexico and other points south, taking the high-paying jobs with them, and leaving the part-time, badly paying jobs behind.

The kid coughed and I turned my attention back to him.

"That still doesn't give you the right to keep them," he told me, pitching his voice over the siren of a second police car.

I took another puff of my cigarette before reluctantly taking up where we'd left off. "If it wasn't for places like this, those birds wouldn't exist. They were bred to be sold."

The boy fingered one of the beads around his neck. "The whole concept of pets is wrong."

A third police car whizzed by. I made a mental note to turn on the evening news when I got home. "Tell me, did you ever have a dog?"

"Yes," Jeff said uncertainly, not sure of where I was going with this. "We have a golden."

"Do you love that dog?"

"Yes."

"Do you treat that dog well?"

"Of course." The "of course" was indignant.

"Is he happy? Does he love you?"

"She. Amber is a she." The kid shook his head impatiently. "Yes. Amber is happy. She sleeps in my bed, my mom takes her everywhere, and she has more toys than my kid brother. But that's not the issue. The issue is that she didn't pick us, we picked her. We could be horrible to her. She doesn't have any rights."

"Actually she does under Statute 26 of the New York State Market and Agriculture Law, but let me ask you something else. Did you pick the family you were born into?"

Jeff leveled a finger at me. "Don't confuse the issue."

"I'm not. I'm just trying to point out that things are more complicated than you're making them out to be."

A sneer crept over the kid's face. "Complicated is the word adults use when they know they're wrong. Complicated is the word adults use so they won't have to do anything."

"But you'll do better, right?" I shot back. I wanted to clap my hand over my mouth as the words left my lips. My God. When had this happened? When had I begun to sound like my mother?

"Yes, I will." Jeff went into his pocket and drew out a sheaf of pamphlets. "You should read these," he said, laying them on the counter. "You'll see what I mean."

But I didn't. After he'd gone, I dropped them in the garbage. I'd seen the PETA material before, pictures of rabbits with their eyes being held open so caustic liquids could be dropped in thereby insuring the safety of our shampoo, pictures of foxes caught in traps, gnawing their own legs off to get free, and I didn't want to see them again. It was too upsetting.

I no longer use animal-tested cosmetics and I don't wear

fur or eat baby animals, but I still eat beef and wear leather shoes. Which makes me what? A hypocrite. Me and ninety-nine percent of the other adults on this planet. Despite my resolution not to, I found myself thinking about what the kid had said as I watched a hamster stuff a treat I'd just fed him into his cheek pouch. I was still thinking about it when Manuel and his cousin, Eli "don't call me Elazaro" Bishop walked in and put the cap on an already bad afternoon.

Manuel was wearing jeans, an oversize flannel shirt, an expensive GorTex shell, sneakers with treads large enough to fit a dump truck's tires, both of which I was sure he'd boosted from a local retail establishment, and, of course, his ever-present baseball hat. He'd recently stopped trying to grow a goatee and mustache, contenting himself with long, fifties-style sideburns. They made his face seem thinner than it was and emphasized the narrowness of his chin. At seventeen, he looked like what he was: a street kid who had seen and done more than he should have.

"No," I said before he and his cousin reached the counter.

"No what?" Manuel asked.

I stubbed out what was left of the new cigarette I was smoking in the empty dog food can I was currently using as an ashtray. "No to anything you're going to ask."

Manuel raised his hands in a gesture of mock offense. "How can you say that? You don't even know what I want."

"Exactly. And I don't care. Whatever it is, all I know is that I don't want any part of it."

Even though Manuel was a friend of mine (we'd met under unfortunate circumstances a few years ago), I've come to view him, as one of my Catholic friends would say, as a penance for my sins, which, judging from him, are multiple. Whenever Manuel is around bad things happen. Or maybe

complicated is a better word. I'm talking the kind of complications that usually take me days with the phone pressed to
my ear, while I'm put on hold, to straighten out. The kind
of complications that brings me in contact with people I'd
rather not meet, under which heading I include representa-
tives of various social and law-enforcement agencies as well
as low-level thieves and grifters.

"And," I added, covering another possibility before Manuel brought it up, "if you want to borrow money, you're out
of luck. I'm flat broke." I pointed to the stack of envelopes in
front of me. "I don't even know how I'm going to pay my
bills this month."

Manuel grinned, exposing a gold cap on one of his upper
molars. When had he gotten that? I wondered.

"Which is why today is your lucky day," he told me.

I crossed my arms over my chest. "Manuel, I have neither
the time nor the patience to get involved with another of
your schemes."

"This isn't about me." Zsa Zsa, my cocker spaniel, came
out of the back room where she'd been taking a nap and
ran over to Manuel. He was one of her favorite people,
which shows you what her judgment in people is like. He
took a second to bend down and pet her, before continuing.
"This is about him." He straightened up and gestured in
Eli's direction. "He's got a problem and I told him you're
the man . . ."

"Woman . . ."

". . . that can fix it."

By now Manuel and Eli were across the counter from me.
I regarded Eli. If it had been Manuel that had the problem,
I would have thrown him out, but I liked Eli, even if he was
a distant cousin of Manuel. Over the past year he'd bought
two Jackson chameleons, an iguana, a couple of skunks, and

a small king snake from me. Once in a while he'd stop in, and we'd chat for the odd half an hour or so. He seemed knowledgeable and responsible. At least when it came to reptiles.

He gave me an embarrassed nod and I nodded back. He'd moved here from Florida a couple of years ago. Five years older than Manuel, he was supporting himself working as a prep chef in a restaurant on Erie Boulevard while he finished up an associates degree at Onondaga Community College. With just one more semester to go, he was talking about going on to a four-year school.

He was as fat as Manuel was thin, and as slow as Manuel was quick. He was clean-shaven, and had short brown hair, myopic brown eyes, glasses with thick lenses, a short stub of a nose, and a mouth that was a shade too small for his face. He dressed in normally fitting jeans, flannel shirts, and sneakers. Best of all, unlike Manuel, he didn't seem to be addicted to shortcuts.

He didn't, as far as I knew, sell stolen merchandise, or break into cars and rip off their stereos and CD players. On the other hand, I wasn't putting Eli up for canonization yet. The fact that he had a problem he wanted me to solve was a definite red flag. The fact Manuel had brought him to me for help made the color of that flag go from brick red to scarlet.

Since I've been doing detective work part-time, an employment I backed into over the course of a murder investigation in which I was named as a suspect, I've come to appreciate the truth of what my grandmother used to say to me whenever I got into trouble. She'd shake her finger in front of my nose and intone in her heavily Russian-accented English, "If you hadn't been where you didn't belong, this wouldn't have happened." Which is also true of most of the people that need my help. They need it, because either they were where they had no business being or they were doing something they shouldn't have been.

Manuel cleared his throat. "This is the story . . ." But before he could get into it, I gestured for him to be quiet. "I'd like to hear Eli tell it."

Manuel hitched up his pants and bobbled his chin in and out like a chicken looking for a piece of corn in the dust. "I'm just trying to move things along."

I concentrated my gaze on him. "You have a special interest in this?"

Manuel put his hand up in the air palms toward me, fingers splayed. "I'm just here as one of those . . . those good Samaritans." He flashed me a smile. "You like the word? I'm doing what you said. I got me one of those improve your vocab books . . ."

"Very nice."

Manuel stroked his left sideburn. "I figured I'd help you out. I'd help Eli out."

"I'm surprised. Disinterested generosity not being your usual style," I noted dryly.

Manuel scrunched up his face and did a good imitation of being affronted. "You got no call to talk to me like that."

I had all the call in the world. I was about to remind him of why I did when Eli started talking.

"It's okay." Eli studied the floor for a minute before looking up at me. The thickness of the lenses in his glasses imparted an unfocused quality to his pupils. "I told him that he could tell you."

I scrutinized Eli. "If you don't mind, I'd rather hear the story from you."

Eli bit his lip. I watched the skin around his teeth go from pink to white.

"I can respect that," he said after he'd released his grip.

I glanced over at Manuel. He was tapping his fingers against his thighs and doing a little shuffle dance with his feet.

I motioned to the back room. "Would you rather talk to me in there?"

Eli shook his head and tugged on the edge of his brown corduroy jacket. "It's not really a big deal."

I began to sympathize with Manuel. I wanted to say, if it isn't such a big deal, why are you here? I didn't. Instead, I waited as Eli reached up and reseated his baseball cap on his head, setting it first one way and then another, until he found the exact right place. Then he motioned to one of the tanks sitting alongside the left wall.

"How much would one of those corn snakes set me back?"

"About one hundred and fifty."

"I don't suppose you'd let it go for one hundred?"

I told him I'd think about it.

"Good." Eli smiled for the first time since he'd walked in the store.

I tapped my fingers on the counter. "So, are you going to tell me what this is about or not?"

He let out a titter, then stopped himself. "It's about a suitcase."

"What about it?" I prompted after thirty seconds or so had gone by without Eli saying anything, not that I didn't have a pretty good idea of what he was going to say next. I wasn't wrong.

"I need you to find it for me."

"No kidding."

"That's right." Eli licked his lips. He hurriedly took an envelope from his shirt pocket and held it out to me, an offering, all the while averting his eyes from mine, looking at the fish and the birds and the hamsters and every damn thing in the store except me. This did not inspire confidence. "There's six hundred in here for you now and another six hundred when you give it to me."

I wondered what was in the suitcase. Drugs? Hot merchandise? Certainly not Eli's Armani suit. I repressed a sigh. So much for my ideas on Eli's moral character. What had they been based on anyway? The fact that he liked herps and went to school? I made a steeple with my fingers and lightly rested my chin on it. "What's in this suitcase that's so valuable?"

Eli swallowed and glanced at Manuel. Their eyes locked. Manuel gave the merest suggestion of a nod.

"Nothing important," he replied. "Personal stuff."

I drummed my fingers on the countertop. "Right. And I'm Marie, the queen of Rumania."

"Rumania?" Manuel asked all wide-eyed. "Is that a country or something?"

"No. It's a new planet." I pointed to the door. "That's enough. Both of you. Out."

"Please," Eli cried. "You got to help me. They're going to chop my fingers off if you don't."

Chapter
2

Maybe it was because Eli looked so piteous standing there in front of me—he was practically wringing his hands—that I made what was going to turn out to be the first mistake of many. Instead of telling him to close the door behind him, I asked exactly who was going to chop his fingers off.

Eli licked his lips again. "A guy named Chapman. Robert Chapman." He let out a deep breath, seemingly relieved to say the name.

"You said they," I reminded him while I automatically reached for the pad of paper—it was lavender, a color I loathe, but it had been on sale for ten cents—I always keep paper next to the register and printed Chapman's name in caps. I told myself as I wrote that taking notes didn't mean I was going to take the case, it was just something I'd gotten in the habit of doing.

"That was a figure of speech. It's just this guy, this one guy." Eli was whispering now. I had to ask him to speak up.

"Who is he?"

"The guy that set up the deal."

I underlined Chapman's name, wrote the word *others* next to it, and followed that with a question mark. "Do you have a phone number for him?"

Eli swallowed and shook his head.

"An address?"

Eli shook his head again.

"Anything?"

I tapped the pencil on the counter. The noise caught Zsa Zsa's attention. She tilted her head in my direction, then came over and put her paws on my legs, demanding her due. I scratched behind her ears with my free hand. "All right. Can you tell me what else he does? Where he comes from?"

Eli looked sheepish. "I'm not sure," he stammered. "I didn't ask. Honest," he added when I raised an eyebrow.

"Okey-dokey." Maybe Eli was telling the truth, maybe he was lying. The problem was, I didn't figure him for that stupid, so why tell me a story that was this idiotic? Why not make up a better one, I thought as Zsa Zsa began butting my hand with her muzzle, her way of telling me to keep petting. It would be easy enough to do. I rubbed her chest and told Eli to continue. "Tell me about the deal," I instructed.

Manuel and Eli exchanged another glance. That did it for me. I crossed my arms over my chest. Zsa Zsa put her paws down and began nosing at a dust bunny on the floor. I clicked my tongue against my teeth and pushed the pad of paper away.

"You must think I'm really dumb," I informed them. "Find someone else. I have enough to do without being lied to. You come in and ask me for my help, you offer to pay me what is for you a fairly substantial amount of money, but you won't tell me what this is all about or who the players are. Forget about it."

Eli hung his head. Manuel weighed in.

"Come on, Robin," he said. "Don't be like that. It's not what you're thinking."

I leaned forward slightly. "Exactly what am I thinking?"

"That Eli wants you to find a suitcase full of dope."

"Not at all." I sat back. "Why would I think that? I was figuring that Chapman is some crazed comic book collector who is after Eli because he's gone and lost a suitcase full of Green Hornet first editions."

Manuel drew himself up. "I thought we were friends."

"So did I."

He put his hands on his hips. "Then why are you disrespecting me like this?" he demanded. "I'm really insulted, and I mean this sincerely, that your opinion of me is so low that you think I'd actually involve you in something like that."

"Oh, PUHLEASE. Spare me the act. I'm not in the mood." I rubbed my forehead. My left temple was throbbing. Had I eaten lunch today? I didn't think so. The last items that had gone in my mouth were a cheese Danish and a cup of coffee at nine o'clock that morning. Maybe that was why I was so cranky.

Manuel gestured to Eli and then to himself. "My cousin wouldn't be doing that kind of shit and neither would I. It's stupid. Too much heat for too little return." For a few seconds, his tough guy mask dropped away and he looked like a six-year-old-boy unfairly accused of stealing his baby brother's ice-cream cone. "You do know that about us, don't you?"

"Yes," honesty forced me to concede, "I do." While Manuel had operated on the fringes of the law for as long as I'd known him, he'd stayed clear of dealing dope in any meaningful way, "meaningful way" being the operative terms here. However, he wasn't above doing favors for friends from time to time, the kind of favors where you run a package over to someone for a quick twenty. I just didn't want to be part of one of those favors.

"Good." Manuel's gold crown winked at me as he smiled. "Eli just suffered a small misfortune, is all. We're trying to minimize the collateral . . ."

I picked up my pen again. "Collateral as in a guaranteed loan?"

"No. As in damage," Manuel explained impatiently.

That was me. Damage control. I turned to Eli. "You have five minutes to tell me what this is about." I looked at the clock on the wall. "Starting now."

Eli blinked again. The light reflecting off the lenses of his glasses made it difficult to read his expression. "I just feel like such a moron," he said.

I refrained from the obvious comment and reminded him that the clock was ticking.

Eli fiddled with the bottom button of his jacket for a few seconds. He was just about to tell me why he felt like a moron when the front door opened and a little girl and her mother walked in. Three more people followed. It was a classic. What I want to know is this: Why do customers always come in clumps? Why do they always come when I'm in the middle of something? I predict that anyone who can answer this question stands to make himself a million dollars.

Eli and Manuel moved off to the side and fidgeted while I waited on everyone.

"I've been thinking that I'd like to study geography when I graduate from OCC," Eli said as soon as the last person left.

"Go on," I prompted. I doodled a "C" under Chapman's name. Then I wrote "Who is he?" on the line underneath.

"But that takes money," Eli explained. "Even a state school takes money these days. I'm twenty-three. I don't want to spend the next five years finishing up two years of school. I'm too old for that. I want to go full-time and get it done. You can understand that, can't you?"

I allowed as how I could.

Eli resettled his glasses on the bridge of his nose. They tilted slightly because the left earpiece was connected to the frame by means of a small, gold safety pin. "If my grades are good, I've been thinking I could even get an assistantship and go for my Ph.D. So when I met this guy . . ."

I clarified. "Chapman."

"That's right. Like I said, we were sitting at the bar and we got to talking and I was telling him about how I want to go on to grad school and do all this stuff, but I don't have the money. He tells me that's a shame. He tells me that's the problem with America today, that it's becoming the land of the rich and the bloated."

"And what did you say?"

"I said, 'Amen to that, man. You sure got that correct.' Then he asks me if I'm an American citizen and I say yes, and then he asks me if I have a passport, and when I say yes again he asks me if I'd like to take a little vacation."

"Just like that?" I sneered.

Eli nodded. "Yeah. Just like that."

"Which bar did this conversation take place at?"

"Lefty's."

I wrote Lefty's under Chapman and circled the name. Lefty's is a dive mostly frequented by heavy drinkers and those who liked to place bets on a variety of sporting events. I shifted around in my seat. "What were you doing there?"

Manuel replied instead of Eli. "Hey, Robin, it's the only

place down in Armory Square you can get a beer for a buck."

"Not to mention the fact they don't check ID's too carefully," I couldn't resist commenting. Manuel opened his mouth to reply, but I stopped him. "Let's just get back to the topic at hand, if you don't mind."

Manuel threw up his hands in a gesture of disgust. "I'm just trying to hurry things along, but, hey, no offense taken."

I turned back to Eli. "Where did this guy say he was going to send you?"

"Cuba."

"Cuba, hunh?" I repeated as I added the name to my list. I began to see where things were heading. "How were you going to get there?"

"Through Mexico. Chapman told me he's got this regular operation going with college kids. He sends them over to Cuba and they come back with cigars and he pays them. It sounded perfect." Eli looked at me imploringly. "I mean, Robin, if I did that four times a year it would mean I'd only have to work part-time if I went to someplace like SUNY Albany. How could I say no?"

"Yeah," Manuel interjected. "It wasn't like he was smuggling drugs or anything."

I shushed him and motioned for Eli to continue. "So, what happened next?"

"I gave him my phone number and Chapman told me he'd get in touch with me when he'd made all the arrangements."

"The original conversation took place . . . ?"

"In September."

"And he called you up?"

"The end of December. He told me he'd booked me on a January fifth flight."

I jotted down the date. "How much was he paying you?"

"Three thousand dollars upon delivery. Plus, he'd pick up my plane ticket and pay for my hotel. It was so cool." Eli's eyes lit up at the memory. "It was warm. I got to swim in this enormous pool. The rum and Cokes were great. Everyone was really nice. I didn't have trouble in Customs. They waved me right through."

"But . . ."

Embarrassed, Eli put his hand over his mouth and studied the tiles on the floor. Manuel took over the conversation.

"See, I told him." Manuel jabbed himself in the chest with his finger. "I said, Eli don't tell nobody what you're doing. The less people in your business the better, but he didn't listen. Cause he never listens to me, cause I'm just some uneducated, illiterate street punk who don't know nuthin' till he gets that wide brown ass of his in trouble and then all of a sudden it's: Manuel, good buddy, what am I gonna do? But, hey." Manuel threw up his hands and spread his fingers. "I don't hold no resentments. I just tell myself, Manuel you got to remember, like your momma always say, family is family, blood is blood . . ."

"Get to the point, Manuel," I ordered. "I'm not in the mood to hear a dissertation on family unity at the moment."

"Fine." Manuel leaned on the counter. "The point is that my cousin told his good-for-nothing roommate, Nestor, a person I might add I had told him not to converse with, much less share an abode with. But I'll let that go by." Manuel nodded graciously, magnanimous in victory. "He and his girlfriend done disappeared with the suitcase."

"Disappeared?" I asked, interrupting Manuel's rant.

"As in gone. Vanished. *Desaparecido.*"

"How long ago was this?"

"Four days," Eli said. "We've looked everywhere."

"Meanwhile," Manuel added, "this Chapman dude been calling and calling, and Eli been telling him one thing after another. Finally, I guess he got fed up because he came down to where Eli is working and dragged his ass out of the kitchen."

"I explained what happened," Eli said, taking up the narration again. "I told him, me and my friend we were working on the problem and he said he'd give me four more days, and that if I couldn't find the suitcase by then he wanted the eight thousand dollars he would have made on those cigars, and that if he didn't get it he was going to come and clip off some of my fingers with a bolt cutter and nail them to my forehead."

"That was probably a figure of speech," I said.

"If we thought that," Manuel replied, "we wouldn't be here talking to you."

"Well, what makes you think he was serious?" I asked Eli as I straightened out the "specials" flyers on the counter.

Eli bit his lip. "He kicked me in the balls," he finally admitted. "And then he did this while I was on the floor." Eli held up his hand and took off a Band-Aid he'd wrapped around his finger. "It's a cut."

"I can see." It was a triangle.

"He did it with his pocket knife and he was smiling when he did. He's got a real nasty smile. He said this was just the beginning."

"All right." I could feel myself relenting. "When did this take place?"

"About an hour ago," Eli said. "You can see why I can't go to the police. God." His face crumpled. He looked as if he was going to cry. "All I want to do is finish school. You believe me, don't you?"

Actually I did. More or less. A month or so ago I'd read a full-page article about smuggling Cuban cigars in *Newsweek*.

I mean, if *Newsweek* writes about it, it has to be true, right? The article had explained that with good cigars fetching prices of twenty-five to fifty dollars each, numerous small-time operators were moving in to fill the void created by our trade blockade of Cuba. On their part, Cubans aided the traffic by not stamping American passports. By traveling through Mexico or Toronto, smugglers were able to avoid US sanctions, thus filling humidors across the country.

Manuel tugged his pants up. "You gonna help him or not?" he demanded. "We gotta know."

I picked up my lighter, then put it back down as I considered what I was going to say. I knew I should probably say no. While Eli's story was credible, the odds were strong that he'd left two or three important points out, points that would come back and kick me in the ass. On the other hand, he was scared. He wasn't faking that. And of course there was the money. Twelve hundred dollars would come in handy right now.

"Have you considered taking a long vacation?" I asked Eli, proposing another solution. "It seems, given the circumstances, that might be your best course of action."

"He can't," Manuel answered before Eli could. "He's got these courses that won't come around again till next spring. He'd be wasting a whole year if he did that."

"That's better than losing a couple of fingers."

Manuel held out his right hand and regarded it. "You know, I knew this guy once who was born with his thumb and his pinky and that was all. Actually, he got along okay."

Eli took a step toward him. "Fuck you, man. Just fuck you."

Manuel took a step back. "Hey. I was just trying to make you feel better."

"Well, don't."

Manuel shrugged. "S-ORRY."

"Okay." Eli addressed me. "I'll go if I have to. But I'm hoping it won't come down to that."

Pickles, the store cat, jumped up on the counter and meowed for her dinner.

"Will you help me?" Eli repeated as I poured some cat food into her dish and set it on the floor. "Please." His voice quavered. "I'm beggin' you here."

Of course I said yes. I said yes because I'm a sucker for stray animals and people who do things they know they shouldn't. It's a major weakness of mine. What's worse, Manuel knows it. I remember thinking, as I caught a glint of satisfaction in his eyes, that he'd probably told Eli to feed me this particular line.

"Thanks, man." Eli clasped my hands with both of his. Then he gave me the envelope. "If you get me out of this, I swear I'll never do anything like this again. Ever."

He probably even believed what he was saying. I know I did when I was his age.

I arranged to meet Eli in his apartment after work. I'd just finished writing down the address when Manuel asked to speak to me in the back room. "It'll just take a second," he promised his cousin.

"So," he said when we'd walked through the door, Manuel holding it open for me, an action that made me wonder what he was going to hit me up for. "I've been thinking about the twelve hundred dollars Eli is paying you."

I corrected him. "May be paying me."

"I figure you could, like, maybe, see your way clear to giving me three hundred of it. You know, like a finder's fee. You don't have to pay it all now," he said quickly. "Half would be good. You can give me the rest of it later."

I snorted. "This is what you dragged me back here for?

Try getting a job, Manuel. You might find the experience useful."

"But I do have a job," he protested, putting his arm around my shoulder and giving it a squeeze. "I'm your agent."

I moved away. "If you ever went back to school and put the same energy into studying that you do into hustling you'd do very well."

"I really need the money."

"For what?"

Manuel looked at the floor. "Gambling debt."

"I told you, I'm broke."

"Please, Robin," Manuel cried. "I'm going to get hurt if I don't pay up."

"It looks as if you and Eli should get together."

Manuel put his hands on his hips. "You don't believe me, do you?" he demanded, reading the expression on my face.

"Not one word. Now get out of here before I change my mind about Eli."

Manuel stomped out of my office. A minute later, I heard the front door slam. The truth was, I did have some money. I was just tired of lending it to him and never getting it back. I went out front and slipped the envelope with Eli's money into my backpack. Then I lit a cigarette and studied the notes I'd taken. There weren't many of them. Four words to be exact.

But that wasn't what worried me.

What worried me was that Manuel hadn't been able to locate Nestor.

If he couldn't, with all his contacts, I wondered how on earth I would be able to.

Chapter
3

One good thing about visiting Eli: It was convenient. His flat was located on Westcott Street, which was a little over a mile from my house. In fact, after the original Noah's Ark had burned down, I'd toyed with the idea of relocating the store there. I could walk to work, the mix of residential, student housing, and small businesses was appealing, and, more importantly, there wasn't another pet store for eight miles around. Unfortunately, at the time I'd been looking there hadn't been any space available. Now there were lots of spaces, but even if I could get out of my lease, which I was pretty certain I couldn't, I wasn't sure I would want to move here.

The intervening years hadn't been kind to the area. My favorite bar had closed, as had a bookstore, a supermarket, a hardware store, a restaurant, and a writers' cooperative. Despite all attempts to rent the spaces, they remained empty, their windows gathering layers of posters, a visible testament to a lack of faith in the area.

Other signs of erosion were apparent. Welfare families were coming in, owners were going out. For Sale signs were sprouting like mushrooms on a wet fall day. Every community group in the area had a plan. None of them were working. Which was too bad. Not only did I like Westcott, but on a strictly selfish level, if the street went down, so would the value of my house, which was close enough to be vulnerable.

It was ten in the evening by the time I arrived at 226. A group of kids who, by the looks of them, should have been home in bed by now, were hanging out in front of the convenience store across the way. The bass from the rap music they were playing crept into my car and seeped into my brain as I pulled alongside the curb. I cranked up the radio and blasted them with the 1812 Overture. Zsa Zsa whimpered. I apologized to her, turned the radio back down, and opened the carton of Chinese takeout I'd bought on my way across town.

The streetlamp glare made the orange beef look like something you'd get at a school cafeteria. Not that it mattered. Zsa Zsa and I were both so hungry we would have eaten anything short of pickled cow dung at the moment. As I chewed, I contemplated the trees and the unkempt hedges surrounding the house Eli was living in. Now, with the leaves off the trees, the house was visible, but by summer it would be enveloped in a canopy of green, invisible to a passerby on the street.

The outside front light was on. It cast a dim, yellowish wash on the small, square porch. The more I studied the place the more familiar it seemed. And then, suddenly, I realized why. I'd visited the house a long time ago. My husband Murphy and I had looked at it when we'd moved up from New York City. We'd seen it at the end of a long, tiring day.

The house had been a pleasant, unremarkable, three-bedroom Colonial, owned, if I remembered correctly, by a retired high school teacher who was planning on relocating to Florida. Murphy had liked it. I hadn't. Even though the price had been right and the screen of greenery had been a plus, I'd seen the lack of a garage and the steps leading up to the house as two big negatives.

The steps were too steep, and the idea of having to trudge up and down them all the time, not to mention the amount of shoveling and salting you'd have to do to keep them clear, was less than inviting. I remember saying to the real-estate agent that if I was going to buy a house, at least I wanted one that was convenient. I also remember Murphy telling me I was a fucking idiot, storming out the door, and driving off, leaving me with an embarrassed real-estate agent who had looked everywhere but at me, while launching into a monologue about her cat's medical problems. It had been what they call in film circles a defining moment.

I licked the glop from the orange beef off my fingers. But, of course, I hadn't known that then. Who ever does except in hindsight? If I had, I would have gone back to the city. Instead, I'd stayed. After all, Murphy and I were starting a new life together. I sighed. That fantasy hadn't lasted too long. Four months to be exact. I wondered when the house had been converted? Probably awhile ago. Even when we were looking, the neighborhood had been changing from owner-owned to rental properties.

I opened the car door. Zsa Zsa jumped out. I followed. As I locked up, I caught a stirring of interest coming from the group of kids across the street. They leaned closer together, exchanging words, while their eyes raked me over, methodical, coolly, scanning for weaknesses. I turned, faced them full on, and stared them down. They returned the favor. Then the moment passed and I climbed the stairs. They were steep. A mat of leaves, leaves that should have been raked up in the fall and hadn't been, covered them.

In the intervening months, they'd been tramped down to a wet, sodden, slippery mass. The hand rail that had been installed to prevent falls had rusted out and was now lying across a patch of dead ivy. I'd been right about the steps after all, I thought pettily as I rang the bell. It was a good place to take a fall. Eli opened the door. Zsa Zsa raced in ahead of me. I followed. The house smelled of cheap beer and pine room freshener. He'd changed clothes since the afternoon. His paint-splattered jeans and a tight T-shirt underscored his soft belly.

Manuel emerged from the living room. He was carrying a CD jewel case by a well known rapper.

"Well," I told him as I surveyed him for cuts and bruises. "It looks as if you've been able to escape injury so far."

Manuel bristled. "No thanks to you." He spun the case around between his fingers. "I've been staying off the streets."

Eli hurriedly changed the topic. "I just hope Nestor hasn't gone home."

"Where's home?" I asked.

"Down in the city."

I rested my backpack on the floor and rubbed my shoulder. I really had to take some stuff out of it or I was going to start walking with a permanent slant. "The city's a big place. Do you think you could narrow the location down a bit?"

Eli flushed. "Nestor's family lives down in Chinatown." He shifted his weight from his left to his right foot while he thought. "Or is it Flushing? I'll check. I've got it written down."

"He's Chinese?"

The surprise must have showed in my voice because Eli asked me why it mattered.

"It doesn't. Nestor doesn't seem like a Chinese name is all."

"Eli doesn't seem Spanish," he observed.

"Except," I told him, "your name is Elazaro."

"Well, maybe his name is something else, too," Eli pointed out. Then he went to get the address. Zsa Zsa trotted behind him. As she ran, tiny fragments of the leaves that had become stuck to the fur on her hind legs dislodged and drifted to the floor.

I hung my jacket up in the closet and looked around. The place was different than I remembered it being, but then, given the remodeling, it would have to be. The hallway was gone. The living room flowed into a dining alcove, which in turn led into a narrow galley of a kitchen.

I moved further in. Some waiting rooms I've been in have had more furniture than this place did. A large-screen TV took up one corner of the sparsely furnished living room, a tattered brown-and-green tweed sofa took up the other. Magazines, old newspapers, and piles of clothes lay on the beige carpet next to the sofa. Two white urn-shaped lamps sat on the floor. Batik tapestries hung on all four walls. A small bridge table and four folding metal chairs formed the sum of the dining alcove furnishings. It was piled high with books and papers.

"Nestor isn't big on furniture," Eli observed when he returned a moment later. He was holding a piece of yellow paper in his hand. "Between school and work I'm never here anyway, so I don't care. I wasn't going to buy anything.

I got all I need already. I'm not wasting my money on stuff like coffee tables when I gotta be putting it away for tuition."

Manuel mimed, grabbing on to his love handles. "Or the gym."

Eli patted his belly. It jiggled a little under his caress. "The way I see it, there ain't nothin' wrong with having some meat on your bones. I figure a woman would rather see a man with some money in his pocket and extra pounds around his middle than a skinny loser with nothing."

Manuel stuck his neck out. "No, Mr. Pillsbury Dough Boy, what they like is someone who knows the moves."

"The moves to the Public Safety Building?"

"That is enough," I growled before Manuel could reply. I pointed to the piece of paper Eli was holding. "May I have the address."

Eli handed it to me. I glanced down. Nestor's family resided on Canal Street. Probably in one of those old, six-story walkups. Well, I sure hoped he was still in Syracuse, because unless I spoke Chinese I'd have as much chance of finding him down there as I would finding a lump of coal on a dark night. Even if I did speak the language, nobody there would tell me anything anyway. They didn't take kindly to outsiders.

"We called," Manuel added. "But there was no listing."

I wasn't surprised. "Do you know if he's first generation Chinese-American?" I said, thinking gangs. There were a number down in Chinatown, mostly kids from Hong Kong looking for action.

"Nestor was born over here, if that's what you mean," Eli answered. "But from the couple of things he said, I don't think his parents were."

"How about his girlfriend? You have a residence for her?"

"Yeah, we know where Adelina lives," Manuel said, giving

the address to me. I wrote it down on the back of one of
my business cards. "But nobody there will speak to you. Her
momma run us off when we tried."

"What did you say to her?"

"Nothing." Manuel pointed to his head and twirled his
finger in a circle. "She's just crazy."

"Manuel . . ."

"We didn't say anything." Manuel repeated indignantly,
his voice rising. "We just asked her where her daughter was
and she threatened to shoot us."

"Was she speaking literally or metaphorically?"

Manuel gave me a blank look.

"Did she have a gun?"

"Not that I seen. I think she was just talkin'."

"Maybe I'll have better luck. How about his friends? Can
I have their names?"

Eli hunched up his shoulders and blinked. "I don't know
who they are. Well," he continued in the face of my skepti-
cism, "he always went out."

"Where did he go?"

From the expression on Eli's face I could have been asking
him to translate the Old Testament into Latin. "He didn't
tell me."

"And you never asked?"

"No. Why should I? I'm not his mother."

"You two had to talk about something."

Eli fidgeted. "We talked about stuff."

"What kind of stuff?" I asked while I moved my head in
a circle, trying to work the crick in the back of my neck out.
It didn't help. Unfortunately, what would help—a shot of
Scotch and one of George's back rubs—was still a ways off.

"Stuff stuff. Who called. Who's gonna go out and get
some more milk. That kind of thing," Eli said. "Mostly we

weren't home at the same time, and when we were, I was studying and he was watching TV."

Manuel bent over and scratched Zsa Zsa behind her ears. "You ask me, the less you talk to that guy the better off you are. Wait until you see his room. He's got some seriously weird shit in it."

"Weird as in how?"

He straightened up. "Weird as in seriously disturbed. I mean, I wouldn't live with that kind of crap. It would creep me out." He turned to Eli. "I don't know how you can."

"It's not like he was dancing around with it while I was trying to eat breakfast," Eli snapped. "Anyway, I liked the guy. Okay? At least he liked to read. He always had something interesting to say."

Before Manuel could reply, I gave him a little shove. "Come on. It's late. I want to get this done and get out of here." I'd told George I'd meet him at his house by eleven-thirty, the latest.

We passed by Eli's room on the way to Nestor's. It was too small for the amount of furniture in it. The room must have measured nine by twelve at the most. Into it, Eli had managed to shoehorn his bed, a nightstand, a dresser, a computer table, and the five aquariums holding his lizards and snakes. A bookcase leaned against the wall opposite the doorway. Its three shelves overflowed with books and papers. The top, in contrast, was empty except for a number of carved wooden animals of the kind they sell in places like Haiti and Brazil to tourists off the cruise ships.

I pointed to a wooden tortoise. "Where did that come from?"

"Madagascar. My mother gave it to me."

"And that?" I indicated a Japanese doll dressed in a kimono.

Eli gave an embarrassed little laugh. "That's from her, too. Every time she and my pops go somewhere, they send me something."

"They must lead an interesting life."

"I guess some people would say so. But me, I prefer being in one spot. You ready to see Nestor's room?"

I nodded. It was the last door in the corridor. Manuel clicked on the light as we went inside. "Is this what you were talking about?" I asked him, indicating the black walls and ceiling. A poster of every parent's nightmare, Marilyn Manson, was taped over the bed.

"Fuck, no."

We took another step in. The place was a shambles. The dresser drawers were open. Clothes were strewn everywhere. The bedcovers and the pillows were on the floor.

I looked around. "Did you guys do this?" I asked. The place exuded a faint, but unmistakable odor of weed and incense. The smell brought back pleasant memories of rainy Saturday afternoons spent with friends.

Eli flushed. "I guess we should have been a little neater."

"We were hoping to find something that would give us a lead," Manuel explained.

"And did you?"

"No."

Eli said something else, but I wasn't listening because I'd just seen what Manuel had been talking about. I crossed the room, stepping on Nestor's clothes as I went. Rewashing them should be the least of his problems.

"See, I told you," Manuel said. He was right behind me. I could feel his breath on the side of my neck.

"Yes, you did." For once, he hadn't been exaggerating.

Several large mason jars were sitting on top of Nestor's bookcase. In them floated what looked like a number of

preserved biological specimens. I peered at the nearest jar.
It had a baby bird with three wings in it. The one beside it
sported a two-headed snake. Next to that was a claw from
an unidentifiable animal. It was soft and white, the color
long having been leached out by the chemical amniotic sac
it was floating in. I repressed a shudder as I peered at the
next specimen. It looked like an organ of some sort. I
decided I really didn't want to know where it came from
as I picked up something brown and shriveled. On closer
examination it turned out to be a dried lizard. I put it back
down hastily.

"Maybe he's interested in biology," I said, but even I
didn't sound convincing to myself.

Manuel snorted again. "Yeah. Right. Biology, my ass.
Gimme a break. What he's interested in is weird shit. That's
why he couldn't get no one else to room with him. They'd
take one look at what he got in this room of his and they'd
be truckin' out the door."

"Do you know where he got these specimens?" I asked
as I thumbed through the CDs on the next shelf. Maybe I'd
be able to use them as a means of tracing him. I found I
was having a hard time not looking at the jars, even though
I didn't want to. It's funny how compelling the grotesque
always is.

"He said he just collected them here and there," Eli
replied.

That didn't help much, but in a pinch I was sure I'd be
able to narrow his suppliers down. There was a biological
supply house in Rochester. I could start there. If they hadn't
sold him those specimens, they could probably tell me who
would. Somehow I didn't think the list of people who handled freaks of nature would be very large.

Nestor kept his books on the bottom shelf. I squatted

down and read the titles. He had a lot of books on natural history, books on electronics, a couple of books on chess, several on the Navy SEALS and other Special Ops units in Vietnam, all of Tolstoy's works, as well as those of Faulkner and the economist Adam Smith.

"I told you he was smart," Eli said. "He was saving up to go to school for oceanography."

"Why that?" I asked Eli as I straightened up.

"He said he liked the ocean because it was peaceful."

Zsa Zsa jumped up on Nestor's bed, yawned, and flopped down, giving me her I-am-bored-so-hurry-up-and-finish look. I ignored her and glanced at my watch. It was ten-thirty. I still had plenty of time to get to George's. Which was good. I'd been late the last two times. He'd been pissed. Which had gotten me pissed. Sometimes relationships can be a real pain in the ass. "Where did you keep the suitcase Nestor took?"

"In my room," Eli said. "Under my bed. I didn't keep my door locked," he added. "I didn't think I needed to."

Manuel confined his commentary to rolling his eyes.

A thought occurred to me. "Do you have a current phone bill?"

Eli looked sheepish. "Uh. We just got our phone reconnected a week ago. It's been out of service for the last couple of months. Nonpayment."

So much for tracing Nestor through the calls he'd been making. "I don't suppose you have a picture of him or Adelina?"

Eli shook his head.

Why had I even asked? "Fine. In lieu of that, I want you and Manuel to write down everything you remember about him and her."

"Like what?" Eli asked.

"Like whether Nestor drives. Whether he owns a car. What kind. Where he works. The kind of food he likes to eat. The names of his old girlfriends. The names of Adelina's friends. Where Adelina goes to school. Anything at all that you think would be helpful."

Manuel and Eli were already arguing about what they should include in the list as they walked out the door. After they left, I sat down on Nestor's bed, lit a cigarette, and tried to empty my mind and think about what the room was telling me, beyond the fact, that is, that maybe Nestor had done too much acid. Instead I found my thoughts drifting back to my younger self, to the me who had looked at this house. How had I seen myself? Certainly not as a part-time private investigator or the proprietor of a pet store. More like a happily married mother and a Pulitzer Prize winner.

I curled a lock of hair around my finger. It was still long and red. My weight hadn't changed, either. I was still a size ten. I flicked the stub of my cigarette into an empty beer can sitting on the nightstand and walked over to the mirror hanging above the dresser. I tilted my head to the right and then to the left. I had wrinkles around my eyes now and my jawline was beginning to soften, but overall I'd held up rather well, if I did say so myself. If I put on some makeup and wore something other than jeans, tees, and flannel shirts I'd still be passable.

The thought should have made me happier than it did. Maybe it was the way the orange beef I'd eaten was rolling around in my stomach. After all, the Chinese say happiness begins with good digestion. I lit another cigarette and got up. The sooner I began, the sooner I'd get out of here. I started with the clothes lying on the floor of Nestor's closet.

It didn't take me long to go through them since there were only four pairs of pants and an old starter jacket. After

I searched their pockets, getting a handful of lint for my trouble, I threw them back down and checked the drawers. They were empty, their contents having migrated to the floor. With the toe of one of my boots. I prodded the mismatched socks, raggedy boxers, and stained T-shirts heaped on the rug. The only thing they told me was that Nestor didn't use bleach with his laundry detergent.

I stuck my head out the door. "Did Nestor have a lot of clothes?" I asked.

"You got me," Eli replied, his voice floating back to me from the living room.

I sat down on his bed and studied the top of his nightstand. An old Kodak, faded with age, was wedged underneath a lamp. I held it up to the light. It was a picture of a basset hound. "How about a dog?" I yelled out to Eli.

"If you're talking about the picture on the night table," Eli replied, "that's Suli. He died about five years ago."

I slipped it into my pocket anyway and opened his nightstand drawer. The smell of weed rose to greet me. But except for a few seeds scattered in the corners, the drawer was empty.

I pressed my finger down on one of the seeds. It stuck to my skin. I lifted my hand back up and contemplated the little seed. So many people rotting in jail because they possessed its progeny. I got up and walked into the living room.

"How heavy into dope was Nestor?" I asked Eli, showing him the seed on my finger.

"He smoked a joint now and then. That's all," Manuel said, answering for Eli.

"You're sure of that?"

"Sure I'm sure."

"Because I don't want to find I'm dealing with something other than what I signed on for."

"You're not, Robin. I swear," Eli said vouching for Manuel.

"I better not be," I told them both. I'd listened to Manuel's oaths before. It wasn't that he lied. He didn't. He just left things out.

I went back into Nestor's room and checked out the only place I hadn't looked, under his bed. I sneezed as the dust from under the bed tickled my nose. Sweeping had not been one of Nestor's primary activities. A collection of socks had taken up residence, along with magazines, torn scraps of paper, dust bunnies, and some small black pellets. Probably mouse droppings. Perfect. The way my luck was running I'd probably get the Hanta virus from them and die.

I used a wire hanger that was lying on the ground to sweep everything out into the open. The socks needed to be washed. The magazines, dog-eared with use, were all *Penthouses* and *Playboys,* and the paper seemed to be of the junk mail persuasion. As I was getting up, my eyes fell on a torn envelope. Something was scribbled on the bottom in pencil.

I picked up the envelope with the tips of my fingers. The writing was smudged but decipherable. Phone numbers, three with an NYC exchange. They'd probably prove to be nothing, but at least it was a start. I turned the envelope over. The mailing address was ripped off, but the left-hand side still sported a local return address. Happy Trails. Sounded like a travel agency to me. One that specialized in dude ranches? I guess I'd find out when I called.

I was just heading out of Nestor's room when the phone rang.

"Answer it," I could hear Manuel saying.

"No," Eli replied.

"Then I will."

"Don't get it."

"It could be for me."

The ringing stopped.

"Here," Manuel said. "It's for you."

There was a moment of silence, then Eli started to speak in a quavering voice. "I'm not trying to avoid you," he was saying. "Yes. Yes. No. I don't have any news. Yes. I know what you said. Hey. I'm doing everything I can. I hired someone to find it." There was a pause. "She's here now. You want to speak to her? I'm not sure she'd like that," Eli stammered.

"Who wants to speak to me?" I asked as I came into the kitchen.

Eli licked his lips and held the receiver out to me. "The guy I told you about." And he made a scissoring motion with his fingers.

Chapter
4

I cursed under my breath and slammed on the brakes as a car going up University Avenue sped through a red light. Didn't anyone in this town believe in traffic signals? I was pissed at Eli, I was pissed at Manuel, but more than anything, I was pissed at myself for having allowed Chapman to railroad me into meeting with him tonight, when I wanted to be with George.

"You want me to come down and cover you?" George had asked when I'd called to explain why I was going to be late coming over to his house after work.

"No. I'll be fine."

"It'll just take me a minute to get my clothes on."

"The meeting's in a public place."

"So? You don't know what this guy is like. What happens if he forces you out of there?"

I lit another cigarette. "Why should he do something like that? All he wants to do is talk to me. Anyway, don't you have work to do? Aren't you supposed to be writing a paper or something?"

George sighed. "I'm always supposed to be writing a paper. That's what graduate students do. But what you're doing sounds more interesting than correcting tests."

I smiled. "Once a cop, always a cop. What's the test on?"

"The French Revolution. You wouldn't believe what these kids don't know. Listen to this." He paused for a minute while he looked for the paper. " 'The French Revolution took place in the early nineteen hundreds.' " He groaned. " 'I think they should have used other means to resolve their differences. After all, violence never works.' Where do these people come from?"

"You were probably like that, too, when you were that age."

"Oh, no, I wasn't."

I closed my eyes. I could picture George sitting on the sofa, phone in hand. The TV would be on. *The New York Times* would be lying on the coffee table. One, not both, of the lamps on the end tables would be lit.

"Are you sure you don't want me to come down?" George asked again.

"I'm positive."

"Come over when you're done. I want to talk to you about something."

"What?"

He laughed. "That would be telling."

I leaned against the wall. "Come on."

"You'll like it," he teased.

"Creep." But it was too late. George had hung up.

I kept wondering what George wanted to speak to me about as I headed downtown. I had half a mind to turn around and go over there now, but I really couldn't. After all, I'd agreed to help Eli. I'd accepted his money. Now I wanted to get the job done as quickly as possible.

Given that context, I couldn't say no to Chapman. I couldn't give up the opportunity to possibly negotiate a settlement on Eli's behalf or at least buy him some time, which would make my job a hell of a lot easier. The good part was the place Chapman had proposed wasn't over in some godforsaken part of town where I'd have to worry about getting out of my car, I thought as I made a left onto East Fayette. Interesting that it was the same place he and Eli had met in. Perhaps Chapman was a man of regular habits. I hoped so. It would make him easier to find if I needed to track him down.

Lefty's was housed in a run-down, narrow, three-story brick building that squatted between two alleys, on the ass side of Armory Square. I parked illegally across the street and Zsa Zsa and I went in. A red "e," the only letter in the neon sign in the window still working, blinked a welcome. At eleven-thirty at night there were five people in the bar, and from the description Chapman had given of himself, he wasn't one of them.

I hoisted Zsa Zsa onto a stool and signaled to the bartender, who was watching a flickering black-and-white TV down at the far side of the bar. Rangy, gray-haired, with pockmarked skin and a scraggly ponytail running down the back of his neck, he looked as if he was counting the seconds till he could go home.

He took his time coming over. I had to call him twice to get his attention, and even when he did walk over he was still watching the TV out of the corner of his eye.

"I'll have a Rolling Rock," I said when he was standing in front of me. "And a small plate." He looked at me for the first time. "For her." I pointed to Zsa Zsa. "So she can have a little beer, too." And I handed him a ten.

He shrugged and walked away. I had a feeling I could have told him I was going to have sex with a doberman and a monkey on the bar and his response would have been the same.

"Do you know a guy named Chapman?" I asked when he returned.

"Never heard of him." His eyes darted back to the TV as he put the beer and the saucer in front of me. The saucer had several small black spots on it.

I didn't say anything about it. I figured that since Zsa Zsa drank out of the toilet bowl her immune system was pretty strong.

"How about someone called Nestor Chang?"

"You some sort of cop?"

"No. Chang's my brother."

He lifted his eyebrows up to his hairline to convey his disbelief. The gesture made the whites of his eyes glisten like the whites of two poached eggs. "You just said his last name is Chang."

"He's my stepbrother."

The bartender grinned, exposing a mouthful of bad teeth. "Of course he is."

"What's the matter? You never heard of adoption?" I took a business card out of my wallet and slid it across the bar. He gave it a perfunctory glance.

"If you see him," I told the bartender, "give me a call. It's a family thing. It'll be worth some money to you."

"Will it now?" His hand hovered over the bar's surface. I guess he wanted to make sure I could see what he was doing, because he waited till he had my attention before he dropped my change down on top of a puddle of spilled beer.

"Sorry about that," he said and moved away, leaving the card lying where it was.

"I can see you are." I picked up the bills and glanced around for a napkin to blot them off with. Naturally there wasn't one. I used my jeans. I was going to wash them anyway. *No tip for you, buddy,* I thought as I put my money away. Okay. It was late. I was tired. So maybe I could have come up with a slightly better story, but mine hadn't been outside the realm of the credible. No. The guy was just a schmuck. If he hadn't wanted to answer me, he just had to turn and walk away. Instead he'd pretty much written up a large placard that said "I know Nestor Chang and I'm not going to tell you" and hung the damn thing around his chest. Why? Because he was stupid? Because he had a chip on his shoulder? The truth was, I was too tired to care. I flicked my lighter and watched the flame shoot up. After a few seconds the skin on my thumb began to prickle from the heat and I put the cap back down.

Of course, I could always ask Chapman when he showed up. If he showed up. It was looking more and more as if he wouldn't. I glanced at my watch. Chapman was ten minutes late already. I'd never met the man and already I hated him. If he hadn't arrived by the time I was done with my beer I was leaving. I poured a little into the saucer for Zsa Zsa, wiped the rim of the beer bottle off with my shirttail and took a sip. It wasn't great, but then, given the selection the bar had, it was probably one of the best of the bunch. I stamped my feet. It was cold in here. A draft from the inch space between the door and the floor eddied around the room, stirring up a fug of stale beer, old cigarette smoke, and dust.

I took another sip of beer, lit a cigarette, and studied my surroundings. The place looked as if it hadn't had a dust rag or a mop taken to it since it opened twenty years ago. The mirror tacked up on the wall behind the bar was filmed with a layer of grime, as were the mementos of a better time, faded photographs that had been stuck up at random on the wall of smiling, sunburned men in shorts holding up strings of fish. The red upholstery covering the bar stools was a patchwork of duct tape, the bar itself was a mass of nicks and scratches, and the linoleum on the floor had long since had its design ground out of it.

Lefty's only possible claim to fame was that it hadn't been turned into a fern bar yet, *yet* being the operative word. Ten years ago Armory Square had consisted of a handful of old warehouses, a few stores, and four or five bars attached to SRO housing. The bars had sported names like The Watering Hole, Joe's, and The Red Dog, and catered to a clientele that worked hard at staying as drunk as possible for as long as possible.

Then things began to change. As with most things, whether the change was for the better or not depended on your point of view. Now the area was awash in the detritus of yuppie life—art galleries, microbreweries, pricey pasta joints, Thai restaurants, French bistros, and nightclubs. Now the bars had names like Ciao Bella. College students trolled the streets and middle-management types ordered Scotches with pedigrees longer than those of most of the dogs I've owned.

Ten years ago, if you went into a bar and ordered something like an apricot wheat ale you'd have been thrown out on your ass. Of course, I reflected as I took a sip of my Rolling Rock, a beer I now remembered why I no longer drank, ten years ago good American beer was an oxymoron.

If you cared at all, you drank German or English. I was thinking about that when someone tapped me on my shoulder.

I turned around. A man was standing behind me. "I'm Robert Chapman," he said.

He wasn't what I'd expected. Even though he'd described himself on the phone, the picture of him I'd conjured up on the ride across town was a cross between Simon Legree and Charles Manson, but the man standing in front of me was strictly suburban. He could have been one of those guys you see out in the 'burbs mowing their lawn or washing their car on a Saturday morning.

I put him at about five years younger than me. He was medium build, medium height. He was wearing a ski parka, a green cotton turtleneck, and a pair of faded blue jeans. He had short, light-brown hair, brown eyes, and regular features.

Chapman held out his hand and we shook. His grasp was firm, his skin warm on my skin. He looked into my eyes and held my hand for just a fraction longer than necessary. Then he smiled, grinned really, and I could tell from the way he did that he knew that he had gotten to me, and that fact put me in an even worse mood than I was already in.

"Somehow I thought you'd be older," he said as he sat down on the stool next to me. I could smell his cologne. It was something foresty.

"That's all right. I thought you'd be scummier."

He laughed and pointed to Zsa Zsa. "She's yours, I take it?"

I nodded.

"I used to have a cocker when I was a kid. She loved bread. She'd sit in front of you and bark and bark until you gave her some. I was really broken up when she died."

"What happened?"

"One of my neighbors poisoned her." He waved his hand in the air. "But I'm sure you're not interested in my childhood. I'm sorry to drag you down here at this time of night." His eyes really weren't bad at all, I was deciding when he said something that brought me up short. "I just thought since you're working for me, we ought to meet."

"Excuse me?" I cocked my head. I was sure I hadn't heard him correctly. "Would you mind repeating that?"

He smiled again. His teeth were white and even. I noticed he had a dimple on his left side. *Robin, this is not a nice man,* I reminded myself. Ted Bundy looked like a sweetie, too.

"Well," Chapman continued, as if what he was saying was the most logical thing in the world, "Eli is working for me, and since you're working for him, I figure that makes you part of the team."

"Is this your version of the new math?" I looked at him incredulously. My thoughts of negotiating faded. This guy was playing by a set of rules they didn't teach at Harvard.

"On a temporary basis, of course."

"I don't think so."

"I see." He folded his hands on the bar. They were large and well tended. The word *capable* came to mind. A few seconds later the bartender came over. Without being asked, he put some ice in a glass, took down a bottle of Jack Daniel's, poured out a shot, and put it in front of Chapman.

"Come here a lot, do you?" I observed.

"Once in a while." He took a sip and made an appreciative sound with his lips. "Mick and I are old buddies, aren't we? We go back a long ways."

Mick nodded and moved back down the bar.

"Did something happen to his vocal chords?"

Chapman shrugged. "He just doesn't like to talk much.

Never has." Chapman took another sip of his drink and put it back down. I stubbed my cigarette out on the side of my beer bottle and flicked the butt into it. My stomach was starting to bother me again.

I turned toward him. "What is it, exactly, that you want from me?"

"Like I said, I just like to meet the people I work with."

"And like I said, I'm not working for you."

He pursed his lips. "That's a pity, because I know in here"—and he hit his chest with his fist—"that we'd make a first-rate team. But you know what? One thing I've learned in this world in the time I've been in it is to never say never. Maybe in the future you will be. Everyone can use a little extra cash once in a while. And I'm always in the market for new couriers." He took a pen, wrote something down on the paper napkin next to him, and pushed it toward me. "Here. It's my pager number. I'd like you to take it. That way you can tell me how things are progressing with the suitcase. Or maybe we could just meet for a drink. Or dinner. There's a nice little restaurant I know near Ithaca that I think you'd like."

I left the paper where it was. "Thanks, but I don't think so."

"Why?" The smile on his face made it clear he wasn't used to refusals. "It's Eli, isn't it?" Chapman took a sip of his drink.

Zsa Zsa barked. I leaned over and scratched her rump. "Among other things, yes. Maybe this is just my hang-up, but having dinner with someone who kicks someone in the balls, cuts them, then threatens to cut off their fingers when a business deal goes bad is not very appealing."

"I just wanted to show him I meant business."

"I think he got the message."

"Good." Then Chapman chuckled. "God. You should have seen his face when I told him I was going to cut his fingers off. I thought his eyes were going to fall out of his head. I didn't think people actually looked like that outside of bad movies." He lifted his glass up and put it back down. "I can't believe that he really thinks I'm going to do it."

"And you think that's funny?"

"In a manner of speaking."

"I don't."

Chapman moved slightly closer to me. His thigh brushed against mine. "I'll apologize to him."

I flushed. What the hell was the matter with me, I wondered as I moved my leg away. This guy was playing me. I knew that. But it didn't seem to matter. "So then nothing will happen if I don't find the suitcase?"

"You will," Chapman said confidently.

"But if I can't. Hypothetically speaking."

He smiled again and stood up. "Let's not talk about that now."

"What's in it?"

"Didn't Eli tell you?"

"Yes, he did. I just want to hear your version."

Chapman squinted. "Cuban cigars. A lucrative commodity thanks to the stock market. I don't smoke them myself, but lots of people these days do."

"Fine. But still we're not talking vast amounts of money here. How about my client gives you half if the suitcase doesn't show up. It sounds to me as if you can afford to take a four-thousand-dollar loss without too much grief."

For a split second the pupils of Chapman's eyes turned flat and reptilian. Then the second was gone, leaving me to wonder if I'd really seen what I thought I had.

"That's right," he said, now looking merely irritated.

"We're not. We're talking about something more important. We're talking about principle."

"The principle being?"

"Honoring your word." He slapped the bar with the palm of his hand for emphasis. "That's very important to me. When I give my word I abide by it, and I expect the people I deal with to do the same."

"Really." I felt as if I was listening to a wolf preach vegetarianism. I found myself absentmindedly chewing on my cuticle. I put my hand down. "And if, through no fault of their own, they can't?" I asked.

"I don't accept that kind of negative thinking. Negative thinking leads to weakness, it leads to moral rot. Listen," he continued. "I made a deal with your friend. I was prepared to pay him a fair amount of money for his services. In return, I expect him to abide by our agreement. That's how I run my business. That's why I'm a successful entrepreneur. It's that simple."

I stood. Looking up at him was making the crick in my neck worse. "Adam Smith would be proud of you."

The corners of Chapman's mouth turned up. "I see you're well read. That's a nice quality in a woman. As a matter of fact, I like to think he would be. I'm not ashamed to be a capitalist. I'm just doing what everyone else is doing. Earning a living, and in the process I'm giving your friend, among others, the chance to earn enough money to go to college. There's nothing wrong with that."

"You're a philanthropist, too."

"Yes, I am," he said with complete sincerity, choosing to not respond to the sarcasm in my voice. "Let me tell you what makes me a success," he continued, answering a question I hadn't asked. "Just like the Japanese, I subscribe to the concept of the team. If the team is successful, then everyone shares in the rewards, but if one person screws up that means everyone screws up. If one person makes a mistake, everyone bears the consequences. And that includes Eli and anyone he subcontracts with."

"Are you threatening me?" I demanded.

Chapman made a vague gesture in the air with his hands. "Actions have consequences. It's time your friend learned that. Believe me, in the long run he'll be better off. Unfortunately, sometimes learning discipline can be a painful process." Chapman reached over, took the paper he'd written his number on, folded it up, and tucked it in the breast pocket of my shirt. The familiarity of the gesture annoyed and excited me at the same time. "Don't forget to call me now. I'll be waiting to hear from you."

"Don't worry." He was turning to go when something occurred to me. "Tell me one thing, Mr. Businessman."

He cocked his head and waited. "Yes?"

"Is Chapman your real name?"

He grinned. "What do you think?"

"I think no."

Chapman imitated the shape of a gun with his thumb and his forefinger and pointed it at me. "Bingo. I knew it when I saw you. You and me we're going to get to be good friends."

"I doubt it."

He laughed. "I don't."

I looked up his name in the phone book after he left. There was a Robert Chapman all right. Unfortunately when I called, his daughter told me, along with a few other choice words, that her father was seventy-five years old and confined to the house with emphysema.

Chapter
5

George was dozing on the sofa when I let myself in. "Wha?" he groaned as Zsa Zsa jumped up and licked his nose. He pushed her off and sat up. "What time is it?" he asked, rubbing his eyes.

"Twelve-thirty."

He yawned. "You want something?" he asked as he levered himself up and padded into the kitchen.

I told him I didn't. The beef was still rolling around in my stomach. "So, what did you want to talk to me about?"

He laughed. "This." George handed me a page from last Sunday's *New York Times* travel section and pointed to a story about Belize in the left-hand column.

I scanned the article and handed it back. "Sounds great."

"One of my cousins just bought some land there. How'd you like to go down for a couple of weeks?"

"Are you kidding?" His expression said he wasn't. I hugged him. "I'd love to."

George grinned. He fixed himself a bowl of cereal and milk and sat down at the kitchen table. "Good. I'll call him tomorrow. So tell me about the meeting you just had." He ate as I talked. "I don't like it," he said when I was done. "Eight thousand is chump change. This guy is putting way too much effort into recovering it."

"I know."

"It sounds to me as if something else is going on." He spooned up the last of the milk and pushed his bowl away. "You have any idea what?"

"Not yet."

"But you're sticking with this?"

"For the moment."

"Can I ask why?"

I picked Zsa Zsa up and sat her in my lap. I'd been thinking about that question on the way over. "A couple of reasons." I plucked a twig off Zsa Zsa's ear.

"Which are?" George prompted.

"I feel bad for Eli and I really don't like Chapman." I scratched Zsa Zsa's chest. "I figure I can always opt out if things go sour."

"Fair enough." George clicked his tongue against the roof of his mouth. "See if you can set up another meeting with this guy."

"Any reason?"

"So you can get his license plate number. I'll have one of my friends run it through the computer and see what comes up. At least then you'll know who you're dealing with."

And on that note we went to bed.

I spent the night dreaming about beaches and butterflies and blue-green waters, so it was doubly painful to wake up and contemplate the gray sky out the window. I burrowed my head into my pillow and looked at George sleeping. God, I wished I didn't have to get up, but I did. I had to be at Lawrence Junior High at ten o'clock.

About a month ago, one of my customers, a nice lady who teaches in one of the city junior highs, and I had gotten talking about how tough it is to teach these days in the city schools. What with all the budget cuts, there's no money for books and paper anymore, let alone field trips. While the suburban kids still have Mommy and Daddy to take them to the zoo and the park, her kids don't. So she asked me if I'd ever be willing to come into the school with some of my reptiles and give a talk. I'd said sure, no problem. She'd called back the next day. And now I had to face a class full of thirty twelve-year-olds. I was not looking forward to this.

I stopped at a 7-Eleven and got two jelly doughnuts for Zsa Zsa and a couple of glazed doughnuts and a large coffee for myself before heading to the store. Tim was already there when I arrived.

"What are you planning on taking?" he asked.

After a fair amount of thinking, I'd come up with four specimens that wouldn't hurt the kids or be hurt by them. "One of the pythons." The Burmese I was thinking about was fairly docile and at seven feet was large enough so he could be handled without being stressed out. "Iggy the Iguana." He loved people and would curl up on your shoulders whenever he could. The people who had him had moved overseas and hadn't been able to take him along and I'd been trying to find a good home for him. "One of the monitors." The one we had in the store was four feet long, with impressive claws and a tail that could inflict serious damage. People liked them because they looked like dinosaurs. In fact, in the fifties, filmmakers had used them as stand-ins.

"How about a corn snake?" Tim suggested.

I nodded. "That was my last choice." A native Southwest snake, they were not only fairly sturdy, but with their yellow and red coloring, attractive as well.

"Have fun," Tim said as I packed the four reptiles up in newspaper-lined cloth bags, newspaper being great insulating material, because the one thing that you can't do with reptiles is let them get cold.

"Who knows? Maybe this could be the start of a new career," I said as I left.

Things began well. The kids gasped when I took the python out of its bag. I told them how they eat and how you can keep them in your house and how their skin really feels dry and what marvels of evolutionary efficiency they are. Then I invited anyone who wanted to, to come up and touch him. After some hesitation about ten kids did. Next I talked about Iggy and about how iguanas were good lizards to start out with if you were interested in owning one, because they weren't as fussy about their eating habits as some other lizards were. They eat a wide variety of fruits and vegetables and seemed to be able to withstand more variations in temperature. The corn snake went well, too. Even the girls liked him, because he was pretty.

When I took out the monitor, one of the kids in the front row said, "Wow, he looks like a Komodo dragon."

"I guess you watch the Discovery Channel."

The kid smiled.

"He does look very similar. He comes from the same family, except he's not on the CITES list." And I went into the little speech I'd prepared. "Every year, thousands and thousands of animals die thanks to the wildlife black market. Many species are in danger of being wiped out. Some, like the Komodo dragon attract attention because they're so dramatic, but others, like beetles and butterflies, don't." By now the lizard was moving his head around trying to bite me. I moved my right hand further down his back away from his mouth and made sure I had a good grip on his underbelly with my left hand. Then I turned him around so they could get a good look at his tail, which was whipping back and forth. "Now if he was bigger," I told him, "his tail could really hurt you." I lifted him up a little and indicated his claws with a nod of my chin. "And these could send you to the hospital with stitches."

The kid who'd spoken before leaned forward. "How can I get a Komodo dragon?"

"You can't and you wouldn't want one. CITES species are protected under international law." I was about to say more when the monitor lizard did something I'd only read about. When monitors get nervous they sometimes do something similar to projectile vomiting, except it comes out the other end.

Well, this one must have been really nervous, because suddenly he started spraying the room. Before I knew it, kids in the first five rows had lizard feces over their hands and faces and clothes. Everyone was screaming. Kids were dropping down on the floor and crawling for cover. The hall monitor and the school cop ran in and they got a dose of it, too. By the time I managed to get the lizard back in the bag, my hand was bleeding from the clawing I'd received and my shirt and hair were caked with lizard shit, which, let me tell you, smells really, really bad.

I looked at the teacher who'd asked me to come in. She was standing there with her mouth hanging open, her white shirt smeared with dark greenish-brown excrement. I looked at the school policeman and the principal. They were yelling at each other. I looked at the kids. Some were screaming and some were crying. No one was paying any attention to me. It seemed like a good time to leave. I packed up my reptiles and ran out into the hall. It was crowded with kids and teachers, most of whom were positive someone had been shot—which in a sense was true.

Tim's mouth fell open when I walked in the store. When I told him what had happened, he started to laugh. He was laughing so hard the tears were rolling down his cheeks.

"So much for your educational career," he said when he got his breath back. Then he thought about it some more and went off into another gale of laughter.

After a minute, I joined him. Who would have thought one lizard could wreak so much havoc? We both ended up sitting on the floor cackling like maniacs, while I fended off Zsa Zsa, who was trying to lick me clean. When I got my breath back, I got up, went home, and practically sterilized myself. The first thing I did was get a garbage bag and strip off my clothes and threw them in it. Next, I went upstairs and took a long, scalding hot shower, making sure to scrub every inch of myself. My skin was bright pink by the time I was done. Then I washed my hair twice, put on new clothes, and went back downstairs. As I brewed a pot of coffee, I wondered if George had talked to his cousin yet. Belize was sounding better and better all the time.

I was struck once again by what a nice guy he was and how scary he looked. The scowl he habitually plastered across his face would have made someone who didn't know him move to another part of the known universe. Maybe it was like the big dogs. Most of the really big breeds are sweethearts, because they don't have to be mean. Everyone defers to them automatically.

"It's not my fault if I'm big and I'm black and I scare the shit out of everyone," George had once bragged to me five beers into the evening. He'd been grinning at the time he said it.

But that had been when he'd been on the police force. I wonder if he felt the same way now that he was in grad school. History grad students don't look like he did. Maybe that's why he was trying to lose weight and had taken to wearing blue denim work shirts and corduroy pants. Which made me think about the paper he was working on. He'd given it to me to read a couple of days ago. I'd been putting it off, "The function of popular political songs in France in the 1800s" not being what I considered an easy read, but now seemed as good a time as ever.

"I call these songs eighteenth-century rap," he'd said, tapping a page with his finger. "These were songs made up by the common man to protest social conditions, in the same way that rap protests today's social ills, by today's disenfranchised."

I took my coffee into the living room, along with the paper, and settled down to read it. Actually, it turned out to be more interesting than I thought. I was on the second page when Tim called to tell me that one of our suppliers had just called to say that our shipment of crickets and mealworms would be delayed by a couple of days. Which wasn't good because we were short as it was.

"Who do you want me to call?" he asked.

"Call Mike," I suggested. "See if he'll sell us some to tide us over."

"Are you coming in?" Tim asked.

"Do you need me?"

"Nah. It looks like it's going to be a slow day." And he hung up.

He was right. It did. Around twelve o'clock the weather had turned bad. The sky had gone from gray to black. The streetlights had come on. It started sleeting. Last night the weather announcer had predicted we'd get a mix of sleet, freezing rain, and snow today, which would continue into the evening. Unfortunately, it looked as if he'd been right. Weather like this was not good for business. If we took in twenty dollars today we'd be lucky. People don't come out when it gets like this, which made it a good day to see what I could do about finding Eli's lost property.

I finished off George's article, penciled some questions in the margin, corrected a few typos, then went to get the envelope I'd found in Nestor's room. The numbers turned out to be the phone numbers of a flower shop, a Kinko's, a dry-cleaning store, two no-longer-in-services, and a Chinese restaurant down in New York City. Nobody there, naturally, had heard of a Nestor Chang or a Robert Chapman. I tried the travel agency next and got a recording telling me to leave a message and they'd get back to me as soon as possible. I looked at my watch. Two-thirty. I called the number Chapman had given me and left a message for him, after which I decided to take a ride over to Adelina's house and see if she had come back home yet.

According to the address Eli had given me, Adelina lived over by Thorden Park. The area had once been middle class. Not anymore. The houses looked wearier than I remembered them being, as if they'd given up the fight against the elements. Driveways buckled. Cars were parked on front lawns. Tipped, empty trash cans lolled around on their sides in front of houses. Sodden newspapers and beer cans lay on the grassy divides.

Adelina's house, a two-family, blue Colonial, still had Christmas decorations in the windows. I parked across the street in front of two, large, dead pine trees, stubbed out my cigarette, put the collar of my jacket up and ran for the house. The wind had picked up since I'd left work. The sleet stung my cheeks and numbed my hands. I blew on them after I rang the bell. A moment later, a woman who I assumed was Adelina's mother opened the front door halfway and peered out at me.

"Yes?" she said. The woman was short and stocky. Her black hair was pulled back, but at some point in the day wisps had escaped and now floated across her lined forehead and her cheeks. Her dark-brown eyes were underscored by deep circles. Her skin was pale and blotchy. Large brown freckles were splattered over her chin and nose. She looked tired and harassed. One of her hands was clutching the collar of the old quilted coat she was wearing. Evidently I'd caught her on her way out, or she'd just come in.

I introduced myself. "My name is Robin Light." I had to raise my voice so I could be heard over the sounds of the TV and fighting children coming from inside the house. I handed her one of my pet store cards. "I run a pet store called Noah's Ark and I'm talking to people in the neighborhood about my store. We have some specials this week you might be interested in."

She furrowed her brow as she read. Her mouth silently formed each word. When she was done, she handed my card back to me. "We don't have any pets here."

"You have children, don't you?"

She crossed her arms over her chest and stood square in the doorway, a stone blocking my path. "Yes."

"Young ones?"

She nodded again. The sleet was blowing across the porch, wetting and darkening the floorboards.

"You should consider buying them something. Animals provide wonderful educational opportunities for children.

Even something as inexpensive as a hermit crab or a hamster can give them a window into a new world."

Adelina's mother stifled a cough. "This isn't a good time. You wanna talk, come back later." Her voice was flat and impatient. It held faint traces of a Spanish accent.

"I understand your eldest daughter is an animal lover. Maybe you can put her in charge."

The woman's breath caught in her throat. "How you know about my daughter?" she demanded.

"Adelina came into my store," I lied. "She told me you wanted to buy something for your children. You just didn't know what."

Uncertainty danced in the woman's eyes. "Well, she's not here now."

"Really? Where'd she go? Is she off on a trip somewhere?"

The woman brushed a tendril of hair away from her eyes and frowned. "Yes. She's traveling." She nodded toward the inside of her house. "I got her brothers and sisters to take care of." She began to close the door.

"Please." I put my hand on the door and leaned against it to keep it open. "Five minutes. That's all I'm asking. Just five minutes."

She kept pushing. "I got laundry to do. I got dinner to make."

"If you don't let me in," I blustered, "I'm going to be back here with the police."

The door stopped moving. "You ain't got no right . . ." she protested.

"I got all the right in the world," I informed her. "Your daughter is involved in the theft of a large amount of money." Not that eight thousand dollars was a large amount these days, but it was still a felony. "Now," I continued, "my client doesn't want to involve the police."

"Elazaro." The woman spat out Eli's name. "You work for that *hijo de puta*. He should be ashamed."

"Of what?"

"Of causing all this trouble."

"That's an interesting point of view, blaming the victim for the crime."

Her eyes flashed. "He said bad things."

I didn't ask what. "That's why I'm here," I lied again. "He sent me to apologize."

The woman opened her mouth and closed it again.

"I didn't tell you the truth at first because I didn't think you'd listen to me." I slid my foot in the doorway, hoping she wasn't going to slam it shut. "All Eli wants is what's rightfully his back. He doesn't care about anything else."

The woman tucked a loose strand of hair behind her ear. "I got to unpack the groceries," she said, and she flung the door open and beckoned for me to follow her.

The heat embraced me as I walked inside the small entrance hall. I unbuttoned my jacket and stepped over and around the coats, boots, hats, gloves, scarves, and book bags strewn on the floor. The living room was on my right. I glanced in. The walls were painted a light green. White curtains hung from the windows. A sofa and a love seat, both in a matching checked print, were arranged around a large, square, wood coffee table that was covered with books, papers, crayons, and toys. Two end tables held lamps and a number of pictures. Three children, two boys and a girl, ranging in ages from four to twelve, were sitting cross-legged on the carpet in front of the television set squabbling with each other while they passed a big bag of tortilla chips back and forth between them.

The woman paused by the doorway. "I don't want no crumbs on the floor," she said.

The kids nodded. Their eyes never left the TV screen. They were watching the cartoon channel. A show I'd never seen was on.

"I mean it." The woman's voice rose slightly, the way it always does when someone isn't paying attention to you.

The youngest child, a girl, replied, "We won't, Mommy."

The woman snorted and continued on into the kitchen. It was a small, bright room. The plants spilling over the window ledges and the children's drawings and paintings on the walls contributed to its cheerful appearance. A round table over in the corner was piled with brown paper bags full of groceries.

The woman unbuttoned her coat and slung it over the back of one of the chairs. I wanted to do the same, but something told me I wasn't going to be here that long. I read her name off the tag pinned on her uniform.

"Where do you work, Donna?"

She started putting groceries away. "At the Jewish old age home. I'm an orderly there. I got the early shift." She whirled around as a thought occurred to her. "Why you wanna know? You gonna come out there and make trouble? Make me lose my job?"

"No. Of course not." Her reaction made me wonder if she had a green card. I reached into one of the bags and handed her a jar of peanut butter. She took it reluctantly, as if doing so would compromise her in some way. "I just want to know about your daughter."

Donna put the peanut butter away. Then she opened the refrigerator and carefully placed two gallons of milk and a half-gallon of orange juice on the top shelf. "I haven't heard from my daughter since she walked out of this house."

"Aren't you worried?"

The woman shrugged. "It's not the first time she's left

home like this." She stowed three boxes of macaroni and cheese in the bottom shelf of the kitchen cabinet by the refrigerator.

I leaned against the back of one of the chairs. "You don't strike me as the kind of mother who loses contact with her daughter," I observed.

Donna took two rolls of paper towels out of the bag. "My daughter and I didn't get along so good." Her tone was unconvincing.

"What are you afraid of?"

She looked off to one side. "I'm not afraid."

"I don't believe you. Your daughter could be in a great deal of trouble from a man called Chapman."

"Chapman?" The woman went over to the table and folded up one of the brown paper grocery bags. She ran her fingers over the creases, making sure that folds in the paper were sharp. Then she started on the second one. "Who is this man Chapman?" Her air of studied innocence was about as convincing as a hooker playing a schoolgirl.

"The suitcase that your daughter's boyfriend stole. It's his property."

Donna straightened up and folded her hands across her chest. "She has nothing to do with any of this."

"Possibly." I sighed. "But she has to do with Nestor, and Nestor is in big trouble."

Donna's jaw muscles tightened at Nestor's name. She didn't like him much. I asked her why, hoping her answer might give me a way in.

She turned and began stowing cans of tomatoes in one of the upper kitchen cabinets. "It's not me. It's my husband. He doesn't like that he is Chinese."

Somehow I'd expected a different answer. "What's wrong with the Chinese?"

"My husband says they eat cats and rats. He says they are dirty."

"You believe that?" It amazes me how frequently I hear comments like that, often from people who should know better.

She shrugged again.

"What do you think of Nestor?"

"I think he thinks he is smarter than anyone else."

"Did you tell your daughter that?"

Donna slammed the cabinet door shut. "She won't listen to anything I have to say about him."

My way in was turning into a dead end. I gave it one last shot. "You want your daughter to go to jail for him?" I asked, adding to the sum of lies already told.

Donna favored me with an impassive look.

I put one of my cards on the table next to the remaining bag of groceries. "Could you at least tell her to call me?"

"How can I tell her, if I don't know where she is?"

I took Donna's hand in mine. "Do her a favor and do what I ask."

"Favor?" Donna removed her hand. "That's funny. Why should I? You get money for finding her, yes?"

"Yes," I agreed reluctantly.

"So you are just like everyone else."

"No, I'm not. Believe me, Adelina will be a lot better off with me than with Chapman. Or the police."

Donna snorted derisively. "I have nothing more to say to you."

Strike three.

The phone started ringing. She walked over and picked it up. I left while she was talking about what she should bring for Teacher's Appreciation Day at one of her children's schools. There didn't seem to be much point in staying. On the way out, on impulse, I stopped in the living room. The kids were still watching TV. I stepped in front of it.

"Hey," the oldest one, a boy, yelped.

"I'll move in a second," I assured him, taking care to speak in a low voice. Their mother would kill me if she knew I was talking to them. Of that, I had no doubt. "Any of you heard from your sister?" I asked.

Okay. I knew it was a tacky thing to do. I'm in a tacky business.

"My mommy said she went to visit someone," the youngest of the three volunteered. She had chubby cheeks. Her long black hair was braided into two pigtails. Two large red bows covered the rubber bands. Like her sister and brother, she was wearing a parochial school uniform.

I felt like a creep for using her. I knelt next to her anyway. I heard crackling. I looked down and saw I'd knelt on the tortilla chips. The little girl covered her mouth with her hand and giggled.

"Did your mommy say who?" I asked as I moved the bag to one side.

The little girl shook her head and popped one of her fingers in her mouth.

"My mom didn't tell us," the oldest boy said. "We don't know."

"That's right," the older girl agreed. She had her mother's eyes, but they were still soft. She hadn't inherited their suspicion yet.

"Addie used to read me stories," the little girl said wistfully. "All the time. Sometimes she even let me sleep in her bed with her."

"Is your father around?" I asked.

The boy shook his head. "He's back in DR. The Dominican Republic," he added when he noticed the blank look on my face. "Visiting our *abuelita*. Now you going to let us see our show or what?"

I got up. This wasn't going to get me anyplace. It was time to go. The kids went back to watching TV. On the way out, a grouping of pictures on a table over by the far end of the sofa caught my eye. I walked over and studied them. They were family photos. Mother and father at the beach with baby. Mother and father in front of a palm tree with two babies. Mother and grandmother with three children. I picked up the most recent photograph.

It showed the three youngest children, plus a girl that I took to be Adelina, standing in front of the house I was now in. Adelina's resemblance to her mother was unmistakable. She had the same long black hair, dark eyes, and perfectly oval-shaped face, but she looked confident, ready to take on whatever was going to come. She hadn't been beaten down by life yet, a fact her clothes, a black leather jacket, a tight sweater, and jeans that she must have needed Vaseline to get into, proclaimed.

I glanced at the children. For all the attention they were paying to me I could have been invisible. I slipped the photograph, frame and all, in my jacket pocket and turned to go.

Donna was standing in the doorway, watching me.

The bright red patches on her cheeks and the way her hands were balled up into fists told me she'd seen what I'd done.

I tried to think of some way I could talk my way out of the mess I'd just made for myself.

I couldn't.

There didn't seem to be any way around it.

"Here," I said, holding the picture out.

Chapter
6

The kids took one look at their mother and scattered. Donna didn't notice. All her attention was focused on me.

"You . . ." Donna spluttered. "You . . ." Her English failed her and she lapsed into a string of Spanish curses as she barreled toward me.

Half of what she was saying I understood and half I didn't. Judging by the half I did understand, I didn't want a translation of the rest.

Before I had a chance to do or say anything, Donna ripped the picture of her daughter out of my hand and slapped me across the face. The blow stung. For a little lady she packed a lot of force.

I edged around her. "If you'll let me explain." But I might as well have been talking to a hurricane for all the effect my words had.

The little girl began to cry. Her mother ignored her.

"Get out!" she shrieked at me. "Get out of my house. Next time I see you, I tell my husband to shoot you."

"I'm going."

I stumbled over the children's boots and toys and coats as I backed out of the living room and into the hallway. I wasn't taking my eyes off this woman. Not even for a second. Donna followed me, screaming curses as she went.

I was a couple of feet from the front door when she bent down and picked up a baseball bat one of the kids had left lying on the floor. This was not good. I didn't have anything on me that I could protect myself with.

"You don't want to do that!" I cried.

"I show you." Donna grasped the bat with both hands, and started swinging. I jumped back just in time. I could feel the wind from the bat whooshing by me. A second later and I would have been writhing on the floor. The bat hit the wall instead. A hole appeared in the wallboard.

"Hey, calm down." I'd heard that Dominicans were hot-tempered, but this was ridiculous.

"I calm down all right." Wham. She took another swing. Another hole in the wall.

I ran out the door, jumped down the steps, and bounded into my car. Donna was right behind me. Fortunately, I was faster. I had my car started up by the time she reached me. She raised the bat over her head and swung at my wind-shield. I yanked the wheel to the left, threw the car into reverse, put my foot down on the gas, and went up on the curb. I heard a crack as the bat came down on my sideview mirror. Donna raised the bat again. I shifted into forward. The car shuddered as she connected with the rear. I floored it. The car leaped ahead. I spun the wheel to avoid a tree. A man standing in his driveway stared at me openmouthed as I drove toward him on the sidewalk.

"Sorry!" I yelled as I went back on the pavement.

I checked my rearview mirror. Donna was still behind me. Who would have imagined someone that chunky could run that fast, I thought as I sped off. As I rounded the corner, I caught a final glimpse of Adelina's mother. She was standing in the middle of the street shaking the bat at me. Her hair was plastered to her head. Her mouth was opened. She was screaming something at me. Fortunately, I couldn't hear what it was.

I stopped at a convenience store half a mile away and got out to examine the damage. I ran my hand along the crumpled mess that had been my side mirror and over the dent near where the gas cap was and told my car everything was going to be all right. The dent wasn't a big deal. Sam, the guy at the body shop, could bang that out, and he could probably scavenge a mirror, too, but I still felt a tug in the pit of my stomach.

I love my car, maybe because it reminds me of my youth. It's an old, New York City yellow Checker taxicab. It has well over 150,000 miles on it and I'm hoping to get 300,000. When it goes, I won't be able to replace it. Last I heard, there were only three or four left in the state. Of course, it is only a piece of machinery, we weren't talking my firstborn here, and given the option of the cab being in the service station or me being in the hospital, the choice is obvious. Nevertheless, I was still really pissed.

I was impervious to the sleet as I walked to the convenience store. The icy rain numbed my fingers, worked its way down my back, caked my eyelashes, and clung to my hair, but I was too busy being angry at Eli to care. He should have warned me about Adelina. But as I bought a couple of Almond Joys I had to admit to myself that he had.

Eli had told me Adelina's mother was nuts, he'd told

me she'd run him and Manuel off, but I hadn't asked for clarification, because I'd thought he was exaggerating. Obviously, he hadn't been. I wondered if there were any other surprises in store for me as I unwrapped one of the Almond Joys and bit into it. If my next couple of stops were like this one, I was going to give Eli his money back. Twelve hundred dollars wasn't enough to pay for a fractured skull. As it was, I figured Eli owed me the repair job on my cab. At the very least, which is why I stopped over at the garage next.

"Can you give me a rough estimate?" I asked Sam.

He looked at the cab with sorrowful brown eyes. He ran his hand over the damage gently and shook his head slowly. "You shouldn't be driving it like this. The water is just going to make the problem worse."

"I don't have another ride."

Sam gestured toward the parking lot in front of the garage where twenty used cars in varying states of decrepitude sat. "Take your pick."

I chose a '90 Honda and left the cab in Sam's capable hands.

My second stop of my day was The Happy Trails Travel Agency. Hopefully, things would go more smoothly this time. The agency was located across the street from a car dealership in a small, run-down strip mall on Burnett Avenue. The shop was flanked by Henri's, "all dog breeds welcomed," and The Clip Joint, "walk-ins accepted, manicurist on premises." Very convenient. It was good to know that if an emergency struck, Zsa Zsa and I could get our hair done at the same time. A kitchen appliance store and a pizza place completed the line-up. At four o'clock in the afternoon, three cars were parked in the lot. Business wasn't exactly booming here.

I ran into the pizza shop and ordered a soda and a meatball sub. While I ate, I noticed some snowflakes were mingling with the sleet. By the time I was through talking to the guy at Happy Trails I'd probably have to scrape the ice off my windshield. The thought did not cheer me. I finished the last of my food, paid, and went into the travel agency.

From what I could see from the doorway, Happy Trails was a strictly shoestring operation. The office had two standard-issue fake wood desks in it, a row of folding metal chairs along the far side wall, a couple of cheap plastic plants, and beige carpeting on the floor. The rest of the furnishings consisted of three large garishly colored travel posters of Disneyland, Hawaii, and Cancun tacked on the walls.

The store was empty except for a man behind the desk nearest to the door, eating a slice of pizza. When he saw me he took another couple of bites before he put the remainder down, and wiped his hands on a napkin.

"Can I help you?" he asked, his mouth full of food.

For some reason he looked familiar, although I couldn't place him, but maybe that was because he appeared the same as a hundred other tired, rumpled-looking, middle-aged men. He had a round face, a bristly mustache decorating his upper lip, and a receding hairline. The plaid sports jacket he was wearing could have used a cleaning, as could his tie.

"I hope so." I walked over to his desk. Its left side was stacked high with travel brochures. Looking at them made me want to whip out my credit card, book a trip to someplace like India, and take off.

"We have some nice trips to Mexico," the man continued in a monotone that would have deadened the most enthusiastic traveler. "The fares are great. You're not going to be able to do better. Or how about Miami?" He favored me with a wet smile. "Or the Virgin Islands? We have a fantastic weekend package. Two hundred bucks for three nights, everything included."

"Sorry. Maybe another time." I held out the envelope I'd found in Nestor's room. "Is this yours?"

A flicker of concern crossed his face as he took the envelope. He studied it for a minute before handing it back. "That's our name on the corner. Why? Is there a problem?"

I gave him my card.

He held it at arm's length and squinted at it. "Inquiries? What kind of inquiries?"

"I was hoping you could help me out with some questions I have concerning a Nestor Chang."

"Nestor Chang, hunh?" A cagey expression crossed his face. He tapped his fingers on the desk in an unconvincing parody of thought. "I'm not sure. Offhand, the name doesn't ring a bell."

Right. I wondered how much he'd want. Probably a double sawbuck, I decided as I sat down. It seemed to be the going rate these days.

I leaned over and read his name off the plate on his desk. "Mr. Landen, I got this envelope from his room. I'm hoping you can tell me where he went."

He scratched behind his ear. "It's hard to remember. I'd have to go through my files . . ."

I managed to say, "I can see where in a booming business like this it would be hard to keep track of all your customers," with a straight face. I took a twenty-dollar bill out of my wallet and laid it on the desk.

He looked at it regretfully, as if the sight of it pained him.

"Ordinarily I wouldn't ask this, but my time . . ." He sighed and put the money in his wallet.

I finished the sentence for him. "Is in demand."

"Exactly. Especially now that February break is coming up." He stuck out his hand. We shook. "Call me Dale. Everyone does."

"So, Dale. About Nestor Chang. Did he take one of your trips to Miami?"

"Let me check." He rose, went over to a file cabinet sitting in the corner, rifled through it for a couple of seconds, and picked out a folder, which from where I was sitting looked as if it had never been used. "Here we are. My memory isn't as good as it once was."

Landen pretended to look through the folder before he returned it to the file cabinet and closed the drawer. He sat back down. "Mr. Chang was in here a month ago. He talked about going to Disney World. I mailed him some brochures, detailing a nice package, direct flight, four nights, three days, deluxe accommodations, I assume that's what was in the envelope you found, but that's the last I heard of him. He never called me back. As to his going someplace? Your guess is as good as mine."

"Thanks." I put the notebook and pen I'd taken out of my backpack away. A couple of years ago, paying twenty and getting nothing for it would have annoyed me, but I've become resigned. Sometimes you get taken, sometimes you don't. That's just the way it goes. And anyway, it wasn't my money, it was Eli's.

Landen leaned forward slightly. He licked his lips in anticipation. "What did this guy do anyhow?"

"Killed a travel agent," I deadpanned.

Landen's eyes widened for a fraction of a second. Then he got the joke and favored me with a wet smile. "Seriously."

"Seriously, he stole some money."

Landen's smile turned rueful. "There seems to be a lot of that going around these days. If I think of anything, I'll be sure and tell you. Here." He handed me one of his cards. "Ring me up if you change your mind about that vacation. We really do have some good deals."

"Thanks, but frankly the thought of going to Cancun doesn't excite me."

"Oh, we have trips all over the world. South America, Central America, Japan, Indonesia, Borneo. You name it. I can get you there."

I made a noncommittal comment and walked out the door. The way my life was going these days I couldn't afford to fly down to Newark, much less someplace like Japan.

I paused in front of the cage with the dead iguana. The two-foot lizard was lying on its back, its four claws pointed skyward. I bit my cuticle. Well, it was nice to know that things hadn't changed at Animals Galore, the pet shop chain from hell. I'd reported them three times in the past couple of years to both the ASPCA and the State Police. The store had been fined each time for improper housing of livestock, specifically their dogs and cats, but it was cheaper for the shop to pay the fine than it was for them to clean up their act. The company that owned the chain had deep pockets. It would take a lot to get them into compliance.

I wondered if Jeff, the kid who had been in my store the other day, had been in here as well. I don't know why PETA doesn't demonstrate in front of them. I'd even join in. The place gives the rest of us a bad name. The shop sells puppy mill puppies. Their reptiles are so badly stressed, they usually die as soon as people get them home, if not before, and most of the fish they have swimming around have contracted ick from the crowded conditions and poor water filtration in which they're forced to live.

My opinion of Nestor hadn't gone up when Eli had told me this was the last place he worked. It also impacted, as they like to say in the corporate world, on my information-gathering ability. Especially since the manager of the store, a moron named Hal Salt, from whom I wouldn't buy a can of tuna fish, had somehow or other found out that I was the one who'd issued the complaints. He hadn't been pleased. I started on my next cuticle while I tried to remember what he'd said when he'd phoned to let me know how he'd felt. Something like: did I think I was goddamned Joan of fucking Ark? Or had it been fucking St. Francis of Assisi?

I wasn't sure. It didn't really matter. What mattered was that Hal Salt didn't like me very much. Which is why I'd left Animals Galore until this time of the day. I'd been hoping he'd be on his dinner break and I'd get one of the clerks, but, of course, given the way my luck was running, that wasn't how things turned out.

Salt must have been in the back, because I didn't see him when I walked in. The store was empty, a fact that cheered my heart. I was standing by the reptiles looking around for someone to talk to when I heard a man say, "I thought I told you not to come in here anymore."

I turned and there Salt was, a vision of beauty in his polyester pants and Izod shirt. I nodded toward the dead iguana. "Still maintaining your normal high standards of care, I see."

Salt's jaw muscles started working. "Get the hell out."

I did my tough-guy imitation, not that anyone ever takes it seriously. "I will as soon as you tell me what you know about Nestor Chang."

Salt threw back his head and let out a roar of laugher.

"I'm glad you think I'm funny."

"I think you're hilarious." He mined his ear with his finger and wiped the wax off on the hem of his shirt. Watching him made me want to throw up. "In fact, I think you're so funny," he continued, "that I'm going to call security and have them arrest you."

"On what charge?"

"Shoplifting. You took . . ." He made a clicking noise with his teeth as he looked around. "One of those." He pointed to a box containing a heat rock. "Not that I need a charge. The guys are my friends."

"You have friends?"

Salt went over to the counter, picked up the phone, and began to dial. "Let's see," he said as he waited for someone on the other end to pick up.

I left before anyone did.

Maybe I should have stayed. Maybe he was just calling the local weather information line, but I didn't want to take the chance. I had too much to do to play games with security right now. A session with them could eat up an hour. If they decided to call the cops and I got taken downtown, that would be another two right there. At the minimum.

Salt watched me go. He was grinning as I walked away. It took every ounce of self-control I possessed to refrain from turning around and belting him in the mouth. He and his store were like warts. You cut them out and they just came back. But then, maybe I just hadn't found the right knife.

The store could afford the fines, but what about public opinion? I headed for the phones down by the door and called Calli, my friend who works on the Syracuse newspaper. She'd been out in California when I'd called the ASPCA last time, but she was back now. People may not care about dead lizards and fish, but they care about abused puppies. Let's see what Salt would do in the face of an exposé? Calli and I chatted for a little while and she promised she'd run my idea by her editor and get back to me.

I felt better after I hung up. The feeling lasted until I dug the list I'd asked Eli and Manuel to compile out of my backpack and looked at it. I still had five people to talk to. Something told me I wasn't going to get any more out of them than I had out of the first three. I decided to take a breather and get a cup of coffee before I began.

I was sitting in Cup O Java—one of those mall-franchised coffee shops that sells black dishwater and calls it espresso—trying to decide whether adding a fourth packet of sugar would help the taste of the swill I was drinking, when someone tapped me on the shoulder. I turned my head.

"Yes?" I said, glancing up.

A teenage girl was standing in back of me. She looked like a wraith. She was so thin, her thigh was probably as big as my wrist. Her eyes were two large dark black pools, her skin was dead white, and her hair resembled straw. The green T-shirt and the faded denim overalls she had on served to underscore her thinness and her youth. She looked like a street urchin in need of a hot meal.

"My name is Myra. I was in the back of the store when Salt was yelling at you," she said.

I motioned for her to sit down. She slipped into the chair next to me.

"Can I get you anything?" I asked. "A piece of cake? A sandwich?" *All the food in the store* I wanted to add, but didn't.

The girl shook her head. "I told Salt I was just getting a soda, so I can't stay too long, but I have to know. Nestor is in trouble, isn't he?"

"Yes, Myra." I pushed my coffee away. It was undrinkable.

"He stole something from someone and they hired me to find him and get it back."

The girl wrinkled her nose. "He's such a sleaze." She ran her finger over the metal clasp on her overalls. "I'm amazed Hal waited as long as he did to fire him." She stopped for a few seconds and then continued, the words tumbling out of her mouth in a rush. This wasn't someone who needed any prompting. "He was always calling in sick and leaving me to close. According to him, he was dying. He always had something wrong with him. He had the flu or strep throat or he sprained his ankle or whatever. Not that it mattered when he was here. He never did anything except talk on the phone. If I were the manager, I would have run his ass out of here a long time ago."

"Really?" I reached for a cigarette before I remembered I couldn't smoke in the mall. Watching this girl, listening to the enmity in her voice, made me wonder what Nestor had done to her to make her dislike him so.

"Yes. Really." She glanced behind her as if she was fearful of being seen talking to me. Given the way Salt felt about me, she probably was. "He was stealing stuff from the store and selling it himself."

"Livestock?"

"Everything." The girl tugged at the neck of her T-shirt. "He wasn't even smart about it. I mean, I think Hal would have overlooked a little stuff like that. But stealing cases of dog food? Come on. Hal may be stupid, but he's not brain dead."

I leaned back and toyed with the spoon lying across my saucer. "Do you have any idea where Nestor's gone?"

"He'd never tell me anything like that. We didn't talk. But if you really want to find out about him, go speak to his friend, Sulfin Olsen. Maybe he can tell you what you want to know. And then there's that animal guy."

"Animal Guy?"

"You know." The girl scrunched up her face while she tried to recollect the name. "The one that keeps all that strange stuff."

"You mean Parker Littlebaum?" I'd supplied things to him once in a while over the last three years. And the girl was right. He did have strange stuff. A lot of it.

She nodded. "I'd talk to him, too. Nestor was always over there."

I wrote the names down on the top of the paper Eli and Manuel had given me. "Can I ask how come you're telling me all of this?"

"No, you can't." She pushed her chair back abruptly, got up and left.

I watched her stride by the empty stores. When she turned the corner, I left, too.

Chapter
7

I probably would have spent more time wondering precisely what Myra had against Nestor if I hadn't stopped at the phone on my way out of the mall and called Tim.

I jingled quarters in my hand and listened to the wind whining through the cracks in the doors as I waited for him to pick up the phone. The weather had worsened in the half hour since I'd called Calli. The sleet had changed to snow, but this wasn't the gentle drifting sort that poets rhapsodize about. This was the kind that insinuated itself down your collar, lashed your cheeks, and made you blink. It wasn't a good evening to be outside. Judging from the way two couples were huddled in the doorway, peering out into the storm, they agreed with me.

Tim answered on the fifth ring. "Noah's Ark," he said, sounding slightly out of breath, as if he'd been in the middle of doing something and had had to drop it and hurry over.

"Zsa Zsa okay?" I asked after I'd said hello. She was

barking in the background. She had a small dog's bark, high-pitched and annoying. I could see her in my mind, reddish-blond fur, stubby tail, flopping ears, dancing around the floor, her eye firmly fixed on something too small for me to see. I hadn't taken her, because I hadn't known how long I was going to be in the mall.

Tim suppressed a cough. "She just wants some more potato chips, but I'm not giving her any. She's had half a bag already."

Which is why she weighs thirty-eight pounds, six pounds above the ideal weight for cocker spaniels. "Any problems?"

"Aside from the fact that Manuel has been driving me nuts phoning the store every ten minutes, wanting to know where you are, no."

I unslung my backpack and rested it on the marble floor. I was definitely going to have to see a doctor about my shoulder. "What does he want?"

"He didn't say. He just said to tell you it's an emergency."

I groaned. "Emergency, hunh?"

"That's what he said."

Tim sounded as skeptical as I had. Maybe that was because everything with Manuel always is an emergency. He could be calling because he found a severed foot or he could have gotten himself stranded and need a ride home. On the other hand, he had told me he owed someone money. Now I wished I'd asked him who the guy was and how much he owed.

"He says you should come here right away." And Tim read off an address on the west side of town.

"Do you have the number?"

"He wasn't calling from there. He was calling from a pay phone."

I hung up and tried the number Tim had given me. All

I got was a recorded message telling me this phone didn't receive calls. Great. I called Tim back. He answered on the first ring.

"So, now what?"

"I'm not sure." I could see the rest of my plans for the evening dissolving into the muck of Manuel's needs. I sighed and twisted a lock of hair around my finger while I thought about my options.

I watched one of the men standing by the front door muscle it open. I could feel the cold air through my jeans as he gestured for the woman who'd been next to him to follow. She hesitated. He gestured more forcefully. I was just about to yell for him to shut the friggin' door when she gave in. Gathering her coat around her, she hunched her shoulders and stepped outside.

Tim began coughing again, a deep hacking, wheeze of a cough that left him breathless and spent. I'd watch him doubling over with spasms for the past week and it didn't seem to be getting any better. I hope he didn't have pneumonia. There was a lot of it going around lately. "So, when he calls again, what should I tell him?" Tim asked when he could speak.

The couple ran for their car, shoulders tilted against the snow beating down on them.

I knew what I wanted to tell Manuel. The last thing I felt like doing was driving to God knows where in my loaner. Especially since the tires were bald. Unfortunately, the way I saw it, I really didn't have a choice.

Manuel could be in serious trouble.

Or not.

Probably not.

I didn't want it on my conscience if he was, though. The

hours of self-torture I'd inflict on myself as a penance weren't worth it.

In a way, I hoped he was in trouble. Because if he wasn't . . . If he wasn't, well, he would be, I vowed, as I told Tim to tell Manuel I was on my way the next time he called. "Once you've spoken to him, you might as well close up shop and go home. There's no point staying open in weather like this."

"With my luck, he probably won't call and I'll be stuck waiting around," Tim groused. Static crackled across the line. I pictured the telephone wires swinging in the wind. "I'll take Zsa Zsa home with me so you don't have to come back and get her. Drive safe," he said, and hung up before I could say the same to him.

When had "drive safe" replaced God bless? I wondered as I dialed my answering machine to collect my messages. Chapman had returned my call. I phoned him back and left another message telling him I wanted to set up a meeting and I'd try to get in touch with him tomorrow morning. Then I dialed George's number, hoping he might want to come along with me. I got a busy signal. I tried again ten minutes later, then minutes after that before I gave up. He was probably online, cruising the web. There was no point in waiting. George could be on his computer for hours before he logged off, especially if he was playing Avenger.

I hung up, shouldered my backpack, and walked toward the door. I leaned against the frame, smoked a cigarette, and watched the white flakes swirling under the parking lot lights. It looked as if the Nor'easter the weather people had been predicting had finally blown into town. These storms, which seem to get more frequent each year, rampage up and down the eastern seaboard, usually leaving a substantial amount of damage in their wake.

As I finished my cigarette, I considered the fact that I should have pruned the dead branches off the crab apple in front of my house and topped the spruce near the kitchen window this fall. Now the storm would probably do it for me. And on that note, I buttoned my jacket, turned my collar up, opened the door, stuck my hands in my pockets and ran. The cold air sucked at my breath. Snowflakes clung to my hair and eyelashes. The world became white.

I really do hate this weather, I decided as I scraped the ice off the car's windshield. It's true it's not as bad as tornadoes or floods or forest fires or earthquakes, but it's bad enough. The other day it had been in the forties, and now this. You go out wearing jeans and sneakers and get caught in a blizzard. No wonder everyone around here was always sick. By the time I got in the car I was chilled to the bone. My mood didn't improve when I got on Erie Boulevard.

The driving was terrible. I had to hunch forward to see out the window. The snow was greasy, and as if that wasn't bad enough, the sleet had laid down an undercoating of ice. I chugged along, following the headlights of the car in front of me and tried to ignore the asshole in the SUV riding my tail. It's amazing. Give a guy a four-wheeler and any sense he has vanishes.

Normally the trip to Sullivan Street would have taken me fifteen minutes at the most. This time I was betting it would take forty-five. It turned out I was wrong. It took an hour. When I turned onto Montgomery, I was down to five miles an hour. A horse could have made better time. When I turned on to West Onondaga, things got even worse. The hill, which was steep enough to make a good ski run, was littered with vehicles.

While I watched, one car got a quarter of the way up the hill and slid back, and another one going down the hill did a three sixty and smacked a third car stuck sideways across the street. No way was I going up there. I backed up a couple of feet and made a left onto Tolliver—at least the street was flat—and clicked on the radio as I concentrated on driving in the tracks the car before me had created. The announcer was telling everyone the southbound ramp on Teall was closed due to an accident, as was the northbound on Thompson. Emergency parking rules were now in effect. Police were advising against unnecessary travel.

"No shit." I clicked the radio off. Nothing like stating the obvious I always say.

Of course I didn't have my boots on. My gloves were at home. I didn't even have a shovel in the trunk, let alone kitty litter, boards, or flares. That was me—always prepared for all contingencies. If I got stuck, it was going to be a long, cold wait. It was nights like these I regretted not replacing the cell phone I'd lost. Not that calling the AAA would help much. In a storm such as this, it would be three or four hours until they could get to me. Why couldn't Manuel have had an emergency on a good night? We hadn't had more than a dusting of snow all winter and he had to pick the night we had a blizzard to need to be rescued.

It was beautiful out, though. I'd give the storm that. I'd just rather be admiring the landscape through the window of my house, sipping a Scotch, and feeding logs to the fire. Snow shrouded rooftops, cars, and lawns. It dripped from the telephone wires, capped utility poles, and wrapped up trees. I was in a more philosophical frame of mind by the time I arrived at 1078 Sullivan Street. Then I noticed the driveway was empty and my mood changed again.

I parked in the driveway, because leaving the car in the street was out of the question, opened the glove compartment, and took out the knife Manuel had given me as a birthday present last year. Mostly I keep it in there to appease him, but occasionally, as now, I feel the need to take it with me. As I've said, *emergency* in Manuel's vocabulary is a very flexible term.

I'm always surprised at how heavy the knife feels in the palm of my hand. A butterfly knife. The object's name, the pairing of the word butterfly and knife, has always struck me as willfully odd. The handle is dull metal. It has a series of small holes down the hasp. The blade is seven inches. It's illegal, but not as illegal as an unregistered handgun. On a scale of one to ten, it probably rates a three, if I was going to quantify that sort of thing. What the knife does do is give me a slight edge. It makes me feel a little more secure, but not so secure I get stupid. Plus, there is the fact that I couldn't get a conceal and carry permit for a handgun anyway. In Onondaga County, they're hard to come by, which is, I think, a very good thing.

As I slipped my knife into my jacket pocket, I realized the lights in the house were on. So maybe someone was home, after all. Of course, it could also mean the people who lived there had just forgotten to turn off the lights when they left, but I didn't want to think about that yet.

By the time I slogged my way through the snow to the front door, my shoes were sodden and my jeans were soaked up to the knees. I thought of what I'd like to do to Manuel as I rang the doorbell. While I waited for someone to answer, I glanced down at the mailbox. The name on it read Myers. Okay, Mr. and Mrs. Myers, where are you? Who are you? And what the hell is going on? Out of force of habit, I lifted the lid. Nothing except for a couple of circulars for a pizza shop.

I could hear the bell echoing inside the house, but that was all. No footsteps coming toward the door. No one yelling, "just a minute." No music on the stereo. No voices from the television. This was not good. I put my finger on the bell and kept it there, while I did a little jig to keep the circulation in my feet going. As the seconds mounted and no one came, I couldn't decide whether I was furious or worried. Something might be really wrong. Or Manuel could have gotten tired of waiting for me and left. Since I couldn't call him, I didn't know which one it was. What I did know was that standing out here was not doing me any good.

I took a look around. The houses on the block had all been built close together. If I were measuring, I'd guess they were no more than fifteen feet apart. There was just enough room between them for a driveway and a few shrubs. Most of them were lit up. People were home, all of which added up to a situation that was not conducive to breaking in. All someone would have to do was lift their blinds and they'd see me clambering in and I'd be down at the police station. I didn't need that kind of aggravation for twelve hundred dollars.

But then I decided that, given the weather, answering a call for a B&E was probably low on the police's priority list at that moment. The Syracuse police and the sheriff's department were too busy doing other things—such as unsnarling traffic and pulling motorists out of ditches. On the other hand, there was no point in pushing it. I decided to look for a less conspicuous way in.

I rubbed my hands together and blew on them as I trudged to the back of the house. From now on in, I vowed I was going to keep an extra pair of gloves in the car. I skirted a couple of garbage cans, then paused as I reached the back-yard. It looked as if I was in luck. The Myers had ringed it in with a hurricane fence. I thanked them for making my job easier. Measuring over six feet in length, the wooden slats butted up against each other, blocking any view a neighbor may have had.

I turned and studied the house. Unequal piles of snow building up on the lower peaks of the roof gave it a lopsided appearance. The most obvious points of entry were the two windows on the first floor. Fair-sized, they led, I suspected, into the kitchen. I slogged over to the nearest one and, standing on tiptoe, reached up and gave its sash an experimental push. I cursed as a patch of snow fell on my face. The sash didn't move. I brushed the snow out of my eyes and tried again. It stayed where it was. I looked closer. It had a lock on it. I moved on to the next one. It had a lock, too. Mr. and Mrs. Myers were obviously careful people. I'd have to break the glass to get in, something I was loath to do if I didn't have to—the way my day was going, I'd probably accidentally slit a wrist and bleed out. I decided to check out the basement windows first.

It took me a couple of minutes to locate them. There were three in all. The first two were too small for me to fit through, but the third one seemed like a possibility, even if it did look just a couple of inches larger than a bread box. I knelt down in front of it. The rust on its frame flaked off when I brushed against it. I touched the pane. It jiggled slightly, a sign most of the caulking was gone. Breaking the glass wasn't going to present a problem. It would just take a tap.

I peered through the thick, cobweb-encrusted pane. A brick wall, concrete floor, and furnace came into view. So far, I didn't see anything I couldn't handle. I gave the window an experimental push. It was open. The Myers had slipped up. The frame scraped my back and sides as I wiggled through. If I were ten pounds heavier, I never would have made it. Coming down, I accidentally kicked over four gallons of paint. I hadn't seen them because they'd been stacked flush against the wall.

The cans clattered to the floor, the noise seemingly magnified by the stone. One thing was for sure, if anyone was in the house, they were going to be down here pretty soon. I froze as I listened for footsteps, for someone saying "did you hear that noise?" while I glanced around and tried to figure out where I could hide. But the only thing I heard was the hum of the furnace. After a minute or so, I let my breath out, brushed the snow off my jacket and my pants and took off my shoes and emptied them out. Then I tiptoed up the basement steps.

Even though I was almost certain no one was home, I had my knife in my hand when I opened the door, but I needn't have bothered. No one was on the other side. I found myself in the kitchen. An unremarkable, serviceable room, it had been outfitted with an eye toward economy and efficiency. You could probably see the same wood, Colonial-style cabinets, Formica countertops, and beige tile backsplashes in half the kitchens in the city of Syracuse. Everything looked neat and tidy. Nothing seemed out of order, a fact that, perversely, was making me nervous.

The refrigerator condenser began to hum as I made my way over to the phone mounted on the far wall. Before I went through the house, I decided to try and get hold of Manuel. If he wasn't here, maybe he was at his house or Eli's.

But he wasn't.

He was at mine. He answered when I dialed in to get my messages, hoping he'd left one on my machine.

"Where are you?" he cried when he heard me.

"Where do you think?" I hissed. "I'm at 1078. The place

you told me to go to. What the hell are you doing at my house? I thought you were here."

"No. I never said that."

"You told Tim . . ."

"He must have misunderstood," Manuel protested.

"Right." If Manuel had a specialty, it was misinterpretations. Loopholes were his subspecialty. I sneezed. I was going to get sick. I just knew it.

"Is Eli there?" he asked.

"No one is here. Listen, you better not have broken my window getting in like you did the last time."

"That was an accident." Manuel sounded offended. "You should be glad I'm here. James was stuck outside."

James is my cat, although the "my" sounds too possessive, connoting a relationship based on ownership, a fact that is not true, since he comes and goes as he pleases, a sleek killer who takes delight in decimating the local bird population.

"Are you sure Eli isn't there?" Manuel repeated, leaving a note of urgency hanging in the air.

"Reasonably."

"Jesus." I could hear a catch in his voice.

I shifted the phone to my other ear, noticing as I did that I'd left a trail of wet footprints across the floor. "How about telling me what's going on?" I said as I made a mental note to myself to clean those up before I left.

"What's going on," Manuel told me, "is that Sulfin spotted Nestor and Adelina going into the house."

I absentmindedly reached over, grabbed a paper towel from the roll on the counter, and began blotting my hair. "Well, they're not here now . . ."

"And he told Eli . . ."

"Are you sure about this?"

"No. I'm not fuckin' sure of anything, okay?" Manuel's

voice rose. "But Eli said he was going up there to get his suitcase back. He said he'd call, but he hasn't. That's why I rang you at the store, only you weren't there."

"Well, I'm here now," I said grimly.

"What should we do?"

"I don't think there's anything to do. I'm going to take a quick look around and then I'm leaving—if I can get my car out of the driveway—before the people who live here show. Hopefully, I'll be able to get back. The roads were pretty bad coming up."

"I know. I saw a couple of cars stuck on East Gennie."

"If you hear from Eli, call me here in the next fifteen minutes," I told Manuel, even though I didn't think that would be the case.

"You got it."

I hung up, shucked off my shoes, no sense in leaving footprints on the light tan carpeting if I could avoid it, and took a quick peek around.

The house replicated the kitchen in its orderliness. The magazines on the coffee table in the living room, copies of *Reader's Digest* and *Time*, were arranged in a fan pattern. The arms of the sofa and chairs were covered with plastic sleeves. Reproductions of Degas ballerinas hung on the pale-blue walls. If anything had happened here, someone had done an excellent job of straightening up.

The dining room was equally unrevealing, except that the Myerses' taste in home furnishings and my taste were markedly different. A bowl of plastic fruit sat on a cherrywood table. The six chairs were all pushed in. Two plaster masks, dime store replications of tragedy and comedy, oversaw everything from their place on the wall. I opened the sideboard. It was full of crystal and china. Upstairs didn't yield much, either.

There were no bodies in the upstairs closets and no blood
splatters in the bathroom. A determinedly cheerful room,
it was decorated in bright blues and greens. A seashell motif
predominated. The shower curtain sported seashells and
seahorses. The rings that held the shower curtains on the
rod were topped with tiny white seashells. Seashells were
glued on to the tissue holder, the mirror, and the soap dish.
The motif continued into the bedroom.

The lamps on the night tables were reproductions of
Nautilus shells. A large wicker basket filled with seashells
sat on the dresser. I picked up a copy of a guidebook to
Sanibel Island off one of the nightstands. I wasn't surprised,
Sanibel Island being a place one goes to collect shells. I
wondered if the Myers were down there now strolling along
the beach as I walked into their guest bedroom/office/
sewing room.

Conch shells and dried starfish, interspersed with post-
cards from Disney World, St. Augustine, and Miami lined
the top of an opened four-shelf stand filled with popular
romances and westerns. The bookshelf took up the left-
hand side of the room. The rest of the space was given to
a sewing machine, a desk, a computer, a file cabinet, and a
twin bed with a chenille cover and little hand-embroidered
throw pillows sporting the kind of cheery mottoes women's
magazines seem to specialize in. I took a quick look in the
file cabinet. If there was anything that would help me find
Nestor, I didn't see it.

Then I went in to the last bedroom and got a surprise.
It seemed that Mr. Myers (I was presuming it was he, because
women don't usually get into reptiles as a hobby) was a
collector. Glancing around, I felt a little offended that he'd
never been in my store. I was pretty positive he hadn't. I
would have remembered if he had, especially if he was a

repeat customer, because I make it a point to know my customers' names, as well as their likes and dislikes. It's one of the ways I manage to compete against the chains.

The impeccably clean room contained four twenty-five-gallon aquariums, which respectively housed two king snakes, a large indigo, a beautiful, once common dark blue snake, as well as four baby albino pythons, which were both expensive and rare, three corn snakes, plus two fifty-gallon aquariums that the guy had turned into terrariums. It took a bit of looking before I spotted the poison frogs. Tiny, jewellike creatures, which come in vivid patterns of red, yellows, and blacks, they are surprisingly easy to raise and had recently become quite popular among home hobbyists, especially since you could now buy them through a mail order house for sixty dollars a pop.

I've always loved the little frogs, but I don't sell them because of liability reasons. My insurance carrier would not be pleased if I got sued because someone died handling them. When angry, their skin excretes enough toxin to kill ten men. South American Indians used their skins to poison their arrows. The trick, obviously, is to keep them from getting pissed off. Still, they're perfectly safe to own, if you observe certain precautions. Judging from what I'd seen so far of Mr. Myers's house, he was a careful, meticulous man— for some reason I pictured him as a retired engineer—one that, I would bet, was not prone to taking chances.

Charmed, I watched the frogs for a few minutes more. As I closed the door softly and went downstairs, I briefly thought about why it was that in nature the most beautiful things were frequently the most deadly. Bright colors are always a warning. Too bad humans don't have a system like that. It would make things easier. Then Eli might not have roomed with Nestor and I wouldn't be here now, wondering if they'd been here, too.

So far I hadn't seen any sign that either of them had been and I wasn't inclined to continue looking. If one or the other of them was stuffed in some hidden closet somewhere, let someone else find them. It was definitely time to leave. I'd been here too long as it was. According to my watch, the ten minutes I'd planned to stay had turned into twenty.

I returned to the kitchen and mopped up the water stains on the floor, stuffed the paper towels in my pocket and headed for the side door. I was too tired and stiff to try to get back out the way I'd come in. I was standing in the little vestibule next to the door, putting on my wet sneakers and thinking about what an unpleasant sensation slipping into wet canvas is, and vowing that from now on in I would buy leather sneakers, when I noticed what I thought was a red spot on the floor.

I hunkered down to get a better look.

Thinking back, I don't know whether I heard something or smelled it or felt the air around me move, but suddenly I knew with absolute certainty that someone was behind me.

I remember thinking, *Robin, you moron, you should have your knife out.*

But before I could even move my hand in the direction of my pocket, a pain exploded in my head.

I heard an odd gasp, which I realized was mine. Lights flashed. Then there was nothing.

Chapter
8

I was lying on my side on the floor when I came to. My head was throbbing, my eyeballs ached, my mouth tasted as if it were filled with camel dung, and on top of everything else, I couldn't seem to remember where I was or what I was supposed to be doing. I lay there for a few seconds panicking, before the answer flashed through my mind. I was in the Myers's kitchen, looking for Eli. When I finally sat up, it felt as if someone was playing the marimba on my brain.

Gingerly I ran my hand over my face and scalp. There was no blood. Aside from extreme soreness in the back of my skull, the various parts of my anatomy appeared to be where they were supposed to be, which, given the circumstances, was about as good as I could hope for. As for figuring out who had done this and why, that would have to wait for later when my mind was working again. Right now it felt as if it was stuffed with goose feathers.

I inched my butt over to the wall, leaned against it, and closed my eyes. Little flecks of light danced around my irises. My shoulder was killing me from being on the cold linoleum. The only bright note in all this as far as I could see was that the Myers hadn't come home and found me passed out on their kitchen floor.

It occurred to me, I had to get out of here. Now all I needed was the strength to do it. I was trying to gather it— the sentence brought to mind little strengths playing in the meadow with me trying to herd them together—when I heard two loud thumps, followed by murmured voices coming up through the heat vent in the basement. I held my breath. Whoever had hit me in the head was coming back to finish the job. No doubt about it, it was definitely time to leave. My heart began pounding in time with my head. I reached for my knife as I stood up. It was gone. I looked down and broke out in a cold sweat. The floor did a cha cha in front of my eyes. Bile rose in my throat.

Not a good idea, Robin, I told myself as I lifted my head and concentrated on the clothes hook sticking out of the back of the side door. A few seconds later, the dizziness subsided. This time I kept my head still and just lowered my eyes. The knife wasn't there. Shit. It had to be around here somewhere. Not that it mattered because the way I was feeling it would take me longer to retrieve it then I had available. By now, I could hear feet pounding up the stairs. I backed up out of the kitchen towards the hall closet. Hiding in there may not have been a great plan, but it was the only one I could think of.

My hand was on the doorknob when I heard, "she better be here, that's all I can say."

"George?" I croaked.

He came out of the kitchen, with Manuel trailing behind.

"See," Manuel said to him. He was still brushing snow off the folds of his cargo pants. "I told you."

"What are you doing here?" I cried.

"What does it look like we're doing here? We're rescuing you," George replied. "I told you I had a bad feeling about this." He handed me my knife. "Yours, I presume."

"Where'd you find it?"

He scowled. "By the door. Are you okay? What happened?"

"Someone hit me over the head."

"Did you see who?"

"No."

He reached over and gently felt my skull with his fingers. "Everything seems to be in one piece. Except you have a bump here." And he pressed a little harder.

"Ouch." I ducked my head and brushed his hand away. "Leave me alone."

"Do you feel sick to your stomach?" George asked, ignoring me and continuing with his catechism.

"A little," I admitted. "But I don't have a concussion if that's what you're getting at. Or at least not a bad one."

"How can you be so sure?"

"Experience."

Manuel came up behind us. He was jumpy, looking at the door every few seconds. "Come on." He took his hat off and put it back on. "We got to go. We still got to get her car out of the driveway before people start waking up."

"What are you so hyped about?" George asked him.

"Because I'm on probation, man. I was gonna tell you," he said to me. "I get caught, I'm gonna end up in Jamesville."

"It might knock some sense into you," George observed, but he put his arm around my shoulder and nudged me to the side door. "Come on. We'll go out this way. It'll be easier."

"Just a minute." I got the cold sweats. The room started spinning.

"We ain't got time for no just-a-minutes," Manuel snapped.

George turned toward him. "Shut up," he told him before turning back to me. "You want me to carry you?" he asked.

I took a deep breath. The room settled back down. "No. I'll be all right." Even though I was shaky in the knees, being carried was an admission of weakness I wasn't prepared to make. "What time is it anyway?" I asked, trying to distract myself from the throbbing at the back of my skull.

"Four in the morning. A time most sane people are in bed."

"I got worried," Manuel explained, "so I called George."

Imagining the conversation that must have gone on made me want to smile. Unfortunately it hurt too much. "Wait," I gasped out as we hit the vestibule. I pointed to the floor. "I think I saw a spot of blood over there."

"So what?" Manuel said. "People bleed all the time."

I tried not to raise my voice. "I thought you were worried about Eli."

"Eli is a schmuck," Manuel told me.

"Maybe you should check it out," I told George. "I got hit before I could tell."

"Oh, this is just great," Manuel said. "Just great. James-ville, here I come."

George whirled around. "You think you can be quiet for a minute," he said as he bullied him back toward the kitchen.

Manuel raised his hands in an I-give-up gesture and George went over to look. I leaned against the wall while

George knelt down and surveyed the linoleum. His jacket fell open. I could see he was wearing a crookedly buttoned plaid pajama top with his jeans. He'd run over to get me without bothering to get dressed. The thought pleased me.

"Come on," Manuel whined, constitutionally unable to keep his mouth shut.

George glared at him.

"Well, you're not the one that's going to be doing time," Manuel muttered. But he didn't say anything else.

After a moment or so, George stuck out his finger, brushed its tip against the spot on the floor, brought it up to his mouth, and gingerly touched it with his tongue. Manuel grimaced with disgust.

"Some sort of jam residue, I'd say," George observed.

Manuel groaned. "I don't believe this," he said, giving the belt on his pants a vicious yank.

"It's not as uncommon a mistake as you would think." George got up off his knees. "Let's get out of here."

Manuel practically danced to the door, while George helped me out. A minute later, the three of us emerged from the house. I stopped for a moment and closed my eyes. The cold air felt good on my skin. We made for his Taurus.

"It's amazing. You're like Mary and her lamb," George told me. "Except wherever you go, chaos follows."

"So, now you're telling me I'm a force of nature?" I got in the car.

"No. I'm telling you, you're a pain in the ass," George replied as he reached in the back and got two shovels off the seat. "By the way, I got in touch with my cousin. He'd love to have us come down. See if you can live long enough to make it. And now, if you'll excuse me, Manuel and I have some work to do." And he closed the door. The vibration made me wince.

Maybe, I remember thinking, as I watched flickering images of George and Manuel dig out my car, I did have a concussion after all. After ten minutes, both of them took their jackets off and draped them over the hood of George's Taurus. After twenty minutes, George managed to get my car out in the street and turn it around. Then he hopped out and Manuel hopped in.

Once we hit the main streets, the going was surprisingly easy. George looked over in my direction once or twice, but didn't say anything. For which I was grateful. I spent the trip staring out the window. A sliver of a moon hung suspended in the sky. Tree branches arched over in graceful curves under the weight of the snow. Flutters of windblown flakes sparkled under the streetlamps. At the corner of Ash and Oxford, a black cat slunk slowly along the side of the street, pausing every now and then to shake the snow off its paws.

"Let's drop in on Eli," I said impulsively, breaking the silence, as we came up on Westcott. "I'd really like to hear what he has to say."

"Haven't you had enough for one night? And anyway, we can't." And George pointed out a pickup truck, stuck in snow up to its fenders, lying across the street. A little further back a bus sat at right angles to where the pavement would have been if we could have seen it. The street was blocked. We weren't getting through.

"You know, I've been thinking about Nestor being Chinese," George said as he maneuvered around an abandoned car.

"Yes?"

"Well, one of tongs runs a heroin route up to Toronto through here."

"So what? That's like saying because you're Italian you have connections with the mob. Nestor stole something of Eli's, not the other way around."

"We don't know that for a fact."

"You're right. We don't." I sighed and massaged my forehead. "The only thing I do know for a fact is that I want to go home and go to bed."

"Will you be all right?" George asked as we reached my house. "You want me to take you to the hospital?"

"I'll be fine."

He helped me inside. "I can stay if you want."

I took off my coat. "Manuel's going to be here in a minute. He'll call you if anything happens."

"Promise?"

I nodded and regretted the action instantly. George kissed me good night and left.

I walked into the kitchen and called Eli. No one picked up.

"He never hears the phone when he's sleeping," Manuel observed, having pulled into the driveway just as George was pulling out. He opened my refrigerator door.

I hung up. "*If* he's sleeping."

"How old is that?" Manuel asked, indicating a takeout carton.

"Two weeks."

"Don't you have anything else?"

"Some canned soup." And I took six Advil and went to sleep, leaving Manuel going though my kitchen cabinets, looking for something to eat.

My dreams were all bad. I dreamt about my old dog, Elsie. She was running through the fields and I was trying to keep up with her but I couldn't because I kept on getting tangled up in the tall grass. Then I dreamt about Murphy. In my dream he shapeshifted into different people, only each one told me that they were leaving me for someone else.

Chapter
9

Four hours later, the telephone rang. I had tears on my cheeks when I woke up.

It was Chapman returning my call. "You have something for me?" he said.

I groaned.

"Bad night?" he asked.

I wondered if he'd been the one responsible for what had happened last night as I struggled to sit up. "You could say that."

"So what's going on?" His tone was impatient, his voice clipped. I could hear the sounds of a TV going in the background.

I struggled through the fog of my sleep to remember what I'd planned to say to him.

"Well?" he prompted.

My mind clicked in. "Nothing. I thought we got off to a bad start the other night. I figured we should begin over."

"And how do we do that?" He sounded interested, but wary.

"We could meet over coffee and bagels."

He was quiet, probably running my suggestion in his head for traps. When he didn't find any, he agreed.

I suggested a chain store in a nearby strip mall, figuring I'd get there a little early and wait for him to come in and read his license plate. He said he'd see me there in an hour and a half. It was sooner than I would have liked but doable.

I hung up the phone and rolled over. Given the night before and the lack of sleep, I felt better than I had a right to. I was still a little stiff in the shoulder and the spot in my head where I'd been hit was still tender, but the nausea, dizziness, and pain had subsided. I dragged myself into the shower and stood under it until the hot water ran out. Then I got dressed, made myself a cup of coffee, left a note for Manuel, who was still sleeping, telling him where I was going, and drove over to where I was going to meet Chapman.

The main roads were all plowed, and traffic was moving at a slow but even pace. The strip mall's parking lot was a quarter full, a normal amount for this time in the morning. I put my car four rows away from the store, between a minivan and an old Saab, and waited. The sky was a cerulean blue. It was a little over thirty degrees, with the temperature supposedly rising to forty later in the afternoon. The only reminder of yesterday's storm was a hill-shaped cloud off in the distance. If I were sports-minded I would have said it was a perfect day for cross-country skiing. I put my mind in a holding pattern and waited. I figured Chapman for being late and he was.

Fifteen minutes after our appointment was scheduled, I watched a green Jeep Cherokee drive up off Nottingham Road. The driver made his way toward one of the spots in front of the dry cleaner. He parked and got out. It was my man. After he went inside the bagel place, I noted down his license plate number and joined him.

Chapman was sitting at a table drinking his coffee and looking annoyed when I came in. Waiting wasn't part of his plan. I knew he wasn't happy that I'd flipped things around. I bought a cranberry-orange bagel and a cup of coffee and sat down next to him.

"You must have had some night," he observed as I lowered myself into the chair. "You look like shit."

I shrugged. Asking him if he'd been the one who'd knocked me out seemed like a waste of time "Well, you look very pretty."

He didn't respond, taking another sip of his coffee instead. "So?" he said. "What did you have in mind?"

"Nothing, really. I just wondered why you weren't looking for Nestor yourself?"

Chapman put both hands around his cup as if to warm them and gave out with that schoolboy smile of his. "Simple. I have better things to do."

I took a bite of my bagel. "You do a lot of this kind of activity, do you?"

He gave me an assessing look, before answering. "No. This is a part-time gig. So, have you found Nestor or not?"

"Not. But I'm working on it. Of course, he could be out of here by now. If he's down in the City, all bets are off."

"You and your client better hope that's not the case." Chapman looked at his watch and told me he had to go. I got the feeling he was thinking that if he couldn't make me wait, at least he could leave me sitting here.

I watched him walk out the door. Mr. All-American in his Gap jacket, turtleneck, and jeans. I think I would have liked it better if he wore leather and was decorated with jailhouse tattoos. It would be easier to remember what I was dealing with. After he left, I finished my bagel and coffee and called George. He wasn't in so I left Chapman's license plate number on his answering machine, told him everything was fine and that I'd call him later. Then I checked in at the store, and drove over to Eli's. I was interested to hear what he had to say about last night.

The snow from last night's storm had filled in the risers on Eli's steps, transforming the stairs to his flat into Mount Everest. I took a last puff of the cigarette I'd been smoking, flicked the butt away, and started up. By the time I'd hauled myself to the top I was wheezing. Rivulets of sweat were running down my sides.

George would have said it served me right for smoking and George would have been correct. I unzipped my jacket and brushed the snow off my pants while I caught my breath. A couple of men were digging their cars out from the piles of snow the plow had created when it came through. Directly across the street, four little kids were having a snowball fight while their mother shoveled the driveway. School had been canceled for the day. Watching them made me wish I were ten again.

At ten, I still had the knack of expectation. I was wondering when I'd lost the ability as I knocked on Eli's door. He answered a couple of minutes later wearing a tatty blue terry-cloth bathrobe. It was hanging open, revealing paint-stained shorts slung low over his hips and a torn Donald Duck T-shirt that rose up, leaving a patch of white belly exposed. His hair was mussed. He yawned without covering his mouth. I could see his fillings.

"Yes?" he mumbled, peering at me through sleep-encrusted lids. He wasn't wearing his glasses. His eyes looked naked without them.

I pushed my way in, kicking the door shut behind me. "Where were you last night?" I demanded.

"W-w-why?" He stammered. "What's the matter?" He shivered and clutched his bathrobe to him. I noticed he had red marks on his skin where his face had been in contact with his pillow.

"The matter is that someone knocked me out last night while I was looking for you and I want to know why."

I'd expected him to stutter something about "What do you mean, looking for me?" But instead he squawked, "You were at 1078?" while his fingers battened on the terry cloth the way a child holds on to his favorite blankie.

"Yes, I was. Unfortunately. Now where were you?"

"I . . . I . . . never got there. Why were you there?"

"Manuel called me."

He swallowed. "Oh."

"Are you going to answer me."

"What did Manny tell you?"

"It doesn't matter." Eli smelled stale, as if he needed a bath. His flesh jiggled unattractively under my hands as I pushed him into the living room. The place looked the way it had the last time I was here, except now the window blinds were up. A limb from one of the maples planted close to the house had cracked in the storm. Dangling toward the ground at a right angle, the exposed wood was a raw, white slash against the grayish-brown bark. "I want to hear what you have to say."

Eli put his hands up. "Just a minute," he protested. "I have to get my glasses."

"You don't have to see to talk," I told him.

His shoulders slumped. "I just feel better with . . ."

"Frankly, I don't care what you feel. Tell me what I want to know."

He scrunched his face up. He looked as if he were going to cry. I didn't care. He could have thrown himself on the ground and sobbed and I wouldn't have felt a tingle of sympathy for him. It probably had something to do with my getting hit on the head.

"You know," I told him, "I'm inclined to take the money you've given me and just forget about this whole mess."

"No. Don't do that," he cried. Small bubbles of saliva formed at the corners of his mouth. He wiped them away with the back of one of his hands.

"Then talk to me."

"I'm going to," he whined. "I don't have anything to hide. It's just that you woke me up." This was said truculently, as if I was supposed to feel sorry that I had.

"You're up now." I watched mounds of snow falling from the cedars. They made soft, plopping noises landing. "Tell me. Did you see Nestor last night?"

"No." Eli shuffled over to the sofa and sat down. "I didn't." The cushions sank under his weight. I stayed standing.

"He wasn't at the house?"

"I don't know." Eli began nervously fingering the ends of the belt on his robe. "We never got there."

"We?"

"Sulfin and me. We never even got near the hill. We kept on getting stuck."

At least that matched up with what Manuel had told me. "Sulfin is a friend of Nestor's, right?" I asked Eli.

He nodded. Then he smoothed his hair down. I noticed the seam of his robe was ripped under his arm.

"So, why should he be taking you to Nestor?"

"Nestor owes him some money. He wants it back."

"Is that what he told you?"

Eli nodded again.

"And you believe him?"

"Why shouldn't I?" Eli demanded. "Nestor owes every-one money. He's bad that way. He never pays unless you lean on him."

"All right." I folded my arms over my chest. My head was starting to ache again. I probably should have stayed in bed and rested. Unfortunately that wasn't an option at the moment. "Go on," I ordered.

Eli pulled at a loose thread in his bathrobe. "There's nothing more to say. We kept on getting stuck. Finally Sulfin turned around and took me home."

"How'd you get through?" I asked, thinking about how George and I had almost gotten stuck on Westcott last night.

"Broad was clear. We went up that way."

"What time did you get in?"

"I don't know. Late," he added. "I didn't look."

"I called around five. You didn't pick up."

"I must have been sleeping. When I'm sleeping I don't hear anything."

"That's what Manuel said." I wondered if that were true or if Manuel was just protecting his cousin's ass as I watched Eli rub his left eye with the knuckles of his left hand. The white looked pink when he stopped. It was too bad George and I couldn't have gotten through the street last night, I reflected. It would have cleared a lot of things up. I studied Eli before going on. He looked miserable slumped on the sofa, a quivering mass of flesh spilling out of his robe.

"Who are the Myers?"

"Myra's parents."

"The skinny girl who works at Animals Galore?" I thought about what I'd seen in the third bedroom of her house. "She keep any reptiles?"

"A few." And he asked if he could get his glasses.

"Why were Nestor and Adelina going up there?" I inquired when he came back in the room.

Eli shrugged. He was holding his glasses in his hand and was fiddling with the safety pin that held the earpiece onto the frame with the other. The little gold wire was almost lost in the white, fleshy mound of his fingertips. "Maybe they had to water the plants or something like that."

"No doubt. It's something everyone does in the middle of a blizzard."

Eli didn't reply. He kept working on his glasses. "You didn't happen to see the suitcase when you were up there, did you?" he asked, trying for casual, but Eli was casual the way an elephant was.

"No, but then I wasn't looking for it."

"Why not?" Eli's voice quavered.

"Because I was looking for you." I went into the kitchen to get a glass of water. As I reached for a glass, I brushed against the stove. It was warm. "Hey," I said. "Did you know your oven is on?"

Eli came in and turned it off. "I was heating up some pizza last night. I must have forgotten to turn it off."

"You'd better be careful. You don't want to start a fire."

Eli rubbed his lips with the back of his hand. "Nothing is going right for me these days," he grumbled.

I didn't say anything. Eli was back sitting on the sofa, trying to readjust his frames when I left. They were never going to fit together perfectly, but maybe Eli didn't care. I drove over to the store next. Zsa Zsa came running out to greet me, yipping in a delirium of joy. I crouched down to pet her. She put her paws on my knees and licked my face. Her breath was hot. Her tongue was warm and rough. She pressed her teeth lightly against my skin, raking it occasionally, which was her way of telling me she loved me, but not to leave her again or dire consequences might ensue.

Tim seemed amused by her display. "From the way she's carrying on, you'd think she'd spent the evening pining away for you. She slept on my bed and had steak for dinner."

"You're saying she can be bought?"

He snorted and ran a hand over his bald scalp. It gleamed. He shaved it every four days, which seemed to me to be a lot more work than having hair. "Come on. Admit it. She's a biscuit slut."

"I'm not admitting anything of the kind." Loyalty wouldn't let me, even if it was true. I petted Zsa Zsa for another five minutes before getting up. Then I took off my coat and checked yesterday's receipts. I'd been right. They were abysmal. "Does the name Myra Myers mean anything to you?" I asked Tim when I was through.

"Aside from the fact that someone in her family had an obvious, unfortunate fondness of alliteration, no. Should it?"

"Not really. She's a skinny kid. Works over at Animals Galore."

Tim grimaced at the name.

"She's got a couple of albino boas, some poison arrow frogs. Not run of the mill stuff. I was just curious."

"Name doesn't ring a bell. You want me to ask around?"

"Please." Tim had assumed the presidency of the Herpetological Society of Syracuse six months ago.

"This has to do with Manuel and his cousin, doesn't it?" he asked.

"Probably not. I'm just checking." I scanned the mail and put it aside. It was all bills and circulars. Then, because I figured I might as well cover all my bases, I asked Tim about Nestor.

"You mean Nestor Chang?"

I nodded.

Tim picked up a broom and began to sweep. "Sure I know him. He was in my ethics class at OCC. Why?"

"He's the guy that stole Eli's suitcase."

Tim's eyes widened slightly. He scratched his chin with a finger. "I never would have pegged him for something like that."

I began cleaning out the gerbil cages. My meeting with Chapman had put me behind with my chores. "Obviously the class didn't do him much good."

"He was smart. Really smart."

I remembered what Adelina's mother had said about Nestor always thinking he knew more than anyone else as I scooped the old bedding out of the cage and poured the new bedding in. "Sorry, guys," I told the four milling gerbils. They were distressed because I'd taken their store of food. I gave them some pellets and watched as they stuffed them into their mouths.

"Anything else?"

Tim stopped sweeping and thought. "Not really. We talked about assignments a couple of times, but that was about it. I saw him at the Jazz Fest this summer. He was with this pretty Latina and a little girl."

I took out the water bottle. "That must have been Adelina and one of her sisters."

"We just said hello."

"Did he talk to anyone else in your class?"

Tim shook his head and went back to his sweeping. "He kept pretty much to himself. He usually came in right before the class started and left right when it ended."

"Maybe I should talk to his teacher."

"He's in California now," Tim informed me as he started on the floor around the front door.

So much for that idea. I went in the back and refilled the water bottle. I was starting on my third cage when the phone rang. Tim was still sweeping, so I caught the call.

It was George. "Have you watched TV recently?" he asked me before I could say anything.

"Since I don't have one strapped to my wrist, no. Why?"

"Because I think we have a problem."

Chapter
10

George was right. We did have a problem. A big one. He'd just caught a breaking news story while he'd been channel surfing. A reporter had come on to announce that a West Side man taking a shortcut on his way to work through an abandoned lot had stumbled over the body of a male, who was later identified as Nestor Chang. Police were investigating. Anyone with information was urged to come forward.

"Shit," I said.

"My sentiments exactly," George agreed.

"But we don't know Nestor was killed in the Myers's house," I said, anticipating George's next comment.

"We don't know he wasn't," George replied.

Tim stopped sweeping. "Someone killed Nestor?"

"It seems so."

He put his hand up to his eyes. "That's horrible."

I agreed with him that it was.

"You don't sound as if you care," Tim observed.

"Well, I'm not breaking out in sobs, if that's what you mean. But of course I care. I don't like to hear about anyone dying. It's just hard to feel really bad for someone you've never met." *Especially,* I wanted to add, *since he's someone you haven't heard anything good about.*

Tim put down his broom. "I'm going to take a couple of minutes to myself." He walked into the back.

"What was that all about?" George asked.

"Tim's upset about Chang."

"He knew him?"

"Vaguely. They took a class together, an ethics class."

George snorted.

"You know," I pointed out, "that newscast didn't say anything about homicide. For all we know, Nestor could have gotten drunk, passed out, and died of hypothermia," I continued. "I looked through the house. Everything was in place. If Nestor was killed there, whoever did it should give clean-up lessons."

"Believe me, I sincerely hope you're right. I'd have less trouble believing that if you hadn't gotten hit on the head."

"Because if we go down to the Attorney's Office . . ."

"We can keep Manuel out of it," George said, anticipating my line of thought. "No reason why he should get his ass handed to him because he was worried about you."

"But what about us? We could be charged with a B&E."

"They won't do that."

"Maybe not to you, but the DA's office doesn't like me very much."

I didn't hear George disagreeing.

I peeled a fingernail. "Let me talk to Eli again before we go downtown. Let's see what he has to say. Then I'll get back to you."

"And if he's not there?"

"I'll phone you either way and we can go from there."

George wavered.

"Come on. Nestor's dead. A couple of hours one way or another aren't going to matter much."

In the end, George gave in. I was about to hang up when I remembered about the license plate number.

"Yeah. I was going to call you about that. My friend got an ID."

"Great!"

"Not really. The car Chapman is driving is registered to a Zachariah Block down in Westchester."

"Did you . . ."

"Yes," George replied. "I tried phoning him. Unfortunately, Mr. Zachariah's number has been disconnected. We have a dead end."

I sighed. Maybe I should light a candle to change my luck, I thought as I went into the back to tell Tim I was leaving. He was leaning against the sink with Slick, an eight-foot boa, curled around his arm.

"At least you know where you stand with these guys," he said, looking up at me.

The snake's tongue flicked in and out of his mouth smelling the air.

"Not always. You could have a snake for ten years, feed him once a week, handle him every day, and then—bam—for no reason at all he'd turn and nail you."

"They eat what they kill," Tim said. "You can't say the same about people."

I couldn't argue with that. I told Tim where I was going and left.

As I drove over to Eli's, I replayed my morning's talk with him over and over again in my head. No matter what construction I gave his words, I just didn't make him for a killer. But then, I reminded myself, people always said that about the guy who turns around and murders his wife and kids.

"I can't believe it," the neighbor would say, putting his hand to his mouth. "He was such a nice, quiet man. So helpful. When I was away, he always took in my mail and watered my plants."

Well, I hoped Eli wouldn't fit into that category as I parked my car and walked up his steps. "Eli!" I yelled as I banged on his door. "I need to speak to you."

"He ain't there. He's gone."

I turned. A kid decked out in a bright-red snowsuit was standing down on the street looking up at me. I started down the stairs. "When did he leave?" It couldn't have been that long.

The kid began flipping the scarlet hood of his snowsuit up and down in time to a tune playing in his head that I couldn't hear. "A little while ago. He said he'd pay me for shoveling his steps when he came back."

I hoped Eli wasn't paying him a lot. The kid had shoveled a narrow path up the middle of the stairs, while leaving snow on either end. The steps looked as if they'd been given a reverse mohawk.

"And when was that going to be?" I asked as I reached the pavement. I brushed flakes off my jeans.

"He said he'd be right back," the kid answered. "But that was a couple of hours ago. You a friend of his?" he asked, wiping his nose with the back of his hand.

"Not really. Was he carrying anything with him when he left?"

The kid squinted up at me. His gaunt face, thin mouth, and deep-set, watchful eyes had poverty stamped all over them. "But you know him, right?"

"Yes, I know him," I allowed.

The kid made a hole in the snow with his heel, then hit me up for some money. "I could use me a couple of bucks for a candy bar."

I handed him two ones. The cost of doing business.

"That's it?" he complained.

"Are you buying chocolate wrapped in gold?" I complained, but I pulled out two more ones and handed them to him. "That's four dollars, three more than you should be getting."

He looked at the crumpled bills lying in the palm of his hand disdainfully. "These bills is old. Ain't you got anything newer?"

I fought an urge to lift the kid up by his hood and hang him on the fence post. "I can take them back if you want."

"No. That's okay." He hastily tucked my money in his snowsuit pocket. Then he pointed to my backpack. "He was carrying one of those. A big one."

"Anything else?"

"Not that I seen."

"Which way did he go?"

He pointed down the street in the direction of East Genesse. "That way."

"Walking or driving?"

"Driving." The kid gave me a look of pure disgust. "You think Eli's gonna walk anywhere? He was in that old Chevy of his."

"Did he say anything to you?"

"I already told you. He said I should shovel the stairs and that he'd give me twenty bucks when he came back." The kid lifted up the snow shovel he was carrying. It was bigger than he was. "How about you pay me? Then you get the money from him," he said, gesturing up to where Eli lived.

I laughed. "Twenty bucks for what you did? You have to be crazy. That's worth about five. Tops. And anyway, how do I know you're not scamming me?"

The kid called me an asshole and left.

"That's not very nice," I yelled after him.

He flipped me the bird over his shoulder and kept walking. I guess things could be worse, I thought as I got back in my car. I could be a teacher and have to deal with behavior like that all day.

So, had Eli skipped out or hadn't he? It looked to me as if he had, but I wasn't ready to admit that yet. I decided to wait another half an hour, then go back and check one last time. If he hadn't returned by then, I'd give George a call. In the meantime, I decided to get a cup of coffee at a café over on Harvard Place, a three-block walk.

Chapter 11

A blast of flamenco music hit me when I pushed the door open. The owner had painted the walls an Atlantic Ocean blue-green. A white fan whirred overhead. A couple of people, grad students from the look of them, were sitting at a table toward the back, talking and passing papers back and forth, but outside of that, the place was empty. I ordered a quadruple espresso and a hazelnut biscotti and took them over to a seat by the window. Across the street, a man wearing a bathrobe, pajamas, and boots was dragging two garbage cans out of the pile of snow they had been buried in.

I dunked the biscotti in the coffee and took a bite. As the biscuit dissolved in my mouth I considered what would happen if George called the police. It would not be good. I lifted the little white cup up to my lips and took a sip of coffee. It was bitter enough to make me shudder.

As I stirred some sugar into my espresso, I contemplated the distasteful fact that I should probably call my lawyer when I got back to the store. Now this is not something I like to do, because he is expensive. The money I'd gotten from Eli would cover about two hours of his time, unless of course his rates had gone up again, in which case, it would cover less. What was that saying about: if it looks too good to be true, it usually is?

I sat in the café, nursing my coffee for as long as possible, before climbing Eli's stairs again and knocking on his door one last time. There was no response. I wasn't really surprised. I was having a run of bad luck, and in my experience those things tend to stay around for a while. And I was right. On my way over to the store, I stopped off at the garage to see how the cab was coming along. Naturally, she wasn't ready.

"I'll have her for you in another couple of days," Sam said, wiping the grease off his hands with a dirty cloth.

He was a good, honest mechanic and those are hard to find these days. Unfortunately, he took forever to get anything done. I sighed and drove back to the store. Not that there was anything wrong with the car I was driving, not really, not if you didn't count the fact that it had no acceleration and it cornered lousy.

"Eli there?" Tim asked me when I came back in. He had our hyacinth macaw perched on his shoulder. She was a beautiful bird I was trying to find a home for.

"Nope." I fed her and Zsa Zsa each a dog biscuit.

"George called."

I reached for the phone, but Tim wasn't finished yet. "And the teacher from the junior high school class . . ."

I supplied the name. "Nettles."

"Yeah." Tim snickered. "She wants you to pay the cleaning bills for everyone's clothes."

"Great. Anything else?" As if that wasn't enough.

Tim consulted his pad as the macaw nibbled on his ear. "A guy named Chapman phoned."

"What did he want?" I was betting that he'd heard about Nestor, too.

"Just that you should call him. Is that the one with the scissors?" Tim asked, making a clipping motion with his fingers.

"You got it." I slipped out of my jacket and stuffed it under the counter. The macaw nipped at my hair as I went by him. I gave him another biscuit and dialed the beeper number Tim had given me. A moment later, Chapman called back.

"Was there something you forgot to tell me at our breakfast this morning?" he asked.

"Like what?" I asked, playing dumb.

"So you don't know?"

"About what?"

"About Nestor being dead."

"That's terrible," I told him, putting what I hoped was the appropriate amount of emotion in my voice. "What happened?"

Chapman's laugh was malicious. "I don't believe a word you're saying."

"Why would I lie to you?"

"I don't know. It's a good question. Maybe you can give me the answer over dinner tonight."

I leaned against the wall and closed my eyes. Suddenly I felt exhausted. Last night was catching up with me. "Yeah. Right."

"I'll pick you up at nine. I know a nice little joint out in Fulton."

"Don't bother."

"It would be a mistake on your part not to be there,"

Chapman told me, his voice oozing through the phone like sugar syrup.

"And why is that?"

"You'll find out." And he hung up before I could tell him to fuck off.

I tapped the phone against my teeth while I thought.

"What are you going to do about him?" Tim asked.

"I don't know yet." I pulled myself away from the wall and went into the back and made myself a cup of coffee. I took it into my office, sat down, put my feet on my desk, and lit a cigarette. What I needed was a vacation, I reflected as I studied the toes of my sneakers, a nice long one. Belize couldn't come soon enough for me. I wondered when George was thinking of going down. I reached for the phone and punched in his number, but no one answered.

I was about to leave a message when the bell that signals the opening of the front door went off.

"Where's Robin?" I heard Manuel say.

"She's tired," Tim told him. "Leave her alone."

"I got to speak to her."

"Have to," Tim corrected. "You have to speak to her."

"Who gives a fuck?"

"Your attitude sucks. I'm just trying to help."

I sighed, picked up my coffee, took another drag of my cigarette, and walked out front. "What do you want, Manuel?"

He moved toward me. "It's Eli," he cried. "He wants to turn himself in for Nestor's murder."

"Murder?" I echoed. So much for my insights into human nature.

"Wow," Tim said.

"Wow," the Hyacinth macaw cackled. "Wow. Wow. Wow."

"I know," Manuel agreed. "I told him to wait till I spoke to you."

I rubbed my forehead. "You want me to get him a lawyer?"

"No." Manuel resettled his baseball hat on his head. "I want you to talk him out of it."

I stared at Manuel. "Why?"

Manuel pulled up his pants. "Because he didn't do it."

"But I heard you say he's confessing," Tim said.

"Yeah," Manuel said.

I pushed my hair out of my eyes. "I'm confused."

"He thinks it would be a good idea."

"Instead of what?" I snapped. "Going to Florida? Do I confess to a murder or take a bus trip?" I made a weighing motion with my hands. "Gee. I don't know. Let's flip a coin and find out."

"Here." Manuel took what looked like a shoebox wrapped in the Sunday comics out of the shopping bag he'd been holding and pushed it across the counter. "This will explain things."

I eyed it warily. I haven't looked at packages in the same way, since some moron had UPSed a viper to the store.

"Go on," Manuel urged. "Open it."

I unwrapped the paper and gingerly lifted the lid. Nestled inside the folded sheets of white tissue paper were a large pair of pinking shears, an alarm clock, and something black I couldn't recognize. I picked it up.

"Jesus." I dropped it back in the box.

"That's disgusting," Tim spat, cold fury in his voice.

We both stared down at the amputated paw of a cat.

"Here. There's this, too." Manuel reached in and handed me a typed note. It read: "Don't be a cat's-paw. Not all feet are lucky. A deal is a deal. Time is running out."

"That fuck," I said through gritted teeth. "He is a dead

man." I pushed the box away from me. I didn't want to look at it.

Tim reached over and picked up the shears. The polished blades gleamed in the light. They were designed to cut material, my grandmother had used shears such as these when she'd sewn my clothes, but obviously that wasn't what Chapman had in mind. "The man is crazy," Tim said, putting the scissors back.

"He's dead is what he is." I took a deep breath and told myself to calm down. "I'd like to use them on him," I added as I ground out my cigarette on the lid of the soda can I was using as an ashtray. I gestured toward the box. "When did Eli get this?"

Manuel unzipped his jacket and tipped his baseball hat back on his forehead. "A little while after you left. It was right outside the door."

I wondered if the kid in the red snowsuit had seen Chapman putting it there. Then I wondered if it mattered.

"Eli's at your house, waiting for you to call," Manuel said.

While I'd been looking for him, he'd been sitting in my living room watching TV. It figured. I lit another cigarette and inhaled. Then I blew a smoke ring and watched it dissolve on the air. "So, let me get this straight. He wants to confess to a murder he didn't commit."

Manuel nodded.

"Because he thinks he'll be safe from Chapman in jail."

"Exactomundo."

"And then do what? Tell the police he was lying when I find the suitcase."

"Something like that."

I put the lid back on the shoebox and pushed it toward Manuel with one finger. "I have another suggestion. How about bringing that in to the cops and lodging a complaint about Chapman?''

"For what?''

"Harassment . . . menacing are two words that come to mind.''

Manuel raised his eyebrows. "This guy Chapman will be out the next day. And that's if they can find him.''

I massaged my temples and blew another smoke ring. "Manuel, tell me something.''

He shifted his weight from his right to his left foot. He didn't know what was coming, but he didn't like it. "If I can.''

"What the hell is in this suitcase?''

"Cigars.'' I flicked an ash into the empty dog food can by the register.

"Try again. No one goes to this much trouble for something like that.''

"They're Cohibas or some weird name like that.''

"That is the wrong answer.'' Normally I would have been more tolerant, but the last couple of days had not put me in the best of moods.

I walked around the counter and grabbed Manuel by the front of his blue Tommy Hilfiger jacket. "Thanks to you, I now have someone calling me for a dinner date, someone who cuts paws off cats. Not to mention the fact that I broke into a house because of you, a house someone may have been killed in. My fingerprints are all over the walls and the phone and, oh, yes, I got knocked out, and last but not least, George is now involved in this whole mess. Now, I want you to tell me what's going on.''

"Chill.'' Manuel pried my fingers off the material. "Don't be doing that to me. This is new. You're going to ruin the material. I already done told you I don't know. All I know is Eli's in trouble and he's really scared. I'd tell you if I knew anything else. Believe me."

"Is that the same as 'trust me'?"

"Why you gotta take that tone with me?" he objected. "You really put people off actin' like that."

"Manuel, can the crap." But I took a step back and looked him in the eye. He returned my glance. Not that that meant anything. It would take a better person than me to get Manuel to talk if he didn't want to.

I stubbed my cigarette out and fought the urge to light another one. "All right, Manuel. Here's a question you might be able to answer."

He carefully brushed off the front of his jacket, inspecting it as he did. "Are we on *Jeopardy* or something?"

"Don't be cute. How do you know Eli's telling the truth about not killing Nestor? He certainly has a motive."

"Sulfin says he was with him last night."

"And you believe Sulfin?"

"He's got no reason to lie."

"You don't know that."

"I don't not know it," Manuel countered.

"It, it, it," the macaw echoed.

I raised my voice. "You know, we don't even know Nestor has been murdered. So far, the death has been listed as suspicious. That's all."

Manuel shrugged. "Given what Chapman is gonna do, big deal."

"Making a false statement to the police is a felony. Eli could go to jail for something like that."

Manuel looked up. "They can do that?" he said, sounding surprised.

I yielded to temptation and lit another cigarette. "They most certainly can."

"I didn't know that."

"Contrary to your opinion of yourself, there are a lot of things you don't know. And here's another thought for you. What if it turns out that Nestor was murdered? And what if the police believe his confession? What if they put together a circumstantial case on him? What if he goes to trial on a murder two beef? You know innocent people have been prosecuted before and found guilty."

Manuel bit his lip. "I don't think that's occurred to him."

"I don't think a lot of things have."

"That's why I want you to talk to him." Manuel looked at me expectantly. "Please, Robin."

It was the *please* that did it. "All right. But first I want to speak to Sulfin."

"Eli isn't lying," Manuel said, his eyes asking me to agree with him.

"He probably isn't, but it would make me feel better if I knew a little more first."

"All right." Manuel said this reluctantly. "Can I come along?"

"No."

Manuel's shoulders sagged. His mouth turned down. I put my hand on his shoulder. "I need you to talk to your friends. See if any of them have heard from Adelina."

"Why?"

"Because if Chapman doesn't have the suitcase and Eli doesn't have the suitcase, then Adelina probably does. And I want it." I thought about what Chapman had done to that cat. "I want to see what's inside it." Now I was hoping there was something in it that would help me turn Chapman over to the police.

Manuel smiled and began a tuneless whistle. The macaw

imitated him. "Hey, wait a minute," he said, a new thought occurring to him. "What if Adelina killed Nestor?"

"*If* Nestor was killed," I corrected Manuel. "In that case, I'm sure Adelina is going to be one of the first people the police want to talk to. Now I need you to tell me where can I get hold of Sulfin."

"At work. He does stuff for that weird rich guy. The one with all the animals. You know the one I'm talking about?"

"I do indeed."

After Manuel left, I tried George again. This time the line was busy. Next I called Eli and extracted a promise from him to wait before going downtown, then I took a drive over to Jamesville to Parker Littlebaum's house.

He met me at the door with a shotgun in one hand.

But that was okay.

It was the lion he was holding on to with his other hand that made me nervous.

Chapter
12

The lion mesmerized me. I couldn't move. My heart was thudding. My mind did what it always does under pressure. It ran for cover.

For some reason, I thought about how wild animals always look bigger in the flesh than they do in the movies, and how movie stars always look bigger on the screen than they do in real life.

Then I thought about how people say animals are supposed to be able to smell fear. If that's true, then this one was definitely getting a noseful.

The lion and I stared at each other for what seemed like forever. Its eyes were flecked with gold. Its ears were pricked forward. Its mouth was drawn back in a tight little grin. I noticed the white tufts of hair growing out of its ears, I noticed the way the tip of its pink tongue showed between its teeth, I noticed the powerful slope of its shoulders, the thickness of its bones, and the sheen of its coat, but most of all I noticed that it didn't look happy. Which made two of us.

"I haven't seen you for a while," Littlebaum said. He spoke casually, as if we'd just run into each other in the street.

I took an effort, but I wrenched my gaze away from the lion. "At least a couple of years."

Judging from his appearance, they hadn't been a good two years. The man looked as if he had been living in a cardboard box on the street. He was even skinnier than I remembered him being. His clothes, a dirty flannel shirt and a ripped pair of jeans, were a couple of sizes too big. The veins in his neck stood out like cords and his cheeks were sunken. The whites of his eyes were marbled with red lines and his left eye had a slight squint to it. His beard and mustache were flecked with remnants of the meals he'd eaten. His scraggly blond hair was fixed into a ponytail that ran down his neck.

He moved his lips into something that he probably thought was a smile. "Has it been that long?"

"Maybe even longer," I told him, trying to disregard both the penetrating, low rumble coming from the big cat's throat and the fact that in the present circumstances Littlebaum's grip on the lion's red leather collar was a lot looser than I would have liked it to be.

"She make you nervous?" Littlebaum asked, his grin widening.

"Not at all," I lied. Littlebaum was a bully. Show a bully you're afraid and they act even worse.

"Good." He scratched his ear with the business end of his shotgun. "I figured, you handle six-foot monitor lizards. She's not that much different."

"She's larger."

"I thought women liked big things." And he sniggered like a little boy telling a dirty joke.

I tried not to grit my teeth. "Not when it comes to cats." I indicated her with my chin. "You've made your point. How about putting your playmate away?"

Littlebaum wrinkled his nose while pretending to think about my suggestion. "Maybe later."

"I'm guessing you're still angry about the lizard." The last time Littlebaum had been in the store he'd left in a snit because I wouldn't sell him a four-hundred-dollar monitor on credit. I'd figured he'd forgotten about it by now. Obviously, I'd been wrong. "You don't strike me as the kind of guy that holds a grudge."

"Hurt might be a better word. You know how much she cost me?" He pointed to the lioness. Her tail was swishing back and forth, the way a tabby cat's does before it pounces on a mouse. I now knew how a slave in Roman times felt before it was thrown to the lions.

"How much?" I asked automatically while my mind was busy wondering whether or not Littlebaum would use his shotgun on her if she attacked me and how much damage she would do before he did.

"I paid eight thousand." Littlebaum looked and sounded smug, like a collector who'd gotten a good deal on a painting. "Not bad, hunh?"

"No. Not at all." The guy had definitely gotten taken, the part of my mind that wasn't busy picturing myself as a patchwork quilt, decided. Five thousand was the going rate for a lion cub, but I sure wasn't going to tell him that under the circumstances. "Where'd you get her?"

"From a firm down in Texas. Wildlife Specialists. Heard of them?" I shook my head. "They shipped her to me. *On credit.* No questions asked. I paid as soon as I got the invoice.

Now we're talking about a baby giraffe," he boasted. "What do you think about them apples?"

Why not say them oranges or pears or pineapples? I found myself wondering while staring at Littlebaum's face. The two sides didn't quite match. Which could be a metaphor for his personality.

"Well?" he demanded, waiting for my answer.

I gave it to him. "How's it gonna get here?"

"By truck. You know, I've always wanted to have one."

And I'd always wanted to own a jet plane, but that didn't mean I was going to go out and buy one even if I did have the money. Jesus. A giraffe! The guy was a moron. I'd heard he'd gone around the bend. I just didn't think he'd gone this far. If I had, I would have phoned instead of dropping by.

What the hell was he going to do with a giraffe anyway? I couldn't even imagine what feeding an animal that large would cost. And where was it going to live? It couldn't stay outside in this kind of weather. As far as I knew, Littlebaum didn't have a barn on his property. Was he planning on cutting a big hole in the ceiling of his house?

As far as I'm concerned, people should stick to cats, dogs, hamsters, birds, and reptiles as pets. When you keep wild animals, the results are almost always predictably tragic, usually for the animals, which either die from improper care or have to be put down when their owners, tiring of the novelty, don't want them anymore. Sometimes, though, the results are tragic for people, too. Like now. For me. Becoming the only person in the history of Syracuse to be mauled by a lion was a distinction I could do without.

Of course, I didn't share this with Littlebaum. I may have a big mouth, but no matter what some people say, I'm not suicidal. Instead, I told him I was sorry for the way I'd treated him. "I should have sold you that monitor. I don't know what I was thinking about."

"I guess maybe you should have." He rested his left shoulder against the doorframe. His shoulders relaxed. He was expansive now, a CEO graciously accepting the mistake of a subordinate. "If you'd been smarter, you could have made a lot of money off of me."

"I made a mistake," I conceded, groveling a bit more.

Littlebaum scratched under the big cat's collar. His gnarled, blue-veined hands were the hands of a man of seventy, not forty. "Yes, you did make a mistake." My admission seemed to please him. "Meet Matilda." He took his hand off the collar, thought better of it, and grabbed hold again. "If you move slowly, everything will be fine."

Actually, I wasn't planning on moving at all. Or at least I wasn't until the cat's tail stopped twitching. Even with Littlebaum holding on, I doubted he'd be able to restrain her if she really wanted to go. She probably weighed almost as much as he did, plus she had the advantage of having four legs and a lower center of gravity.

"She's a little nervous around strangers," he observed.

"So don't take her to parties," I retorted, nervousness making me facetious. It was the wrong thing to say.

"Parties," he spat out. His hand tightened on the shotgun. "For years, no one could be bothered to give me the time of day. Now that I got my money, it's Oh, Parker, let's go to the bar and have a couple of rounds. Only of course I'm doing the paying." His voice rose. "People are just a bunch of good-for-nothing pricks. Well, I say fuck 'em. I say we'd be better off without any of them around." He punctuated his rant by punching the air with the hand that was holding the shotgun.

Matilda let out a low, angry growl of commiseration. She was matching Littlebaum's tone and going him one better.

"Matilda is a nice name. How did you choose it?" I asked, hoping to cool down the emotional climate.

"It was my mother's name." Littlebaum's voice softened. He lowered his arm. "She's beautiful, isn't she?"

"Yes, she is." I meant it, too. I could see why Littlebaum had fallen in love. Matilda was a golden poem of muscle and sinew, but a poem penned in the wrong time and place. "How old is she?"

Littlebaum stroked the lioness's head. She rubbed the side of her face against his leg. "She was two months when I got her and that was five months ago. She's not going to reach her full weight for another eight, nine months. I'm thinking about having a fence built around the place, so she can run free." He chuckled. "Anyone sneaking in would definitely get a surprise."

I made a crack about the postman not being a happy camper.

Littlebaum looked annoyed. "I'm talking about letting her out at night. Like a watchdog. She'd be my watchcat."

"A pit bull might be simpler."

"I'm not interested in simple."

"Obviously." Somewhere or other Littlebaum had turned the corner from animal admirer to animal fanatic. It wasn't enough for him to love animals anymore. He had to possess them. I'd heard about people like this, willing to sacrifice house, money, and family to possess a chimp or a big cat. I'd just never met anyone like that until now.

I'd named my store Noah's Ark, but Littlebaum seemed determine to build one. A Vietnam vet, he'd spent most of his time since the war pumping gas, bagging groceries, and working on a novel no one had ever seen. Then a distant uncle had died and he'd taken the very sizable inheritance he'd received from his death and bought a house with a quarter acre of land attached. After that, Littlebaum had gone on a buying spree.

He'd proceeded to acquire, if what I'd heard was true, several monkeys, a small baboon, snakes, lizards, several potbellied pigs, a goat, many parrots, and a couple of alligators from a variety of sources, which included breeding farms and small circuses. These places sell off their surplus stock to anyone who can pay for it, although they would deny it if asked. Lions, for example, are easy breeders. There's always a surplus. The cubs are either sold or killed. This is the side of the game parks and zoos no one wants to talk about.

"So, what do you want?" Littlebaum demanded. Oinks and squawks floated through the doorway. "Why are you here? I'm not selling anything."

"I hadn't heard you were."

Matilda made a move to sniff me. Littlebaum took his hand off her collar. I remained absolutely still. I was aware that my nose itched. I made no move to scratch it. As the lioness stepped forward, I realized how big her paws were, and then I thought about the scratches my cat, Jamie, could inflict with his. A faint odor of musk rose from Matilda as she came closer. I wondered what Jamie would think as Matilda rubbed her head against the side of my jeans, marking me with her scent. Then she licked my hand. Her tongue felt rough enough to scour the skin off my bones. I reached over and scratched her under her chin. She half closed her eyes and began a big, rumbly purr.

"See," Littlebaum said. "She really is a big kitty."

The cat leaned against my leg. Her whiskers trembled in

the breeze. Her smell enveloped me. I could feel the hardness of the muscles under the fur. "I never said she wasn't."

Littlebaum went on. "Lions are easy to train."

"True." They were more like dogs than cats in that regard. That's why so many circuses used them in their acts.

"They're much more reliable than those fifteen-foot pythons you handle. One of those could strangle you before anyone could get it off your neck."

"I don't handle fifteen-footers by myself, and secondly, I don't let them get around my neck."

"That's good."

Matilda gave me a last cursory sniff and turned and padded back to Littlebaum. He scratched her back. His fingers made whorls in her fur. She stretched and leaned into him. "The funny thing about her is she doesn't like women very much. You're the exception. I think she was mistreated by a couple of them when she was a cub."

"Usually it's the men that do the mistreating."

Littlebaum shot me an odd look. "Not always. You'll forgive me if I don't ask you to come in. I'm not set up for company."

Now that was a surprise. I shifted my weight slightly. "I wasn't going to ask to. The only reason I'm here is that I'm looking for Sulfin Olsen. I understand he works for you. I need to speak to him for a moment."

Littlebaum rested the rifle against the wall. "He isn't here. He didn't show up for work today."

I asked if he had his address.

Littlebaum pressed his lips together. "I forget. Look it up."

"I tried that on the way over. Sulfin Olsen isn't listed. But then you probably know that. Listen," I said when he didn't volunteer the information, "I'm doing you a favor. I want to speak to Sulfin about a police matter."

"What kind of police matter?" Littlebaum asked suspiciously as he picked a Cheerio out of his beard and flicked it away.

"Nothing that has anything to do with you," I hastened to reassure him. "But if I don't find him, the police might come here looking for him and I don't think you want that."

Littlebaum digested the piece of news in silence. "Will it—this police matter—put Sulfin in jail?" he asked after a moment had gone by.

"No. I just want to know if he was with someone last night."

"It was pretty bad out there."

"I know. I was out in it."

Matilda swished her tail impatiently. "So, who was Sulfin supposed to be with?" Littlebaum asked as he began scratching the top of her head.

I didn't see the harm in telling him. "Eli Bishop."

Littlebaum smacked his lips while he thought. "The name sounds familiar."

"He was friends with someone called Nestor Chang."

"Now that one I know." Littlebaum flicked another piece of debris out of his beard with his free hand. "He's been here a couple of times. I buy stuff off of him once in a while."

I didn't correct Littlebaum's use of tense. Obviously, he hadn't flipped through the morning rag, because if he had, he wouldn't be referring to Nestor in the present tense. But then, when I thought about it, I realized that Littlebaum probably wasn't a paper-reading kind of guy. Which was just as well, since I wasn't interested in getting involved in a conversation about Nestor's death at the moment.

"He gives me a good price on stuff," Littlebaum added. "Better than yours."

I didn't ask how he knew what my prices were. "I'm sure." He probably did, too. It's hard to compete with stolen merchandise, not that I cared. In fact, I enjoyed the idea. Animals Galore deserved all the bad luck it could get.

"What's he done?"

"Sulfin hasn't done anything."

"No." Littlebaum frowned. "I mean Nestor."

"He took off with a suitcase that wasn't his."

Littlebaum petted Matilda some more.

I gave him a closer look. "You wouldn't happen to know anything about that, would you?"

"Are you accusing me?" Littlebaum's tone was belligerent.

"Not at all." I moved to calm him down. "I just need Sulfin's address. Please," I added.

Littlebaum's expression softened. "If you find him, tell him to come in," he said after he'd told me where I could locate him. "I need him. I can't clean all these cages by myself."

I was promising him I would when Matilda sneezed.

A worried expression flickered over Littlebaum's face. "I shouldn't have been standing out here like this. She's going to catch a cold," he said. He began closing the door. Then he stopped as a thought occurred to him. "You're not going to tell anyone about her, are you?" he demanded.

I assured him I wouldn't.

"Because my neighbors don't know."

"That seems wise." I pictured what my neighbors would say if they knew that they were living next door to a lion.

"You don't like me, do you?" Littlebaum said suddenly.

"Of course I do."

"You're lying." Littlebaum's eyes got smaller and meaner. The cords on his neck stood out. "You're here to take my animals away."

I held up my hand Boy Scout style. "I swear I'm not."

"You know," he told me, his words tumbling out so quickly it was difficult to understand him, "these animals are a hell of a lot better off with me than in some goddamned circus."

"Oh, I agree." My palms were starting to sweat. I bobbed my head up and down hoping to calm him down. It didn't work.

He pointed at Matilda. "No one wants her. I'm the only chance creatures like her have. Think of that before you open your mouth."

The cat began to growl.

"I told you I wasn't going to," I protested. I could have saved my breath.

He jabbed his hand in the air. "Anyway, you're one to talk," he continued as if I hadn't spoken. "Selling hamsters and gerbils to kids that are going to pet them to death. Please. Please, Mommy. Can I have one." His voice rose in a savage mimicry of a little child's. "Mommy, Mommy, it isn't moving! I just fed it a Snickers because I thought it would like it. Why can't I put the snake in the oven to warm it up? You said they liked the heat."

"You're exaggerating."

"Am I?" Matilda's growling was getting louder. She tossed her head. Her tail began to twitch in earnest now. "You know what I think," Littlebaum continued. "I think that it would be a good thing if the whole human race just died . . . was wiped off the face of the earth." He threw his arms out. "It would serve us right. We have been the scourge of this planet. . . . Do you know how many species we are killing? How many plants and animals disappear each day?"

The funny thing was, I agreed with him. Theoretically. We are killing our planet, and by extension we are killing ourselves. I just didn't want to be a martyr to the cause. But I didn't say that. First of all it, wouldn't have helped— Littlebaum was off on his own private tear, and, secondly, I was too busy watching Matilda.

The louder, the angrier Littlebaum got, the more agitated she became, and when cats become agitated, they do not go for a walk to cool down. They remove the cause of their agitation. Which was me. The time for telling Matilda she was a nice puss was gone. Her tail was in full twitch mode. She'd shifted her weight to her hindquarters and gone into a crouch. She was getting ready to go straight for my throat.

I fixed her with my eyes and waved my hands in the air and made myself as big as possible.

I did this because the books I've read on wild animals say that's what you're supposed to do when you meet a puma in the back country. It shows them you're not prey and they go off and look for something easier.

"You are a bad, bad cat," I told her in the loudest, sternest voice I could manage.

Matilda stopped for a second while she considered my statement.

Then she sprang.

So much for theory.

Chapter
13

All I can say is, thank God Littlebaum's door was partially shut.

I wondered if I could get my money back for the book as I kicked it closed.

I heard the lock click a second before I heard the thump of Matilda's body against the wood. The door shivered, but held. In another couple of months, it probably would have come off the hinges.

Then I turned and ran to the car, slipping and sliding in the melting snow. I didn't look back. If Matilda was going to get me, I didn't want to see it coming. But Littlebaum didn't let her out. He probably didn't want her to get her feet wet.

Once I got onto James Street, I pulled over to the side, and had a smoke to settle my nerves. Then I went looking for Sulfin. It took me a little over an hour to track him down. He wasn't at his place on Clarington or at the three other addresses people gave me. I finally found him over on the North Side in an overheated apartment off Lodi, killing rats.

He answered the door stripped to the waist. He was holding two large, dead rats by their tails. They dangled down from his left hand. I guess he'd taken his shirt off because he didn't want to get it dirty. He was a runt of a guy, five feet two inches at the most, with a pigeon chest and an oversized, flat head that looked as if it belonged on someone with shoulders three times as broad as his. His hair, fixed in a series of marceled waves, and skin were so pale they were almost white. The only thing that saved him from being an albino were his eyes, which were a dark brown. The contrast was disconcerting, reminding me of two raisins set in a sea of dough.

"I'm busy," he said after he answered the door. "And Stan ain't here. Come back later."

"I don't want to speak to Stan. I want to speak to you." I stepped inside the apartment. It stank of dirty laundry and pine-scented air freshener, but most of all it stank of rodent. I nodded at the rats he was holding. "Maybe you should get the city in here."

His brow wrinkled like the marceled waves in his hair. "For what?" Then understanding hit. "No. I raised these. They're for snakes. Now, what do you want?"

I could have told him, peace, prosperity, and good will to men, but I didn't. I told him I had a message for him from Littlebaum.

Sulfin's nostrils flared. His eyes went deeper into his head. "He wants me to come in now, right?"

I nodded.

He scowled. "For God's sake, I told him yesterday I'd be in this evening."

"Don't get mad at me," I protested, glancing around the apartment. It looked as if it should have been condemned. "I'm just telling you what he told me to say." One wall was covered with graffiti. There was a hole in the other. The window I could see was covered up with Saran Wrap. The linoleum on the floor rippled like waves in the ocean. The only attempt at decoration was a picture of a deer painted on a velvet background hanging on the wall across from me. "Maybe Littlebaum forgot. He looks like a man with a lot on his mind."

"What mind?" Sulfin muttered. "The guy's a total burnout. He's migrated to a different planet." I lit a cigarette as Sulfin casually shifted the rats to his right hand. The smoke helped mask the smell of the place. "When did he tell you this?"

"I was just there. He told me he's been calling you all morning," I lied.

His mouth tightened. "Yeah, he thinks I should be at his beck and call. Well, I got my own stuff to attend to."

As I took a puff of my Camel, I realized I could hear squeaking noises coming from the direction of what I took to be the bedrooms. "I had a boss like that once."

Sulfin held up the rats. "If these work out I'm gonna have people working for me soon." The thought seemed to cheer him and he smiled. Each canine had a small diamond chip in it. "Did you meet Matilda?"

I allowed as how I had.

"She's cute, isn't she?"

I tried not to grimace. "Adorable."

"Did Littlebaum say anything else?"

"Just that he can't clean all the cages by himself."

"Of course he can't," Sulfin groused. "I told him he has to hire more people, but he won't listen."

"Maybe he can't afford to."

"Oh, he can afford to all right. He's just too cheap to do it."

I stubbed my cigarette out on the floor. Given their condition, I didn't think Sulfin would mind. For some reason, the smoke was making it harder to breathe, not easier. "How much are you getting for those anyway?" I asked, gesturing to the dead rats.

"Two-fifty a pop. The little ones are a dollar." He gave me a speculative look. "Why? You interested. Most women don't like this kind of stuff."

I told him who I was.

Sulfin giggled. "Gee. The way Tim described you, I figured you for older. You don't look so bad."

"Thanks." I made a mental note to have a word with my employee. "How do you know him?"

"I talked to Tim about advertising in the herp newsletter."

That made sense. The herp newsletter ran features, convention news, and a sprinkling of ads, all having to do with reptiles of one type or another. I gestured toward the rats with my chin. "Do you sell them locally?" I was curious to know from a business point of view.

He shrugged. "I got a couple of people in the city, but mostly me and Stan freeze 'em and then ship 'em out to places in Madison, Chenango, and Oneida counties. Places where you have to drive to get to a pet store."

I walked into the living room, with Sulfin trailing behind me. I had the feeling he would have liked to tell me to leave, but he wasn't going to say that because he didn't want to make me mad if he didn't have to. After all, I might be a customer of his someday.

There was a pile of maybe ten dead rats in the middle of the coffee table and another ten in a box over by the TV.

He dropped the two he was holding over in that one. I went over and looked inside a cardboard box sitting on the chair. It was full of mice, both adults and pinkies. A size for every variety of snake.

"I try to freeze them right away," Sulfin explained.

"This is quite a business you have going."

He grinned proudly. "I got the idea from the back of *Reptiles*. One of those little ads. I sent for this booklet for $5.99. Told me everything I needed to know. It was the best investment I ever made." He shrugged. "Reptile ownership is going up. And, hell, snakes got to eat, too. I'm just helping out the people who don't like to kill things themselves."

Of which there are a plentiful supply. Enough to support companies that specialized in shipping frozen dead mice, rats, and rabbits.

"We got a superior product here." Sulfin wiped his brow with the back of his arm. "One whole bedroom is breeding tanks." Which explained the persistent squeaking I was hearing. "I feed them good stuff. All high-grade, organic food. I get the leftovers that the supermarket is throwing out from a friend of mine. We got a big freezer in the kitchen set really low, so we put them right in there. I figure if things keep on going this way and we keep expanding, I'll be able to give up delivering pizza and working at the store and concentrate on doing this."

"What pizza company do you work for?" I asked so I'd make sure not to order from them again.

He gave me the name. It was one of the major chains. Maybe this was how urban legends get started.

"Excuse me, but I gotta get back to work."

I followed Sulfin as he went into the kitchen.

If he minded my tagging along, he didn't show it. The smell of fear hung in the room. I thought of Matilda as I took a sniff and recoiled at the sour odor. I wondered if the rats knew what was going to happen to them as Sulfin grabbed a small one by its tail. He lifted it out of the aquarium it had been in.

"So, if you don't want Stan, what do you want?" he asked as he cracked the wriggling animal's neck. He threw it back on the table and went over to get another.

"I want to talk to you about last night."

He looked up. "What about it?"

"Eli told me you drove him up to the Myers house," I lied, curious to hear what he'd say.

"I don't know why he said that." He picked the next rat by the tail. The thing squeaked and flailed around as it dangled above the floor. "We tried, but the weather was so bad we never got there."

I averted my eyes. Why this slaughter was bothering me, I didn't know. But it was. Maybe it was the numbers. Or the smell. After all, it isn't as if I hadn't done this for the snakes in our store. I have.

Ironically, you're not supposed to feed caged snakes live animals. They can get bitten, which leads to infections that are both difficult and costly to treat. But their food still has to be warm, because snakes, fussy creatures that they are, don't like cold meals. People get around this by either killing the mouse and giving it to the snake or, in the case of Sulfin's customers, by taking the mouse or rat, defrosting it, and warming it up on top of the heating lamps. Sometimes that works and sometimes it doesn't. It depends on whether your snake is an easy feeder or likes its prey with its heart still beating. Which is one reason I've come to appreciate animals such as hamsters and gerbils. Their diets are vegetarian.

"So, how come you took Eli up there? I thought you were Nestor's friend?" I asked, getting back to the matter at hand.

Sulfin gave me a lopsided grin. "Eli tell you that?"

"Actually, Myra did."

He cocked his head. "Where'd you meet her?"

"At the store." I decided if I took shallow breaths in through my mouth, maybe the smell wouldn't be so awful. "I got the impression she doesn't like him too much."

Sulfin giggled. "That's one way of putting it. So, what else did she say?"

"Not much. That Nestor was stealing from the store."

"He steals from everyone." Sulfin killed another rat and tossed it on the table and wiped his hands on his pants. "The guy is a klepto. I wouldn't let him in my house."

"Do all of his friends feel that way?"

"Nestor doesn't have friends. He has business opportunities. Why do you care anyway?"

"For several reasons. The first one being that I did reach the house."

Sulfin shot me a look. "The house again. What does that have to do with anything?"

"I'm trying to tell you."

He crossed his arms over his chest. "Go ahead."

"I got a call from someone"—I left Manuel's name out—"telling me they needed help. They gave me that address."

Sulfin licked his lips. They were so thin they were almost invisible. "I don't see where this is going."

"I went through the house. No one was there. On the way out, I bent down to look at something and someone hit me on the head."

"So?" Sulfin uncrossed his arms and put his hands on his hips. His head looked even larger. "What does that have to do with me? Hey," he cried, finally picking up my train of thought, "are you saying I did that?"

I hadn't been going to, but as long as he suggested it, it didn't seem like a bad idea. "No. I'm asking."

I watched a tinge of red blossom on Sulfin's cheek. "The answer is no. Why the hell would I want to do something like that? And even if I had—not that I would—big deal. You look all right. I mean you're walking around, ain't ya? I don't see what the big whoop is. Actually, this is pretty funny. Yes, it is," he insisted when I didn't say anything. "You broke in, and now you're pissed because you got hurt. I love it."

"That isn't the issue." And I explained about Nestor's death and Eli.

Sulfin took a step back. "You're kidding, right?" he asked in a shocked tone of voice.

"No."

"So when was he . . . ah . . . when did he die?"

"Early in the morning."

"Oh." A quick smile flitted across Sulfin's face and was replaced by a look of studied indifference.

I clicked my tongue against the roof of my mouth and studied Sulfin. He fidgeted under my gaze. "He's alive, isn't he?" I guessed.

"Hey, you just told me he was dead."

"I think I made a mistake. Do you mind if I look around?"

Sulfin did belligerent. "Yeah, I mind."

I ignored him. My eyes roved around the room and lit on a list of numbers posted on the wall over by the phone. I walked over to get a better look.

"Come on," Sulfin whined, "you're holding me up."

I pointed to a number with the letters *Ne* written in neat

script in front of them. "Would that *Ne* stand for Nestor by any chance?"

Sulfin came up behind me. I moved down wind. "So what if it does? I never said I didn't know him."

I picked up the phone and began dialing the number for the hell of it.

"What are you doing?" Sulfin squeaked.

"Just seeing who picks up."

Sulfin's shoulders sagged. "Okay. I spoke to Nestor about an hour ago."

"How'd you speak to him?" I asked as I wondered whose body the police had.

"The usual way," Sulfin replied peevishly. "By phone. What you think? I was using a Ouija board or channeling through one of these?" He picked up a dead rat and held it to his ear.

"Very nice."

Then before I realized what he was doing, Sulfin dropped the rat, reached up, tore the paper off the wall, and ripped it to shreds. "There," he said, dropping the pieces in my hand. "Now you got no reason to stay."

"That was remarkably stupid," I told him.

Sulfin smirked at me. That was the last straw. I walked over to the table, took a garbage bag that was sitting there, and swept the dead rats into it. I did the same with the next lot.

Sulfin ran over to me. "What are you doing?" He grabbed my arm. "I had those sorted and everything."

"Too bad." I shook him off.

He snatched at me again. "Give them to me."

"No." I dropped the bag and peeled his hand off me.

He came at me, arms windmilling. I pushed him away. I guess I used more force than I intended, because he flew

across the room, smacked against one of the kitchen cabinets, and slid partway down. His face collapsed. He looked
as if he was going to cry.

"I'm taking these and the ones in the living room and
then I'm getting on the phone and calling the health department," I told Sulfin. "They're going to shut you down.
Being a small businessman, I think you understand the consequences of disruption. People are fickle. They tend to go
elsewhere if you don't have what they need and, unfortunately, they usually don't come back. However, if you want
to give me Nestor's number, I'll be happy to stay out of your
way."

Sulfin stood up and reached around with his right hand
and rubbed his back. The gesture made his ribs stand out
even more than they already did. "You didn't have to do
this," he whimpered. "You have the number."

"No. What I have, thanks to you, is a handful of confetti,"
I corrected.

"I have to go get it. I don't remember what it was." He
turned and left the room. I was noticing he had a red welt
running across his back from where he'd smacked up against
the cabinet when it occurred to me, I shouldn't have let
him go in the other room by himself. For all I knew, he
could have been going to get a knife or a gun. I went after
him. We met in the hall as he was coming back out.

"Here," he said, handing something to me.

I breathed a sigh of relief as I looked down.

He'd put a grimy crumpled-up piece of paper in the palm
of my hand. "This is what you want," he told me. "Now,
can I have my stuff back?"

I smoothed the paper out. It had a number written on it
in pink Magic Marker. "Pretty color," I commented before

folding the paper back up. "And sure you can have your stuff back after you do two things."

"That's not fair," Sulfin groused.

"Too bad. First, I want you to tell me everything you know about Nestor, and when you're done with that, I want you to ring him up and put me on the line."

Chapter
14

The blinding blue of the morning sky had muted during the day, vanquished by the slow but steady gathering of dark, gray storm clouds. The streetlamps had come on around four, shedding feeble rays of yellow light onto the gloomy late afternoon. I gazed out of my living-room window at the five crows squabbling amongst themselves as they circled above the branches of the crab apple tree, settled down, then rose again with a flap of their wings only to land on another tree limb a few yards away.

There seemed to be more and more of them and fewer jays, robins, cardinals, and sparrows every year. Now it wasn't uncommon to see flocks of a hundred or more roosting in the trees above my house filling the air with their raucous cawing. It was enough to make me wish I had a shotgun.

Across the street, a neighbor, attired in a tatty housecoat and unbuckled galoshes, hanks of blond hair sticking out from her head, was scattering salt on her driveway and talking to herself. The white specks fell from her fingers like rice at the wedding party that would never be for her. The temperature had dropped fifteen degrees in the last two hours and the melting snow had turned to ice, making walking treacherous.

I closed the blinds, turned away from the window, and bent down to give my cat, James, another pet. Ever since I'd come home he'd been winding in and out of my legs, rubbing his head over every inch of my jeans that he could reach. Between the lion and the dead rodents, I was evidently irresistible. He meowed and I picked him up. His black fur eclipsed my arms. At twenty pounds, he weighed more than some of the smaller wild cats. He purred and rubbed his face against my cheek and neck. He cocked his head to the left and then to the right as I scratched behind his ears and thought about what I was going to do next.

I'd had a plan mapped out when I'd walked in the door, but the plan had depended on Eli and Eli wasn't here. No one was. Despite the fact that I'd asked him to stay put and wait for me, Eli had taken off.

I was still scratching the cat and thinking about where Eli could have gone when James turned around and bit me.

"Son of a bitch," I cried and threw him on the sofa.

He gave me a reproachful glance, got up, shook himself off, and pointedly cleaned where I had touched him. Then he delicately picked his way across the pages of the morning paper Eli had left strewn around. I watched the pages crumple under James's weight as I sucked the side of my hand. It was a good thing, I decided, I was dealing with something that was twenty pounds instead of five hundred, because when you come right down to it, no matter what some people say, all cats, whatever their size, act pretty much the same—unpredictably. You can almost always read a dog's intentions. You can't always read a cat's.

And, unlike dogs, cats don't have a sense of shame, a fact demonstrated in this case by James, who was now curled up on a sofa cushion, sleeping the sleep of the innocent. He'd become tired of being petted or maybe he hadn't liked the way I was going about it, although he had seemed to, so instead of walking away, he'd bit me. And now his fit of pique was over. He wasn't going to waste valuable energy agonizing over whether he should have performed the action or not. He didn't feel a scintilla of guilt or doubt over what he'd done.

I sat down next to him. He opened one eye, then closed it again. He curled his tail around his nose and went back to sleep. I decided there was a lot to be said for that kind of ruthlessness as I touched his tail. His eyes snapped open. I stopped giving him a hard time and called George again. I'd been trying to get him since I walked in the house, without success. This time wasn't any different.

Maybe he was on campus. Or he could be at the library. I reached for the remains of the candy bar sitting on the coffee table while I waited for his answering machine's beep. When it sounded, I left a message telling him to call me ASAP and hung up. Then I peeled the silver paper off the two remaining squares of chocolate and ate them. As the candy dissolved on my tongue, I thought about what the police were going to say when they found out that the guy they had in the morgue was the guy who'd stolen Nestor's wallet.

If Nestor and Sulfin were to be believed.

The explanation Nestor had given me for the mix-up was iffy, but not so iffy it couldn't be true. I leaned my head back and closed my eyes as I remembered our conversation.

"My wallet got stolen, okay?" Nestor had said. "BFD."

"Did you report it?"

"Of course I did. Not that it matters. The mall police don't do jack shit. They couldn't find their asses with their hands tied behind their backs. I'm glad that putz croaked. Saves me the trouble. He got my jacket, too. A new one. I had it over a chair at the food court and he just took off with the whole fucking thing. I had a hundred bucks in my wallet. Not to mention my driver's license. You know what a pain it is to get another one of those?"

"Yes, I do." My wallet had gotten stolen a couple of years ago. It had taken me months to straighten out. I was still getting bills for things people had bought under my name months later. Now I just carried my license and a credit card, period. It was easier that way.

"I think you'd better call the police and tell them they made a mistake."

"Yeah." The yeah was halfhearted at best.

"I mean it. They need to know."

"Of course I will." Nestor did righteous indignation. "What the hell do you think I am?"

"How about a scum-sucking bottom feeder."

Nestor's righteous indignation rose to biblical proportions. In the end, I allowed Nestor to convince me that he would make the call. The truth was, I'd wanted to believe him because it was easier that way, even though deep down I knew Nestor probably had as much intention of phoning the police as I did of quitting smoking.

It wasn't in his interest to. But then it wasn't in my interest, either, considering Chapman's little gift this morning to Eli. Which is why I'd allowed myself to be convinced. Or at least it wasn't until I had the suitcase in my hand, because if Nestor got himself tied up at the PSB—a definite possibility.

The guy could have a warrant out on him for all I knew—
it might be awhile before we could get our business cleared
up. The bottom line was, whoever was lying in the morgue
could wait another five or six hours to be identified. It wasn't
going to kill them. They were dead already.

I got up, popped a couple of Advil—I couldn't believe
how lousy I felt—then sat back down and called Manuel's
house next. My luck was running true to form, that is to say
bad. His mother told me he'd been there and left without
saying where he was going. I tried Manuel's friends. Two
weren't in and the other three told me they hadn't heard
from him. I restrained myself from throwing the phone
across the room, took a deep breath and dialed Tim.

"Guess what?" I told him. "Nestor is alive."

I could hear him draw in his breath. "You're shitting me,
right?"

"No."

"Good. I'm glad."

"You know, you're the only person I've heard say that."

"I told you I like Nestor. I think he's an interesting guy.
How'd the cops make a mistake like that anyway?"

I told him about the lost wallet.

"You believe that?"

"Stranger things have happened."

Tim digested this for a moment. "I suppose," he grudgingly allowed.

Then I told him about Eli taking off and asked if he called
in.

"No. But Chapman has."

"Great."

"He told me to remind you about your date with him for
tonight."

"He used the word *date?*"

"From the Latin. As in appointment, although the word can also apply to the fruit of the date palm tree. Interestingly enough, that word comes from the Greek word for finger. A word that has obvious ramifications for him. Not to mention resonance."

"I see you've been reading the dictionary again."

"I find it soothing."

There had been a time in high school when I had to. That's when my idea of a good time was a day spent reading at the library. "Did you say anything to him?"

"Other than that I'm planning on consigning him to the nether reaches of hell, no."

"Did you really say that?"

"No. I told him I'd give you the message. What are you going to do about that asshole?" Tim asked.

"I wish I could tell you." So far I hadn't come up with anything that wouldn't land me in jail. I could hear Zsa Zsa barking in the background. "What's she going on about?"

"Nothing. She's barking at one of the angles that got loose."

I told Tim I was going to come by and pick her up.

"You don't have to, you know. She's perfectly happy with me."

"I know I don't. I want to." The truth was, I missed her company. Then I told him about my meeting with Sulfin Olsen.

"I suppose I should have told you." I could hear the tinge of concern in Tim's voice.

I knew he was thinking I might be angry about the ads for feeders in the newsletter, even though I had no legitimate reason to feel that way. I reassured him I wasn't.

"It turns out he was the one that drove Eli up to the Myers

house." I reached for my cigarettes and lighter. "What kind of person would you say he is?"

"Sulfin?" I could picture Tim twirling his stud around in his ear as he framed his reply. "If I had to use one word to describe him, I'd say that word would be ambitious. Very ambitious."

That pretty much summed up my opinion, too. I told Tim I'd be over in a little while to get the dog. Then I hung up. I tried George one last time. He was still out. I left a message on his machine and left my house. I had a few things to do before I met Nestor.

Chapter 15

Nestor and I were supposed to meet in a house over on the west side of town at nine-thirty. I would have preferred a more public place, but Nestor had refused and, given the circumstances, I really felt as if I wasn't in a position to bargain, which was also why I didn't feel I could object to the location he'd chosen.

The feeling I'd gotten off him from the brief conversation we'd had was that either this meeting was going to go his way or it wasn't going to go any way at all. As it was, I'd had a tough time convincing him to see me, and I'd only done that by telling him what Sulfin had told me.

Viking Street was one of those streets that showed up a lot in the local paper when a crime was written about. As in: So and so was beaten up on Viking Street. Or, shots were fired on Viking Street. Or, John Doe remains in critical condition after being stabbed on Viking Street. You'd think the block should have a sign on it—Caution: Walk With Care.

It doesn't, of course. In fact, from the car the street doesn't look any worse than a dozen other run-down avenues in the neighborhood. Almost all of the large Victorians in the area have been turned into multifamily residences. They're dotted in among the neat, single family homes of working-class people who are fighting a losing battle to hold on to their neighborhood. Boarded up and plastic-wrapped windows, shored-up porches, and ripped-up driveways, alternate with picket-fenced yards and clipped hedges. Piles of trash spill out into the road. The only visible things of value here are the expensive drug-money cars sitting next to them.

The street still hadn't been plowed—no big surprise. The rich neighborhoods get done first and the poorer ones last—so I had to drive slowly. Although the cars had packed the snow down in the middle of the road, there were still hillocks along the edges, where it would be easy to get stuck. It was dark by the time I reached Viking, which added to the problem, since several of the streetlights were out, making it hard to read the numbers on the houses that still had them.

This was one of those times when it would have been easier to park the car and walk, but I couldn't do that because there was no place to put it. Vehicles were parked on both sides of the street, shrinking the road down to one lane. If anyone had come along, one of us would have had to back up. And even if I managed to hump my way into one of the few vacant spaces I spotted, I was fairly confident I wouldn't be able to get back out. The car I was driving could barely make it up a hill, let alone anything else.

I finally found a spot two blocks away and let Zsa Zsa out. She trotted along ahead of me, tail wagging, ears flying in the cold wind, pausing now and then to nose at the garbage spilling out from the ripped-open trash bags. Three twenty-five Viking turned out to be a slanting, shambling wreck of a structure that looked as if the city should have pulled it down a long time ago.

A quarter of its second floor had been burned away. Scorched jagged beams reached out to the winter sky. All the windows, except for the two in front, were boarded up. The lawn was still full of the sofas, chairs, and wood the firemen had thrown out of the windows when they'd put out the blaze. The front of the house had a large For Sale sign tacked over one of the windows. Another sign next to it said, "reduced." Good luck, I thought as I mounted the steps, which shifted and sighed under my weight. Given the property values in this area, it would cost more to pull the building down and clean up the lot than it was worth.

Nestor sure knew how to pick them, I reflected as I walked across the porch. If I hadn't been so anxious to wrap this up, I would have turned around and gone back to the store. Instead, I knocked on the door, which, given the condition of the house, was, oddly enough, still intact. It swung open. Zsa Zsa ran in before I could stop her.

Somewhere ahead of me I heard the sound of ska being played. I called for Nestor as I went inside.

I didn't get a reply.

Someone was here, though, because there were lit candles in glass jars set along either side of the hallway. They flickered and waved, casting shadows on the wall. For a moment, I thought I'd wandered into the set from a bad Hollywood gothic. You had to give the guy points for style. He definitely had a flair for the dramatic. Given what was in his room, I was surprised there wasn't something like a skull in the middle of the floor.

I could only marvel at what Nestor thought he was accomplishing with this setup as I followed the path the candles had laid out into the kitchen.

"Hey, Nestor!" I yelled. "Very impressive. You can come out now and stop playing ghoul in the closet. I've got the message. Let's get this thing wrapped up so we can get out of here." I rubbed my arms. "It's too cold to stay here for long." And, besides, the place stank of burnt wood.

He didn't answer.

Except for the music, the crunch of what I was stepping on, and the click of Zsa Zsa's nails on the floor as she trotted along in front of me, the house was quiet. At this point, I should have returned to my car and gotten my flashlight, but I was tired and cold and hungry and irritated. I wasn't in the mood to walk the two blocks to my car and back again. Instead, I picked up one of the candles and used that for a light.

Three more votive candles sat next to the boom box on the kitchen table. Nestor must have bought out the store. I picked up the CDs and read the labels. Ska, reggae, and rap. About what I would have expected. "Come on, Nestor. This is bullshit."

Nothing.

I put the CDs down and looked around. The sink was intact, as were the countertop and the cabinets. "You want to play games, fine with me." I told Zsa Zsa to seek and find, which was pretty laughable if you knew her—the only thing she was good at locating was the nearest bag of French fries—but you gotta work with what you got.

By this time I was beginning to have my doubts about Nestor being in the house, but I decided to give the place a quick look-see anyway. Maybe, through some unbelievable stroke of good fortune, he'd left Eli's suitcase lying around.

I walked over and opened the closet door. Except for a couple of brooms, it was empty. I tried the doors of the lower and upper cabinets next. Most were stuck shut. The ones I could manage to get open were filled with dented cans of food and spilled bags of rotting flour and sugar.

Zsa Zsa and I rapidly went over the rest of the downstairs. As we checked the rooms, it was obvious people had been using the place as a squat. The floors were all filled with trash. I kept on stepping on pizza boxes and tripping over empty soda cans. Occasionally I'd hear a squeak as a mouse or a rat hustled out of the way. There were probably hundreds in the building. I should tell Sulfin. What is that saying about, one man's loss is another man's gain?

The ripped sofas and chairs in what had once been the living room spilled their guts onto the floor. The odor of mold hung over everything. Metal blinds dangled down from single fasteners, letting in the light from the street. In another room, a bed was obliterated by chunks of plaster, as were the nightstands standing next to it. A dresser was covered with a thin dusting of snow. I looked up. There was a hole in the ceiling. Two Metallica posters, the only things left untouched, stared at me from the doorway of the third room. I moved on with Zsa Zsa following gingerly behind me.

The dining-room table was broken in two, each half inclining towards the other like dancers bowing at the end of the dance. The chairs to the set were lying on the floor, their legs splayed out in different directions. A lamp hung precariously from a ceiling wire. Miraculously, a sideboard stood intact, its display of commemorative plates untouched.

After I made my circuit I came back to the kitchen. Maybe Nestor had come and something had happened to make him leave. Or maybe he'd just gone to get something. Whatever the reason, the only thing I did know was he wasn't here now. What was worse was that the suitcase wasn't here, either.

I decided to give him fifteen minutes.

I was sitting, slumped down on the folding chair, with my feet up on the table, listening to Bob Marley and throwing pieces of an old Tootsie Roll I'd found in my backpack to Zsa Zsa, when Eli walked in.

Chapter
16

Later, when I thought about the event, I realized that in a funny way the most amazing thing about it was that Zsa Zsa hadn't barked to let me know someone else was in the house. It was something I always counted on. Her warning me, before I could see something coming. But I guess that was only true if she wasn't eating. This time all her energies had evidently been concentrated on the bits of Tootsie Roll I was tossing her. It made me wonder if anyone else had been there, standing in the dark, watching me go by.

But I wasn't thinking about that at the moment. At the moment, the only thing I was thinking about was Eli. The two of us could have been playing a scene out of an old movie. He stopped dead when he saw me. I sat up so fast, the chair I was sitting on fell over. I automatically reached down and picked it up while keeping my eyes fixed on him.

The flicker of the candles on the table emphasized Eli's mouth and chin, giving them a soft, luxurious cast, while shrouding the rest of his face in darkness. Her attention finally aroused, Zsa Zsa began to bark and dance around Eli, darting in, then backing away, then going in again, the way she did when something frightened her.

Eli ignored the dog. All his attention was focused on me.

"Who were you expecting?" I asked. "Not me evidently."

"I'm sorry. I really am." He took a step back. Out of the corner of my eye I saw the left cuff of his pants leg brush against one of the tapers on the floor. The flame tip reached up and touched the material in a leisurely fashion. A delicate puff of red and yellow appeared.

"Eli!" I yelled.

"It's no good." He shook his head from side to side and kept backing away. The puff became a vine, tracing its way up Eli's leg.

I gestured frantically. "Your pants."

He looked down. His mouth formed a large black O.

I made brushing motions with my hands. "Slap it out."

He didn't. He panicked. His mouth quivered. His lower lip drooped. "Oh, my God," he moaned, jumping back and knocking another candle over in the process.

"Stand still for God's sake. I'm coming."

The fact that Eli was hopping around like a kangaroo on speed did not improve the situation.

I ripped my jacket off as I ran.

The fire was spreading up his pants.

I'd taken two steps, and was about to take a third, when Zsa Zsa darted in front of me. I saw her, but not in time to stop myself from tripping over her and falling, coming down hard on my knees and the palms of my hands. She yelped and ran away. A pain shot up my wrist. I ignored it and concentrated on covering the remaining steps between Eli and myself.

I hit at his pants and knocked off a couple of burning embers. Then I wrapped the jacket around the front of his legs and smacked at it with my hands, beating out the flames, while Zsa Zsa played Greek chorus in the background.

Eli pointed in back of me. "Look!"

I turned. A small blaze caused by the candle Eli had kicked over had started behind me. I stamped the tendrils out. "It wouldn't kill you to help me," I snapped.

Eli bit his lip while I just stood there, bent over, my hands on my knees, inhaling the odor of melted wax and the charred wood, listening to myself wheezing. Suddenly I was very, very tired. All I wanted to do was go home and go to bed.

"But what about my legs?" Eli finally said hesitantly. His hands were fluttering at his sides like birds. He looked close to tears.

"What about them?"

"Shouldn't we go to the hospital?"

It took every bit of spare energy I had to straighten up. "They're probably fine. You weren't on fire long enough to get burned."

"They don't feel so great."

Neither did I as I led him back over to the table and used one of the candles sitting on the table to take a look. The light wasn't great, but under the circumstances it was the best I could do.

"You can go if you want, but they look okay to me," I reassured Eli after he'd rolled his pants up to his knees.

I'd been pretty sure he would be. In reality, he'd been on fire for no more than a few seconds. The denim was scorched, but from what I could see, aside from a superficial burn on the front of his calf, Eli was okay.

"It's a good thing you're not into polyester," I cracked. "Otherwise you'd have diamond-patterned skin."

Eli didn't laugh. I couldn't blame him. Picking my jacket up, I wondered if the cleaner's would ever be able to get the smell of smoke out of it. Then I wondered if it was worth cleaning and repairing. Given what it had cost, maybe it was time to retire it to the dustbin.

"At least it's not my leather one," I told Eli as I inspected it. As far as I could see, the jacket had three small holes in the outer shell, not to mention the ripped zipper. And that was what I could see in the candlelight. God knows what I'd find when I looked at it tomorrow morning, but I put it on anyway, smell and all, because now that I'd stopped moving I was getting cold.

"Eli," I repeated when he didn't reply.

He shivered. "I have to go."

"I don't think so."

"I can't stay here." And he turned and started for the door. "I'm late. I have to do my work."

"And what kind of work is that?"

"My schoolwork."

"It's going to have to wait," I flung at his back. "Don't even think about leaving."

He kept lumbering along. I caught up with him and grabbed him by the arm.

He shook me off the way a bear shakes off a gnat. "I told you, I have to leave." Eli's voice rose, quivered, and broke. "I could have . . ."

"Could have what?"

"Died."

I ran in front of him and blocked his way. "You still might if you don't tell me what you're doing here."

He hung his head. The candlelight made him look denser,

harder, as if the dark had compacted his flesh. "I can't believe it," he whispered.

"What can't you believe?"

"What just happened."

"You know what I can't believe," I told him. "What I can't believe is that you're here."

Eli started to move again. "Really. I gotta go."

"Of course. I forgot for a moment. You're an important man. You have things to attend to." I moved out of his way. "Go ahead." The reality was, I couldn't stop him. "Just tell me why you're here. You owe me that much."

My eyes must have become accustomed to the dark, because I could see his forehead wrinkling.

"After all," I reminded him, "I did just save your life. You'd be a cinder by now," I added unkindly when he didn't say anything.

Eli wiped his mouth with his jacket sleeve. "I . . . I . . . got a call."

"From whom?"

"From Adelina. She told me Nestor wanted to meet me here."

"Adelina, hunh? And how did she know to get a hold of you?"

"I . . . I . . . don't understand."

"It's very simple. Where did she phone you? My place? Yours? Sulfin's? Where?"

Eli didn't say anything.

"Come on. Where?" I insisted. "Or can't you decide?"

Eli cleared his throat. "Why are you so interested?"

"Because I'd like to get at least one thing in this mess cleared up. Remember. You were supposed to be waiting at my house for me to call."

Eli looked away. "I would have. I was going to. Only

George came by. He said he was taking me downtown. To make a statement. I told him I didn't want to go, but he told me I had to."

Good Old George, I thought bitterly. And I'd been trying to get hold of him all day to tell him what was going on. Too bad he hadn't extended the same courtesy to me.

"Go on," I prompted.

"We got in his car. He said he had to drop something off to get copied, someplace downtown first, before we went to the PSB. The place was on East Gennie. He told me to wait in the car. He said he'd just be a moment. But while he was inside, I saw this bus coming. We were parked right in back of the bus stop. I got out of the car and got on it and the bus took off."

"And you just rode off?"

He nodded. "That's right."

I laughed incredulously. "Just like that."

"Yeah."

"I can't believe George didn't make you go inside the copy center with him." The guy was definitely slipping up in his old age.

Eli shrugged. "I don't know. I guess he thought maybe I was just this big tub of lard." His tone was bitter. "Maybe he thought I was like some dog. Tell me to do something and I will."

I wondered if that was what he thought of himself as I pushed a lock of my hair off my forehead. "And he didn't look for you?"

Eli shrugged again. "I don't know. Maybe he did. Maybe you should ask him."

"I will when I see him, but for now I'd like to concentrate on you. So then what did you do?"

"I went over to Sulfin's."

"You must have just missed me."

Eli blinked and crossed his arms over his chest. "He didn't say anything about your having been there."

"I just bet he didn't."

"What's that supposed to mean?"

His story stank, but I didn't say that. I didn't say anything.

Eli continued after a few seconds, his voice hesitant and nervous. "I was eating a slice of pizza when Adelina called. . . . And that's when I found out about Nestor wanting to meet me here."

"And that's your story. The one you're sticking to."

"I don't understand," Eli stammered.

"I just want to make sure."

"Why is that?"

I shrugged. "Curiosity. I just wanted to see how far you'd go." Then I casually added, "I know what's in the suitcase."

Eli stared at me. I could hear his rate of breathing increase.

"Your pal Sulfin told me."

"Told you what?" Eli countered.

"About the tortoises."

He gasped.

"Manuel's right. You should be careful whom you tell your business to. Madagascar tortoises. I'm impressed." I kept my voice level. "No wonder Chapman is so interested. How many do you have in there? Ten? Twelve? How much are they worth anyway? A hundred thousand all together? A hundred and twenty thousand? That's a tidy piece of change."

Eli just stared at me.

"If they're alive." But they probably still were. That was one of the things about tortoises. They could survive for a very long time in adverse circumstances, which is why, like snakes, they're a favorite with animal smugglers. Warm-blooded mammals have a much higher rate of attrition, attrition being a nice word for death.

"It wasn't my idea," Eli whined. "It was Chapman's. Honest."

"Honest isn't a word I'd be using right now if I were you."

"But it's the truth," Eli protested. "He told me all I had to do was take them over to Japan. He had the buyers and everything all set up and waiting."

"I see." I motioned to Zsa Zsa. She followed me outside. "So you kind of told me the truth. You just changed a few trivial things. Like the countries. And the contents of the suitcase."

Eli looked down at the ground.

"And Chapman, he just picked you up at the bar because he liked the way you looked. The whole thing was pure coincidence. You've never done anything like this before."

"I really didn't know."

"You mean you never looked in the suitcase? You didn't have to take the tortoises out?"

"I—"

I cut him off. "Don't even bother trying to make up a story. I don't want to hear it. The only reason I haven't turned you and Chapman over to Fish and Wildlife yet is because I wanted to make sure this was real."

"But . . ." Eli began.

I interrupted again. "Do you realize you and your friend could be responsible for the extinction of a species? How does that feel?"

"Well . . . I . . . didn't think . . ."

"That's right." I poked my finger in his chest. "You

haven't thought. At all. At least tell me this. Did Manuel know?"

"No," Eli whispered. "I wasn't going to tell him anything, but he came by a half hour after I discovered what Nestor had done. I was really upset. And he asked me what the matter was. I had to tell him something. I don't know why, but I didn't want him to know about the tortoises. The story about the cigars just slipped out. One of the guys at work told me he was thinking of doing it. Somehow it just seemed better. More . . . dignified. And when he suggested you . . ."

"You figured, hey, why not mess up her life, too? Cigars. Tortoises. Snakes. Who gives a fuck? It's all the same."

"I'm sorry." Eli's voice was low, floating on the air. "Really I am. But if I'd told you the truth, you wouldn't have helped me."

"You're goddamned right I wouldn't have." I reached in my jacket pocket for my cigarettes, but all of them were crumbled from when I'd beaten the fire out on Eli's pants leg. What was that saying about no good deed goes unpunished? I finally found one that looked salvageable. I straightened it out carefully and threw the rest of the pack down on the floor. "I think what you're doing is beyond redemption."

Of course, not a whole lot of other people shared my conviction. The buying and selling of endangered species protected by the CITES Act, officially known as the Convention on International Trade in Endangered Species, an act signed by one hundred thirty countries, is a growth business these days. Collectors in Japan and Germany are particularly avid, bidding up prices for hard-to-get species to record levels. For those who like shelled things, Madagascar-radiated tortoises are a particularly hot commodity. Their yellow head and domed shell with its bright yellow-and-black starbursts, make them walking art, one of the rarest and most prized tortoise species on earth. Especially since no two have the exact same pattern. Their shells are as individual as snowflakes.

The markup on them is extremely lucrative. The tortoises sell for anywhere from ten to twenty thousand apiece at their destination. They've usually been purchased for five hundred. The markup is actually better than the markup on cocaine. In addition, the penalties are a whole lot lighter. If you're caught, three hundred thousand dollars in smuggled animals might earn you two to three years jail time max (with probably half of that off for good behavior) and a ten- to fifteen-thousand-dollar fine. Sometimes, most times, if it's a first offense, you get away with a warning and a fine. Compare that with what you get if you smuggle drugs and you can see the attractiveness of the proposition to a person with certain proclivities.

Especially since it is so easy to get the animals—if you have the right contacts. Farmers in places like Madagascar, Borneo, and India, who are eking out a subsistence living on small plots of stony land, can earn enough money selling two or three snakes or one tortoise to feed their families for a year. If you were they, which would you choose? Food for little Consuela or the tortoise? Let's guess. Everyone benefits. Except the animals, of course.

But what the hell.

There are too many species around anyway.

I walked out onto the porch. Eli came after me.

"Did you find the suitcase?" he asked at my elbow.

"Nope." I pressed my cigarette into shape, lit it, and took a puff. "No Nestor. No suitcase. No nothing. It looks as if you're out of luck."

"But Adelina said . . ."

"Maybe Adelina was lying," I told him. "That is, if you really spoke to her." A fact I wasn't prepared to bet on.

"I did," Eli protested. "She said Nestor wanted to work out a deal."

"Why would he want to do that?" I asked, curious to hear what Eli was going to say.

"I think because he realized he didn't know what to do with the tortoises. He didn't know where to sell them."

"Why didn't he call up Chapman?"

"Maybe he's scared to." Eli shivered. I didn't think he was shivering from the cold, although I could have been wrong. A slow, penetrating wind had kicked up since I'd gone inside.

I put my collar up as I watched the wind ruffle the fringes of a piece of cloth hanging over the back of an armchair squatting in the front yard. Even though it was chilly out and I couldn't close my jacket against the wind's fingers, I still preferred the outside to being back in that house with the candles burning.

I flicked an ash off my Camel. George was right. This whole thing had been a waste of time from beginning to end. Running around. Getting involved with stupid people doing stupid things. I should sell the store. Leave the city. Go back to the newspaper and the life I used to have. Move on. The thing to do would be to notify the proper authorities and see if they could get the suitcase back from Nestor. Maybe they could find him before he sold the tortoises.

"Why would Adelina do that?" Eli asked, breaking the silence.

"Do what?" I replied.

"Lie. Why would she lie?"

"Lots of reasons."

"Like what?"

But I didn't reply. My attention was taken up with Zsa Zsa. She'd run down the front steps and was barking at a sofa off to the left. Her left front leg was crooked and off the ground, her tail was out, her back was straight. She was pointing, her bark telling me to look.

I yelled at her to be quiet. She didn't listen. I told myself that, knowing Zsa Zsa, she could be carrying on about anything. A shoebox. A ball. A bag full of garbage. A rat. It was all the same to her. I'd had enough for one evening. I didn't want to look. I didn't care.

On some level, I think I knew that what I was going to find wasn't going to be good. I think I figured if I didn't see whatever it was, if I played monkey with its hands over its eyes, I wouldn't have to do anything about it.

This time I ordered Zsa Zsa to get her ass up on the porch. She ignored me and kept barking. I hate when my dogs do that.

"Obedience school for you," I told her. Her barks, high and yapping, were beginning to get on my nerves. Evidently I wasn't the only one, because a minute later I heard a window open. I looked up.

The man next door had his head stuck out. "Shut that fucking thing's yap before I come down and pound you!" he screamed. "I'm trying to watch TV."

"Screw you, too!" I yelled back. But I went and got Zsa Zsa anyway.

She was barking at what had been Nestor Chang.

One of his hands was covering his face, as if shielding it from the light, while the second one was resting on his chest. He could have been taking a nap.

Only he wasn't.

The blood seeping through the fingers on his chest told me that.

It turned out the police had been right all along.

Nestor was dead.

They'd just gotten their times mixed up.

I walked back up to Eli. "Are you sure Adelina told you to come? Is that the story you want to stick to?"

"What do you mean?" he stammered.

"You tell me." And I guided him over to the sofa.

Chapter
17

Eli's fingers frantically plucked at the sleeve of my jacket. "I didn't do this," he wailed. "It wasn't me. I swear. It wasn't me. Why would I show up here if I did something like this?"

I shook my head. "I don't know. But I'm sure the police will come up with a dozen or more reasons."

"It doesn't make any sense."

"Actually, it does." And I recited the lines about guilt, remorse, and the killer returning to the scene of the crime.

"No." His eyes had gone wide with terror. Before I could stop him, Eli fell to the ground and put his arms around my knees. "Please help me," he sobbed. "You have to."

"Jesus." I pulled him up. "What the hell is the matter with you?"

He wiped his nose with his jacket sleeve. "Just give me half an hour."

"To do what?"

He made a vague gesture toward the street. "Leave. That's all I'm asking."

I sighed. "Eli, it won't matter if I do. The police will find you anyway. It'll look better if you go in voluntarily."

"But they're going to put me in jail," he cried.

"Not necessarily. You haven't been indicted."

"But they will. Why shouldn't they? I'm their best suspect."

I didn't disagree.

Eli went on. "I'm never going to finish school at this rate," he lamented.

I tsked. "My grandmother used to say everything happens for the best. Maybe she was right. I understand the state offers correspondence courses you can take from prison."

He recoiled as if I'd hit him. I massaged my wrist. It was throbbing. I must have sprained it when I tripped over Zsa Zsa.

"Do you have money to pay for a lawyer?" I asked, thinking I might call mine.

"I told you I don't. If I had money why would I have done this?" he demanded sullenly.

"Then the court will appoint one." Mine didn't do pro bono work. The word free wasn't in his vocabulary.

"Fine." Eli hung his head. His shoulders slumped. He put his hands in his pants pockets. "If that's what you think is best." His tone was meek. He looked like a dog that's been kicked one too many times.

"I do. Really." Absurdly, I felt bad for him. Eli seemed to have the ability to evoke that feeling in me. I was going to pat him on the shoulder when I saw the gun he was pointing at me. "Where'd that come from?" I said stupidly. It looked as if I should have been feeling bad for myself.

"In here." He gestured down to his pants pocket with his chin. "I'm sorry, Robin. I really am."

I didn't answer.

"Aren't you going to say anything?" he asked.

"Like what?"

"Anything." This time his voice was a little more desperate. If he was looking for absolution, he wasn't going to get it from me.

"All right." I hunched my shoulders up against the wind. It was picking up. The scent of snow was suddenly in the air. "So this whole thing with you down on your knees. Begging? What was that, exactly?" I asked as I watched a piece of newspaper tumbling across the street. "An act?"

"No." Eli's gun hand was shaking slightly. His voice rose. "I meant it. I didn't want to do this."

I snorted. "I'm forcing you? Is this something like the robber saying to his victim, 'If you weren't wearing that Rolex on your wrist, I wouldn't have had to rob you.' "

"Come on, Robin." Eli's voice had taken on a wheedling quality. "I tried to give you an out. I begged you to let me go. You wouldn't listen."

"I wasn't holding you. You could have walked anytime."

"You would have come after me."

"Not necessarily. So now what? Are you going to kill me, too?"

"No." Eli sounded genuinely shocked. "Of course not. I could never do anything like that."

I nodded toward Nestor's body. "Except for the occasional slip."

He took a step back. "I didn't kill him. I already told you that. A half hour. That's all I'm asking. Now give me the keys to your car."

For a few seconds I toyed with the idea of not handing

them over, but in the end I did. I believed what Eli had said. I didn't think he would shoot me if I didn't give them to him, but I wasn't prepared to bet on it. After all, I hadn't thought he had a gun, either. Plus, Eli's hands were shaking. Which meant he was nervous. Which made me nervous.

I wasn't in the mood to gamble with the consequences of not doing what he said. I wasn't in the mood to try and take the gun away from him. That was the way accidents happened. And I didn't need another one. I didn't want to spend time in the hospital recovering from a gun shot wound in God knows what part of my anatomy. I'd done too much of that all ready. Pain had long since lost its charm for me.

"Now what?" I asked.

"Now this," Eli said, pitching my keys into the yard as he would a baseball. Fortunately, he didn't have a very good arm because they didn't go very far.

Then he turned and ran. I didn't try and go after him. There didn't seem to be much point. Instead, I watched Eli go out of the front yard and down the block. He shambled rather than ran, his legs bowing out slightly. When he was almost at the end of the block, he stopped and got into a car. I'm not sure what kind, because as I told the police, I was too far away to see the make and model. I heard the engine cough and sputter a few times before it turned over. A moment later, the car's headlights came on. A few seconds after that, Eli nosed the car out into the street, made a U-turn, and sped away.

The block was quiet again, the only sounds the mewling of a cat and the rustle of sheets of newspaper blown by the wind.

I ambled over in the direction Eli had thrown my keys. Calling the police a little later rather than a little sooner really wasn't going to make that much of a difference when it came to locating Eli, and it certainly wouldn't matter to Nestor—given the condition he was in, he was beyond timely matters—but it would make a big difference to me.

I had my house and my store keys in addition to my car keys on the ring that Eli had tossed away. What was worse was that they were my spare set of keys, since I'd lost my other pair last month. Having a duplicate made was one of the things on my list I hadn't gotten around to doing. Once I called the police, they'd rope off the area and I wouldn't be able to get them. Which would be a real pain in the ass for me. Not that the police would care.

It took me ten minutes of lighting matches and cursing while I pricked my fingers on sharp-edged objects as I felt around through rusted soda cans, sodden clothes, and crumpled-up newspapers before I located them.

After I put the keys in my pocket, I walked over to the house next door and rang the bell.

I figured, what the hell, the guy who'd yelled at me from out the window was probably still up anyway. And if he wasn't, then he should be, given what he'd called Zsa Zsa.

I stared down at George. He was sprawled out on his back in his bed. His left hand was gripping the edge of his quilt, while his right hand was resting on his chest, just the way Nestor's had been.

The thought gave me the heebie-jeebies.

I took a deep breath and refocused.

I made myself study George's face instead. I noticed what looked like the beginning of a mole near his chin. I noticed he had a crease in his left earlobe. I noticed his lips were slightly parted. A low whistle was coming out of them. Zsa Zsa jumped up on the bed and licked the edges of his mouth.

He brushed at her with his hand, mumbled something, and turned on his side.

I leaned over, grasped his shoulder, and shook. He snorted and buried his head in his pillow.

"Get up."

He didn't stir. According to George, he could sleep through anything, and had, a fact he'd demonstrated by snoozing through a fire in the kitchen of his apartment when he was twelve.

I shook him harder, my irritation mounting by the second. I was not in a good mood. It had been a long, crappy day, climaxed by an even longer, crappier night. The only reason I was here at all instead of down at the police station was because I was lucky enough to know one of the detectives that had caught the call.

I'd given him a good deal on a couple of king snakes for his son last year. He returned the favor by cutting me some slack. He took my preliminary statement and let me go instead of dragging my ass downtown.

He'd pointed a finger at me. "First thing tomorrow morning."

"Without a doubt."

"I mean it."

"So do I. How's your kid?"

He broke a smile. "He's doin' okay. So are the snakes. Now get out of here."

I didn't have to be told twice. By now the area was crawling with the crime-scene crew. Neighbors, awakened by the commotion, were standing outside, watching the show and doing running commentaries among themselves. They'd seen enough of these to have a perspective. I spotted the man who'd yelled at Zsa Zsa over by the side of the yard. He was carrying on to a fat woman with her bathrobe peeking out of her overcoat about how he had to get up early to go to work the next morning. She told him to shut up and moved away, leaving him standing by himself.

I didn't feel much sympathy. Short of the winos and the hopheads, everyone had to get up early. I should have gone home and gone to bed, but I didn't. I was too tired to sleep. Instead, I'd driven over to George's and let myself in. There were a couple of things I wanted to get straightened out.

"George. Wake up, goddamn it." By now I was practically yelling in his ear.

He opened one eye a crack. "Wha?" he mumbled.

"I want to talk to you."

His other eye opened. He ran his hand through his hair. Black strands curled around his fingers. "What time is it?" His voice was hoarse with sleep.

"Two o'clock."

Zsa Zsa nipped in and licked his chin. He pushed her away, then rubbed the dog saliva off with the back of his hand and lifted his head off the pillow. "Jesus," he groaned. "What's going on? What's wrong?"

"Nestor's dead."

"This is what you woke me for?" George put his head back down and closed his eyes. "He was dead before."

"Not really."

His eyes snapped open. "What do you mean 'not really'? The newspaper said . . ."

"They made a mistake."

"Friggin' morons," George grumbled. "I'm surprised they even get the date right. Just a minute." He got up. He was wearing his usual pair of ratty boxers.

I watched him pad out of the room. A moment later, I heard the toilet flush, followed by the sound of water running. Then that was gone. George returned. "You want to start again," he said as he crawled back into bed.

"Someone shot Nestor. I just had the pleasure of finding his body a little while ago."

"That doesn't make for a nice evening."

"Not unless you're a necrophiliac."

"So who's the other dead guy?"

I shrugged. "Got me."

"I'm surprised the SPD let you go."

"Pete let me go. I have to be downtown early tomorrow morning."

"That was nice of him." George yawned. The corners of his eyes were still crusted with sleep. He rubbed his face with the palm of his hand.

The lights from a passing car briefly illuminated a yellow maple leaf stuck on the storm window. I wondered where it came from; there were no maple trees around George's house.

"Do we know who the shooter is?"

"No, we don't. But Eli was at the scene."

George shook his head in disgust. "I told you we should have turned his ass in when we had the chance."

"Don't go putting this on me. And, anyway, I thought you tried."

"What the hell are you talking about?" George demanded.

"I'm talking about the fact that you tried to haul Eli downtown despite the fact you gave me your word that you wouldn't. Then you let him get away."

"Is that what he told you?"

"Yes."

"Wow." He sat back a little. "Stop right there. I didn't take him away."

"He said . . ."

"He's lying."

I bit my lip.

George scowled. "You really don't trust me at all, do you?"

"God, let's not get into that again." This was an old argument, one that was never resolved.

He grabbed my wrist and pulled me to him. "Let's. This guy tells you a story about me and you believe it. I don't like that. I don't like that at all."

"All right. I apologize. It's been a long day. I tried calling . . ."

"I've been out."

"I know."

"Anyway, an apology isn't the issue."

"Then what is?"

"Your pervasive and ongoing lack of trust." George loosened his grip. I pulled my wrist away. "I'm getting tired of it. Look, I know you had a rotten marriage. I know what Murphy did. I should. He was my best friend. It's true. He treated you like shit. He lied to you all the time. Fine. You had a bad deal. But it's time to move on."

"Please. Stop with the two-bit psychology. I'm not in the mood for it right now. Let's just stick to Eli."

"I'm serious about this."

I folded my arms across my chest. "You really want to get into this now?"

"Yes," George said. "I do."

"So you're telling me I should trust you without hesitation?"

"Yes."

"And you'll be there for me."

"Yes."

"If I were sick? If I needed someone to support me?"

George gave me a puzzled look. "Robin, what are you talking about?"

"It's simple. You're telling me I can trust you. To me trust means being able to rely on someone. So can I rely on you? Will you always be there for me whatever the circumstances? If you can't say that, then I think you should stop with the trust bullshit of yours."

"Robin, you're asking for a big . . ."

"Commitment. Exactly. And I've never seen that coming from you. This Belize thing is the first time you've mentioned taking a vacation together. We don't usually celebrate holidays together. You go down to the Bronx to do that. I don't see you asking me to come down with you. So what you're telling me is a load of crap."

George's eyes flashed. "You're the one that's full of shit. I never thought you wanted to come down. You've never given me the slightest indication that you were interested, and as for the vacation thing—forgive me, but I didn't think you golfed. You're just doing what you always do. Turning things around and blaming me. Well, you should look at yourself for a change."

"That's not true."

"Isn't it? All right, let's talk about your level of commitment." George put up his left hand and touched each finger with a finger from his right hand as he made his point. "You don't listen to what I say. Ever. Or take my opinions or feelings into consideration. But you want me to treat your opinions seriously. That's not fair. Half the time I don't even know where you are. When I ask, you get annoyed. The fact that I'm asking because I worry about you doesn't seem to occur to you. You treat my concern as an intrusion. And you're always busy. You're always tired. You're always stressed. You don't have time to do the simplest things, like feed yourself, let alone me—once in a while. I never come first. Ever."

"I . . ."

George held up his hand before I could say anything else. "You started this, now let me finish what I have to say. It's not that I'm asking you to cook me dinner every night or take my shirts to the laundry or see me every night of the week. I'm not. But I would like to come first once in a while. I would like you to make time for me. Planned time. Not come rushing in—like this evening—when things haven't gone well and you need some propping up.

"There's nothing wrong with just spending time with someone, you know. That's what a relationship is. And one last thing," George said as I opened my mouth, "you can't expect me to jump every time you snap your fingers. Just because you've finally decided you want to change the terms of our relationship doesn't mean that I do now. Maybe I've come to like things the way they are. Have you ever thought of that?"

Instead of answering, to my mortification I burst into tears.

It was probably low blood sugar.

Chapter
18

I yawned and checked my watch again. Twenty minutes had gone by and no one had come in to take my statement. First they had sent a squad car to my house to bring me down to the Public Safety Building—now there's an optimistic name for you—and then they'd stuck me in a room by myself and made me wait. Which was supposed to do what? Make me nervous? Intimidate me? Well, the only thing it was doing was getting me irritated.

I slumped further down in the uncomfortable, dilapidated wooden chair I was sitting in. It had the dreary, institutional look of furniture used in prisons, churches, and schools, as did the scarred green-topped table in the middle of the room. I contemplated the No Smoking sign pasted on the wall in front of me and read the graffiti scribbled around it, mostly sad musings from people who wanted recognition and were never going to get it.

When I was tired of doing that, I started biting at the

cuticle on my thumb. When I'd ripped it off, I began on the next finger. I knew what I was doing was going to hurt later. It didn't matter. I couldn't stop myself. I found my mind drifting back to George, something I'd been doing since I'd woken up, despite trying not to. Maybe it was because I hadn't had a chance to talk to him since last night. He'd left by the time I'd woken up. Instead of him, I'd found a note on his pillow.

It had read: Had to get an early start. Took Zsa Zsa out for her morning walk already. Will call you at the store later this afternoon. Coffee's in the coffee machine. There are bagels in the breadbox and cream cheese in the fridge.

And that was it. Cheery. Upbeat. Businesslike. He could have been talking to his departmental secretary. He hadn't signed the note, Love, George. He hadn't signed it at all. There was no mention in it of last night's conversation, no mention of my breaking down. George hated scenes. He liked cool. He hated losing his temper. He liked intellectual jousting. I'd made him lose his temper and sobbed hysterically when he had. I wondered if he hated me for that?

Maybe George thought if he didn't mention it, the scene had never happened: kind of like the old philosophical chestnut about how if a tree falls in the forest and no one hears it does it still make a noise? Fuck, yes. Or maybe he wanted to pretend what I'd said had been a late-night dream. Or the kind of thing that happened when you'd had too much to drink.

One thing was for sure. I couldn't feel worse if I had spent the night tossing back shots of Scotch. I rubbed my temples. The pounding headache I'd woken up with was beginning to subside, the Advil I'd taken had seen to that, but I could still feel it there, lingering, ready to jump out again at the slightest excuse. After I'd read George's note, I'd staggered into the bathroom and glanced at myself in the mirror. I looked awful. My hair was matted and sticking up in odd directions. My eyes were red, the lids puffy from crying. My complexion was mottled. It also seemed to have developed a greenish tinge, which went so well with my red hair. My stomach was queasy. I felt as if I wanted to throw up. I brushed my teeth, washed my face, and combed my hair— all of which helped. But not enough.

Emotion may be good for the inner soul, but it sure didn't do much for the outer person, I'd decided as I walked back out into the bedroom. Since it was after eight already, I put on my clothes and went home, intending to change there. I'd gotten as far as the front door when two detectives I didn't know had swooped down on me. They'd been waiting in a car parked across the street from my house. I'd just been too distracted to notice. So much for letting me to come in on my own.

They'd allowed me to put Zsa Zsa in the house before they'd hustled me downtown. On the ride all I could think of was that I should have showered at George's house. At least then I would have felt semihuman. Not to mention not looking as if I'd spent the night sleeping out on the street.

The coffee they'd offered me when I arrived didn't make me feel any better. It was bitter, weak, and stale, a difficult combination to achieve. Maybe bad coffee is one of the tactics they used to soften people up. If it is, it was sure working for me. I'd managed to take three sips before I had to stop. What I needed was something solid in my stomach.

I was just about to ask for a doughnut—they had to have one of those here, right?—when the door opened and a man I hadn't seen before walked in. He was bulky, in a high-school-quarterback-gone-to-seed kind of way, with a bad hairpiece and a self-important look on his face, the kind that people who spend too much time in positions of power and start believing their own PR tend to get. Right behind him was someone I had seen before.

Quite recently.

Chapman.

I startled. Then I recovered. But it was too late. The damage had been done.

He grinned at me. It was the grin I had noticed first. A schoolyard grin. Cocky and self-assured. The kind of grin that said, Aren't I clever and aren't you the dumb schmuck?

I noticed Chapman's clothes next. Gray suit, black, polished shoes, white shirt, narrow, conservative tie. Fed clothes. The nametag in the plastic holder clipped on to the breast pocket of his jacket confirmed my guess.

I couldn't take my eyes off him. The first guy, a detective, introduced himself. I don't remember the name he gave me because I wasn't paying attention. Then he introduced Chapman.

"Agent Chapman," he said, emphasizing the word agent. "From Fish and Wildlife. He wants to talk to you about possible violations of the Lacey Act."

One thing was evident as I watched Chapman walk around the detective and perch on the edge of the table in front of me. The guy was definitely enjoying himself, which was more than I could say for myself.

"You know what the Lacey Act is, don't you, Ms. Light?" he asked, while he swung his right leg back and forth like a metronome. It was an irritating gesture, but then I'm sure Chapman knew that.

"Yes, I'm familiar with it," I replied, trying to keep a strictly neutral tone to my voice. Had this guy been setting

Eli up, and me along with him? Was that it? "Isn't it the law that protects cats from scum-sucking assholes?"

Chapman flushed. "Try again."

"Sorry. I must have gotten my statutes mixed up." I pretended to think. "Oh, I know," I said after a minute. "It's the trafficking in endangered or protected species that have been illegally caught. Do I get an A?"

"You might." Chapman straightened his tie and leaned forward. His cologne, the same scent I'd smelled in the bar, washed over me again. "I'm glad you reported the contents of the suitcase last night."

"Are you?" I met his eyes. They were expressionless, giving nothing away.

"Of course. Why wouldn't I be?" His smile dared me to say something about our previous meetings.

He knew that I wouldn't. There was no point. All I had were unsubstantiated allegations. He had the weight of the federal government on his side.

"I'm surprised you got here so fast, Mr. Chapman."

"I'm based in this area." His jaw muscles tightened a bit.

"Really?"

"Yes. Really. I suppose you want to know why I'm down here?"

"I thought I was going to give a statement about what I saw last night." I folded my hands in my lap.

Chapman's smile wavered slightly, then came back full kilowatt. "I was hoping you could tell us some more about the suitcase as well."

"The suitcase? I'm afraid I can't do that," I replied, forcing myself to give his smile back to him.

Chapman leaned a little further forward. I hoped he'd fall over, even though I knew he wouldn't. "And why is that?"

"Obviously, because I don't know anything."

"Obviously." He straightened up and ran a finger down his tie. I noticed his nail was bitten down to the quick. "But you *will* call me if you hear anything."

The sound of his foot hitting the table leg filled in the silence.

"Won't you?" he said more sharply when I didn't answer.

I nodded. He smiled again. I returned the favor, even though my stomach felt as if it were twisting into a figure eight. Then Chapman left the room and the local guy took over. All told, I was in the police station for the better part of an hour, although the meeting seemed as if it had gone on for days.

I had just gotten out and was standing by the curb in front of the Public Safety Building, fishing around in my backpack for my cigarettes and waiting to cross the street, when a green Cherokee pulled up beside me.

"Hey, Light!" the driver called.

I looked over. It was Chapman. He made a come closer motion with his fingers. "Let's go for a ride."

Of course I didn't have to go with him. The man wasn't holding a gun to my head. I could have walked away. But I didn't. I figured that Chapman and I were going to have this conversation. It could be now or it could be later. But it was going to happen. I preferred it happen sooner rather than later. The more information I had, the easier it would be to figure out a way to do something about that sonofabitch.

I opened the Cherokee's door and slid in. A faint hint of bubble gum hung in the air, then I smelled the leather from the seats. There was a fancy CD player in the dashboard. I was just about to ask him if it had come with the car when Chapman roared away from the curb without checking to see if anyone else was there. I gasped as he missed an oncoming Civic by inches.

"Jesus," I couldn't stop myself from saying, "you almost hit that car."

Chapman laughed and sped through a yellow light. "I'm not worried," he told me. "The accident would have been on your side of the vehicle."

"You really are a sweetheart," I observed.

"I know. That's why you love me." His jaw went up and down. I realized he was chewing gum. "Apropos of which, you missed our date last night. I was hurt."

"I was busy."

He blew a bubble and popped it. "I just bet you were."

"Why did you lie about your name not being Chapman?" I asked as he nosed the Cherokee through downtown traffic. An old woman, dressed in rags and wildly waving her hands in the air, dashed in front of the car. Chapman slammed on the brakes and cursed.

"I didn't lie. I suggested. You ran with the idea."

"Why bother?"

"It amused me."

"You like games?"

"Let's just say I'm good at them." Chapman gave me a speculative look. "You're not wired, are you?"

"You've got to be kidding."

"Unbutton your shirt and let me see."

"Fuck you."

Chapman braked suddenly. I lurched forward. My head almost hit the windshield. "Do it," he barked. A car beeped in back of us. Chapman ignored it. "Go on," he prodded. "Either that or get out of the car."

What the hell, I decided, complying. At least I was wearing a bra for a change. I opened my shirt. "Satisfied?"

He grinned salaciously and started up the car again. "Not bad." By now the single beep had grown to a chorus. "Now you can ask me what's going on," he told me as I buttoned up.

I reached in my backpack, got a cigarette out, and lit it. "Is that why you picked me up? Because you wanted me to know?"

"In a way." He blew a bubble and popped it.

"That's very considerate."

He smiled again. He could have been a thirties magazine illustration for the wonders of modern life: straight white teeth, regular features, clear eyes. If he was subject to bouts of self-doubt in the middle of the night, it didn't show. "I've got a different idea."

"What's that?" We were heading toward the highway. I studied the gray sky. It gave the sensation of pressing down on the city, bending it under its weight.

"Why don't you tell me what you know first and I'll tell you if you're right or wrong."

I shrugged and took another puff of my Camel and looked around for an ashtray. There wasn't one. I opened the window and threw it out. The tobacco was making me nauseous. I really needed to get something in my stomach. "Why not?"

We headed up the ramp onto I-81. Chapman pointed the car north toward Watertown. Traffic was sparse and he threaded his way around the cars that were on the road. I guessed we were doing about eighty-five miles an hour by now.

"So?" Chapman prompted when I didn't continue. He blew another bubble, a bigger one, and popped it. A small strand of gum stayed on his lip. He picked it off.

"It's not very complicated. When you came into that room

earlier I figured that you'd entrapped Eli, but that's obviously not the case.''

"And why is that?"

"Because you would be trying to charge me, too, if it were. Incidentally, have they arrested him yet?''

Chapman checked his rearview mirror and switched into the left lane. "Not as far as I know. Not that I really give a fuck if they get that fat slob or not.'' And he smiled that smile of his again, the one that made you think you hadn't heard him correctly, before motioning for me to go on.

"I figured, working for the people you work for, having the contacts you must have, you set up this deal and then used Eli as your mule.''

Chapman didn't say anything.

I read the expression on his face. "That's not right, is it?''

"You're partially correct. Eli was doing this in a low-level kind of way. He'd been doing it for a while. Not very successfully.'' Chapman broke off talking and concentrated on the road as the car next to us pulled ahead and moved into his lane. Chapman sped up and bore down on the pickup truck. I grasped my seat and involuntarily stiffened my legs against the coming impact. Soon there was less than a car length separating us. The truck finally gave it up and moved over. I exhaled. "Can't let someone get up on you,'' Chapman said as he adjusted the rearview mirror. Then he went on with his explanation. "Eli was smuggling poison frogs and albino boas into Japan. But he's such a screw-up he couldn't even do that right.''

I bit my fingernail and thought about the frogs and boas I'd seen at the Myers house. Those frogs could go for up to a thousand dollars in Japan. They were illegal there, the government having deemed that reptiles with the word poison in their names were probably not a good thing to have living in someone's house.

"Of course most of them died," Chapman continued, his voice filled with scorn at Eli's incompetence. "I caught him on the way back in with a load of turtle eggs. Instead of turning him in, I gave him an option—do a couple of runs for me or get arrested."

"That was very nice of you."

"I thought so."

We were now passing Mattydale. The parking lot at the Northern Lights strip mall was practically empty. The stores looked sad and neglected in the thin morning light, as if they knew they were slated for the wrecking ball.

I stated the obvious. "And everything would have been fine if Nestor hadn't taken the suitcase."

"Exactly," Chapman agreed.

"For which he has paid."

Chapman gave an elaborate shrug. "So it would seem. As my mother used to say, greed kills."

It was hard to believe this guy had a mother someplace. He probably never forgot to send her flowers on her birthday, either. I leaned slightly forward and searched his face. If there was any regret or guilt there for Nestor's death, I didn't see it.

"Don't you care at all?" I asked.

"No. And if you're honest, you don't, either."

"That's not true," I protested.

Chapman shrugged, as if the topic were too boring to discuss.

I sat back in my seat. "What do you want with me anyway?"

He gave me an astonished look. "I thought I'd made that abundantly clear earlier. I want you to find the suitcase."

I picked at one of my nails. "Why don't you go out and find it? It would be easier for you, being a Feddie."

"I could, but it wouldn't be an efficient use of my time. And anyway, Eli made this mess. It's only right that I give him a chance to clean it up."

"You're so generous."

"Don't push it," Chapman warned.

I thought about the cat and put a lid on it. "It isn't as if I haven't been looking," I answered. "The fact that Nestor is dead certainly isn't going to help matters any."

Chapman pursed his lips as if to say that wasn't his problem. I studied the scenery. In the summer it would have been a pretty ride. Now it was grim. The trees were bare, their branches twisted and gnarled. The grass was a dried-out brown. Sheaves of dead reeds stuck out of the marsh. Flocks of crows circled overhead, their cawing filling the air.

"You know," Chapman said after about thirty seconds had gone by, his tone as light and conversational as if he'd been discussing the arrangements for a summer dance, "when I was in the Army I found that most people aren't afraid of dying. They're afraid of two things: pain and loss." He lingered on the last two words, caressing them with his voice as if he were talking about old friends.

"How long did it take you to come to that brilliant conclusion?"

He shrugged. "Not too long." Then he reached a hand out and squeezed my shoulder. "I've really come to admire you."

I gave him a sharp look. He put his hand down.

"No. It's true," he protested. "I have. You've been dealt a rough hand, but you've managed to make it work for you. It's not easy keeping a business going. No one knows that better than I do. All that pressure. It must be your relationships that sustain you, wouldn't you say?"

I didn't answer. Chapman didn't care. He hadn't been expecting one.

"Some people, I'm told, get a lot of reassurance from their dogs. Now me, I wouldn't know about that. I don't feel that way about dogs—maybe because I used to eat them when I was in the Philippines." He gave me a sidelong glance to see if I was taking in what he was saying. "I can tell you one thing—they didn't taste like chicken. The farmers used to break their legs and hang 'em over a pole and leave 'em like that until someone came along who wanted one. Then they'd chop their heads off." He smiled again. "Of course my stay in the Philippines changed my mind about a lot of things."

I managed a fairly cool "Really" despite the fact that at the moment I was trying not to gag.

"Yeah. You really are lucky. George. Tim. Manuel. Zsa Zsa. They all care for you."

"That's nice." My throat felt dry. *This guy isn't just conning you—he's playing you,* I told myself. Too bad I wasn't listening to me.

Chapman continued as if I hadn't said anything. "And you care for them. Which is important. Especially with your husband dying the way he did." He tsked tsked. Then he blew a large bubble and popped it. "I understand you were there when it happened. Something like that, watching someone you love die, it must leave a mark inside. Here." And he made a fist and smacked himself on the chest. "I imagine it's something you probably never want to see occur again."

"Are you threatening them?" I demanded hoarsely.

"Is that what you think I'm saying?"

"If you're not saying that, then what are you saying?"

"I'm merely suggesting you redouble your efforts looking for the suitcase. Before . . ." And he stopped himself.

"Before what?"

"Before nothing."

"How would you suggest I go about this task? Any helpful hints?"

"One."

"What's that?"

"Simple. To quote the French, *Cherchez la femme.*"

And with that, he pulled over onto the exit ramp and put me out of his car.

Chapter
19

George shook his head. "So Chapman's a Fed?"

I corrected him. "Fish and Game."

"Well, whatever the agency he's working for, it still brings things to a whole new level," George observed as he scooped up some hummus on a piece of pita and bit into it.

"I know," I said gloomily.

"You think he killed Nestor?"

"Probably not." I moved the grains of cracked wheat in my tabbouleh salad around with my fork. I don't know why I'd ordered this in the first place. I wasn't hungry. Chapman had taken away my appetite. "And if he did, it didn't help much because he didn't get what he wanted."

George took a sip of his coffee. "Which is why he wants you to find Adelina. He figures she has the suitcase."

I nodded. She'd been hovering on the edges of this mess, like an unseen presence, sensed but not felt, ever since I'd gone looking for Nestor. I leaned back in my seat and shoved

my plate away. The oil glistening on the stuffed grape leaves
gave them a slick, greasy look.

"You're not eating those?" George asked, pointing at my
food.

I shook my head and took a sip of my soda.

"You're positive?"

"Absolutely." I was afraid I'd throw up if I took another
bite. I pushed the plate over to him. I hoped I wasn't coming
down with the flu. There was a lot of it going around. "Be
my guest."

We were sitting in Little Jerusalem, a Middle Eastern restaurant about two blocks away from the university. I glanced
at the oversize generic travel posters on the wall as I hooked
my feet around the rungs of my chair. They were the kind
of posters establishments of this type always have, the kind
of posters that promote foreign lands as exotic and different,
but not too different, just like the food in the restaurant.

In the first one, a smiling couple was seated on a camel
in the middle of an oasis filled with palm trees. The pyramids
loomed in the background. The message underneath said:
Come, experience the romance of the Middle East. The
second poster featured a picture of a beach, blue water, and
more palm trees. The inscription underneath read: Enjoy
Yourself. I thought about the exhortation for a minute as I
surveyed the room That's what my therapist used to tell me.
You should get out and have some fun, she'd say. Go bowl-
ing. Learn how to quilt. When I told her if those were my
alternatives I'd rather be depressed, she told me I had a
bad attitude, a line I'd been hearing for the better part of
my life.

At two o'clock in the afternoon, Little Jerusalem was
almost empty. The waiters were sitting at a table in the back,
eating their lunch and joking with each other, readying

themselves for dinner's onslaught. The place had been here for twenty years and showed no sign of folding. It had everything the students wanted: cheap, fast, edible food, okay service, and large tables where you could sit and talk.

I unhooked my feet from the chair and shifted my weight around. For some reason, I was having trouble getting comfortable. As I watched, George started eating the grape leaves off my plate. He was dressed for the class he'd just finished teaching—blue shirt, tan cords, and fun tie—casual, but not too casual. George always got his clothes right, whatever the occasion, unlike me, who always got them wrong, whatever the occasion.

I'd arrived at his undergraduate class in European history fifteen minutes early. I'd waited in the hallway for him, leaning against the wall and listening to him talking to an undergraduate class about the implications of the Edict of Nantes. It was the first time I'd heard him lecture. His voice, animated and assured, seeped out through the space between the floor and the door, putting me in mind of when I'd gone to college. It seemed like a lifetime ago. Once in a while, a burst of knowing student laughter would erupt and I'd wonder what the joke was that I was missing.

George exited the classroom five minutes after the period was over. A group of ten students milled around him. He looked happy, as if he'd finally found someplace he belonged. I was pleased for him and sad for me. Watching him, I realized I was tired of working alone. I wanted to go back to working at the newspaper. It had been so much easier. I missed the joking around over coffee. The drinks after work. The benefits. I was wondering if they'd hire me back when George spotted me.

He was surprised to see me, which I suppose was to be expected, given that he didn't know I was coming. Childishly, I wanted his face to light up when he saw me. It didn't. Maybe I was reading too much into his look. Or too little. I seemed to have lost my ability to judge people correctly, an ability I'd prided myself on once upon a time in my life. I was thinking about that as George conveyed more hummus to his mouth.

"So what are you going to do?" he asked, wiping his fingers on a napkin.

"I know what I should do if I'm smart. Try and find Adelina."

"You agree with Chapman? You think she has the suitcase?"

"She might." I brushed some crumbs off the table. "Then there's always Littlebaum." I thought about the way he had greeted me again. I'd assumed he was just paranoid. But maybe he wasn't. Maybe he thought I'd been there to get the suitcase. "And if he doesn't have it, I'm willing to bet he knows who does."

"I can't believe Chapman hasn't been down there already," George protested between mouthfuls of spinach pie.

"He could have been, but until now, from what I've heard, Littlebaum hasn't been buying anything he'd need a CITES certificate for, which means there's no reason for him to have come under Chapman's scrutiny."

"You're saying it isn't illegal to own a lion?" George's voice rose in disbelief.

"It's not. At least, not according to Federal laws. It's illegal only if the place you're living in has a law on the books against owning exotics. It's strictly a local ordinance type of thing."

"Unbelievable."

"Not really. Think about it. Most locales have laws on the

books against owning farm animals in the city, because at the time those laws were passed, there were people who were keeping chickens and sheep in their backyards, whereas—"

George interrupted. "You're telling me I can't have a chicken in my house in Syracuse, but I could have a tiger cub?"

"Until recently, when the Common Council amended the law, yes. Actually, more and more legislative bodies across the country are passing laws banning exotics because more people are buying them, which is turning out to be a problem for people who own large boids. Boa constrictors and pythons to you," I told George. "This is mostly a dog and cat country. There aren't many Littlebaums around." I reached across the table and snagged the rest of my pita bread. "Given the circumstances, I'm sure Littlebaum wouldn't hesitate to avail himself of the opportunity to buy a tortoise at a discount rate."

"And Nestor would know about him?"

I ate a piece of the bread. It was slightly stale. "He has to have. He was friends with Sulfin. Sulfin works for Littlebaum. How could he not know?"

"True." George drummed his fingers on the table. "Are you going to talk to him?"

"Eventually."

Littlebaum was my backup plan. The truth was, I wasn't exactly anxious to go back there given the way my last talk with Littlebaum had ended. All things being equal, I didn't want to renew my acquaintanceship with Matilda. Adelina might be hard to find, but at least the chances were she didn't have the kind of bodyguard Littlebaum did. Plus, I had the feeling that Chapman had told me to find her for a reason.

George took a sip of his beer "What, exactly, do Madagascar tortoises look like anyway? What makes them so unique?"

"Their coloring and the fact that there aren't that many of them left. Maybe three to four thousand. Tortoises aren't what you'd call fast breeders." I took another bite of pita and put the rest down. I was hungry, but not for this. I'd get an ice cream later, I decided.

George loosened his tie and unbuttoned his collar. "If you find them, we can have some of Chapman's crew watching him take delivery of them from you through binoculars. The moment he takes the suitcase they close in."

"Then he'll claim he was working a deal on me."

"He can claim he's the Tooth Fairy. We'll have you wired."

I told him about Chapman checking me out.

"Okay. So we'll set up a listening post. God knows, with all the junk that's on the market, that shouldn't be too hard."

"I think it will be. This guy is hipped to all this stuff. Given his job, he has to be. What if he won't talk? What if he wants to do the exchange in the middle of someplace with no cover? Then it'll come down to a 'he said, she said' situation." I wound a lock of hair around my finger. "He'll stick me with a felony rap. I don't need that type of trouble. I can't afford the thirty thousand, probably more given how much my lawyer charges per hour, it would take to get me out of it. Not to mention the time and the energy."

George frowned. The vein in his neck was sticking out the way it always did when he was stressed. He knew I was right. He just didn't want to admit it. He pushed his plate away.

I rooted around in my backpack for a cigarette before I remembered I'd smoked my last one on the ride I'd hitched back to my car. "I've played this every which way and the bottom line is, I don't think I have a choice. I have to do what Chapman says. At least on the most obvious level."

George nibbled on his lower lip. "Meaning?"

I leaned forward. "Remember how a little while ago you suggested it might be helpful if we knew a little more about this guy."

"What sort of things are we talking about here?" George asked, cautious and interested at the same time.

"Like where he's staying. Like what he does with his spare time. Like whether he has any interesting hobbies."

George didn't say anything. I watched him tear little pieces off the leftover pita.

I persisted. "Okay, the car didn't pan out, but you have the contacts. Maybe it's time to have a couple of drinks with some of your old buddies."

"This guy could be serious bad news." George pushed the pita aside. The pieces spilled over the table. "It might be better for you to just go along."

"No." I surprised myself with my ferocity. "Chapman is scum."

George gave me a no-kidding look.

"I want to nail his ass to the wall. Doesn't he offend you?"

"How can you ask me that?" The vein under George's eyes twitched. "You know what I think about guys like that. I'd like to hang the prick up by his thumbs."

"But?"

"But sometimes it doesn't work that way." George made clicking noises with his tongue against the roof of his mouth. "I'll tell you what really worries me. What worries me is the speech he gave you about Tim, Manuel, and me. I don't like it. I don't like it at all. It means he's gone to the trouble to find out about you."

"It wouldn't take him very long to get that info," I pointed out. "All he had to do was ask a few questions. I don't think it means that much."

"Except that he's interested," George said.

"That's why I figure we need to even the balance by finding out a little bit about him. As to his threats—You and I can look after ourselves."

"What about Manuel and Tim?"

"I'll take care of Manuel and I'll talk to Tim. See what he says."

George cracked his knuckles twice in a row. "And Zsa Zsa? What are you going to do with her?"

"I have a friend that lives south of Dryden. She has three dogs and a horse, some chickens. I thought I'd ask her if I could leave Zsa Zsa there for a little while." There was no point in taking chances. I couldn't bear it if something happened to her.

George chuckled. It was the first time he'd laughed since I'd met him. "Zsa Zsa and the country. This I'd like to see."

"She *is* a dog after all. She'll like it," I said doubtfully, because I wasn't sure she would. After all, she was used to beer and barstools, not horses and hay. "It'll be like a vacation."

George and I fell silent. We watched the street. Except for a few students hurrying by, the sidewalk was empty. It had begun to snow. Flakes were drifting down from the sky.

"I don't know if I'll even be able to turn up anything," George said after a minute had gone by.

"I realize that. Which is why I plan to start searching for Adelina."

"Do you know what she looks like?" George asked as he idly traced a pattern in the leftover hummus on his plate with a sprig of parsley.

"I've seen a picture of her. Of course, it's a couple of years old."

"People can change a lot in that period of time," George pointed out. "They can dye their hair. Cut it. Lose weight or gain it. Get glasses or switch to contact lenses. Get a nose job."

"I have Manuel. He's seen her."

George nodded.

As I left the restaurant, it occurred to me that sometimes George and I made a good team. It was a shame it didn't happen more often.

Chapter
20

I stopped at the garage on my way back to the store. Sam had the cab ready. I wanted to kiss him when I saw her.

"See," he said, pointing to the side mirror. "It's not exactly the same, but I don't think anyone else could tell the difference."

"It's fine." I did kiss him. I hummed all the way to Noah's Ark.

Tim looked up as I walked in the door. "What's got into you?" he asked.

"I just picked up the cab."

He went back to wiping the counter. "You and that cab. I could never figure it."

Neither could most other people. But that was all right. I couldn't understand why they wanted to drive around in something like a Taurus. "It's a sentimental decision." I told Tim about Chapman.

"Is that so?" And he reached under the counter for the

baseball bat I've taken to keeping there and rested it on top of the counter. "I don't think I'll have a problem."

"You're sure?"

"Believe me, I'm positive."

We talked about it for a little bit longer and then I went in the back and called Joan and laid out my dog situation. Fortunately, this was her night to come in to Syracuse to do some shopping. We agreed that she'd drop by the store and pick Zsa Zsa up later in the afternoon. I spent the next half hour making up Zsa Zsa's "suitcase." I packed her toys, her food, her bedding, a couple of my old shirts, and some treats for her and Joan's other dogs in a big blue laundry bag.

"My God," Tim said as he watched me tuck another package of rawhide bones into it. "She's not going away for that long."

"I know." It didn't matter. I wanted her to be as comfortable as possible. I knelt in front of her.

Zsa Zsa came over and licked my chin.

"I love you," I told her as Tim rolled his eyes.

She wagged her tail.

"And I'll come and get you as soon as I can."

She wagged her tail again. I now knew how mothers felt when they had to leave their kids behind. I took one last look at her and walked out the door. As I got in the cab, it occurred to me that if Chapman touched her I would kill him. And then I thought how some people would say she was just a dog. But I didn't care.

It took me a little while to locate Manuel, but I finally ran him down at a friend's house over on West Street. He and a couple of his buddies were clustered around one of those "entertainment centers" in a living room so packed with plastic-covered sofas and chairs and wood-veneered pieces, it reminded me of a showroom in a cheap furniture store. The guys were all decked out in their parkas, jeans, and baseball hats, doing what they usually did: drinking cheap beer, eating pretzels, and watching a video on TV.

"At least wait till the good part is over," Manuel pleaded with me when I told him why I was there.

"Which part is that?" As far as I was concerned, the movie he was watching, an old Godzilla movie from Japan, had no good parts.

"The part where Godzilla smashes in the apartment complex and tears a train in two."

"Five minutes." It's hard to argue with good taste. I maneuvered around a coffee table and leaned against the fake wood-paneled wall next to the sofa and waited. "You haven't seen Eli, have you?" I asked in a casual do-you-know-if-it's-raining-out kind of way.

"No." Manuel kept his eyes glued to the TV. His friends didn't look up, either. I could have been the Invisible Man as far as they were concerned.

A cell phone started ringing. The guy sitting next to Manuel whipped one out of his pocket and briefly spoke into it. "Dynnel," he said to everyone by way of explanation before he lapsed back into silence.

"You know, the police are looking for him," I said to Manuel. "They want to question him in connection with Nestor's death."

"That's a load of crap," he shot back without looking at me. "He didn't have anything to do with it."

No one else in the room showed a flicker of interest.

"You're sure?"

"Yeah, I'm sure."

My eyes drifted over to the images on the screen. The movie was dubbed. The lips of the Japanese were out of sync with the American voices. As a child, I'd always wondered what the Japanese were really saying. No one else had cared. I'd entertained myself by making up imaginary dialogue, but after a while the novelty wore off and I stopped watching the movies.

"How'd you hear?" I inquired.

Manuel grunted. "Some kid. I forget who."

"It would be better for all of us if he turned himself in."

"If I knew something, I would tell you," Manuel assured me.

"Of course you would," I replied, sarcasm dripping from my voice. "You always do."

Manuel held out his hand and put a finger up signaling for me to be quiet. "Come on, Robin. This is the scene I've been waiting for." He leaned forward, propping his elbows on his knees, rapt with attention.

I went back to studying the picture on TV. The images were choppy, the faces elongated, the photography bad. It must be a guy thing, I decided, a teenage-guy thing, because the movie left me cold. I'd felt that way twenty years ago and I felt that way now. When the scene was over, I tapped Manuel on the shoulder and motioned for him to follow me.

"Now," I said.

He picked a piece of lint off the front of his jacket as he reluctantly got up. "Why the rush?" he asked fretfully as he stopped in front of the hall mirror to adjust his baseball hat. He put it on and took it off three times, maneuvering the brim a slightly different way each time. When the fourth time came, I couldn't stand it anymore. I dragged him out of the house by his elbow.

"For God's sake, you're worse than my mother," he protested, pulling his arm away from me. "Lighten up, Light."

"Ha. Ha." As I stepped around a crack vial lying on the pavement, I wondered exactly how cool he was going to be when I told him what Chapman said.

"So, this guy is gonna do what to me?" Manuel asked after I explained.

"I don't know. He might not do anything." I brushed the snow off my hair.

"Damned right he won't." Manuel adjusted his collar so it stood up fifties-style and put a roll in his walk. "I'm the man."

"Or . . ." I continued.

"Or what?" Manuel demanded. "What's this punk gonna do?"

"Think of yourself as Tokyo and think of Chapman as Godzilla and you get the idea."

Manuel muttered something.

"What was that?"

"Nothing." He put his hands in his pocket, hunched his shoulders, and picked up his pace.

I matched it. "That's funny, because I distinctly heard you say 'I'm going to kill that fat little prick.' "

"No, what I said was Rick . . ."

"Please, Manuel. This is serious."

"Everything with you always is. You ought to change your name to Dark."

"Enough with the names."

"Suits me." He lowered his eyes as if he was searching for something he'd dropped. "Suits me just fine."

"So, you have spoken to Eli?"

Manuel kept walking. We were almost at the cab before he looked up. "It won't do you any good, even if I have. I don't know where he is."

"He didn't say where he was calling from?"

"I just told you that."

"What did he want?"

"To say hello. To ask how things are going. That's it."

"The police are looking for him."

"So you've said. Several times." Manuel got in one side of the cab. I got in the other. He slammed the door. "That's not my problem."

I started the car up and turned on the wipers. "It could be."

"How's that?"

"Aiding and abetting," I replied as I watched the powdery white flakes disappear off the glass. "Your probation officer might not like that."

Manuel viciously attacked one of his cuticles. "No way. I'm the one that tried to keep his sorry ass out of trouble. This wasn't my idea. I'm not getting tagged for this."

I turned the wipers off. "Then maybe you should tell me where he is."

"I don't know." Manuel exhaled. He was practically shaking with indignation. "Eli didn't consult with me before he did this. Whatever happens, happens. It ain't my fault."

"You're right. It isn't." If Manuel knew where Eli was, and despite his words I thought he might, he wasn't telling. I started the cab up. "So you really don't think Eli killed Nestor?"

Manuel gave a snort of disbelief. "Get real."

"Who do you think did?"

"How the fuck should I know? You mind?" he asked, reaching to turn on the radio.

I shook my head. The sound of rap filled the cab.

"Where're we going?" Manuel asked as I pulled out into the street.

"Sulfin's."

Manuel rolled his eyes. "Ratboy's. Terrific. I just bought these." He indicated his shirt and jeans. "I ain't going up there and getting my clothes all smelly," he told me. "His place stinks."

"Fine. Stay downstairs." It was probably better that way. Manuel had a tendency to mouth off when he shouldn't.

I didn't say anything else. Neither did Manuel. He turned the volume control on the radio up. I turned it back down. We drove over to Sulfin's apartment without exchanging another word.

Sulfin wasn't exactly happy to see me, but then, given the way we parted, there was no reason why he should be.

"Get out of here," he said. He'd opened the door partway to see who it was. Now he was trying to close it again. "I don't want to speak to you."

"Obviously." I extracted five twenties from my wallet and waved them in his face. Sulfin fell back and I stepped inside.

"I just want to ask you a question."

"About what?" His eyes flickered from the bills in my hand to my face and back again.

I shut the door behind me and walked into the living room. The squeaking of the rats and mice I'd been hearing in the entryway got louder. "How's business?"

"Fine. No thanks to you."

"Why is that?"

"I almost lost the last batch. If you don't freeze 'em as soon as you kill 'em, they're no good. You should know that."

"I'm sorry. I didn't realize you were on such a stringent timetable."

Sulfin ran his fingers through his white hair. "Well, I am. That's why my business is growing. Because I sell a good product. One hundred percent organic."

Of course his rats were organic. What else would they be? Plastic? Crystalline? But I didn't say that. This wasn't the time for a minilesson in semantics. "That's what Tim told me," I replied instead.

Sulfin's expression softened slightly. "It's true. I do. So what do you want to know?"

"I want to know where Adelina is."

"Why should I know where that bitch is?" he asked sullenly.

"You know everything else."

"Not this."

I waved the hundred dollars in his face. "Are you sure?"

Sulfin reached for the money. I moved it away. "Not until I get some answers from you."

"Is she in trouble?"

"Yes."

"A lot?" he asked gleefully, his eyes glowing like two dark raisins in the doughy white of his face.

I told him it couldn't get much worse.

"Good." He looked as pleased as the kid on Christmas morning who gets what he asked for.

I waited for him to say more. Instead, he extended his hand down, and a black rat that had been sitting on the arm of the sofa climbed onto his palm and scampered up his arm to his shoulder. "This is Barnaby," he said, introducing him to me. Barnaby sniffed the air in front of me. Sulfin scratched his back with a finger. "Try Myra," he finally said. "Last I heard, Adelina was staying with her."

I thanked Sulfin and put the money in his hand. "My pleasure." And he smiled and pocketed it.

When I left, he was feeding Barnaby crumbs of bread off the coffee table.

Manuel was still listening to the radio when I got back in

the car. "Did you get what you needed?" he asked as he fiddled with the dial.

"I hope so." I restarted the cab. "Sulfin doesn't like Adelina much, does he?"

Manuel stopped fiddling. "Why should he?"

"Meaning?"

"She used to be his girlfriend until Nestor came along. He stole her right out from under Sulfin. I heard he was promising he'd take her to Disneyland and shit like that."

"Adelina used to be Sulfin's girlfriend?" I repeated, dumfounded.

Manuel gave me a sidelong glance. "That's what I just said, didn't I?"

I pictured Sulfin. "I can't believe he has a girlfriend."

"Yeah." Manuel grinned. "He's got lots of them. I don't know why he cared so much about Adelina. He's got a couple of others that moved in to fill the slot."

"Are we talking about Sulfin?"

"Amazing, isn't it?"

"Yes."

Manuel's grin grew wider. "Sulfin just goes to prove some things are more important than looks. It's because he's got this giant you-know-what. All the girls are crazy to try it out."

I digested this news while we drove over to the mall to find Myra. I was still digesting it when we parked. I guess the old saw is true about no accounting for tastes.

Chapter
21

It was still snowing out. The flakes were coming down a little heavier now. It looked as if someone was tossing handfuls of Ivory Flakes out of a box. But it wasn't sticking. It was too warm for that. The streets were wet. Tonight, if the temperature fell, they'd become icy, but they were fine for now. It had taken Manuel and me a little over fifteen minutes to drive over to the mall. I parked close to the entrance and we went inside.

I sent Manuel to get Myra while I waited in the bookstore, which was four stores up from the pet store. I was reading a remaindered book about the Masons when Manuel sauntered in.

"Where's Myra?" I asked.

He tugged his pants up. "She'll meet us in the food court in fifteen minutes, when she has her dinner break."

I glanced at my watch. It was five minutes after five. "It's a little early for that, isn't it?"

Manuel shrugged as if to say that that was the joy of working retail.

I bought the book and Manuel and I meandered over there. It was a weekday night and except for the occasional harried-looking mother chasing down a child or a random clump of giggling preteens, the mall was almost empty. Through the windows I could see the store's sales staff standing behind the counter with plastered smiles on their faces and boredom in their eyes.

The food court didn't look any busier. The servers were either chatting with each other or leaning on the counter and daydreaming about what they were going to be doing when they got off. The food choices were the usual fast food American fare we'd given to the world. Fast, cheap, fatty, and tasteless. I don't think there's a stall that sells anything that's not bathed in fat. It's probably a law: no fat bath, no booth. Not that that doesn't earn points with me. The more highly processed what I eat is, the better I like it. Or at least I have until recently.

I ordered a couple of slices of pizza, while Manuel got a portion of bad Chinese food. As we ate, we watched the carousel go around, its horses riderless, its tinny music playing to an empty room. The carousel had been built for a bigger time and it seemed lost here, enclosed in four walls, reduced to a museum exhibition, unappreciated by children brought up on laser tag. I was once again contemplating why anyone would have thought it would be a good idea to bring something like that indoors when Myra materialized in front of me.

She was even thinner than I remembered her being. I wondered if Mr. and Mrs. Myers's baby girl was anorexic.

"What do you want?" she asked as she fiddled with a

silver ring on her finger, turning it round and round. It was so loose it was a wonder she hadn't lost it already.

I told her to get something to eat before we talked. The last thing I needed was for her to pass out on me. She came back with a green salad with no dressing and a slice of pizza.

"I could get fired for speaking to you," she declared as she folded herself into the chair across from me.

"Maybe it's time to get a new job," I suggested. "I'm sure you could find a better place to work."

Instead of answering, Myra devoted her attention to eating a few pieces of lettuce. She then proceeded to methodically remove all the cheese from the pizza, after which she put it in a napkin and dumped it in the garbage. "So I won't be tempted," she explained. Then, while I watched, she blotted her slice with another napkin. To remove any additional fat, no doubt. She threw that away as well.

"Jesus," Manuel muttered. "Give me a break. Do you think you can eat the crust, or does that have too many calories, too?"

Myra pretended she didn't hear him. "Now, what's this about?" Myra asked. "All Manuel would say is that you wanted to talk to me about something important."

"That's right."

"Like what?"

"I think you already know why I'm here," I parried, having decided to go on a fishing expedition.

"I don't," Myra protested. She took another tiny bite of her slice. As I watched her wrinkle her nose in distaste and put the gnawed-on slice back on her plate, I couldn't help thinking that I was glad I wasn't her mother, because I'd kill her if I was. Of course, I still might.

"Then why are you so nervous?" I countered as she began making little tears in the edge of the pizza plate.

"I'm not," she protested.

Manuel opened his mouth to say something and I silenced him with a look. He scowled and went back to shoveling forkfuls of lo mein into his mouth.

Myra took up her fork and ate another lettuce leaf. At the rate she was going, it would take her all night to finish her dinner. "It's about the frogs, isn't it?" she said finally.

"Among other things."

"It was Eli's idea."

"Breeding them?" I guessed, remembering the room in her house.

She nodded. "He said there was a really good market for them." She speared a forkful of lettuce and crunched it down.

"Is there?"

"No." Myra threw her fork down and began playing with her ring again. "I don't know why I listened to him. I should know better. He's such a loser."

"Why is that?"

"Because he can't do anything right," Myra told me, echoing Chapman's sentiments. "I went and spent all this money on setups and breeding pairs and I hardly got enough from him to break even. I would have made more money if I'd worked at Burger King."

"Where was he going to sell them?"

"Japan. Germany." Myra's gaze was defiant. "He said there was a big market for that kind of stuff there."

"How was he going to smuggle them in?"

"In a vest."

"A vest?" I said, trying to picture it.

"One of those ones with all the pockets." She shrugged. "I didn't ask for details. All I cared about was getting paid. He said I'd make a lot of money, enough so that I could quit my job and take off to California. What a crock." Her mouth turned down. The lines between her nose and mouth sprang into view. For a few seconds, I caught a glimpse of the embittered old woman she might become. Myra snorted. "I can't even sell the ones I have. No one wants to buy them. There's a glut on the market. What the hell am I going to do with them?"

"Lower the price. Use them as costume jewelry."

"Very funny." She brightened. "I don't suppose you'd like them?"

I told her I wouldn't. "My store doesn't carry venomous stock. The liability would be too high."

"You know," Manuel chimed in, "my mom would kill me if I had stuff like that in the house with all my sisters and brothers running around."

"Well, my dad doesn't care," Myra said. "Anyway, they're not poisonous unless they're angry."

"How do you tell? I mean, do ya ask them?"

Myra gave him a withering look. Manuel was unimpressed.

"I wouldn't want to live with them," he went on, warming to the subject. "What happens if you forget to lock the room and one of them gets out and hops in your bed and you lie down on it? What then?"

"Then you'd be dead." Myra picked up her fork and put it down again as the implications of what Manuel had just said hit her. "How do you know about the room?"

Manuel gave me a sheepish grin. "Sorry," he said, and he went back to eating.

I made a mental note to have a chat with him later about the joys of silence as Myra turned to me.

"How do you know?" she demanded.

"I was there." And I explained about Manuel's phone call.

"You broke into my house?" Myra's voice quavered with outrage.

"Report me to the police."

She gave me a sullen look and collapsed into her seat.

"Where were you that night?"

She glared at me. "Why do you care?"

"Because I do."

"I was stuck, just like everyone else."

"Who were you stuck with?"

"A friend."

"Does this friend have a name?"

Myra looked at her watch. "Listen. I have to go."

I checked mine. "You still have some time left before you have to be back at the store," I observed. She had about twenty minutes, to be accurate.

In a nervous tic of a gesture, she conveyed her quarter-eaten pizza slice to her mouth and brought it away untouched. "I don't want to talk anymore," she told me.

I crossed my arms over my chest and just looked at her. She was vibrating like a guitar string.

"I don't have to say anything to you," she insisted.

"You're right. You don't. You can say it to the police."

She feigned puzzlement. "Why would they be interested in poison frogs?"

"They're not. And you know it. They're interested in Eli and Adelina."

Myra tried to act cool. She didn't succeed very well. I noticed her hands were trembling. She clasped her fingers together, brought her hands under the table, and rested them in her lap, the way good little girls are taught to do.

"Aren't you going to ask me why the police are interested?" I continued. "Most people would. Aren't you even the tiniest bit curious?"

Myra bit her lip.

"But you don't really have to ask me, do you? Especially since you already know?" I leaned forward slightly. Then I planted my elbows on the table. It wobbled slightly, just like the story Myra was trying to tell me.

"Adelina told you about Nestor, didn't she?"

"I haven't seen Adelina in weeks," Myra protested. Her voice had grown as thin as her body.

"That's not what Sulfin says," I replied. "He says you were with her yesterday."

"He's wrong," Myra cried, half rising from her seat. "He hates Adelina. You can't believe anything he says about her. Or Nestor. Adelina didn't do anything to Nestor."

"I didn't suggest she had," I said mildly. "You did."

"That's not true. You implied it. If anyone did anything to Nestor, it was Sulfin."

"Really? You're saying Sulfin killed Nestor?"

"No. I'm saying he could have. He's never forgiven Nestor for taking Adelina away. He said he'd get him back if it was the last thing he ever did." Two patches of color glistened on Myra's cheeks. "Just leave Adelina alone, you hear me!"

Given Myra's tone, it would have been hard not to.

A woman sitting a few seats down stopped eating and looked at us. I could tell from the expression on her face, she was an inch shy of coming over and asking if everything was all right. Which was the last thing I needed now.

"It's okay," I told her, beating her to it. "Just a family dispute."

She gave me an understanding smile and went back to her taco. I put a hand on Myra's arm and guided her back down to her seat. She came reluctantly. "All right. What you're saying may be true. I'm not saying it isn't, but I still need to find Adelina."

Myra straightened her back and stiffened her neck. She looked straight ahead. She was the warrior queen.

"Is she with Eli?"

Myra shrugged.

"Have they left the area?"

"I told you I don't know." This time Myra's voice was flat and lifeless.

I tried again. "You may think you're protecting your friend," I told her, "but you're not."

"Really?" she sneered.

I explained about Chapman and the suitcase. "Look, in the end, either Chapman, myself, or the police are going to find Adelina. Who would you prefer? Think about it."

She bit her lip.

"One person is dead. Do you want your friend to be next?"

The corners of her mouth began to droop.

"Think how you'd feel if Adelina dies and it's your fault?"

Myra put her hand to her mouth.

"Is it worth the risk?"

I watched her fight with herself.

"Is it?" I insisted. "Do you want to go to her funeral? Be there when they lower her casket into the ground? Watch her mother crying, when all the time you know that this could have been prevented if you'd only . . ."

"All right," Myra finally said, her face going soft. "That's enough."

And she told me where Adelina was.

Chapter
22

The street Adelina lived on had settled down for the evening. Everyone was in for the night. Cars were tucked into their driveways. In the houses, lights were on and curtains were down. Scraps of canned TV laughter lingered in the air, remnants of programs that promise a world where no one is ever unhappy. I watched sleet falling under the streetlamps. It came down desultorily, as if it was too tired to make the effort. Across the way, a white cat crept under a porch.

Manuel and I were parked midway down Adelina's block, watching her house. It was lit up like a Christmas tree. I could see the shadows of people walking back and forth through the curtains. We'd gotten here half an hour ago and had been arguing ever since about what we were going to do to get her outside, a fact that was not improving my mood, which was piss-poor to begin with.

"Why don't you just walk up there and knock on her

door?" Manuel suggested for what must have been the hundredth time.

"Why don't *you*?" I replied, thinking of our last encounter.

"Are you afraid of her mother?" he taunted.

"Absolutely." I turned on the wipers to clear the windshield. They made a squeaking sound as they went over the glass. "Aren't you?"

Instead of answering, Manuel slouched down lower in the seat. "Well, we can't stay here forever waiting for her to come out," he groused.

"Detectives spend hours watching houses," I felt the need to point out. I'm not sure why.

"Good for them." Manuel flicked a piece of lint off his jacket.

"Sometimes eight hours at a stretch without leaving the car."

"What do they do about peeing?"

"They use a bottle."

Manuel made a face. "That's disgusting." He ran a finger down his jacket zipper. "Anyway, we don't even know she's in there."

"Are you saying Myra lied to us?"

"No, I'm not saying that," Manuel replied. "I'm just saying she could have gone out again."

"Let's assume that she hasn't." That was a possibility I wasn't prepared to entertain yet.

"Why should we assume that?"

"Because I say so." And I picked up my backpack and began searching around in it for my pack of cigarettes.

"Good reason." Manuel rolled his eyes, a gesture I particularly dislike. "Seriously, Robin," he said, "how long are we going to sit here like this?"

"As long as we have to." I kept on looking for my cigarettes. They weren't there. Then I remembered I'd left them on the table at the food court.

"My knees are locking," Manuel whined. "It's hot in here."

"Then roll down the window," I snapped. "For heaven's sake, we've only been here for half an hour."

"It feels like three."

"Too bad." Now that I'd found Adelina, I was damned if I was going to move from this spot and take the chance of letting her get away from me again.

Unfortunately, Manuel was right. We couldn't sit and wait. Time wasn't on our side in this case. Aside from the fact that I needed to buy cigarettes, someone was sure to notice us and call the police. It's hard to stay hidden for long when there isn't any traffic and everyone knows everyone else's car.

Manuel sighed loudly. He began tapping his fingers on the dashboard. "We could always call and tell Adelina's mother there's a gas leak and she has to get everyone outside."

"Somehow I don't think that would work."

"Why not?"

"Because she'll wonder where the trucks are."

"We'll tell her they're on their way."

I didn't bother to reply. But Manuel's suggestion had given me an idea. "Do you have your cell phone?" I asked him.

"Yeah." He patted his parka pocket. "Right here."

"Good. I want you to make a call for me."

"To who?"

"To Adelina's mother."

He sat up straighter and smiled. "You go, girl. What am I going to say?"

"Tell her there's been an emergency and she's needed back at work right away."

For once Manuel played it straight and did what I asked. Maybe it was the prospect of peeing in a bottle that did it. Fifteen minutes later, I watched the front door of Adelina's house open. Her mother came out, got into her car, and drove away. I calculated it would take Donna fifteen minutes to get to the Jewish old age home, another fifteen minutes to drive back, and ten to check with the supervisor and realize she'd been had. Which meant we had forty minutes, at most, to do our business before she returned.

I nudged Manuel. "Let's go."

We walked to Adelina's house. The snow, which had almost stopped, had left a glistening residue of water on the pavement. I stood off in the shadows as Manuel climbed the porch steps. When he got to the front door, he turned and looked at me. I gave a little nod and he rang the doorbell. A moment later, someone answered.

"Yes?" I heard a small girl's voice say through the closed door.

"Can I speak to Adelina?" Manuel asked.

"She's not home," the little girl lisped.

Manuel resettled his baseball cap on his head. "This is very important." He dropped his voice to a gentle semiwhisper. It always surprised me that Manuel was good with children, but it shouldn't have. He had enough experience with his younger brothers and sisters. "Tell your sister, Eli's cousin is outside. Tell her he has to speak to her about the suitcase."

"She said not to tell anyone she's here. She'll be mad at me if I do that," the little girl protested.

"No she won't. I promise."

"She will," the little girl insisted.

Manuel spent another few minutes coaxing her. Finally I heard a tremulous okay.

I jammed my hands in my pockets and rocked back and forth on my heels, while Manuel stamped his feet and cracked his knuckles. A minute later, the overhead porch light flicked on, bathing everything in a dim light. The window curtain was drawn back a trifle. An older, harder voice took up where the little girl had left off.

"How did you know I was here?" Adelina asked.

"Myra told me."

"Stupid bitch," Adelina spat out. She said something in Spanish I couldn't understand, then I heard, "What do you want?"

"I need to come in."

"Why?"

Manuel recited the lines we'd agreed on. "Because I need to show you something Nestor left for you."

"Like what?" Her tone was hard.

"You have to see."

I held my breath. This was the moment I was waiting for. If Adelina didn't open the door, I was out of luck.

"This had better be good," she said.

I heard the chain rattle as Adelina took it off its catch. Then she opened the door a crack. "Show it to me," she demanded.

"Here." Manuel pretended to reach into his pocket as I scrambled onto the porch.

I hit the door with my shoulder. It flew open, smashing against the interior wall. Adelina fell back. The gun I hadn't known she'd been holding clattered to the floor. She dove for it, but I got there first and picked it up. As I pointed it at her, I wondered if this was the gun that had shot Nestor.

"You okay?" Manuel asked me.

"Fine." I motioned for him to close the door behind me.

"Interesting toy," I said to Adelina when I got my breath back. "Who were you expecting? I mean, I heard this is a bad neighborhood. I didn't know it was that bad."

She scowled.

"Did you kill Nestor with this?" I lifted my hand with the 9mm up slightly.

"You're an idiot," she told me disdainfully.

I smiled equably. "So people keep telling me."

"It's true. You don't know nothing."

"I know enough to have found you," I couldn't resist pointing out.

Then, before I could say anything else, her sisters and brother came out from the kitchen to see what had happened. They moved slowly, the brother tightly holding the hand of his younger sister as they hugged the walls. I guessed from the furious expression on Adelina's face when she caught sight of them that she'd told them to stay put, but they hadn't been able to stand the wait anymore and disobeyed. Their eyes widened when they saw me. I lowered the automatic, ejected the clip, and slipped it into my jacket pocket. I didn't want to take the chance of having an accident happen in here.

"Everything's fine," Adelina said, trying to assure them, and she smiled a tight little smile that faded on her lips as fast as it had come on.

The children didn't look as if they believed her. The little girl certainly didn't, because she ran over to me and began beating my legs with her fists.

"You leave my sister alone," she cried.

I put out a hand to fend her off and accidentally pulled off one of the ribbons on her braids. "Stop that," I ordered.

"No. I won't." She kept pounding on my leg even though her lower lip was trembling and her eyes were scrunched up. It was surprising how annoying it was. Finally I reached down and scooped her up. She burst into tears and began to wail.

Adelina's eyes flared. "Give her to me," she demanded, reaching out.

"With pleasure." I handed the little girl over to her sister.

"Maria, it's fine," Adelina assured her, stroking her hair. "Don't worry. I'm not mad at you."

Maria kept crying.

"I just need to get something your sister has," I found myself explaining to her. "That's all. I promise."

"It's true, *niña.*" And Adelina put her mouth to Maria's ear and whispered something in it.

Maria's face relaxed. She stopped crying. Adelina whispered something else to her and tickled her tummy. Maria laughed and buried her head in Adelina's shoulder.

As I watched her, I reflected that George had been right about people's appearances changing. Adelina didn't look at all like her photograph. For openers, she'd lost weight, bleached her hair blond and cut it, but those weren't the only things that accounted for the discrepancy. Her mouth seemed smaller, her eyes a little more closely set together, and she had a large scar on the side of her neck that the picture hadn't shown. She was wearing a tight white sweater, tight black pants, and platform boots. Her jewelry, large gold hoop earrings, a wide gold herringbone chain and a matching gold bracelet, all looked real. She appeared old for her years. I was thinking about the fact that I would have pegged her for midthirties if I'd seen her in the street, when her brother tapped my arm. I looked over.

He pointed to the gun I was still holding in my hand. "Is that yours?" he asked.

"No," I told him, ignoring Adelina's glare. "It's your sister's."

"Really." He gave his sister an appraising look before turning back to me. "Can I see it?"

"No, you can't," Adelina and I both said at the same time.

He put his hands on his hips. "But the clip's out."

"No," Adelina repeated.

"I've seen them before," he protested.

"All the worse for you," his sister answered.

"Then how come you have one?"

"She shouldn't," I replied, and put the gun in my pocket, thereby settling the argument. "No one should."

"But everyone does."

"That's not the issue."

He sighed a long sigh that bemoaned the idiocy of adults and walked into the living room. The older sister went with him. I nodded to Manuel and he followed. At least that way I didn't have to worry about them getting on the phone.

Chapter 23

Adelina walked into the kitchen carrying her baby sister on her hip. "What do you want?" she asked me as she took a glass out of the cabinet, filled it with water, and handed it to Maria. The little girl grasped it with both hands and gulped the liquid down.

"I want the suitcase."

"I don't know what you're talking about," Adelina replied, though the crack in her voice told a different story.

It was a lie I'd been hearing a lot lately and I was growing tired of it. "Then why did Chapman ask me to look for you?" I asked.

"Chapman?" she said, widening her eyes to play the innocent, but all the gesture did was draw attention to the large quantity of eye liner she was using.

"Oh, please." I made a rude noise.

She gave me a defiant stare. "Well, the name isn't familiar."

"He's the man whose property Nestor stole. He really isn't very nice. But then, you know that, don't you?" I watched Adelina's face as I was talking. She was trying to make it a blank slate, but she wasn't succeeding very well. She looked scared. A vein under her eye was twitching. "I'd hate to think of him coming to your house," I continued. "I'm positive he wouldn't be nearly as nice to your sisters and brother as I am. Did you know he's a Federal agent?"

Adelina absentmindedly took the glass Maria was holding out and put it in the sink.

I moved a pile of papers off a kitchen chair onto the table and sat down. "He really wants that suitcase very badly. Nestor made a big mistake. He should have stolen from someone else."

"He didn't know," Adelina whispered. For a second she looked on the verge of tears. "He never would have done it if he had known." She put Maria down. The little girl clasped her arms around her sister's legs and lifted her face toward her sister. "Pick me up," she piped.

Adelina smoothed her sister's hair down. "In a minute, *querida.*"

"The best thing for you to do would be to give it to me so I can give it to Chapman."

Adelina bit her lip. "But I don't have it. I think Eli does."

I riffled through the pile of papers I'd moved from the chair to the table. On top was a brochure for Disneyland and another one for Universal Studios. I picked them up.

"Going somewhere?" I asked.

"We were." Adelina gave me a reproachful glance and patted her sister on the head.

I put them down and studied the drawing that had been under them. It was a crayon drawing by Maria, the kind that mothers tack on their refrigerators. It showed a pink house with four windows, each one in a different color, and green smoke curling out of the chimney. Someone, I presume a teacher, had printed "Maria's house" underneath in big bold letters.

I held up the drawing. "If you don't give the suitcase to me, Maria may not have her house much longer."

"Stop it," Adelina cried. "Just stop it." The corners of her mouth quivered. She sniffed. "I'm telling the truth about Eli. He has to have the suitcase. Nestor left with it. He told me to call Eli and tell him to meet him there."

I stopped looking at the drawing. At least that part of Adelina's story checked out. Eli had told me the same thing.

"So why did Nestor do that? Why go to all that trouble for nothing?"

"Because he was getting scared." Adelina took out the other ribbon in Maria's hair and draped it around her neck. "I told him we should go away."

"To Disneyland?" I ran my finger around the rim of a pink plastic mug decorated with little hearts.

"Yes."

"Were you taking the suitcase with you? Or were you going to sell the tortoises here?"

"We weren't going to do either. I told him we should give them back, because if we didn't, we'd always be worrying about Chapman."

"What did Nestor say?"

"He said it was a good idea." Adelina swallowed.

Maria was jumping up and down now in a frenzy of impatience. Adelina told her to stop. She didn't listen.

"He was willing to give up all that money?" I asked Adelina over Maria's wailed, "you promised."

"There are some things that are more important."

"True." I looked at the gold she was wearing. "That's

what some people say." The problem was, I didn't know if Adelina was one of those people.

She opened her mouth to say something, changed her mind, and closed it again. I went on.

"Only now Nestor's dead and the suitcase is missing."

"Sulfin." Adelina reached down and picked Maria up and sat her on the counter.

"Pardon?" I wasn't sure I'd heard Adelina correctly.

"You should talk to Sulfin. He was always carrying on about how he was going to kill Nestor for taking me away from him." Her voice had grown more decisive.

I got up. "It must be nice to be the object of such affection."

Adelina threw me a nasty look.

"Really," I said. "I'm not kidding. Where'd you get the gun?"

"A friend gave it to me."

"How convenient." It appeared as if everyone had friends. Manuel. Myra. Adelina. Of course none of those friends had names. But that would have been expecting too much.

I found myself chewing on the inside of my cheek. My gut told me Adelina was lying. One hundred thousand dollars was a lot of money to someone like her, enough to take a considerable risk for, but, if I was reading her correctly, not enough to put her family in danger. After speaking to her, I was almost positive she still had the suitcase. I was equally positive that it wasn't here. I asked if I could look around anyway. Just to be on the safe side.

"Go ahead," Adelina replied.

She and Maria trailed behind me as I went through the attic and the basement and opened closet doors and looked under beds and in bathrooms.

"Satisfied?" she said when I was done. She had her sister

clasped to her breast like a shield. Her look dared me to do anything to make her cry.

"Yes. I guess I was wrong." I walked into the living room. Manuel and Adelina's brother and sister were sitting on the sofa. They all looked up.

"We're going," I announced to Manuel.

He put the bowl of popcorn he was holding down on the coffee table. "Did you find it?"

"No. I made a mistake."

"A mistake?" His voice rose. "Gee. Thanks a lot. You made me miss the end of *Godzilla* for this?"

"I'll rent it for you."

"Now?" He stood up. "A two-day rental?"

I nodded. We went outside. As we walked down the porch steps, I heard Adelina locking the door behind us. The snow had almost stopped. The wind had blown most of the clouds away. The sky was clearer now. I stopped and studied the thin sliver of the new moon hanging in the sky.

"Let's go." Manuel nodded toward the cab. "I want to get to the video store before it closes."

"You'll have to take a rain check."

"What do you mean?" Manuel yelped. "You just promised."

"And I'll do it. I'm just not doing it now. We're going back to the car and wait."

"Why?"

"Because I think Adelina still has the suitcase. I think she's hidden it someplace and I think she's rattled enough now so that she's going to get it when her mother comes back."

"How do you know?" he demanded.

"Gut feeling." I almost tripped on a crack in the sidewalk where the pavement had heaved up.

"Gut feeling. Great." Manuel rolled his eyes again. "I'm supposed to freeze my ass off because you have a gut feeling."

"Exactly." We got to the cab.

"Have you considered that maybe you're wrong? That maybe she sold it already?"

"I don't think she'd be here if she had, but if I'm wrong we're out of luck." I opened the cab door and got in. "We'll know soon enough," I told Manuel after he closed the door on his side. I consulted my watch. "Her mother is going to be back in another ten minutes at the latest."

"I hope so." And Manuel crossed his arms over his chest, leaned back in the seat, and sulked.

While he did that, I sat and brooded about Zsa Zsa. The more I thought about her, the more nervous I got. Finally I couldn't stand it anymore.

I turned to Manuel. "Give me your cell phone."

"Why?"

"Because I need it."

He handed it over reluctantly. "You make any long distance calls, you pay for them," he said.

I shushed him, while I powered up and dialed the store's number. I wanted to make sure Joan had picked up Zsa Zsa. She had.

"Was she okay with her?" I asked Tim.

"Why shouldn't she be?"

"I just expected . . ."

"What?"

"Nothing."

"Reluctance," Tim asked.

"Maybe a little," I admitted, feeling like a fool. I hung up and called George.

"I found out where Chapman lives," George said without

waiting to be asked. "He's renting an apartment over at the Hilton on Genesee Street." The line was full of static and it was hard to hear him. His voice kept fading in and out. "I'm losing my touch. When I was on the Force I would have had that figured out."

I didn't say anything, but George was right. It was the logical place for Chapman to be staying. The Hilton had two parts. It had its regular hotel rooms and it had its furnished apartments that the management rented out by the week or month. I'd been in one of them once. The walls in the hallway had been a drab ochre, the floor had been tiled, and the apartment looked as if it hadn't been touched since the forties.

"Mike just looked it up for me. He's made himself known around the building and I don't mean in a favorable way."

"Didn't Mike want to know why you were asking?"

"I told Mike I had to speak to him about you. I think he figured I was going to tell him to back off. Which, I also think, he would be happy to have happen."

"He doesn't like him very much, I gather."

"The general consensus is, the man's an asshole." George's voice dissolved in a burst of static then came back. "That no one will be sorry to see him rolling around on the floor with the pigs."

"That's good for us." There was another burst of static.

"Well, let's just say that no one's going to go out of their way for him. Also, he's gone out to the casino a couple of times. Mike thinks he didn't do too well out there." George's voice faded out.

"I can't hear you!" I yelled.

"I know." George sounded as if he was calling from New Zealand. "I'll call later." He hung up.

I powered down and tossed the cell phone back to Manuel.

"What was that all about?"

"Nothing." I started biting my cuticles.

"Why do you want to know where Chapman lives?"

"I'm not sure yet. I just do."

Manuel's face lit up. "Are you going to surprise him and beat the shit out of him?"

"No."

"Why not?"

"Because it wouldn't be a smart thing to do."

"Who gives a fuck?"

"I do. The guy is a Federal agent, even if he is Fish and Wildlife. You don't beat people like that up. The courts tend to frown on that type of behavior. Unless, of course, you like the idea of spending many years in jail."

"Then what are you going to do?"

"I don't know." I was rubbing my eyes when Manuel tapped me on the shoulder and pointed. Adelina's mother was pulling into the driveway.

"Now we're going to see," he muttered.

I held my breath. A few minutes later, the door opened again and Adelina came out, jumped into the car, and started it up.

"I was right," I crowed at Manuel. "Now we can wrap this up and go home."

And I took off after her.

Chapter

24

Despite what Manuel says, what happened next wasn't my fault. It was the fault of the Onondaga Sheriff's Department. Things were going along just fine. I was keeping Adelina's Taurus in view. I was half a street length behind, which, given the time of night, was the perfect distance—not so close that she could see me and not so far away that I'd lose her.

Adelina was driving much faster than the speed limit allowed. She went down Oak and through Willow at a brisk forty-five miles an hour. Then she took a right onto Ash, drove five blocks, and came to a rolling stop at the four-way intersection of Ash and Crescent before speeding through it.

"Where the hell is she going?" Manuel muttered as I pressed down on the accelerator.

"I don't have a clue," I replied.

And I didn't.

I'd expected her to go toward Littlebaum's house, which was in the opposite direction.

I was speeding up because the intersection she'd gone through was a big one, big enough so that there were cars going through it at any time of the day or night, and I wanted to make absolutely sure I didn't lose her. Because all my attention was focused in front of me, I wasn't checking the rearview mirror. Which was too bad. Otherwise, I might have spotted the sheriff's car behind me and come to a full stop at the four-way.

Unfortunately I didn't do either.

The next thing I knew, I saw the lights flashing in the mirror. I cursed and pulled over to the side.

"Good move," Manuel volunteered. "Very smart."

"Be quiet," I hissed as I rolled down my window and waited for the deputy to approach me.

"If the wheels don't rock, you ain't stopped," he told me as I handed him my license and my registration. Terrific. A poet. Maybe he'd write me a haiku instead of a ticket. Or a sonnet. That wouldn't be bad, either.

He looked older than the normal run of guys in that line of work. Most deputies I see are in their midtwenties to thirties. By their forties they're usually sitting behind a desk or collecting their pension and doing something else. This guy looked to be about fifty. Or maybe he was younger and was just having a hard life. "You should slow down," he added as he took in my tapping fingers on the steering wheel. "Speed kills."

I forced a smile. "Yes, you're right. I'm sorry. I'll be more careful in the future, Officer."

But I was so jazzed by the pursuit, I was practically bouncing up and down in my seat.

His eyes narrowed. "Anything wrong?" he asked. His eyes swept the inside of the cab and lingered on Manuel.

I made myself sit still. "Just anxious to get home."

"You're sure? What about him?" he asked, indicating Manuel.

"He's coming home with me. He's my nephew," I added, hoping he wouldn't make us get out of the cab.

He gave Manuel a long, speculative look, then somewhat reluctantly, he took my papers back to his squad car.

"Shithead," Manuel spat out when the deputy was out of earshot. "He thinks I was carjacking you."

"Probably."

He pushed up his sleeve and pointed to his wrist. "He wouldn't have said that if my skin was white like yours."

"You're right, he wouldn't have," I agreed.

"I'm gonna . . ."

"All right, Manuel." I rubbed my forehead. I was tired. I was irritable. I was stressed. I wasn't in the mood to listen to one of Manuel's rants about racial inequality tonight, even if it was true. "That's enough."

"Don't you 'all right' me." His voice warbled with indignation at my lack of empathy. "You wouldn't be liking it if it happened to you."

"You're right. I wouldn't. I apologize," I said to keep the peace. The last thing I needed now was Manuel mouthing off to the officer. Then we'd never get out of here.

"Okay." Manuel slumped down in his seat and began fiddling with the zipper of his jacket. "I still say that's why he stopped us," he repeated.

"And I told you I agreed."

"I should report that prick."

"Go ahead. Just do it tomorrow."

"Maybe I will."

"You should," I said, even though I knew he wouldn't. Doing something like that took the kind of effort Manuel wasn't prepared to make. Instead, he'd mutter and complain until something else came up.

The computer must have been down, because it took the deputy fifteen minutes before he came back, though it felt longer than that. I kept checking my watch every two minutes or so. The hands moved at a glacial pace.

"Now what?" Manuel asked as I shoved the ticket in my backpack.

"Now we're going to Parker Littlebaum's house."

"Why?"

"Because I think Adelina might be there." Even though she hadn't been heading in that direction, Littlebaum's was her logical destination.

"And if she isn't?" Manuel said. "What then?"

"We'll check every other place I can think of."

Manuel groaned. "I was going to a party tonight."

"Not anymore." I pulled out, hooked a left, and drove over to Littlebaum's.

It took me more time to get there than it usually would. I had to drive slowly because the sheriff stayed on my ass for a good quarter of the way. Maybe Manuel was right about him suspecting Manuel of carjacking, or maybe he just figured I'd speed up again.

And he was correct. I did. I went into warp speed as soon as he was gone. We arrived at Littlebaum's house ten minutes later. I parked on the road's shoulder, ten feet away from the house, underneath a large oak, and turned the motor off. The house looked as if Littlebaum had turned in for the night. The lights were out on the first floor, although two rooms were lit up on the second story.

"Maybe Adelina's up there," I said to Manuel, indicating the windows on the left-hand side of the structure.

He threw me a disgusted look. "And maybe Littlebaum can't sleep. Maybe he's watching TV." He gestured to the house. "I mean, I don't see her car around here anywhere. I don't see anyone through the window walkin' around up there."

I'd noticed that, too. "The Taurus could be in the garage. I'm going to check."

"You don't mind if I stay here, do you?"

"No."

"Good. 'Cause it's freezing out there. And I ain't fixin' to get my clothes dirty tramping around outside." He pulled out his cell phone.

"Who are you calling?"

"A friend. I got to do something while I'm waiting. Hey!" he yelled as I took the keys out of the ignition. "Leave those in there. It's cold."

I handed them to him reluctantly. "Don't play the radio and don't turn on the lights."

Manuel bristled. "You think I'm an idiot?"

It seemed better not to answer.

"So I can't go and get me a hot chocolate?" he asked straightfaced as I got out of the car. "Just kidding," he said before I could answer. "Truly. I wouldn't do something like that."

I wasn't so sure. As I closed the car door, I could hear Manuel talking to his friend.

"Whatup, Brooke?" he was saying. "No. I ain't goin' to that jive ass party. I got me something better to do. I got me hired as a private investigator. No shit! It's true. I be here right now staking out this place."

I couldn't help smiling as I started down the road to

Littlebaum's house. As I walked, I hunched my back and put my hands in my pockets. It had grown colder since I'd left Adelina's. It was a beautiful night. A few clouds remained in the sky. The moon and a few stars were visible.

Little flecks of ice glimmered on the fence posts. Frozen leaves crunched under my feet. I walked around the remnants of a pumpkin left over from Halloween that lay rotting on the ground, its face now reduced to an orange mush. In another month or so, not a trace would be visible. The air smelled of smoke. Someone must be running a wood-burning stove, I decided as I walked along the road. When I got to Littlebaum's driveway, I halted and considered what I was going to do next.

What I hadn't noticed the first time I'd been there was that in order to get to Littlebaum's garage I had to cross a wide expanse of open, flat land. There were no trees I could hide behind, nothing I could use for cover. Basically, if Littlebaum set Matilda on me, I was royally fucked.

This was not good. I guess I was either getting older or smarter because I decided to see if I could come up with a more conservative solution to getting a look inside Littlebaum's garage instead of charging over there. I chewed on a lock of my hair and watched my breath turn to smoke in the night air. A plane roared by overhead. I looked up. It was flying low, coming in for a landing, its lights blinking in the sky. Then it was out of sight and I went back to studying Littlebaum's house. Whereas the front was clear, the back was shrouded in shadows.

Then I realized what I should have spotted immediately. Littlebaum had lots of trees on his property. They were just in the back of his house instead of the front. Maybe I could get to his house by heading down, then cutting across. I walked a little farther and came to a large privet hedge that bordered the road. It was thick and well tended, but the people who'd planted it evidently hadn't felt the need to extend the plantings back toward their house. Here they'd put in cedars and arborvitae. I was betting it would be easy to follow the cedars down and then cut over to Littlebaum's house. I bet wrong.

The ground wasn't nearly as easy to walk over as I expected. The terrain had been left to go wild. The cedars were being taken over by maples and honey locusts. The ground was littered with their cast-off limbs, in addition to being full of large rocks and holes. I had to keep looking down to see where I was going. Despite that, I kept tripping. Walking would have been easy during the day, but at night, in the dark, it was tough going. After twisting my ankle for the third time in ten minutes, I leaned against a tree and reconsidered my plan for the second time that evening.

At the pace I was going, it would take me a while to get to the back of Littlebaum's house, which wouldn't even matter, except when I got there I didn't know what I was going to find. This wasn't going to work. I backtracked reluctantly. Maybe this was why I usually took the direct approach. On the way to the car I came up with another idea.

Manuel was still chatting when I got behind the wheel.

"That was quick," he said, interrupting his conversation.

"I didn't go." I reached out. "Can I have the phone?"

He tightened his grip on it. "Don't I even get a please?"

"Fine. Please. This is important."

He pushed his chin out. "And my business isn't?"

I gritted my teeth and restrained myself from grabbing and shaking him by reminding myself that it was his phone. "I really need to make this call now."

"That's all you had to say. Just give me another second."
And he resumed his conversation.

"Manuel," I repeated urgently when the second had
turned into a minute.

He nodded, told his friend he'd call him back, and
handed the phone to me. "What's this all about?"

"Listen," I said, paying him back a little for making me
wait. Then I punched in George's number.

"Speak to me," George said.

"I am."

"Hey, it's you."

"Who did you expect?"

"Mike. He's seeing if he can come up with anything on
Chapman."

"It would be nice if he could."

"Yes, it would, but I'm not holding my breath. So what's
going on at your end?"

I told him why I'd called.

"But that was my idea," Manuel protested after I had
promised George I'd let him know what happened and hung
up. "You were the one that said calling Adelina's house and
telling her mother there was a gas leak wouldn't work."

I patted him on the shoulder. "What can I say? I was
wrong. Here." I gave him back his phone. Then I reached in
my jacket pocket, took out the clip from Adelina's automatic,
and reinserted it in the gun.

Manuel's eyes widened. "You using that?" he said. "I
thought you don't believe in weapons."

"I don't. But I also don't believe in getting ripped to
shreds." I didn't want to shoot Matilda, but I would if I had
to.

A moment later, the lights in Littlebaum's house went

on, bing, bing, bing, one after the other. Evidently, George hadn't wasted any time making the call.

"What you want me to do?" Manuel asked.

"I want you to stay here and call George if anything goes wrong."

"How will I know?"

"If you hear blood-curdling shrieks coming from the vicinity of Littlebaum's house, I think it's safe to say things aren't working out the way I planned." I got out of the cab and jogged toward the house.

I wanted to greet Littlebaum and Adelina when they came out. Two minutes later, the front door opened and a dazed-looking Littlebaum emerged into the night. I noticed that neither Matilda nor his shotgun was with him. A definite plus. I waited a few more seconds for Adelina to appear. When she didn't, I stepped in front of Littlebaum and raised Adelina's gun.

"Close the door," I ordered. "I don't want Matilda out here."

Littlebaum blinked. "But there's a gas leak." He stuttered slightly in his confusion. His voice was still sodden with sleep. George must have roused him out of a sound slumber. "The man that called said someone had reported a gas leak and that a repair crew from Niagara Mohawk was coming with a meter to check it out."

"Guess what?" I informed him. "The crew isn't going to be along, because there isn't any leak. That was one of my friends calling. Now shut the door." I raised my voice and lifted the gun a little higher. "If I have to shoot Matilda because she's attacking me, it's going to be on your conscience."

Littlebaum quickly did as he was told. I motioned for him to come closer.

He ran one of his hands over his face and hair as he took a hesitant step toward me. Stripped of his rage, he had the confused look of a fragile old man who couldn't quite grasp what was happening to him. "Why'd you do that?" he finally asked.

"I wanted to see if someone was inside your house."

Littlebaum wrinkled his face up in disbelief. "What are you, nuts?" he croaked. "Why didn't you call?"

"I didn't think you'd tell me what I wanted to know. But you will now, right?"

Littlebaum nodded docilely. He'd started to shiver. If I was cold in my jacket, he had to be freezing in his T-shirt, sweat pants, and socks, but I wasn't about to let him go into his house and get some more clothes on.

"Was Adelina here earlier?"

He rubbed his arms with his hands. "No. Why should she be?"

I could hear a faint rumble coming from the other side of the front door. Littlebaum cocked his head, smiled, and half turned. "Just a minute," he told the big cat. The lilt in his voice was the kind a man uses to a woman he's in love with, which was too bad, because odds were Littlebaum and Matilda weren't going to have a happy ending. Then Littlebaum turned back to me. "She wants to know what's happening," he explained. "She understands more than you would think."

"I'm sure she does." Maybe she did for all I knew. Zsa Zsa was certainly more perceptive than some, make that a lot, of people I've known. "When we're finished, you can go in and tell her all about our conversation about Adelina. She was looking to get rid of a suitcase full of Madagascar tortoises. I thought she might have tried to sell them to you."

Littlebaum shifted his weight from left foot to right foot and back again. "She called me, let me see"—he stopped and thought—"was it yesterday or the day before? And offered me one, but I didn't buy it."

"Why? I would have thought you would have liked that sort of thing."

He glared at me. "I'm disappointed in you, Robin. You should know me better than that. I'd never buy CITES stuff. And anyway, she was asking too much money. Ten thousand dollars," he scoffed. "You got to be crazy to pay that for a turtle. Even if it does come in pretty colors." This from someone who had spent what he had on a lion cub. He motioned for me to come inside with skeleton-thin fingers. "Take a look if you want."

I debated taking him up on his offer, but in the end I declined. I believed he was telling the truth. Even though he liked reptiles, mammals were his passion.

"Can I go now? I'm freezing my ass off out here."

"In a minute." I coughed. The cold was getting to me. "Do you know who Adelina was going to sell them to?"

He shook his head. "Didn't ask. I stick to my own business. All I ask is that other people do the same."

Matilda roared. I heard scratching.

"She's going to ruin the door if you don't let me get in there," Littlebaum said.

I lowered my gun and nodded for him to go on. "Hey, Parker," I called when he was almost at the door, "maybe it's time for you to relocate the ark."

He turned around. "What do you mean?"

"Sooner or later someone's gonna turn you in and they're going to take Matilda and everything else away from you and hold you for a psych evaluation. I know someone out

West who has a lot of open land they might be willing to rent to you," I added impulsively.

He didn't say anything.

I thought about what Sulfin had said about Littlebaum being cheap. "It would be worth the money."

He nodded.

"You should consider it seriously."

He squinted. His lips began to move as he tried to figure out why I was doing this. Finally he asked.

"Simple. I don't want to see your animals killed or have them end up in some fly-by-night traveling circus."

Maybe conditions for Littlebaum's charges weren't ideal, which they weren't. Maybe he shouldn't have them, but the animals were still better off with Littlebaum than in some of the other places they could end up. And at least Littlebaum cared for them. That had to count for something.

"I'll think about it," he said.

"Don't think too long," I warned.

"Would you like to give Matilda a pet?" he asked shyly, the way a little boy does when he's showing you his special rock collection. "She liked you."

I told him I'd love to, but asked if I could take a rain check for another day. Littlebaum looked disappointed.

"Are you sure?" he said.

I told him I was. Then I slipped the gun into my jacket pocket and took an old napkin and a pen out from the other one and wrote the phone number of my friend out West down. "Here," I said, holding the napkin out to him. An offering. "Take it for Matilda's sake."

The ends of the napkin fluttered in the breeze. Littlebaum extended his hand and took a few tentative steps toward me.

"All right." He grabbed the napkin from my hand and

crumpled it up in his fist. "All right." And he went inside his house before I could say anything else.

As I headed back to the cab, I wondered if he'd understood what I'd been telling him. I hoped he had. I hoped he'd make the phone call, but I doubted it.

"Well?" Manuel asked as I slammed the cab door shut. I rubbed my hands. It felt good to be where it was warm. "What happened?"

"Adelina wasn't there."

"I know. I saw." He yawned. "Now what?"

"We go to Plan B."

"I didn't know you had a Plan A."

"Stop playing the comedian. I already told you. We're going to drive around and look for Adelina's car."

He crossed his arms over his chest and leaned against the door. "That's fucked."

"Elegantly put. What would you suggest? Exactly," I said when he didn't answer. "You don't have a suggestion, do you?"

He fiddled with the brim of his hat. "She's probably home by now."

"Good idea." I tried to make my voice enthusiastic. "We'll begin there."

Manuel groaned. "Robin, have a heart. Why don't you just drop me off? I got a whole lot of shit I could be doing instead of running all over the city."

"No. I like having you with me." Until I got this thing settled, I wanted Manuel where I could keep my eye on him. "First we'll go back to Adelina's place, then Myra's, then Sulfin's," I announced.

It was the only thing I could think of to do.

Chapter
25

Manuel spent the entire hour and a half it took me to crisscross the city and check out Adelina's, Sulfin's, and Myra's houses whining. I half listened, veering back and forth between wishing he'd be quiet to thinking that if he ever went back to school Manuel would make a great courtroom lawyer.

His list was endless. Manuel complained about the fact that I'd made him come with me. He complained that he could have been at a party meeting girls. Or watching TV. He complained that now it was too late to get the Godzilla movie I'd promised him. When I didn't say anything, he told me that my plan was a waste of time, but in less polite language. He told me I should get a new ride. Something cool. Something he wouldn't mind being seen in if he had to go with me. Maybe something like an SUV.

According to him, my cab was Stone Age and I should get with the times, for God's sake. Get a car with air-conditioning and heated seats and killer electronics. Something with a CD player, because how could I listen to the radio anyway? All the stations in Syracuse sucked. The DJs sucked. The music they played sucked big time.

In fact, Syracuse sucked. He was tired of living in this city. He wanted to go someplace where there were some opportunities, someplace warm. He'd told his mother but she didn't understand. All she cared about was that he didn't have a job. She couldn't see that standing around in the mall dishing out slices of pizza wasn't for him. That he needed something interesting and challenging. She didn't understand that getting his GED and going on to a community college wasn't going to help him. After all, look at Eli. He was going to college and it sure hadn't made him any smarter. In fact, it was his desire to go to college that had gotten him in the mess he was now in.

"Ironic, isn't it?" Manuel punctuated his observation with a smug smile, infinitely pleased with himself.

The smile was the last straw. I told Manuel to shut up, not that he listened.

"You're just saying that because I'm right about Eli," he sniffed. "I'm right about everything. You don't want to admit that this whole evening has been a waste of time. Can we go back to your place now?"

"No, we can't." I had one more idea I wanted to try.

"No?" Manuel yelped. "What are we going to do? Drag Onondaga Lake?"

"We're going to check out Eli's house."

"How about letting me off at the corner? I'll walk."

"Forgetaboutit. I told you, you're coming with me."

"Fine." Manuel let out a heartfelt sigh. "But even Eli isn't stupid enough to go back there."

As it turned out, Manuel was wrong.

"Holy shit. What a schmuck," Manuel said when we saw that the lights were on in the flat.

"Maybe Eli isn't dumb. Maybe he wants to get caught."

Manuel snorted. "Where do you come up with this kind of stuff?" he demanded as he reseated his hat on his head. "You sound like that moron of a guidance counselor they made me see in ninth grade. No one wants to get caught. No one."

"I think people want to get caught all the time," I countered. "I think that's why they do what they do."

"And I think you're full of shit."

"You do, hunh?"

"Yeah." Manuel put his hand on the door handle. "You gonna order me out of the car?"

"Stay right where you are. That was a nice try, but not good enough."

Manuel slumped back in his seat. "Well, I still can't figure why he should come back here."

"Maybe he's figuring that that's what the police think and that's why it's a good place to hide out." This time Manuel didn't disagree.

"If it were me," he said, "I wouldn't go near the place. Or at least I'd leave the lights off. The police have got to be checking it out."

"Evidently not. Or if they are, they obviously aren't doing it on a regular enough basis. Who knows? Maybe Eli just dropped in to get something and we were lucky enough to catch him." I pointed at a Taurus parked four spaces down. "And that, I believe, is Adelina's car. What do you have to say now?"

"That we should have come here first."

I drove down a little farther and pulled in behind a pickup

truck. "Come on." I turned off the engine and pocketed my keys. "Let's go."

Manuel sat there stony-faced, fiddling with the zipper on his jacket, while the car wheezed and clanked, the way it always did when I shut it off.

I shook my head. I couldn't figure the kid out. "I don't understand you, Manuel. The way you've been bitching, I thought you'd be glad to get this over."

Manuel scratched at his left sideburn. "You're not calling the cops on my cousin if he's up there, are you?"

"I think I'm going to have to," I allowed. After all, Eli was wanted for questioning in Nestor's death.

Manuel bit his lip while he thought about what I'd said for a moment before speaking. "Because if you are, give me a sign first so I can leave."

"Leave?" My voice sounded unnaturally loud in the silence.

"Before you call them." He clasped his hands together, laid them on his knees, and gazed at them as if they were a crystal ball and he could see his future in it, and he didn't like what he was looking at. "I don't want to have to tell my mother I let Eli get arrested. She'll never forgive me."

"I'll touch the top button of my shirt if I'm going to. Will that do?"

Manuel looked doubtful.

"Come up with something else if you want," I offered.

He shrugged dispiritedly. "I guess that should work." He got out of the car and followed me down the block. He could have been going to his own execution the way he was walking. "Don't expect me to help you," he warned when we got to the bottom of the steps that led to Eli's flat. "Because I won't."

"Fair enough."

Eli was surprised to see us.

Very surprised.

"I can't believe you're here," I told him after Manuel
and I had burst through his door.

We'd tiptoed up the side of the steps, using the trees as
cover. Then I'd knocked on the door. A moment later, Eli
had asked who was there. I'd told him I needed to speak
with him. It was urgent. When he unlatched the door, I
came through with Manuel following me inside. As I pointed
Adelina's automatic at Eli, I began to see why people liked
guns. They reduced complex problems to simple ones. I
have the gun, therefore you will do as I say. Although, judging from Eli's complexion, dead white, and the beads of
sweat on his lip, I wasn't sure this was the best approach.
The last thing I wanted to do was scare him into a heart
attack.

"What are you doing here?" I repeated.

"I just had to get a few things," he stuttered.

I was just going to ask him what, when Adelina came out
of the bedroom. "Nice to see you again," I commented.

She walked over to Eli, put her hand on his shoulder and
gave it a supportive squeeze.

"Solidarity. I like that," I said.

Adelina looked as if she wanted to spit in my face.

Eli took Adelina's hand. "I hope it didn't take you too
long to find your car keys," he said to me in a mock-hearty
voice.

I motioned for him and Adelina to go into the living
room.

"About ten minutes."

"Good." He pushed his glasses up the bridge of his nose
and licked his lips. "I was worried."

"That was considerate of you." Out of the corner of my

eye I saw something moving on the floor. I looked down. A Madagascar tortoise lumbered by my feet with a large piece of lettuce clasped firmly in his beak. Its shell and body looked as if they'd been painted by someone with a sense of humor.

"I'm glad to see they survived their travels," I noted.

"They're really doing well," Eli assured me. He gave me a bleak little smile. He looked paler. He had dark circles under his eyes. His face looked thinner. The last week hadn't been kind to him. "They have remarkable powers of survival, but I guess that's why they're still around. They and the lizards . . ."

I interrupted. Given the way my day had been going, I wasn't in the mood to discuss animal taxonomy. "Have you been staying here all the time everyone's been looking for you?"

Eli shook his head.

Adelina took a step toward me. "He's been in my house. In the attic." She looked as stressed as Eli, even more so, her blond hair and lipstickless mouth pulling all the color out of her face.

"So that story Eli told about your disappearing from home, that was a lie, too?"

Adelina allowed as how it was.

"What did you tell your mother?"

"I told her some bad people were trying to find me. That was enough. I knew she'd protect me from anything that came along. She's better than a pit bull."

"I'd say so," I agreed.

"She got you good, didn't she?" Adelina said, a slight, vengeful smile hovering on her lips.

I corrected her. "Actually, she got my car."

"Lucky for you."

"No. Lucky for *you*. Otherwise your mother would be in jail on assault charges. Who'd take care of your sisters and brother then?"

Adelina glowered at me. "I would. I do now anyway."

While I thought about Donna chasing me with a bat and how lucky I was she hadn't connected, a second tortoise came out of the kitchen and went by us. This one had a piece of apple in its mouth. It was, like the first one, a little larger than the palm of my hand. Manuel stuck his foot out in front of it. The tortoise stopped, considered its options, and went around.

"Neat," Manuel said to no one in particular. Then he squatted down and watched the tortoise crawl away.

"Where are the rest of them?" I asked.

"Nestor's room," Eli said reluctantly.

"Let's go take a look."

"Why?" Eli said.

"Because I want to." And I motioned for everyone to move. After all, it wasn't as if I was going to ever see one of these animals again, outside of a zoo.

Eli and Adelina walked down the hallway and past Eli's room slowly, as if they'd learned a new gait from their charges, with Manuel bringing up the rear.

They stepped inside Nestor's room and stopped. I followed. The room had acquired a slight fishy smell.

"There they are," Eli said, pointing.

From where I was standing I counted six tortoises. Two were eating out of a bowl filled with chopped fruits and vegetables, one was sitting in the water bowl, while the remaining three were basking under a heat lamp. It was hard to believe that these tortoises were worth over sixty thousand dollars. Back in Madagascar people ate them. They were stewpot favorites. An expensive meal.

It isn't as if you couldn't get them legally. You can. Zoos and a few private breeders have set up programs. The problem is, because the species is so endangered, you have to be willing to go through all the red tape that getting a CITES-listed animal into the country entails. And most people aren't willing to do that. They'd rather spend the money. It's simpler. And faster.

Poor tortoises. On top of everything else, their habitat is being destroyed, so even if people did stop eating them and other people did stop collecting them, they probably wouldn't be around in the wild too much longer. They were doomed, like the tiger and the rhino, their world whittled down to smaller and smaller scale, until there was no room left for them at all.

"What's the matter?" Manuel asked.

I realized I must have sighed out loud. "Nothing," I said, thinking that soon the only things there'll be room for on earth are computers and wires and things that don't make a mess. "Where are the other tortoises?" I asked Eli, making myself get back to the business at hand.

He coughed. "What do you mean?"

"I count eight. There are supposed to be ten."

"You're wrong," he countered, while his eyes blinked like a semaphore, signaling his lie. "Chapman gave me eight."

I raised my gun slightly. "Bad answer."

"I'm not lying," Eli protested. "I swear."

"Don't be a walking cliché on top of everything else."

"Why should I lie?"

"I don't know and I don't care." I glanced at my watch. This was taking way longer than I wanted it to. "Who'd you sell them to?"

Eli looked at Adelina pleadingly. She gave him a contemptuous glance. "Tell her," she ordered.

Eli pulled at his fingers. "Sulfin has one."

"Where's he keeping it?"

"At his apartment."

"And the other?" I prodded.

"I sold it to Littlebaum," Adelina said. "So what? Is that a crime?"

"Yes. As it happens, it is," I replied as I inwardly cursed myself.

I should have gone into Littlebaum's house when I had the chance. He'd offered and I'd said no. Why? Because I'd wanted to believe him, so I'd given him the benefit of the doubt. Which made me a fool. Now I'd just have to go back there again. And this time would be harder. I'd exhausted my meager bag of tricks and there was no reason to think he'd let me in when I came knocking on his door, especially since I was taking back someone he wanted and had paid good money for.

"My sister needs an operation," Adelina told me. "That money is for her."

"I see. And which sister is this?"

"My younger one. There's something wrong with her kidneys."

"Right." I took a last look at the tortoises, then told everyone to go out into the living room.

"Don't you believe me?" Adelina said as we passed Eli's room.

I thought about her sister. She looked pretty good for a kid with kidney problems. "No. I don't."

Adelina stopped walking and turned to face me. "You callin' me a liar?" she demanded.

"Let's just say, I think you have a flexible attitude toward the truth." I raised the gun slightly. "Now get moving." Not that it really mattered. Whether her sister did need surgery or didn't need surgery was going to be a social services problem. I was still going to have to get the tortoise back.

Adelina stopped again. "I wouldn't lie about something like that."

"I wonder why. You'll lie about everything else."

Adelina flushed. Her mouth tightened at the corners. She touched one of her earrings, then put her hand down and began to peel her nails.

"I . . ." she began, but I signaled for her to be quiet.

"Where's the money?"

"It's gone." She widened her eyes. "I gave it to my mother."

"And she spent it, right?"

Adelina's tongue flicked out and moistened her lips. "She had to pay the utility bill and the doctor's bills, and she sent the rest to our grandma, because she needed to get her roof repaired."

By now we were in front of Eli's room. "So if I went in there"—I indicated Eli's room—"I wouldn't find anything?"

"No," she replied as her eyes involuntarily strayed to the cosmetics bag lying on Eli's bed.

Keeping my gun pointed at her, I backed into the room, walked toward the bed, and picked up the case with my free hand.

"Don't," Adelina cried. "That's mine." And she took a step toward me.

"Stay where you are," I ordered.

She stopped. Her eyes were riveted on my fingers as I pulled the zipper open. I quickly glanced inside. The case was filled with hundred-dollar bills.

"You can't." Adelina reached for it. "My sister is going to die without that."

I raised the gun. She dropped her hand to her side.

"If your sister needs surgery, I'll give it back," I assured her as I tucked the cosmetic case into my jacket pocket.

Adelina whirled on Eli. "Do something," she urged, a cut-rate Lady Macbeth trying to egg her man on.

Eli studied a stain on the wall. He looked close to crying. "What do you want me to do?"

"How should I know?" Adelina spat back. "Something. Anything."

"All right, children." I raised my voice. "That's enough. We're going to start a new topic of conversation. March."

Adelina closed her mouth. Her face turned sullen.

"Better," I said when we hit the living room. "Now, then," I asked Eli. "Were you at Adelina's house when I went through the place?" It was a little detail, but it had been nagging at me.

He shook his head. "Adelina let me in after everyone was asleep. I'd tiptoe up to the attic, then leave in the afternoon before everyone came home."

I lowered the gun slightly. "It's amazing no one woke up."

Adelina didn't say anything.

I watched the second tortoise circle around one of the chair legs and move into the hall. He was moving at a good clip—for a tortoise, that is.

Eli rubbed his hands against his pants legs. His palms were probably sweating. I knew mine would be. "I went to the library in the late afternoons," Eli said, continuing his recitation as if I was a schoolteacher who asked him to repeat yesterday's lesson. "When that closed, I'd go to the mall and walk around or catch a movie. I think I've seen everything that's playing." He readjusted his glasses. "It's amazing the junk that Hollywood puts out."

"Well, at least that's something we can both agree on." And I told Eli and Adelina to sit down.

They settled themselves on the sofa, while Manuel took up a position against the wall off to one side of them. I carried a chair in from the dining room table and sat on that. It was uncomfortable, but I didn't care. The day was catching up with me. I was too tired to stand.

"Would you like to tell me what's been going on?" I asked.

Adelina and Eli looked at each other and swallowed.

I raised the automatic slightly. "I really, and I do mean really, would like to know."

"You're not going to like this," Eli promised.

I told him to tell me anyway.

Chapter 26

Eli looked the picture of misery slumped on the sofa. "I never meant to hurt anyone," he intoned. If everybody had a theme song, that would be his.

I bit at one of the cuticles on my free hand. "So you keep saying. Over and over and over again."

He sat for a minute as if pondering where to begin. Finally he spoke. "I told you about how Chapman found me."

"Several versions. Eli, get to the point."

"I am. It just takes me a little while. You heard about the frogs?"

I nodded.

He looked mournful. "If I'd wetted them down better, they would have been all right. Frogs need to have their skin moist at all times."

I interrupted. "Eli, I know about frogs."

"I'm sorry. I know you do. I just didn't realize they could dry out that fast. I thought I had more time. They were so pretty, too. I should have wrapped them in moist towels or washcloths and put them in Ziploc bags, with little holes punched in them for air. Then they would have been fine."

"Eli," I said warningly. "Stop crapping around."

My store of patience had long since vanished. On the other hand, I couldn't make Eli talk. The truth was, much as I wanted to, I wasn't going to beat the story out of him, and I think he knew that. He wanted to tell me what happened. That was clear. But it was also clear that he was going to take as long as he felt like to do it in.

"Don't rush me. I don't like to be rushed," he told me. He pulled the edge of his T-shirt down.

"No kidding." I sat back a little in my seat and watched Manuel. He couldn't contain himself. He was rolling his eyes and tapping his fingers against his thighs. I brought my gaze back to Eli.

Adelina leaned over and gave Eli another pat on the shoulder. She was treating him like her baby sister. "You want me to do this?" she murmured to him.

"No. I will." After another minute, Eli took up where he'd left off. "So, Chapman told me if I made this one run for him, he'd leave me alone. He said he had everything fixed up. He said the customs guys were all taken care of. It was going to be a walk-through. A piece of cake. He was even going to give me a thousand dollars for my trouble."

I nodded encouragingly, waiting for him to tell me something I didn't know.

"It just seemed easier to say yes. And anyway, I didn't want to have to call and tell my mother I needed money for a lawyer. She wouldn't understand. She and my dad are missionaries. Baptists." Pride and embarrassment warred in his voice.

I raised an eyebrow.

"That's why I have all those carvings and dolls and stuff in my room. Every time my mother goes somewhere she sends me something."

I remembered the Japanese geisha doll on the top shelf. "Is that how you got the idea to smuggle the frogs into Japan?"

He nodded. "I lived there for a while when I was a kid. The Japanese like anything expensive and strange. At least, that's what my mother used to say."

"I'm sure she'd be delighted to know what her comment sparked," I observed.

Dots of color appeared on Eli's cheeks. "That wasn't necessary," he whispered, ducking his head and looking down at the floor.

One of the tortoises came crawling by. Eli picked it up and put it in the palm of his hand. The tortoise made a swimming motion with its hind legs. Eli hurriedly put it down and rubbed where the tortoise had scratched him.

"They have sharp nails," I observed as it crawled away. "But then, you already know that, don't you?"

Eli didn't say anything.

"Did you set up the buy?" I asked.

"No. Chapman did that," Eli mumbled. "I should never have brought them back to the apartment. If I hadn't done that, everything would have been all right." He said this earnestly, as if saying it would make it true. "Myra was here when I took them out of the suitcase. She'd come over to tell me how pissed she was about all the money she'd wasted on the frogs." He took a deep breath. "I thought she believed me when I told her the tortoises were from the Southwest. I did," he repeated as if I doubted his word. "I didn't think she knew enough to know what they were."

He drew his upper lip down with his teeth and nibbled

on it. "Actually, I don't think she did know," Eli reflected. "I think what happened was, she went home and checked them out in one of her books." He paused again as another thought struck him. "I should have given her the money she asked for, for the frogs. If I'd done that, none of this would have happened, because she never would have come up here." He nibbled on the bottom of his lip. "What pisses me off the most is I think she stole some money from me on top of everything else. I had five hundred dollars in my wallet. And it was gone when she left. All she wanted was three hundred bucks. Why did I have to be so cheap?"

"What does this have to do with anything?" I asked, trying to move the story along.

"I thought you were supposed to be smart," Adelina said to me.

"Obviously not."

"She went and told me," Adelina answered. "And I told Nestor."

"He didn't know what they were before you told him?" I asked.

"Nestor wouldn't have known an asp from an anaconda," Eli observed.

Adelina brought the palms of her hands together and raised them to her lips. "I don't know what I was thinking of, telling him. With all the crazy ideas he had."

Eli leaned forward. "Nestor came to me. He told me he had this foolproof scheme to get the tortoises away from Chapman, without him knowing what was going on. The way he explained it to me, I thought it would work."

I looked from Eli to Adelina and back again. "Let me get this straight. You're telling me that the suitcase was never stolen?" My voice started to rise as I understood the full import of what Eli and Adelina were saying. "That this whole thing was a scam?"

Eli mumbled something and slowly nodded, almost as if he was doing it against his will.

I opened my mouth and closed it again. I didn't know what to say. I couldn't have said anything even if I'd wanted to. I was too angry to talk.

Manuel didn't have that problem.

He sprang away from the corner he'd been leaning against. "You're kidding me, right?" He glared at Eli. "Right? Answer me, you piece of shit."

Eli avoided his gaze, looking everywhere else but at his cousin.

Manuel strode toward him. His jaw was out and his fists were clenched. "I'm going to kill you myself, you little fat fuck."

Eli stood up, trying to get away, but he wasn't fast enough. Manuel buried his fist in Eli's soft, white belly.

Eli doubled over. "Please," he whimpered.

"Fuck you," Manuel said and punched him again.

Eli gagged and went down on all fours. A line of drool snaked its way out of his mouth and onto the floor.

"Do something!" Adelina screamed.

Much as I didn't want to, I grabbed hold of Manuel's shoulder. "That's enough," I told him.

He whirled around. "No, it's not!" he shouted, spraying spittle in my face. "I'm going to beat the crap out of him."

Manuel and I were standing nose-to-nose. Out of the corner of my eye I could see Eli crawling in back of me.

"Take it down a few notches," I ordered, enunciating each word slowly and distinctly. The last thing I needed on top of everything else was to have to take Eli to the ER room.

"He deserves it," Manuel said.

"I agree. You can beat him up later. In fact, I might even help you."

"You wouldn't do that," Eli cried as he scrambled up onto the sofa.

"Shut up," I told him. "You deserve whatever you have coming to you."

Eli gasped.

I kept my eyes on Manuel. His breath was hot on my face. A car honked outside. Finally he took a couple of steps back and turned to Eli.

"You lied to me," he said to him, his face contorted with hurt. "You straight out lied. You used me. You dragged my friends into your mess."

Eli wiped his mouth with the tips of his fingers. "I tried to tell you I didn't need you to help me, but you didn't listen. You never listen to what anyone says."

"What the hell was I supposed to do?" Manuel took a step forward, turned, then took another step back. "What was I supposed to do?" he asked rhetorically. "I hear you carrying on. You come up with this story. What was I supposed to do? Ignore it. You're family. How was I supposed to know you were trying out for the Academy Awards?"

"I want you to know . . ." Eli began, but Manuel cut him off.

"I could have been out dancin' tonight instead of running all over the city chasin' your sorry ass down." Manuel pointed a finger at Eli. "Don't you be asking me for nothing after this. We are quits. Quits." And Manuel stalked back over to where he'd been standing and leaned against the wall.

A few seconds later, he whirled around, brought his foot up, and kicked it. The plasterboard cracked. A hole appeared. "Asshole," he muttered. "Fucking asshole." He kicked the wall again.

"Manuel, that's enough," I said.

By way of an answer, Manuel kicked the wall for the fourth time, then walked away a little ways. No one spoke. Adelina looked shaken. Eli was studying the window blinds. I waited a few seconds to see if there were going to be any more outbursts from Manuel before continuing.

"All right," I said when no more were forthcoming. "Let's get back to where we were. Eli, if I understand you, the total sum of your plan was to tell Chapman that Nestor had stolen the suitcase and assume that he'd write it off?"

"Yes," Eli whispered.

"How could you have been so stupid?" In a way, the sheer imbecility of the plan offended me more than anything else.

Eli looked down at his hands.

"What did you expect Chapman to do?" I continued. "Say, Oh, well. Too bad. I guess I'll call my insurance agent."

"He didn't seem like such a bad guy in the beginning," Eli mumbled. "I didn't think he'd get so upset. I thought he'd just get mad at Nestor, not at me."

"Which presumably wouldn't matter, because he wouldn't be able to find him."

Eli nodded.

Manuel was right, I decided. He was smarter than Eli. "What about Chapman's putting you in prison, or was that just a made-up story too?"

Eli studied a spot on the wall. "Nestor said he wouldn't arrest me. That it wasn't worth Chapman's effort, because I'd get a suspended sentence. He said I was worth more to Chapman out of jail than in it." He recited the sentences, as if he had memorized them a while ago and trotted them out whenever he needed reassurance.

"What did Nestor say about Chapman's threats?"

"He said he was using psychological warfare and that he really wouldn't do anything."

I remembered the beads of sweat on Eli's lip. "But you weren't sure, were you?"

"No," Eli muttered.

"Did you think he'd hurt me?"

"I wanted to tell you," Eli stammered, "but Nestor was afraid that if we did, you'd be so angry you might go to Chapman."

"Nestor thought we could pull it off," Adelina added. "He said that if Chapman couldn't find us, eventually he'd calm down."

"Except that Nestor is dead and your friend here"—I indicated Eli—"is being sought by the police for questioning regarding Nestor's death."

Chapter
27

I studied Eli and Adelina for a moment. They looked as tired as I felt. Even the air in the room smelled tired. I got up and opened one of the windows a crack, then sat back down. It helped a little, but not much.

Eli hung his head and contemplated his hands. "If I had known Nestor would end up dead, I never would have gotten into this. I feel awful," he said again.

"Under the circumstances, I don't think that's nearly enough."

"I know." Eli began kneading one hand with the other.

I massaged the back of my neck to relieve some of the tension in it. It didn't help. My muscles felt like rocks. "Where were you going to sell them?"

"We had a buyer in New York. Down in Chinatown. One of Nestor's cousins. He was going to sell them in Germany and Japan."

"Didn't you think Chapman was going to hear from his

sources that people had bought them and trace them back to you?"

"No, I didn't. Nestor's cousin is in one of the Tongs. They're very secretive. They have connections all over the world."

I shifted my position. My legs were stiffening up. "I think you might have been underestimating Chapman. He has a large network available to him, too."

Eli nervously pinched at the roll of fat around his middle. "Even so. Nestor was doing the selling, so he was taking most of the risk."

"Is that what he told you? Because I think he lied," I informed Eli. "According to the way Chapman looked at it, you were the responsible party."

Eli licked his lips. "Do you think he knew I was lying?"

I shrugged my shoulders. "I'll ask him when I see him." And I changed the subject. "Why did you ask me to meet you at that house?"

"That was Nestor's idea, too." Eli's glasses had slipped down the bridge of his nose. He moved them back up.

"It seems as if everything was Nestor's idea and you just went along for the ride," I couldn't resist pointing out.

"It *was* all Nestor's idea," Eli told me, relieved at finally being able to pass the blame for this mess on to someone else. "All of it."

"Which is why he deserved to die?"

"I never said that," Eli cried. He looked contrite, but Eli's looks meant as much as a fake ID. "Really," Eli said. "I mean it. I'm sorry he's dead. I didn't know that would happen."

Manuel snorted and turned away.

I stood up. "I'm sure that's going to be a great consolation to Nestor's parents."

Eli gulped.

"What do you think they are going to feel like when they find out? What would your parents feel like?" I pointed to Adelina. "Or yours?"

Adelina and Eli both studied the material on the sofa. Adelina pulled at a stray piece of thread that was sticking out of one of the seams.

Looking at them made me angry enough to spit. "What a stupid way to die." As if, I thought, there was a good way.

For a moment everyone was silent. The only sounds in the house were the scritch scratch of the tortoises' claws on the floor. Somewhere off in the distance a dog was barking. I took a big breath and got myself under control.

"Tell me about the house," I ordered, changing the subject.

Eli fiddled with his glasses for another few seconds before answering. "By that time Nestor was getting nervous. We were going to give you a couple of the tortoises to give to Chapman and tell you that the rest had died. We were hoping that would buy him off. That he would figure that twenty thousand dollars was better than nothing."

"I was going to deliver them," Adelina told me, taking up the narrative. "Nestor was coming straight from work and he didn't want to leave them in the trunk of his car. Too cold. Tortoises don't like the cold. Especially these ones." Adelina paused for a second. "Only the fan belt on my car went. Which meant the car wouldn't move. So I phoned Eli and he came over."

"And put on an Academy Award performance for me."

Eli gulped. "I called Adelina when I couldn't find Nestor and asked what I should do. She told me I should give you the tortoises, but I didn't want to do that."

"Why not?"

"Because you'd know what a big liar I was and you'd tell Manuel and he'd tell his mother and she'd tell mine."

"It's nice to know you still have a slight sense of shame," I observed.

Embarrassed, Eli picked up a piece of lint on his pants and flicked it away.

I pressed him. "Then how come you came in?"

"I called Adelina back and she told me I had to. I was going to." He gave Adelina a beseeching glance. She examined a scratch on her bracelet. Eli looked back at me. "But when I saw you looking at me, I knew I was wrong." He hung his head. "I knew I'd made a big mistake." He shuddered. "And Nestor. Lying there like that. The gun. Saying those things. Nothing was right. I couldn't breathe. I had to get out of there."

"Who lit the candles?" I asked.

"Nestor did," Eli said.

"Why?"

Adelina sat up straighter. She gently touched one of her gold hoops, as if to make sure they were still there. "He thought it gave the place more atmosphere."

"Very romantic." I thought about how much I wanted something to eat. Something chocolate. Something chocolate with almonds.

"That wasn't the point," Adelina said. "It was supposed to have made it harder for you to follow him."

"How?"

Adelina looked peeved. "How the fuck should I know? He read it in some stupid book. He was always reading these stupid spy books. He thought that made him so smart. All it did was give him these crazy ideas. People shouldn't be allowed to buy stuff like that. It makes them think about things they've never thought about. If I were in charge, I'd make that kind of stuff illegal and jail the people that wrote it."

"I'm glad to know where you stand on First Amendment rights, but can we get back to the matter at hand?"

"I mean it," Adelina said. "If it weren't for those books—"

I interrupted. "Can we get back to Nestor?" I repeated. "Was he staying with you, too?"

"No. He was staying with a cousin of his out in Mattydale. He was washing dishes in his restaurant and sleeping in the basement of his house."

I studied her face. "Are you sure you didn't kill Nestor?" I asked.

"Me," she cried. She flushed. "Of course not. Why would I do that?"

"The question is, why wouldn't you?"

She crossed her arms over her chest and gave me a defiant look. "You can't prove that I had anything to do with that."

"I'm not so sure." I took a guess. "What about this gun, for instance?" I indicated the 9mm I'd taken away from her at her house.

Adelina patted her necklace and sat up straighter. She was trying to give the impression she had nothing to hide, but she wasn't succeeding very well. "What do you mean?"

"I mean, if the forensics unit does a ballistic test, will they find that the shell that killed Nestor was fired from this barrel?"

She gave an unconvincing little laugh. "How would I know?"

I smiled. "You're right. But I feel certain the police will. I'm sure they're going to want to talk to you." My eyes rested on Eli. "And him, too. I think it's time I called them."

"But I didn't have anything to do with Nestor's death," Eli protested. "I swear."

"After what you've been doing, you expect me to believe you?"

"But it's the truth," Eli insisted.

"A much abused commodity around here," I observed.

"The police are never going to believe me," Eli said.

"Quite possibly," I told him unkindly.

"I've made such a mess of things. Such an incredible mess." Then he buried his face in his hands and began to cry.

"Give me your cell phone," I said to Manuel, trying to ignore Eli's weeping.

He handed it to me.

I touched the top button of my shirt. "Manuel," I said.

He gave me a vacant look.

"Remember. We agreed."

"On what?"

"You're going."

"Oh, yeah." He scratched his sideburn. "I decided I'd rather stay."

"What about your mother?"

He made a dismissive gesture with his hand.

"Who are you calling?" Adelina demanded as I powered up.

"I already told you. The police."

Eli's sobbing filled the background. He was rocking back and forth. "I'm so sorry, so sorry," he kept on repeating over and over and over again.

It was an appalling display. Sometimes there's such a thing as being too in touch with your emotions.

Adelina put her hand out to stop me. "Don't," she said. "Please."

I waited.

"Sulfin is the one you want."

I snorted and resumed dialing. "You hate Sulfin and Sulfin hates you."

"You have to listen," Adelina pleaded. "Sulfin and I had a deal going and Nestor found out."

"You were going back to Sulfin?" My voice crackled with disbelief.

Manuel turned. "Get out of here," he told Adelina.

She looked at Manuel and then at me and nodded.

Eli lifted his head up and stared at her. His eyes were swollen from weeping. His complexion was mottled. She avoided his gaze.

"And you were going to bring the tortoises with you?" I asked.

She swallowed. Then she nodded again.

Eli sniffed. "You were going to do that to me?"

Adelina didn't reply.

"But I thought you liked me," he wailed. "I thought we were friends." He sounded so stricken I had to look away.

"We are," Adelina assured him.

I wondered what Adelina's definition of friendship was as Eli spoke. "Then why'd you do it?" he demanded, curling his hands into fists. "Why?"

"Some things are more important." Adelina pressed her lips together into a thin line and narrowed her eyes. "I needed the money. I started thinking about it when Nestor wanted to give you two of the tortoises to take to Chapman." She lifted her head up. "Eighty thousand dollars is good, but one hundred thousand dollars is better."

"Especially if you split it two ways instead of three," I observed. "Eighty thousand dollars, split three ways or one hundred thousand split two. I can see your point."

Adelina's nostrils flared. "Fifty thousand dollars is enough to give my mother a little peace of mind, a little breathing space. She deserves it. She's had a tough life."

"Don't blame this on her," I told Adelina. "Lots of other people are having a tough time, too, and you don't see them doing what you are. Does your mother even know about this?"

Adelina studied the ceiling.

"I thought not. From the little I've seen of her, I don't think she's going to like it very much, either."

Eli wiped his nose with the back of his arm. "Why didn't you take the tortoises and go to Sulfin's if that's the case?" he demanded. "Why are you here now with me?"

"I'm here," Adelina said, "because I didn't like what he did to Nestor."

"And what exactly was that?" I asked.

"You were right. That is the gun that Sulfin used to shoot Nestor with." She pointed to the automatic I was holding. "I was there. I saw it happen. I arranged everything. I should have left it all alone. I didn't mean for him to die. I didn't. It was an accident." And she started sobbing, too.

"Stop it," I said.

While Adelina was sniveling, Eli took the opportunity to run for the door.

Chapter
28

"Don't!" I yelled.

Eli ignored me and kept going.

"I'll shoot," I warned.

Eli was almost at the front door when I fired a shot into the floor. The noise wasn't loud, but it was loud enough to get Eli's attention.

He froze.

"Get back here."

Manuel sniggered as Eli pivoted and walked toward me.

"Can't do anything right, can you, dipstick?" Manuel sneered.

Eli ignored him. His hand went up and fixed his glasses. His lower lip was trembling. "I don't know what I was thinking," he said to me.

It took every ounce of self-control I possessed not to smash him in the face with the butt of my gun. Instead, I told Eli to get back on the sofa.

"I think I panicked," he told me as he edged around me.

"Shut up, Eli. I don't care."

"I . . ."

"Shut the fuck up!" I screamed.

His eyes widened.

"Next time you do something like that, I swear I'll shoot you," I said as I gave the gun to Manuel.

"You wouldn't," Eli stammered.

"Why not?" I told him. "What's another dead kid? Keep an eye on them," I said to Manuel.

He watched me with surprised eyes as I stalked into the kitchen. I needed to call George, but first I needed to calm down and get myself under control. I filled a glass of water and gulped it down. I refilled it and drank the next one more slowly. Sipping it, I thought about how at one time in my life I couldn't have understood how someone could have beaten the crap out of someone and about how now I could. This was not progress, I decided as I dialed George's number. He picked up on the second ring.

"I'm thinking about Belize," I told him in a tone I normally reserved for talking about sex.

"Good. Because my cousin called. We're on."

"Tell me about it," I implored.

"I'll tell you that if we don't get this Chapman thing squared away, you might not be going anywhere."

"What do you mean?" I put the glass down on the kitchen table and wiped my lips off with the back of my hand.

"Mike called. Chapman is downtown, talking about swearing a warrant out for your arrest."

I cursed under my breath. "For what?"

"I don't know exactly. Something about having something in the store that you shouldn't. Do you?"

"No. But I bet that bastard's going to put something

there. Probably tonight when the store is closed." God only knows it would be easy enough to jimmy open the door and leave something behind. I closed my eyes. I felt a pain in my gut. This was Chapman's way of letting me know what he was going to do if I didn't do what he asked.

"Wouldn't you notice?"

"Not if I weren't looking for it. Some of the CITES stuff . . . well, you wouldn't know what is was if you weren't looking for it . . . but Tim's good. He'll be able to pick it out."

"Where the hell are you anyway?"

"At Eli's."

"You've got to start checking your answering machine," George complained. "I've been leaving messages on it for the last hour and a half. Did you get the tortoises?"

"I have eight. I have to get two more."

"Where are they?"

"One is at Sulfin's. The other is at Littlebaum's." I opened my eyes and reached for the package of matches sitting near the stove and started lighting them one after another. "I have to go get them."

"And then what?"

"Then I call Chapman. I'm going to crucify the son of a bitch."

"Robin, what are you going to do?"

"I don't know yet. When I do I'll let you know." And I hung up.

There were only two things I was certain of: One, I wasn't going to let Chapman get those tortoises, and two, I wasn't going to let Chapman ruin my life. I lit a few more matches and watched the arc of their flames as I flicked them into the sink. By now the kitchen was beginning to smell of sulfa, a smell I liked. I pondered over what that said about me as I called Tim.

"Yeah?" he said in a voice that was sodden with sleep.

"It's Robin."

There was a short pause, then he said, "Do you know what time it is?"

Why did people always say that when you woke them up? I wondered. Would it be better to wake them up if you didn't know the time?

"Sorry. I have a favor to ask."

Tim coughed, but didn't say anything. I heard the bed creak and bed sheets rustle. He must be sitting up.

"It's important. Please."

"What do you want?" Tim finally asked.

"I want you to get dressed and go down to the store and go through our stock and see if you can find anything that needs a CITES certificate."

"Have you started doing drugs again?"

"Chapman is setting up a raid on our store. He's planting some stuff there."

"Like what?"

"That's the problem. I don't know."

"Jesus." Tim groaned. The sheets rustled again. I wondered if anyone else was there. "How do you know this?"

"George told me. So will you?" I asked after another interval of silence had gone by.

"I told you not to get involved in this." I swear, sometimes Tim reminded me of my mother.

"And you were right." I lit another match and watched it burn until the flame was almost down to my fingertips before I blew it out. "You're always right. Now will you go?"

"If I find anything, what do you want me to do with it?"

"Take it to Eli's house and leave it in the living room. I'll leave the key in the mailbox for you."

"You should be glad you have me working for you," Tim said.

"I am," I told him, but he'd already hung up.

As I replaced the receiver, I contemplated what I was going to do with Adelina and Eli. Ordinarily I would have called the police and let them sort everything out, but I didn't want to do that before I got the tortoise from Sulfin, which was why I'd marched Eli and Adelina and Manuel down to my cab.

I would have preferred to drive over to Sulfin's apartment by myself, but that wasn't feasible. I had to take everyone with me. I couldn't leave Adelina and Eli in the flat and expect to find them there when I returned. And I couldn't leave Manuel behind to guard them because I was afraid he would beat up Eli. Anyway, I was thinking it would be interesting to hear what Adelina and Sulfin had to say to each other.

We were cutting across Teall when Adelina leaned forward and tapped me on the shoulder. "You're not taking us downtown?"

I stopped for a red light. "Don't worry. You're going, but we have a couple of stops to make first."

Manuel leaned his head against the front seat, and closed his eyes. "These seats are really uncomfortable, Robin. You know that? I think you got a broken spring."

I ignored him and turned my head slightly toward the back. "We're going to Sulfin's to pick up the tortoise."

"He's probably sold him," Adelina said.

"I hope for your sake he hasn't," I replied as I turned onto Burnett.

Adelina compressed her lips and sat back.

It turned out Sulfin kept two places, the one where he

lived and the one where he bred his rats. One was conveniently located next to the other.

About five minutes later, Adelina leaned forward and tapped my shoulder again.

"Yes?" I said.

"Sulfin's going to lie," she informed me. "He's going to say he didn't have anything to do with this, but don't believe him because he has."

Manuel snorted. "But you, of course, are telling the truth."

"Keep out of this," Adelina snapped at him. "I ain't asked your opinion."

Manuel twisted around in his seat to face her. "Well, I'm giving it. You know, girl, you should keep your mouth shut. Everything you touch turns to shit."

Adelina put on a hurt face. "You got no cause to say that."

"I got every cause. You fucked up my cousin. That gives me every right. Look at him."

I could see Eli in the rearview mirror. He was hiccuping and quietly crying at the same time.

"He was fine until you got to know him," Manuel continued. "Now he's a mess."

"What do you care?" Adelina taunted. "Given what you said to him."

We came to a stoplight. I told everyone to shut up.

Manuel turned back around and faced front. "Well, I'm only telling it like it is," he replied. "She fucks over everyone she meets. Eli, Sulfin, Nestor. Man, I'm surprised . . ."

"Don't go any further," I ordered, cutting him off.

Manuel shut up, but a few minutes later, he and Adelina started in again. By the time I parked the cab, I was deeply regretting having done this. Unfortunately, the evening's fun really began when we got inside Sulfin's apartment.

His apartment building hadn't gotten any better since the last time I'd been here. It was still a wreck of a place, a large asphalt-shingled house that had been subdivided into several apartments. Sulfin's was number two. The place where he bred his rats was number three. We walked up a narrow set of worn down steps to the first landing. I told Adelina to knock on Sulfin's door. When he opened it, Adelina and I stepped inside. Manuel and Eli reluctantly followed.

"We're here to clarify a few things," I said to Sulfin, who was dressed in jeans and a tight T-shirt that made his head look even larger and his chest punier.

He looked at all of us. "At this time of night?"

"Why not? Are we disturbing you?"

"No. I was just watching TV." And he indicated the set, which was on.

"How come you're up?" I inquired.

He shrugged. "I don't go to sleep until late. I never have. I like the night better than the day. Not that it's any of your business."

"So ratboy is a vampire," Manuel commented to no one in particular.

"Shut up," Sulfin told him. "At least I've got me some plans, which is a hell of a lot more than I can say for you."

"I got plans," Manuel shot back.

"Like what?" Sulfin demanded.

"Like going to OCC, right, Robin. Right, Robin," Manuel repeated when I didn't immediately reply.

"Of course," I replied absentmindedly as I glanced around the apartment. "Absolutely."

Sulfin's place was small and somewhat messy, but it

appeared rodent free. It also looked as if someone had run amok with paint samples. In the living room someone had painted two walls pale orange and the other two bright green. The ceiling was yellow. None of the colors went with the purple cloths draped over the love seat and sofa. The red rug, one of those cheap ones you get from a roadside stand, with a picture of the pyramids embossed on it, added another pleasing touch. The effect was enough to make me seasick.

"Interesting decor," I commented as I walked over to the coffee table. It was covered with parts of a model airplane, a couple of knives, and a tube of cement.

"Thanks. I like it."

I picked up a gray plastic wing.

"I'd appreciate if you didn't touch that," Sulfin said, and took it out of my hand. "It's delicate."

The model box had a picture of a World War II German Messerschmitt on it.

"Where's Barnaby?" I asked.

"Sleeping in his cage. Now what do you want? I want to get back to my program."

"I want the tortoise for openers."

Sulfin put his hands on his hips. "I bought him."

"Then I guess you made a bad purchase."

"You can't take him from me."

I laughed. "Of course I can. You shouldn't have him in the first place. Now where is he?"

Sulfin folded his arms across his chest and planted his feet on the floor.

"Come on. Make this easier. It's not as if I'm not going to find it."

"It's not here."

"I think it is."

Sulfin remained silent.

"Manuel, go see," I ordered.

He straightened up. "Why me?" he whined. Then he took a look at my expression and left.

Sulfin's mouth looked like a prune as he watched Manuel leave. "I want my money back," he told Adelina.

"Talk to her," Adelina said, indicating me with a toss of her head.

"Don't bother asking, because it's gone," I informed him.

"That's not right," Sulfin protested.

"Neither are a lot of other things," I said, thinking of Nestor. I was about to say something else when Manuel returned. He was carrying the tortoise in his hand. It was a little larger than his palm. The starburst pattern of its shell was lost in the room's bright colors.

"Where was it?" I asked him.

"In a box in Sulfin's bedroom. Now what?"

"Call George and tell him to pick you up and drive you back to Eli's. I want you to leave the tortoise there."

Manuel grimaced.

"And be sure and wrap the tortoise up in something before you take it out—I don't want it getting cold."

"Anything else?" he asked sarcastically.

"Yes. You can hand me the phone when you're done."

While Manuel spoke to George, I watched Adelina, Sulfin, and Eli. They were all glowering at each other. Their brief partnership had dissolved like sugar in hot water. Now all they wanted to do was save themselves.

Chapter 29

It took George ten minutes to drive over to Sulfin's. During that time the silence in the room was broken only by the sound of the TV. We all kept our eyes fixed on the screen. The air was thick with unspoken recriminations. No one said anything. We were all too tired. Everyone looked up when George walked through the door.

"So, this is what the fuss is about," he said, taking in the tortoise in Manuel's hand. "I mean, it's pretty. But ten thousand dollars?" He shook his head. "I don't know."

"There are probably no more than two thousand of these species left in the wild. For all practical purposes, it's a museum piece already." I shrugged. "It's all about supply and demand."

"What isn't?" George gestured to Adelina, Manuel, and Eli. "What are you going to do with them?"

"As soon as I hear from Tim, I'm going to take them downtown." Eli opened his mouth and I told him to close it. "Tim just got to the store," I continued. "Hopefully, it won't take him long to find what Chapman left."

"All right, then." George gave me a peck on the cheek. Then he and Manuel left.

I suppressed a shiver as the door closed. I didn't know whether I was cold because it was cold in here or because I was tired and hungry.

"So, we just have to sit here and wait," Sulfin complained, having suddenly become reenergized.

"That's right." I massaged my wrist and leaned against the wall. I hoped Tim would call soon. I was so tired my teeth were hurting. And the colors in this room weren't helping things. The red rug and the acid-green walls pulled at my nerves.

"Why?" Sulfin demanded. His eyes had sunk further into his head. They looked like two raisins that had been left in the oven for too long. "Why take us downtown? You have what you want. Let us leave."

"There's the slight matter of Nestor," I reminded him.

"I didn't have anything to do with that," Sulfin retorted. "It's not my problem."

"You're wrong," I answered, trying to work the kink out of my neck, tilting my head first to the right and then to the left. "Someone is dead. That's everyone's problem."

"Not mine," Sulfin insisted.

"You're a liar," Adelina told him, her face flushed.

"And you're crazy."

Adelina pointed to me. "She has the gun. Now what do you have to say?"

"What gun?" Sulfin asked, feigning ignorance. "I don't know what the hell you're talking about."

"She's talking about this." I took the 9mm out from my pocket, and showed it to him.

Sulfin barely glanced at it. "Get real," he sneered. "I wouldn't kill anyone—not even Nestor. Not that that two-bit piece of shit didn't deserve it. She just wants to get me in trouble because I dumped her." He grinned. "What's that line about don't dump your lady, 'cause they'll come back and do you? Well, she wants to do me good."

Adelina walked over to where he was standing. "No, Rat-boy," she spat. "Remember. I dumped you."

He wiggled his tongue inside his mouth. "You couldn't get enough of me."

Adelina put her hands on her hips and thrust out her breasts. "You're a freak! I just slept with you because I felt sorry for you and I thought you needed something in your life for a little while besides those disgusting rodents of yours."

Sulfin took a step toward her. "That's a lie and you know it."

I showed them the gun. "Enough."

Sulfin bounced up and down on the balls of his feet. "All you got is talk."

Adelina pointed to the automatic in my hand. "You gave that to me, remember? You told me to keep it safe."

Sulfin looked incredulous. He turned to me and indicated Adelina. "She's lying, just like she always does. I don't think I've ever heard the truth passing through those lips."

"It's passing through now. Eli and me, you'd better believe we're not getting stuck for something you did."

Eli cringed at being pointed out.

"I didn't do anything," Sulfin reiterated. "I don't have a clue what you're talking about."

"You certainly do, you fucking liar."

I turned to Adelina. "One question. Did you actually see him shoot Nestor?"

"No."

"Then you don't know that he did."

"He told me." She jabbed her finger in my face. "Why would he tell me if he didn't?"

I turned to Sulfin.

"The bitch got wax in her ears. She should go to the doctor's and get it cleaned out. Look around, you'll see I ain't got nuthin' to hide."

"That's a good idea," I said. "I think I will."

"What?" Sulfin squawked.

"Look around your apartment. Let's go. All of you." I didn't expect to find anything, but at least it would give me something to do while I waited for Tim to call.

"Why do we have to go?" Eli protested. It was the first time I'd heard him open his mouth since we'd left the house.

"So I can keep an eye on you." And I herded them in front of me.

I wandered into the kitchen first. There was nothing much of interest in the room, unless you liked dirty dishes, evaporated milk, Golden Grahams cereal, and macaroni and cheese.

"This is disgusting," Adelina said to no one in particular.

I hustled them out and tried the bathroom next. It was hot pink, not a color I would have chosen, but at least the walls were painted one color. I kept one eye on the three of them as I opened the medicine cabinet door.

"Hey, you're invading my privacy," Sulfin complained.

"Too bad," I told him as I scanned the contents. Plenty of sunscreen, which, given Sulfin's pallor, made sense, a vial of medicine for seasickness, iodine, which was unusual until I remembered you could dilute it and use it to treat infections from rodents, and a can of shaving gel and a razor blade. In short, nothing.

We tried the bedrooms next. The first one was almost austere. The walls were white. It was furnished with a twin bed and a desk. A water bowl, a food dish, and a heat lamp were arrayed against the far wall. A half-fixed-up aquarium sat in the middle of the floor.

"I was going to put Zeus in that," Sulfin explained, looking genuinely sad. "It would have been nice."

Somehow I didn't feel sorry for him.

I motioned everyone to go on to the next room. I caught my breath when I saw what was inside. I could have been in Vegas. The focal point of the room was a king-size, canopied, four-poster bed. The sheets were black satin, the blanket was some sort of white, shaggy, fake fur. The walls were a deep red. The ceiling was mirrored. I've never been in a bordello, but this is how I imagined one would look. It was amazing, but Manuel had been right about Sulfin after all. Either that, or the guy had an incredibly active fantasy life.

Eli's jaw had gone slack when he caught the view. He kept looking around, taking everything in. Adelina's face, on the other hand, showed no expression, but then, why should it? She'd been here before. The thought of her and Sulfin together in this room was enough to make me shudder. Maybe there was something to be said for good taste.

"Now that you've had the tour, can we go?" Sulfin said, hands on hips. I watched as he stalked over to his closet and threw the door open. "See," he said. "Nothing there. Or here, either," he continued, striding over to his dresser.

He was about to open one of the drawers when Adelina pointed to something small and silver, sitting next to a box of cookies. "What's that?" she demanded.

"Nothing." Sulfin's smile flickered along the edges of his mouth and went out. "Nothing." He picked it up, but before he could get it in his pocket, Adelina had swooped down and pried it out of his hand.

It was a silver, monogrammed lighter.

Adelina held it up. "This was Nestor's. You have Nestor's lighter. I can't believe you took Nestor's lighter."

Sulfin planted his feet apart and folded his arms across his chest. "He gave it to me."

"He'd never give it to you," Adelina answered, her face swollen with emotion. "He hated you. His father gave it to him. That's why he had his initials engraved on it. So he wouldn't lose it. You shot him and you took his lighter. Like a trophy. Like he was some sort of animal."

"I wouldn't do anything that dumb. He gave it to me," Sulfin insisted. "And you can't prove otherwise." He smiled. "You're going away for his murder. For a long, long time," he added maliciously. "By the time you get out, you're going to be old and fat and no one will look at you."

"You fuckin' faggot!" Adelina screamed, attacking him with her nails.

Sulfin tried to punch her and missed, his blow glancing off her cheek.

"Stop it!" I yelled as Adelina picked up a lamp off the dresser and threw it at Sulfin. He ducked and it crashed against the wall, missing Eli by inches.

Sulfin tackled her and threw Adelina to the ground. She grabbed his hair and pulled. He screamed as she came away with a handful. As she brought her hand toward his eyes, he grabbed it and bit down as hard as he could. She shrieked and punched him in the face with her free hand. He let go.

I grabbed the back of Adelina's shirt and pulled. The

material stretched. For a second, I thought it was going to tear. She whirled around and scratched me. I slapped her across the face as hard as I could. My hand stung. She gasped. A line of blood snaked down her nose. She let out a roar and charged me. I sidestepped. She crashed into the side of the bed. I was on her. I reached around from the back and pinned her arms to her sides.

"Goddamn it," I cursed as she kicked at my ankles. "Calm down."

"Let me go."

"No." I gritted my teeth. I was dragging her out of the room when Sulfin got up and kicked her in the belly. She fell against me and I tottered and went over, too, hitting my head on the side of the dresser. Adelina tried to get up. I grabbed for her foot. She kicked my hand loose and then aimed a kick at my ribs. I rolled to avoid it and reached for my gun, but it wasn't there.

The next thing I knew I heard a shot.

I looked up. Sulfin had my gun.

"Give me the money," he said to me.

I got up. My ankles hurt. So did my wrists. I'd had it. "It's in my backpack. Go get it."

"If you think you're taking all the money, you're out of your mind!" Adelina screamed. "It's mine. I worked for it. It's mine."

"Shut up, Adelina," I cried. Sulfin's hand was trembling. I watched his finger.

"Don't," I told him. "Take the money and go."

He was breathing hard.

"Please," I pleaded.

He opened his mouth to say something when we heard a crash, followed by—"Police."

Sulfin dropped the gun and ran for the window.

Chapter 30

It was a raw, overcast day, the kind of day that makes you want to stay inside and feed logs to the fire. The temperature was hovering in the low thirties as I pulled into the store's parking lot. The sky was a mottled dark gray. An icy drizzle was falling. The few people out on the street walked hurriedly, hunched over, anxious to get where they were going. Even the crows and the pigeons were huddling under cover. But I wasn't complaining. I was just happy to be out of the Public Safety Building. This was the second time in less than two weeks I'd been in that place. It was getting to be a habit I'd prefer not to cultivate.

The aroma of the store, a combination of cedar shavings, hay, and brine shrimp, washed over me when I opened the door to Noah's Ark. I smiled and took a deep breath, chasing the last bit of the air from the PSB out of my lungs. Tim nodded when he saw me. He had a cup of coffee in one hand and a Pop Tart in the other. He also had large dark circles under his eyes from having been up all night. His lips were chapped, something that always happened when he didn't have enough sleep.

"Any luck?" I asked as I walked toward him.

He shook his head and took a gulp of coffee. As he did, I noticed that faint stubble was growing on his skull. I hoped that meant he was going to let his hair grow in. I liked it better that way.

"If Chapman put something here, I can't find it. Are you sure about this?"

I repeated what George had overheard.

"That could mean anything," Tim pointed out.

I rubbed my eyes.

"Here." Tim pushed the box of Pop-tarts toward me. "Have one. You look as if you can use something to eat."

"Thanks." I ripped the foil covering open with my teeth and took the pastry out. "Strawberry," I said, looking at the light pink icing. I took a bite. It was so sweet it made my teeth ache. I was so hungry I wolfed it down anyway.

"Take this, too." He indicated his coffee. "I'll pour myself another one."

I accepted the offer gratefully. I'd had a couple of cups since I'd gotten out of the PSB, but I'd need a lot more to get me up to speed. A moment later, Tim returned from the back room, new mug in hand.

"It didn't even look as if anyone was here," he informed me. "Everything was exactly the way I left it."

I took a sip of lukewarm coffee. I still thought I was right. Chapman had put something here. If Tim hadn't found it, that didn't mean it wasn't here. It just meant it was something unexpected. But what? Livestock was hard to hide, so it had to be something else, something small, something that was worth a lot of money, something like vials of pow-

dered black rhino horn or tiger bones. Said to promote
male potency, sold by Chinese herbalists, there was a big
market for stuff like that down in Chinatown. The glass vials
the powders came in were usually about eight inches long
and no more than an inch around. They'd certainly be easy
enough to hide here. Maybe in the ceiling tiles, I mused.
The air vents were another possibility.

"Where were you anyway?" Tim asked, interrupting my
train of thought. "I kept waiting for you to call."

"I couldn't. I was at the Public Safety Building." And I
told him about my evening.

"I was wondering how you got those scratches on your
face."

"And you haven't seen the black-and-blue marks on my
leg." I touched my cheek and chin gingerly, Tim's comment
having brought them to mind. I couldn't believe how much
the scratches still stung.

"Poor Nestor." Tim took another sip of his coffee and
shook his head. "I liked him."

"It seems as if you are one of the few that did."

"He always had plans."

"In this case, it would have been better if he hadn't."

Tim wiped a drip off the rim of the mug. "So what's going
to happen? Is Sulfin being charged?"

"Who knows? No one has told me anything. And, believe
me, they won't. I'll read about it in the newspaper along
with everyone else, unless George's friend tells him and he
tells me."

Tim raised an eyebrow.

I put my cup down. "Listen, I'm just glad I wasn't charged
with anything. I expected Chapman to walk in at any second.
Thank God he didn't. But it wouldn't surprise me if they
do charge Adelina and Sulfin. Let's put it this way. They

released Eli and me. As far as I know, Adelina and Sulfin are still downtown being questioned. You mind?" I asked, pointing to the Pop-tarts.

Tim pushed the box toward me. "Be my guest."

I unwrapped another one and took a bite. A trickle of raspberry jam slid down my chin. I wiped it up with my finger, then licked my finger clean.

"Why did the cops let Eli go?" Tim asked.

"I'd say because Chapman hasn't informed them about the implications of the tortoises. What a surprise." I finished off the Pop-tart, collected the two foil wrappers and threw them in the trash. "I wonder where he's going."

"Chapman?"

I nodded.

"What makes you think he's going anywhere?"

"Because he's just here on some sort of special assignment. According to George, he lives down in Fort Myers. I bet he's going home as soon as he gets the tortoises."

"Why should he do that?"

"Why should he stick around?" I countered. "What's here for him? The beautiful weather?"

Tim grunted.

I realized I was drumming my fingers on the table. I gulped the rest of my coffee down and brought the mug out back. It was time to start looking for whatever Chapman had hidden.

"Where's Eli?" Tim asked as I stood in the middle of the store, thumbs hooked into the loops on the waistband of my jeans, considering where I was going to start my search.

"He's back at George's place." I rocked back and forth on my heels.

"What about the tortoises?"

"They're there, too."

Tim ran his fingers over the top of his skull. "I bet George is pleased."

"Well, I didn't want to leave them at Eli's."

"I can see that. And Manuel?"

I gnawed on my fingernail. "He's at George's, too. Tim, did you go through all the bedding and rocks when you searched?" I asked, changing the subject.

He looked offended. "Of course I did. I went through every single one of the reptile cases, I looked through all the bedding in the rabbits, guinea pig, hamster, and gerbil cages, and I looked in the gravel and moved all the rocks in the aquariums. Let me tell you, there is nothing in any of those things that shouldn't be."

I held up my hands. "Okay. I was just asking."

"Go ahead. Look." Tim gestured around the store with his right hand. "Maybe you'll have better luck than I did."

"I hope so," I replied as I walked to the shelves. Since Tim had gone through the livestock pretty thoroughly, I decided to concentrate on the rest of the stuff.

I began with the shelving. First I took every box of fish food, every can of gerbil treats, every piece of stock in the store off the shelves and put them back on. Nothing. I got down on my hands and knees and eyeballed the floor. I ran my hands underneath the shelves. Still nothing. I got up and went over to the vents in the walls and removed the plates and stuck my hand in them and felt around. The only thing I got for my trouble was a lot of dust.

"Told you," Tim said as I sneezed.

"I know," I said when I'd stopped. "But I have to try." After I replaced the covers, I went out back and brought out the stepladder and checked the light fixture coverings.

"That's taking it a little far, don't you think?" Tim observed as I climbed back down.

"Maybe." Another thought hit me. The window display. Hidden in plain sight. I climbed up and ran my hands through the gravel in the aquarium. I inspected the stacked bags of dog and cat food for holes. They were all sealed.

"You don't even know he's done this," Tim said. "Look at yourself."

I caught a reflection of myself in the mirror. My hair was plastered to my head. My shirt and jeans were covered with dust. I had black smudges on my forehead and nose.

"I don't not know it, either," I told him, and I went in the back and started looking there.

Actually, the back was worse because we had things piled everywhere. I went through the utility closet and the bathroom. I looked in the freezer, where we keep the brine shrimp, and the barrels where we keep the live grasshoppers. I looked in the coffee can and the sugar bowl. I inspected the boxes of deliveries we hadn't gotten around to shelving to see if any of them had been opened. I surveyed the bags of dog food, cat food, and cedar shavings. All of them appeared intact.

Almost two hours had passed since I'd begun and I had nothing to show for my work but a pulled muscle in my shoulder, aching feet, dirty hands, and a runny nose from all the dust. Maybe I was wrong. Maybe George had misunderstood his friend. Or maybe his friend had misunderstood Chapman. Check any or all of the above.

I pulled out the chair from my desk and sat down and watched one of the geckos we let run free to keep the roaches in check wander up the far wall. It occurred to me I kept on saying I hated this store, that it was a pain in the ass, but the truth was, I didn't want to see it go. It'd invested too much of myself in it now. Or if it did go, I wanted to be the one making the choice. I sighed and rolled a pencil around on the desk with the flat of my hand and watched the yellow color go round and round, while I surveyed the top of my desk. It was piled high with bills, brochures, samples, empty soda cans, candy wrappers, and copies of *The New York Times*. You could have buried an elephant in the debris and never found it.

Damn. I leaned back in my chair and contemplated the mess I'd made. Why was I such a slob? I was taking a deep breath and settling myself to get to work when I noticed what I thought was something small and white in the air vent on the far wall. My heartbeat went into overdrive. I got up, walked over, and knelt in front of the vent. It hadn't been a trick of the light. There was something in there all right. I pried the cover off, reached in, and took out what was inside.

"Hey, Tim," I cried. "Come in here. I found it."

Chapter
31

"Those are eggs," Tim said, looking at what I'd found. "Those are eggs stuffed in a shoe bag." He seemed bemused by my find, but then, so was I.

"I know." I continued contemplating them. There were twenty eggs in all. They were linen colored with a light speckling of brown spots, each one individually wrapped in newspaper. It was the white of the paper that I'd spied sitting in my chair. "The question is, what kind."

"I'm guessing not chicken."

"I'm guessing you're right." I started rewrapping the eggs. I was assuming they were viable, so I didn't want them to get chilled. The air vent had been warm enough to work as an incubator. The temperature was chillier in the store.

Tim picked one up and held it to the light. "What are you going to do with them?"

"Take them to George's." He had an electric oven. Set

at 150 degrees, with the door ajar, it could do as a stand-in for an incubator.

Tim handed the egg to me. "He's going to be pleased," Tim observed, crooking one side of his mouth up in a half-smile.

I knew Tim was right. George wouldn't be pleased at all, but there was nothing I could do about it. "They're not going to be there for that long."

"So, what do you think they are?"

"Bird. They're too large to be reptile."

"Maybe a parrot? A hyacinth macaw? Some sort of cock-atoo?"

"Could be." Egg identification was not my specialty.

"But why not just go out and buy a bird?" Tim asked. "You can buy captive-born ones at any store. What's the point?"

"Trophy hunting. Some people like to keep theirs on the wall and others like to keep theirs in cages."

"That sucks."

"Agreed. But most people don't care." And I went outside to warm up the car so that the eggs wouldn't catch a chill. Then I called George and told him I was coming over.

George greeted me at the door. He was wearing a pair of jeans and a red pullover and looked better than I did, having shaved and showered and changed his clothes since he'd picked up me and Eli at the Public Safety Building earlier this morning.

"So these are them?" He pointed to the shopping bag. "This is what Chapman hid?"

"You got it," I said, stepping inside.

"Eggs?" George's voice rose in disbelief.

"Eggs that are probably worth ten to twenty thousand."

"That much? How do you figure that?"

"Because any less and it wouldn't be worth Chapman's while to set me up."

George meditatively rubbed his chest with his right hand. His face looked like a judge's—a judge I wouldn't want to be standing in front of. "Believe me," he said. "He's going to be sorry he did this."

"I know."

"I've got the stuff. It's in the hall closet."

"That's good."

"I hope so."

I stopped in front of the living room and said hello to Manuel.

He took his eyes off the TV for a few seconds, gave me a wave, and went back to his program.

"Nice to see you're improving your mind," I told him.

He grunted. I continued on into the kitchen.

"Where's Eli?" I asked George, who was right behind me.

"Upstairs asleep. I feel like I'm running a combination day-care center and zoo here," George complained as I went over to his stove.

I set the shopping bag down. "You did say you wanted to help," I reminded him.

"I know. It's just that I didn't have this in mind," he answered as he watched me turn the oven dial on his stove to warm. "Why can't we switch places?"

"Because Chapman is expecting me, not you." I opened the door, and gently laid the shopping bag on the middle shelf. "This should work," I told him. "My grandmother used our stove once for a baby squirrel. Just make sure and leave the door ajar so it doesn't get too hot in there."

"Yeah," George intoned. "I wouldn't want to bake the

suckers. I wonder what twenty thousand dollars worth of hard-boiled eggs would taste like."

"Cute." I went over to the kitchen sink and got myself a glass of water. Usually George's sink was immaculate. Now it was full of dishes. "Boys getting to you?" I asked.

"They'd get to Martin Luther King. How long do you think I'm going to have to play Dr. Doolittle? When is this thing going down?"

"That depends on Chapman. I have to call him and set up the meeting, which I assume he will want to take place as soon as possible. After that, I figure things should go pretty fast."

George shook his head. "Anyone who would pay ten thousand dollars for one of those things . . ."

"Irridiated tortoises . . ."

"Whatever . . . that I have in my bathroom is nuts."

"Let me ask you this? Would you pay five thousand dollars for a baseball signed by Babe Ruth?"

"No."

"What would you pay for?"

George stroked his chin while he thought. "I don't know . . . maybe a first, signed edition of Richard Wright's *Native Son* or one of Chester Himes's books."

"That's my point. The people that are willing to pay ten thousand dollars apiece for those tortoises probably don't even know who Richard Wright is."

"I suppose," George allowed grudgingly.

"So, you talked to Mike?"

George nodded. "Everything's all set."

"Okay then."

"Can you stay and have some coffee?"

"I'd love to, but I have to get the last tortoise from Littlebaum."

"You'll call?" George asked.

"As soon as I know anything," I promised.

We kissed. George nuzzled my neck.

"A half hour won't make any difference," he whispered in my ear.

He was right. It wouldn't. We tiptoed up the stairs.

"You want to do me a favor?" he asked when we came back down.

"Sure."

"Take Manuel with you. I'm going to commit severe bodily injury if he stays here any longer."

"He does tend to have that effect on people," I observed.

When I walked into the living room, Manuel was sprawled on George's gray leather sofa with his feet on the teakwood coffee table and the remote in his hand watching the Home Shopping channel. A lady was selling a silk blouse paired with a velvet skirt.

"I think you'd do better in a different style," I said, leaning over and taking the remote out of his hand. I clicked off the TV.

Manuel looked up at me resentfully. "What you have to do that for, Robin?"

"Because you're coming with me. Let's go."

"Why?" he whined. "I'm tired. Thanks to you I didn't get any sleep last night."

"Too bad." I nudged his feet off the table with my leg. "Neither did I. You can sleep in the cab."

"The cab sucks." Manuel reluctantly sat up. "How can you expect me to sleep with that broken spring stabbing me in the back? I need to stay and help George."

"George is the one that asked me to take you," I told him.

Manuel pulled his hat further down on his head and folded his arms across his chest. "Where are we going anyway?"

"Back to Littlebaum's."

"Fucking great."

"Get going." And I pointed to the door.

Manuel glared at me. Then he grabbed his jacket and strode out the door. I followed him out of George's house.

"What were you doing upstairs anyhow?" he demanded as I started up the cab.

"Talking."

"Yeah. Right." Manuel reached over and clicked on the radio. He turned the dial to the rap station. Then he leaned against the seat, and closed his eyes.

I didn't pursue the topic. As I watched him, I wondered how he could relax to music like that. It just made me jumpy. Then my thoughts drifted on to how I was going to handle my upcoming visit with Littlebaum. I wasn't looking forward to it, not with Matilda at Littlebaum's side. The weather didn't help my mood. It hadn't improved since this morning. The sky was still a study in gray. Raindrops dripped from bare tree branches. The asphalt on the road was shiny with water and occasional patches of black ice, making me drive slower than I normally did. When I turned off the main road, the cab skidded out. For a moment, I thought I was going to go into a fence post before I got it back under control. Manuel opened his eyes as he fell forward.

"Jesus," he muttered, gripping the dashboard to steady himself.

I brought the cab to a stop. "Don't say anything," I warned him.

"Like what?"

I made a U-turn and got back onto the road.

"I knew I should have stayed at George's," Manuel muttered to the window.

Five minutes later, Littlebaum's house came into view. As I drove down the access road, I realized that something about the house looked different, but I wasn't sure what it was. Then, as I got closer, I realized what was bothering me. There was no smoke coming out of the chimney. The window shades were down. The doors to the garage were closed. The house looked vacant. Then I spied a couple of cardboard boxes, the kind you use for packing, laying outside the front door and I knew.

Littlebaum was gone.

And he wasn't coming back. He'd taken my advice and left town.

"I'm staying here," Manuel told me as I parked the car.

I handed him his cell phone. "Call 911 if there are any problems."

He snorted and powered up. By the time I'd closed the door of the cab, he was talking to a friend. I turned my collar up against the sting of the rain and jammed my hands in my pockets. Snow would almost be better than this, I thought as I started toward the door. I was halfway there when I saw another vehicle turning down onto the road. I rocked back and forth on my heels and waited for it to come closer as the rain dripped down my hair. The car, a beat-up green VW bus pulled up next to the cab.

Jeff, the kid from PETA that had been at my store a couple of weeks ago, got out. He was swathed in a black overcoat big enough to have accommodated two of him.

"What are you doing here?" I asked as he came toward me.

He did a double take and wiped the rain out of his eyes. "What are you?"

"I'm looking for Littlebaum."

"He's gone."

"So I surmised. I repeat. Why are you here?"

He rummaged around in his pocket and came up with a large, filled key ring. "Myra asked me to pick up a couple of tapes she forgot."

"Myra?" My voice rose in surprise. "How do you know Myra?"

"She's my half-sister. Only I live with my dad."

I looked at Jeff more closely. He and Myra both had the same body type—long and lean, and the same punk sensibility. I thought I detected a similarity around the eyes as well, but before I could make up my mind, he turned and unlocked the door and went inside. I followed.

Jeff and I were standing in a small entrance hall. The floor, dirty black-and-white tile, was muddy with water dripping off both of our jackets. The walls were covered with a collage of pages from the Sunday comics that someone, I assume it was Littlebaum, had pasted on. I glanced into the living room. A flowered sofa sat in the middle of the room. A TV stood to the left. The rest of the space was bare. I sniffed. The room smelled musty like the ape house at the zoo.

"He used to keep his monkeys in here," Jeff said, as if reading my mind. "All caged up. See, that's what I'm talking about. People thinking animals have no rights." He brushed the water off his hair and shook it off his coat. "He shouldn't have done that."

"You're right. He shouldn't have."

My answer appeared to mollify Jeff slightly because he stopped scowling. "Myra came over as often as she could and took them out and played with them. Monkeys need that or they go crazy—just like people."

"She never said anything about that to me."

"Maybe she didn't want you to know," Jeff suggested.

"Maybe," I murmured.

When I didn't say anything else, Jeff continued. "There was a spider monkey she particularly liked. Leo. She wanted to buy him from Littlebaum but my dad wouldn't let it in our house. He said it would make too much of a mess."

I thought about the Myers house, all neat and tidy. Somehow I didn't see a monkey fitting in there. I'd known someone who'd had one once. He'd specialized in jumping on people's heads from the curtain rod. It hadn't been fun.

I walked into Littlebaum's dining room. It was filled with stacks of newspapers and books. A chair lay on its side on the floor. A coat was draped over it. It looked as if Littlebaum had left in a hurry.

"Boy, my mom's gonna be pissed," Jeff said.

"Pardon?" I turned around. I'd been thinking about how fast Littlebaum had acted. Two days ago, he'd been here and now he was gone. I'd thought he might call my friend, but I'd never expected this. I hadn't figured him capable of organizing anything like this himself. Obviously I'd been wrong. I reached in my bag for Manuel's phone to call my friend Steve in Arizona and realized I'd left it in the cab with Manuel.

"When my mom finds out what Myra's done," Jeff explained, "she's gonna make her go to some boarding school or something when she gets her back. I know it."

"Why'd she go?"

"Just to help Littlebaum get settled. He offered her a lot of money to come. And anyway, she's never been out West before."

"How'd they move?"

Jeff gave me a boy-are-you-dumb look. "U-Haul. The usual way. I figure the animals will be better off out there. Littlebaum said he was going to build a big cage for the monkeys with bars to swing on and everything."

I nodded while I thought about Matilda. She'd probably like it out there, too. Then I thought about the tortoise Littlebaum had taken with him. I wondered if that had anything to do with his decision to leave at this particular time.

"You're not going to try and stop them are you?" Jeff asked anxiously, jingling his key chain. I knew he was thinking about Myra.

"No. I'm not. And anyway, I don't think I could even if I wanted to." His sister wasn't my problem, and since I knew where Littlebaum was going, I could always get the tortoise back.

"Good. Because he said not to tell anyone."

"Aside from your parents, I don't think many people are going to care."

Jeff moved into the kitchen. The place looked as if a cyclone had hit it. All the cabinet doors were open. Drawers were ajar. Paper bags littered the floor.

"Good," said Jeff, looking toward the far counter.

I followed his glance.

"Myra's Pink Floyd tapes," Jeff explained, going over and stuffing the tapes in his pocket. "She wants me to keep them till she gets back. Listen. I gotta go."

I stayed for a few minutes more. I went upstairs and poked around. I didn't find anything of interest, but then, I hadn't really expected to.

Littlebaum had left all his furniture behind, not that there was that much of it to begin with.

But, still.

He'd just taken what was important to him: his animals. As I closed the door to his house, I wondered if he saw himself as a modern-day Noah bopping down the Interstate, heading for the safety of the desert before the rains came.

I hoped he and Matilda made it.

Chapter
32

I could hear the music from the radio blasting outside the cab. Manuel turned it down as I got in.

"You're going to go deaf," I told him.

"That's what my mom says."

I wondered if "you're going to go deaf" had replaced "you're going to lose an eye" in the annals of maternal advice as I held out my hand. "Could I have the phone, please."

Manuel gave it to me reluctantly. "Why can't you get your own?"

"I will."

"When?"

"When I have a chance." And I called Steve in Arizona.

"You're calling long distance?" Manuel yelped. "Do you know how much that costs?"

"I'm charging it to my calling card, so be quiet," I snapped as the operator came on.

But I could have saved myself the bother. Steve wasn't home. I left a message on his voice mail.

"Now what?" Manuel said as I cleared the number off.

"Now I'm dialing my house and seeing if I have any messages."

I'd expected one on there from Chapman and I wasn't disappointed. I took a deep breath, dialed his beeper number, and left Manuel's number for him. I had an idea that things were about to heat up.

Chapman called back almost immediately. "I heard you had fun last night," he began, never one to let an opportunity to get a dig in pass.

"I missed you. I expected to see you there."

"Nah. I figured you didn't need me to remind you of what you have to do. How's our project coming?"

"Well."

"That's good. I was beginning to worry you were getting other ideas."

"Why would I do that?"

"A misplaced sense of chivalry."

Chivalry. The word sounded odd coming out of Chapman's mouth. I was surprised he knew it. I wondered if Chapman was going to allude to what he'd hidden in my store, or was he going to get me to give him the tortoises and have me arrested anyway? If I had to bet, I'd say the latter.

"Good. Let's meet in an hour," I said.

"An hour?"

"Do you have a problem with that?" Suspicion made his voice bristle.

"No. Not at all. I want to get this over with and go back to things the way they were."

"At Eli's."

"No. In a public place."

He laughed unpleasantly. "Why? What do you think I'm going to do?"

"I don't know and I don't want to find out."

"If I'd wanted to do anything, I would have done it already."

I didn't say he had.

"At Lefty's then," Chapman said after a moment's silence.

"Works for me. And we'll be quits?" I couldn't help adding.

"Absolutely."

The scary part was, he really sounded as if he meant it.

I hung up and phoned George. "I'm meeting Chapman down at Lefty's in an hour."

"Don't worry," he said. "I'll have everything packed and waiting."

It had stopped raining by the time I got to Lefty's and the temperature had moved up a couple of degrees. According to the weather forecaster on the radio, it was supposed to be in the forties tomorrow, five degrees warmer than usual for this time of year. He was almost done with a spiel tying the weather we'd experienced this winter into the trend towards global warming as I pulled into a parking spot across from the bar. I wondered if that meant I'd own beachfront property right here in Central New York in twenty years as I clicked off the radio and checked my watch.

I was exactly on time. As I crossed the street, I scanned it for Chapman's car. It didn't take me long to spot it. It was parked a few feet down from the bar, away from the bar's window. I glanced back quickly. George was double-parked down the block, in front of the parking lot. I pretended not to notice and went inside. Chapman was waiting for me. In his white turtleneck, tan corduroy pants, and blue ski parka, he looked as if he belonged on the slopes of Aspen. He grinned when he saw me and patted the stool next to him.

"Drink?" he asked. "It's the least I can do."

"Sure. Why not? Scotch, please." I sat down and handed him the suitcase. "Here you go."

"They're all here?"

"All of them," I lied. "Count them if you don't believe me."

"Oh, I do."

I dug my cigarettes out of my backpack, tapped one out of the pack and lit it.

"You should quit," Chapman observed. "It's an expensive, dirty habit."

"That's what people tell me." I took the smoke deep in my lungs and exhaled. "So, are you going home?" I asked.

"In a couple of days. I have some odds and ends to clean up."

I felt like saying, "Is that what I am to you, an odd and end?" But didn't.

Chapman cocked his head and studied my face. "You seem remarkably unupset about this."

"What do you mean?"

The bartender put my drink down. I picked it up and took a sip. It tasted as if it had been bottled in Passaic, New Jersey.

"I'd expected . . ."

"That I'd carry on?" I said.

"Something like that."

"That I'd call you a scum-sucking worthless piece of shit? What would be the point? You already know it."

Chapman knocked the rest of his drink back. "Believe me," he told me. "I'm not doing anything that anyone else isn't."

"You're saying that I'm quixotic?"

"I'm saying you're antediluvian." And he slapped a ten down on the bar. "Have a couple more on me." And he picked up the suitcase and left.

I pushed the glass away, took another puff of my cigarette, and waited. Three minutes later, I heard the crash. I smiled and walked out the door and down the block a few feet to get a better view.

George had rammed straight into Chapman's car. The door of Chapman's car was caved in. His bumper was hanging down. The street was covered with broken safety glass from Chapman's front window. One thing is for sure: they definitely don't make cars the way they used to. George hadn't even been going that fast. I hoped the tortoises and the eggs were all right. But then, I decided they probably were. There was a lot of insulation in the suitcase they were in. Both men were standing in the middle of the street. Chapman was screaming at George.

"You fuckin' son of a bitch!" he yelled. Chapman's mouth was distended. His teeth were bared. He didn't look so nice anymore.

"I said I was sorry," George told him.

"Sorry. Sorry?" Chapman's voice rose in a crescendo of rage.

He was reaching back in his car when George's friend Mike, drove up. He'd been waiting around the corner. He stepped out of his car, badged everyone and called it in. Chapman took out his badge and showed it around as if it were the Holy Grail. Mike shook his head. Chapman practi cally stuck the thing in Mike's face. Mike shook his head again and said something. I couldn't hear, so I moved a little closer. I saw George pointing to the backseat. Mike opened the door and pulled out a small suitcase and opened it up. I didn't have to move any closer to see what was in it. I already knew. Several bags of fertilizer and two blasting caps. People take explosives a lot more seriously than they take endangered species.

"I don't know how that got in here," Chapman squawked. Mike looked skeptical.

"He did it!" he yelled, pointing at George.

"Why would I do something like that?" George demanded.

Chapman came toward George. "Because you're a friend of hers."

"Who is her?" George asked.

I heard sirens. More squad cars were on the way. This was going to take a while to sort out. I looked at my watch. George had already alerted Fish and Wildlife. I wouldn't be surprised if someone wasn't up here by tomorrow. In the meantime, the tortoises would most likely be passing their time at the zoo. I went back in the bar and ordered a beer. While I was waiting for it, I called Joan and told her I was coming out tomorrow to pick up Zsa Zsa. Sitting at the bar just wasn't the same without her.

Chapter
33

"Look," George said. He pointed to a flock of parrots sitting in a tree alongside the dirt path we were bouncing down.

"Sure beats the crows," I said. We were three days into our vacation in Belize and had another seven to go. I wished we had a month or more. "Littlebaum would like it down here."

George grunted and maneuvered the Land Rover he was driving around a ditch in the road.

Of course, Littlebaum liked it in Arizona, too. At least that's what he'd said when I'd flown down to pick up the tortoise.

"They leave you alone down here," he'd told me as he'd fiddled with the water tank on his trailer.

Steve had sold him a large tract of land out in the desert. There was nothing there but cactus and dirt and a view of the mountains, which, as Littlebaum said, suited him fine. The land was flat and good for building. He'd already contracted to have a well drilled and had put up the cage for the monkeys, who, judging from the amount of chasing that was going on, seemed to be having a good time in their new home.

Matilda seemed to be enjoying herself, too. She'd been lying on the ground, in a patch of shade the trailer was throwing off, having a peaceful snooze when I'd driven up. Myra had been sitting beside her in a folding chair, also dozing in the sun. At the sound of my wheels, both of them had awakened, stretched, and turned to face me.

"You have a tan," I told Myra while I gave Matilda a pet. Her fur was warm and smelled of hay.

Myra grinned and drew a line in the dirt with the toe of her sneaker. "It's nice down here. All this sun." She did a half pirouette. "Do you think I look too fat?"

"No. I think you look good."

"That's what my uncle says, too. He wants me to stay with him. I don't know." She wound a lock of hair around her finger. "Maybe I will. Listen," she continued. "I want to apologize."

"For what?"

"For hitting you over the head."

"That was you?"

She fidgeted.

"I thought you'd come to get the stuff I took from Eli's apartment." She gave a slight shrug. "I guess I got paranoid."

"But I didn't see you."

"I know. I was next door. I saw you snooping around through the window." Myra drew a circle in the dirt with her toe. "I was angry." Then she added, "I was angry a lot."

"Look at that," said George, interrupting my thoughts and bringing me back to the present.

I watched a large iguana run across the path and vanish into the undergrowth.

"This is amazing," George remarked as we hit another bump.

"Isn't it, though." I grabbed on to the seat and brushed a branch from a tree away from my face.

We'd gone to town to get supplies and the day's mail for George's cousin, Andre. Now we were returning. The path we were following, more of a track really, was just above the Macal River. When we got to the drop-off spot, we were supposed to use the CB radio mounted on the dashboard to contact Andre, at which point he'd come get us with the outboard and ferry us back across the river.

"So you still think what we did was wrong?" I asked as we went over another rut. I winced as my head hit the Land Rover's ceiling.

George kept his eyes firmly fixed ahead of him. "If I had thought it was wrong I wouldn't have done it." He bit his lip as we went over another ditch. I remembered what Andre had said about this road sometimes being impassable during the rainy season. "However," George continued, "I'm not proud of it. I don't think manufacturing evidence is the way to go. Even in this case. Even when we're right."

"Even when the guy is a murderer?"

"Even then."

I nibbled on my fingernail. Of course we hadn't known that Chapman had killed Nestor. No one had, especially not Sulfin, who'd already confessed to the shooting, or Adelina, who'd accused him. Then the ME had done an autopsy and found two different bullets in Nestor's chest, one of which matched Sulfin's gun and the other of which turned out to match the gun the police found in the nightstand in Chapman's bedroom.

Evidently Chapman had come along after Sulfin had shot Nestor and decided to take the opportunity to finish the job. Why? If you listened to Chapman, it had been an accident. According to the story in the local paper, Chapman maintained he'd just been trying to help Nestor. He'd been bending over when his gun had gone off accidentally, putting a hole through Nestor's heart.

Sulfin's charge was being downgraded to assault, while Chapman was being charged with manslaughter because the DA didn't think he'd be able to make a murder charge stick. He was probably right, I decided, brushing a mosquito away from my ear. But it didn't really matter, because what with the other charges being lodged against him, Chapman wasn't getting out anytime soon. Besides the manslaughter charge, he was up for violations of the Lacey Act, trafficking in endangered species, as well as possession of explosives without a license.

George gestured at the undergrowth. "I wonder if those tortoises could live here?"

"Probably." Given what they'd been through, they seemed pretty tough.

Right now they were down in Miami awaiting shipment back to a preserve that was being set up for them in their home country. I couldn't say the same for the eggs, though. They weren't going anywhere. I guess we hadn't packed them as well as we thought we had. Not one of them made it.

"How does it feel to be the savior of a species?" I joked.

George grinned.

I glanced down at the river. We were about two feet above it. The black water was rippling over the rocks. I remembered Andre saying he'd already torn the bottom out of one boat on the shoals.

"Don't worry. We still have plenty of time to get across," George said, reading my thoughts.

After sunset, travel on the river would be even more difficult. It was already six. It would be dark by six-thirty. Night came quickly in the tropics.

"I'm not worried." I leaned back in my seat and smelled the flower-scented air and listened to the birdsong. "You know," I said, "I could definitely live here for a while."

"Doing what?"

"What Andre's doing."

"Running a guest house? You don't even like to cook."

"I used to do it rather well."

"Andre and his wife both worked in the hotel business. You've never done anything like that."

"I never ran a pet store, either."

George grunted.

In the distance, somewhere ahead of us, a howler monkey roared in the jungle. I smiled as I watched the sky turning a brilliant crimson. Tomorrow, we were going to go visit the Mayan ruins of Xunantunich.

For now it was enough.

Please turn the page
for an exciting sneak peek of
Barbara Block's newest
Robin Light mystery
BLOWING SMOKE
on sale in July 2001!

To clarify in case you're wondering, I'm not a licensed New York State private detective. I don't work for an agency. I don't advertise in the Yellow Pages. My business comes to me strictly by word of mouth. I also don't carry a gun, although I can shoot one if I have to. And have. I also run a pet store called Noah's Ark, which specializes in exotics—read reptiles—though these days I seem to be doing more detecting and less pet storing, if I can coin a word.

I started doing investigative work to save my own ass and turned out to be good at it, good enough so that people keep asking me to help them and I keep saying yes. I usually work a handful of cases a year. Mostly, I find lost children and animals and leave the high end sexy stuff to the big boys.

It was almost eleven-thirty at night by the time I walked through the door of my house, and I was not in a good mood, possibly because I hadn't had anything to eat since ten o'clock that morning. When I saw the blinking light on my answering machine, I was hoping it was Bethany's parents calling to tell me their daughter had come home by herself. But it wasn't. It was someone called Hillary Cisco, wanting to hire me to do a job for her.

Normally, I would have turned her down. I prefer giving people their money's worth by concentrating on one thing at a time. But with the proverbial wolf at my door in the form of quarterly tax payments to good old New York State, I figured it was time to make an exception to my rule. The next morning, before I went to work, I phoned her back.

"How'd you'd get my name?" I asked her while I let James in and got a can of cat food out of the cabinet.

"Calli gave it to me."

Calli was an old friend of mine who'd gone out to California and was now back. At the moment, she was covering the Metro section in the local paper.

"She said you'd be perfect for this."

"Really?" As I set James's food in front of him, I filled her in on my fees and how I worked.

It sounded fine to Hillary, so I told her I'd swing by her place later that afternoon. As I hung up, I noticed that James's ear was torn.

"Fighting again, I see."

He answered me with a growl. I wondered why I kept him around as I went to get the peroxide. Of course, he'd disappeared by the time I'd come back, and after searching the house for five minutes or so, I gave it up as a bad job and called Calli.

I wanted her to fill me on this Hillary Cisco, but either Calli wasn't home or she wasn't picking up. I left a message on her machine, got Zsa Zsa, and finally left the house. I was only twenty minutes late.

Tim, the guy who works for me, and I spent the rest of the day restocking shelves, cleaning cages, and feeding the snakes. Bad day for the mice, good day for the snakes. In between, I popped into the back, arranged to go in and have a TB test, and made calls about Bethany while I tried not to listen to the asthmatic wheeze of the store's air conditioner.

The temperature was in the nineties, and the machine was not happy. It probably wanted a vacation, but then didn't we all, a fact I was reminded of when I stepped outside. I was drenched in sweat by the time I walked to my car. Which didn't improve my mood any. If I wanted heat, I'd be living in the Southwest instead of central New York.

On my way to Hillary Cisco's, I swung by Warren Street, but Bethany wasn't there, and after about twenty minutes or so, I gave up and drove over to Starcrest, the development in which Hillary Cisco lived. When I saw her leaning against the porch railing, I was reminded of a kid who'd been locked out of her house and was waiting for her mommy to come home. Even though she wasn't a kid. Not even close. And 113 Wisteria Lane was her house.

Listening to her voice on the machine, I'd pictured her as blond and big-boned, but this woman was as small and brown as a wren. Her gauze dress, incongruously long-sleeved and high-hemmed, fluttered around her thighs as she came down the steps to greet me. She moved with a slow, languid pace, but then, I reflected, it was too hot to move any other way.

Her hair, straight, black, and chin-length, hung like a curtain on either side of her face. But it was her eyes I noticed. They looked as if they belonged to someone else. A pale grayish blue, they were too light for her complexion, casting a vacant expression over her features. Her eyeliner and mascara had run in the heat, smudging into dark cir-

cles underneath her eyes. Beads of moisture ringed her
hairline. She looked tired, as if she'd been wrestling with
something for a long time and lost.

"Robin Light?" she asked. In person, she sounded breath-
ier, less self-assured than she had on the phone.

I nodded. "Hillary Cisco?"

She bobbed her head and nervously plucked at the hem
of her dress, trying to make it longer. "You're late. I thought
you might have decided not to come."

"I got lost." I'd been circling around streets that all
looked the same for the last twenty minutes, kicking up
plumes of dust and growing more and more irritated by the
second.

"Everyone does." She swiped at her forehead with the
back of her hand. Her arms, I realized, were exceptionally
long. "They designed these roads like a maze, you know.
That's so the blacks from the inner city can't come up here
and rob us." For a moment I couldn't tell if she was serious
or not. Then the corners of her mouth formed a slight
smile. She shook her head as she contemplated the houses
on either side of her. "As if they . . . or anyone would."

I followed her gaze. The place didn't seem so bad to me,
just raw in the way that new housing developments are.
They were popping up all around Syracuse, siphoning off
its population. In twenty years, when the trees and the
hedges grew in, it would be a pleasant enough place. At six
o'clock, the day was just beginning to cool off. Somewhere a
cardinal was singing his song over and over again, the notes
rising and falling away like a benediction.

His notes mingled with the happy shouts of children
chasing each other with water guns while their parents, still
in their suits from their day in the office, were busy adjusting

and readjusting the hoses and sprinklers on their lawns before they went inside and changed into shorts and T-shirts.

Hillary snorted her opinion of them and beckoned for me to follow her. "My brother and sister are anxious to meet you," she told me, as if she'd invited me to tea instead of to discuss a job. "Nothing big," I remember she'd said on the phone. "We just need to clarify a few issues."

Issues. Right. The new buzzword. As in, he has issues with alcohol or she has issues with men. Meaning he drinks and she sleeps around. I wondered what particular issues Hillary Cisco had in mind. They had to be substantial. People don't hire a private detective otherwise. Then I thought about how much I wanted it to rain as I mounted the three steps that led to Hillary's house.

A small white colonial, 113 Wisteria Lane was indistinguishable from the ones sitting to its left and right, even though Hillary had made a stab at decorating. Two wind chimes constructed from spoons hung from the eaves of the porch. A blue banner with several white music notes stitched to it jutted out from the porch beam. Half-dead red geraniums lay wilting in the ceramic pots lining the path to the house.

"The banner is my sister's handiwork," Hillary explained. "She does crafts," she continued, making the word crafts sound like some arcane sexual practice. "I sing, you know. Professionally. Teaching is my day job."

I nodded politely. I guess I should have acted more impressed, because a spasm of irritation rippled across her face. She compressed her lips, pulled the door to her house open, and stalked inside. But I didn't feel bad. I got the feeling she got irritated a lot.

The air in the hallway smelled faintly of cooking grease, room deodorizer, and kitchen trash. It had a dank, underwater quality to it, the kind you get in cheap motels in which the windows don't open and the air vents need to be cleaned. The living room was done up in a Chinese motif.

The rug, furniture, and walls were all white. Badly painted Chinese scrolls hung on three walls. A lacquered screen, dotted with someone's idea of a bamboo tree, stood off in the corner of the room, while a matching black lacquered coffee table sat in front of the sofa. Even the cabinet housing the television had an Asian motif. It looked like the kind of room they advertised on TV at two o'clock in the morning. Five pieces for seven hundred dollars. No money down. Two years to pay. By which time it would have come apart.

"My brother, Louis," Hillary said, pointing to the man in Bermuda shorts and a polo shirt sprawled on the sofa, watching television.

"At last." He clicked off the program he'd been watching, hoisted himself up, came forward, and shook my hand, engulfing it in his. "And yes," he said, laughing. "We have the same mother and father. Everyone always wonders."

It was easy to see why they did. If Hillary was the mini version, Louis was the jumbo king-sized. A bear of a man, everything about him was big, from his ears, beaked nose, and lantern jaw to his hands and feet. Looking closely, though, I could see a similarity in the shape of the mouth between him and Hillary.

"I'm glad you could come." He was about to say something else to me when a woman burst out of the kitchen and planted herself next to Louis.

"I still think this is wrong," she told him, ostentatiously ignoring me.

Hillary took a deep breath and let it out. "My sister," she explained as her eyes lightened to an even paler shade of gray. "Evidently, Amy still has a few doubts about the wisdom of what we're doing. Although I thought we'd straightened that out."

Amy flushed. "No, we haven't." She drank from the can of soda she was holding and brushed a strand of frizzy hair off her face. She seemed as if she were one of those women who always looked permanently disheveled. The jewelry she had on, a squash-blossom necklace and matching wristful of silver bangles belonged on someone five inches taller. The peasant-style white blouse and pleated gauze skirt she was wearing accentuated her pendulous breasts and stomach. She was as short as Hillary, but she outweighed her by a good seventy pounds or so. "Listen," Amy went on, "all I'm saying is that Mom is going to be furious if she finds out."

"She's not going to," Louis snapped.

"She always does," Amy countered.

Louis glowered at her. "Don't you think it's time you grew up," he said. "She's not God."

Amy's face turned sullen. "That's not what I'm saying, and you know it."

"Amy," Hillary said, tugging at her sleeves. "Please. We've already had this discussion. We've decided—"

"You decided," Amy snapped.

"No. You agreed. We all agreed."

"I never said—"

"Yes, you did," Louis replied. "If you can't remember, maybe you'd better change those antidepressants you're on."

"That's a lousy thing to say," Amy flung back at him.

"You're right," Louis apologized. "It is." Even though he didn't look particularly sorry.

Amy put her can of soda down on the coffee table and

began fiddling with her bracelets. "All I'm saying is that I'm not sure that this is the right thing to do."

"Well, I am." Exasperation underlined Louis's words. "Why do you always do this?"

"Do what?"

"Say yes and then change your mind?"

"But what if she finds out?" Amy wailed.

"So what?" Hillary's eyes flashed. "Big deal. So what if she does. We're certainly not going to be any worse off than we are already."

When Amy started to reply, it was all I could do not to say, Hey, people. Why don't you all shut up. Instead, I picked my backpack up off the floor and said, "Call me when you've decided what you want. I have other things I have to attend to. " Like finding Bethany. Like finishing restocking the shelves. Like repairing one of the filters in the big fish tank. Like ordering five more geckos.

"Please." Hillary took my hand and began leading me to the sofa. "Don't go."

"Only if we can get down to business."

It was the money that made me stay. Though if you asked me, I'd say that what these folks really needed was a therapist instead of a private detective.

Hillary glanced at Amy. Amy shrugged.

"All right," she said. "But I'm not taking the blame for this."

"How novel," Louis sniped. "It's not as if you ever take the blame for anything."

"Both of you stop it," Hillary ordered. "It's the heat," she said to me. "The heat is making everyone crazy. Let me get you a drink," she continued. "An iced tea." And, without waiting for my answer, she went into the kitchen.

As I listened to the air conditioner's rattle and hum, I

watched Amy wind a lock of her hair around her finger. Her face was round. She looked younger than her siblings and paler, as if she never got out in the sun. The outline of a faint mustache was apparent above her upper lip.

"It must be nice to still be able to do that," she said wistfully, referring to the high-pitched screams of the children playing outside that were seeping into the room. Then she sighed and sat next to me. A faintly sour smell came off of her. "Do you believe in life after death?" she asked suddenly.

Louis rolled his eyes and flopped down on the armchair to the left of the sofa. "Ah . . . we're back to the great unknown."

Amy sucked in her cheeks and straightened her back. "What's wrong with that question?"

"Well—" I began when Louis interrupted. Doing that seemed to be a bad habit of his.

"Anyway, what she thinks is besides the point," he said.

"It most certainly is the point."

"No, it isn't. The point is that we don't want Mother taken advantage of."

"That's right," Helen agreed, entering the room. As she handed me an iced tea, I could see that her nails were bitten down.

"I was just curious," Amy said, but her tone had changed from defiant to defeated.

"You'll have to forgive my sister," Hillary told me. "She's just concerned about our mother."

"As are we all," Louis chimed in.

I took a sip of my tea and put it down. It had that chemical aftertaste of the powdered instants. "Does your mother have a name?"

"Oh." Hillary paused. "I thought you knew."

"Should I?"

"Of course not. Why should you?" She gave a dismissive little laugh at her own foolishness. "It's Rose. Rose Taylor," she continued, idly caressing her arm with her hand.

The name sounded familiar, but I couldn't place it, and I didn't ask, figuring I could always do that later.

"I suppose," Hillary continued, "I could go to one of the larger detective agencies, but that seems like overkill."

"Not to mention expensive," I couldn't help volunteering. As an unlicensed part-timer I charged bargain basement prices.

"That, too," Hillary conceded, her gray eyes widening a fraction. "I won't lie about that."

"One hundred dollars an hour is a lot on a postal worker's salary," Louis griped.

Hillary fingered the hem of her skirt. "Actually, I thought we needed a more personal touch."

"So what is this job about?" I asked.

Louis and Hillary exchanged glances as Hillary sat down on the other side of me. She crossed and uncrossed her legs. She seemed to like the way they looked. I noticed she had a small half-moon tattooed on her left calf.

"Tell me," Hillary asked, turning her head in my direction. "Do you believe in psychics?"

"Psychics? You mean people who communicate with the dead?"

"Yes."

"No." I'd tried one after my husband Murphy had died. It had cost me a hundred bucks and left me feeling like a fool.

Hillary and Louis exchanged another look. "Do you believe people have the ability to talk to animals?" Hillary asked me.

"I think we can communicate." My dog, Zsa Zsa, was pretty good at letting me know what she wanted.

"I mean talking."

I looked to see if she was joking. She wasn't.

"As in my cat telling me, watch out, the lady down the street is in a bitchy mood today?" I asked

"Something like that."

"Not outside of the movies."

"Well, my mother does."

"She believes she can talk to animals? I don't think . . ."

"No, she believes a woman named Pat Humphrey can." Hillary spread her hands and studied what was left of her fingernails.

"Go on," I finally prompted.

"This is so embarrassing."

I waited.

Hillary sighed and brushed a strand of hair off her forehead. "All right. Three months ago—more or less—my mother's cat disappeared from the house. At first, we thought someone let it out by accident. Now, of course—" Hillary stopped. "Well, you decide. My mother was hysterical. She's very attached to . . . this animal. Anyway, the next morning at nine o'clock, this woman—"

"Pat Humphrey?" I asked.

Hillary nodded. "She appeared at my mother's door with the cat in her arms. She said she was a pet psychic. She said she'd found the cat wandering in the park and the cat told her where my mother lived."

"So you're saying you think this woman might have stolen your mother's cat and then brought it back?"

Hillary gave me the kind of smile a teacher bestows on a promising pupil.

"She said she didn't want any money," Louis continued, "but my mother insisted on giving her a reward."

I leaned forward. "How big?"

"Five thousand dollars."

I whistled. "Five thousand dollars is a fair chunk of change— even these days."

"Not for our mother," Amy blurted out. "She's rich."

Hillary glared at Amy, who turned her eyes downward. "Comfortable," Hillary corrected. "She's comfortable."

While Amy bit her lip, Louis took up the narrative.

"In any case," he said, "our mother talks to her every day now. Sometimes twice a day. We're worried. We think our mother is giving this woman money."

"I assume you think this woman is running a scam."

Hillary nodded.

"So, then, why don't you go to the police?"

"We will if we have to," Hillary said. "But we're hoping to avoid that. We don't want to upset Mother unnecessarily. She's a very private person. She would be furious if she thought we involved the authorities in her private business."

"It would be like saying we thought she's losing it," Louis said.

Hillary nodded her head in agreement.

"But going to me wouldn't be?"

"She's not going to know."

"I'm confused here. Now, what is it exactly that you want me to do?"

Louis looked at Hillary, and Hillary gave a nod.

"We've been thinking about that," Louis said. "And this is what we've come up with. We want you to get an appointment with this Humphrey woman. And then we want you to tape your session with her. I don't care if it takes one, two, or five times. We want tangible proof that this woman is a fraud."

It seemed as if that wouldn't be too hard a task to accomplish.